GOTREK & FELIX:
SLAYER

In a blink of motion the Bloodthirster was there beside Gotrek. It cupped the Slayer's scalp in one mighty hand and bent the dwarf's neck back to lift his face off the deck. Kolya did not think that anything would prevent the daemon from doing exactly as it had promised it would – cracking Gotrek's skull like an egg and consuming his brain.

Then an odd shadow passed across the daemon's face and it let the Slayer drop, gnashing its teeth like a dog denied a bone. It withdrew to wrap itself up in its wings and snarl in frustration.

'No,' it said, its voice growing measured to once again become that of Be'lakor the daemon prince. 'Your doom is to be at the hands of one mightier even than I.'

'I will accept no doom,' Gotrek grunted, hefting his axe.

WARHAMMER®
THE END TIMES

SIGMAR'S BLOOD
The Prequel to the End Times
A novella by Phil Kelly

THE RETURN OF NAGASH
Book One of the End Times
A novel by Josh Reynolds

THE FALL OF ALTDORF
Book Two of the End Times
A novel by Chris Wraight

THE CURSE OF KHAINE
Book Three of the End Times
A novel by Gav Thorpe

THE RISE OF THE HORNED RAT
Book Four of the End Times
A novel by Guy Haley

THE LORD OF THE END TIMES
Book Five of the End Times
A novel by Josh Reynolds

GOTREK & FELIX: KINSLAYER
Book One of the Doom of Gotrek Gurnisson
A novel by David Guymer

GOTREK & FELIX: SLAYER
Book Two of the Doom of Gotrek Gurnisson
A novel by David Guymer

DEATHBLADE
A Tale of Malus Darkblade
A novel by C L Werner

*Visit blacklibrary.com for the full range of Gotrek & Felix novels,
novellas, audio dramas and short stories, as well as many other
exclusive Black Library products.*

WARHAMMER®
THE END TIMES

DAVID GUYMER

GOTREK & FELIX

SLAYER

BLACK LIBRARY

A BLACK LIBRARY PUBLICATION

First published in Great Britain in 2015 by
Black Library,
Games Workshop Ltd.,
Willow Road,
Nottingham, NG7 2WS, UK.

10 9 8 7 6 5 4 3 2 1

Cover by Slawomir Maniak.
Map artwork by Nuala Kindrade.
Additional artwork by Winona Nelson.

A CIP record for this book is available from the British Library.

UK ISBN 13: 978 1 84970 840 1

US ISBN 13: 978 1 84970 841 8

See Black Library on the internet at
blacklibrary.com

Find out more about Games Workshop
and the world of Warhammer at
games-workshop.com

Printed and bound by CPI Group (UK) Ltd, Croydon, CR0 4YY

The world is dying, but it has been so
since the coming of the Chaos Gods.

For years beyond reckoning, the Ruinous Powers have coveted
the mortal realm. They have made many attempts to seize it,
their anointed champions leading vast hordes into the lands of
men, elves and dwarfs. Each time, they have been defeated.

Until now.

The Three-Eyed King has come. With the Empire in flames, Archaon
Everchosen has marched south with all the armies of ruin at his heels to
claim his birthright and usher in the Age of Chaos. The city of Middenheim, one of the few bastions remaining to men, dwarfs and elves, is his
target, for buried deep in the mighty rock upon which it sits is an ancient
weapon with which he will bring about his ultimate victory.

The last hope lies with a few heroes. With the great vortex sundered,
the Winds of Magic have been freed, and each has found a mortal host.
Only the power of these 'Incarnates' can prevent the cataclysm that
Archaon seeks to unleash. But they are scattered, and even if they can be
gathered, they may not be able to work together.

Far from the growing storm, Gotrek Gurnisson and Felix Jaeger lead a
ragtag army through the ruins of the Empire in search of Felix's family.
Their deeds in these dark times are as heroic as any from their legendary
journeys, but their friendship has been riven by words that cannot be
unsaid and actions that cannot be undone.

And Gotrek's Doom approaches.

These are the End Times.

Claus

North of Here Lie The
Dreaded Chaos Wastes.

Erengrad.

Here Be Trolls...

Praag.

middle mountains.

heim.

Kislev

Kislev.

Wolfenburg.

Talabheim.

The Empire

ldorf.

Karak Kad

Nuln.

The
Moot.

Sylvania.
Dracken
-hof.

Zhufbar.

Averheim.

Black
Water.

Black fire Pass.

rak
Norn.

'If this journal is found, if the day was won,
then remember this – here a Slayer lies.'

From *My Travels with Gotrek*, unpublished,
by Herr Felix Jaeger

PART ONE

REDEMPTION
IN THE EYES
OF MY ANCESTORS

Early Spring 2527

ONE

He Who Changes

The gods themselves had ridden to the defence of Altdorf, so it was rumoured, but not even Taal had a finger to raise for this corner of Hochland's Great Forest.

'Doomed!' howled Markus Weissman until his voice cracked, one more broken note amidst the clatter of cloven hooves and screaming men.

The men of his unit pressed in more from either side. He could smell their sweat, the soil in their green and red livery, could feel the shivers passing down their spears as they recovered their schiltron formation at the top of the hill and raised shields. There was a splintering crash as a shield split apart under a blow from a beastman's club, then screams of terror before two men could rally to drive the creature back and seal the breach in their formation.

'Blood of Hochland!' roared Sergeant Sierck. His doublet sleeve had been torn off up to the shoulder. His reversible red and green cloak showed the red side to hide the blood that made a circus horror mask of his face, his beard and even his teeth as he bellowed for courage.

'Doomed,' Markus sobbed again, blindly driving his spear into a beastman's neck. The goat-headed beast brayed and fell back with Markus's spear point still lodged in its throat. He let the weapon go with a cry and struggled to free his katzbalger, the short, unfamiliar blade of last resort of the Emperor's infantry.

He studied the cheap, impurity-riddled weapon for a moment, transfixed. How appropriate.

A spear stabbed over Markus's shoulder and took a charging beastman through the eye. The monster stumbled witlessly on and somehow fell on Markus's sword. Hot, stinking bile washed his hand and splashed over his boots. It reminded him of the birthing fluids that he used to see puddled on his neighbours' fields at calving time. It was like that. Except in the one important way. The gutted beast emitted a deafening bray until another man's spear skewered it through the mouth. Sickened, Markus snatched back his sword and bossed the dying animal with his shield. The beastman bumped and rolled down the slope and for a second Markus stood unopposed.

He gasped at the close, copper-sharp air. His ribs felt like a vice around his lungs. He couldn't breathe! The need for air was overwhelming and he pulled his dented helmet from his head. He let it drop. The alpine wind moved blissfully through his beard. Unblinkered by the cheek-guard of his battered helm, he saw the herd in its terrible entirety.

They were doomed.

The rocky clearing in which General von Baersdorf had thought to make his stand against the beastmen that had been harrying them since Hergig was close to a league in length and about a quarter of that wide, rising steadily to this low hill at its northern end. In all that, there wasn't a scrap of bare rock that didn't harbour a dozen braying nightmares. The archers and outriders that von Baersdorf had hastily redeployed to defend the column's gun carriages and supply wains had been wiped out and now beastmen boiled through the wreckage. Every so often a scrap of red fluttered over the broken wagons, a remnant of the general's banner taken by his killers as a trophy.

The screams of women and children carried weakly through the chaos. Markus looked over the column's mutilated heart to the rearguard, ranged up under the eaves at the southern end of the clearing. A beleaguered ring of halberdiers held the beastmen at bay while terrified wagoners pulled their vehicles into a defensive circle around the soldiers' families. Working under a pall of black smoke that obscured the wagons' tops from view, the famed Hochland handgunners poured death and thunder over the halberdiers' heads.

A long, bone-throbbing bass note boomed over the infernal din.

Standing like an icon to all that was unholy above the beasts that served him, came the Chaos warrior. Mounted northmen flanked him on stout, ill-tempered ponies. Their muscular bodies writhed with weird, unsettling tattoos and they bore an array of banners, gongs and other instruments, but even as a group they could not match their champion for size or sheer presence. His heavy armour was the deep blue of the northern sky and blazed with icy white runes that, though Markus could not read them, vouchsafed the ultimate understanding in death. From a sealed helm, twin discs of witchfire shone the cold contempt of the immortals onto their earthly demesne. His slow advance was the opening of a pit, a great maw, a chasm that resounded to the footsteps of doom.

He appeared to be searching for something. Or someone.

Markus moaned with dread. He was a farmer, not a fighter. When the Hergig soldiers had come through his land on their way to Wolfenburg he should have stayed behind. Better to die where his wife and baby daughter had died. Why should Ostland have fared any better than their neighbour? He looked up, tears in his eyes and an imprecation to the gods in his breast. Even the sky was damaged, the blunt banks of morning cloud scarred by comets that still fell months after Morrslieb's destruction.

What sanctuary could there be in Wolfenburg, or even in Middenheim, when even the heavens were not safe? There was–

A strong but not unkind hand pulled Markus back from the front rank. Ernst Höller forced Markus's useless helmet back over his ears, muffling the screams and narrowing the terrible view to that which lay immediately in front of him. Höller's lined, red face looked at him worriedly. He had been a cobbler, the best that a farmhand's coin could afford. Markus was still wearing one of his boots.

'Look,' yelled Höller, pointing towards the forest on the battlefield's long eastern edge.

Broken in every meaningful way, Markus could do little but limply do as he was told. As he turned to watch, arrows scythed through the running beastmen from behind, carving out a thin crescent of killing ground into which a ragged mass of soldiers roared from the treeline. They wielded swords, maces, halberds and hammers. Some men had shields, though no two bore the same colour or motif, while others hacked into their foes with two axes and a berserker zeal. Their clothing, similarly, had passed under the great grinding wheels of war. Markus picked out the colours of Ostland, Talabheim and others that must have been from even further afield than that because he didn't recognise them. And it was a jumble at that. Markus watched a wildly bearded axeman in black-and-white Ostlander trousers and a ripped burgundy doublet block a beastman's axe with his own and then clobber it down with his shield. If there was a uniform then it was brown and red – blood, rust and the forest's clinging mud.

One of the newcomers seemed to wear his sorry state more loosely than the others, and despite the fight that still raged around him Markus found his gaze drawn to that man.

He was tall, clad in mail that looked tough but well used and was covered by a shred of red cloak. A crown of blond hair illuminated his head, shining golden in the weak morning light that made it through the clouds. Brandishing an ornate longsword with the skill of a tournament knight, he glided through the beastmen as if their hooves were shod with lead, shouting encouragement to those around him. Amazingly, those men seemed to fight a little harder and a little better when he passed them.

'Who says the north has no heroes?' said Höller.

Markus looked back. His heart fluttered as he watched the swordsman in the red cloak throw himself between a beaten-looking soldier and the three beasts that assailed him. One beastman went down in short order. Then two. Watching that swordsman's runic blade conduct its work, Markus was put immediately in mind of one of the mighty runefangs, but the Goblin-Bane of Hochland had been lost. *Hochland* had been lost. The third beastman fought as if its gods were watching while more of its horrifying brethren closed in. Markus couldn't watch, but just as it looked as though the swordsman was certain to be overwhelmed, it was the beastmen that were screaming and animal parts went flying as if a bomb had just gone off underneath them. A gory crest of bright red hair emerged from the carnage and the biggest and bloodiest dwarf that Markus had ever clapped eyes on threw himself into the suddenly routed beastmen like a battle-mad minotaur with an axe.

'Steady,' barked Sierck, and Markus thought for a moment that it had been the glimpse of that barbaric dwarf that had led his comrades to waver.

But then he saw the true reason, and he trembled as the brief hope that had begun to fill him ebbed away. Ernst Höller clutched his shield and moaned.

This was not a time for men: these were days of legend and destiny, of gods adopting mortal flesh to renew again the great struggles of the elder days.

They were the End Times.

And the Chaos warrior had reached the hill.

A madness of shapes and sounds blurred around Felix Jaeger as he fought. Screams and butchery hemmed him in and simply breathing left the taste of uncooked offal on his tongue. The clash of blades reverberated like the hammering of a blacksmith's forge.

Too close and too dog-tired for the elegant swordplay he had swooned over as a youth, he kicked, bit and clubbed out with his blade using every instinct and dirty trick that he had accrued like scars over two decades chained to the Slayer's shadow. A rusted sword slid through the flailing scraps of his Sudenland wool cloak and banged his shoulder blade. His armour absorbed the worst of it, but the recent bruise underneath left him in no doubt that he'd been hit. Gritting his teeth through the pain, he got his sword up to meet an in-swinging glaive with a numbing parry, then massaged the blow across his body and kneed the bull-headed gor in the kidney. An arrow whistled inches past Felix's face as he ignored the snap of pain in his back to shoulder the beastman aside. The braying creature fell straight into the path of an axe meant for the struggling swordsman to Felix's right.

Blood sprayed Felix's overgrown beard and painted the right side of his face with a warm mask.

The soldier, all damaged ringmail vest and muddied burgundy and gold doublet, looked at Felix with awe as though Sigmar himself had just arrived to smite his foes. Felix would have gladly introduced the soldier's skull to the heavily ornate dragonhead hilt of Karaghul had another beastman not immediately burst from the melee with a halberd. Felix turned it on the flat of his blade and struck open the beastman's ribcage with his return. When Felix glanced over his shoulder the man was gone, the fight having already dragged them apart. Trapping his scrappy red cloak between his cheek and his shoulder Felix mopped sweat and blood from his face.

Felix was too old for this; too, too old. He had an old warhorse's joints and they still ached from the last battle – with a Kurgan warband over the ruins of a forester's winter station, after which they had decided that even the forest's back roads were too dangerous to move an army on. He let his stiff muscles guide him, parrying faster than he could think. He thought it quite probable that he would be dead in the next ten minutes; fifteen, perhaps, if the men around him could remember what he had tried to drill into them.

Mentally applauding his keen view of any situation's bright side, Felix quickly scanned the melee for a sign of the Chaos warrior. In Felix's experience – and how he hated that he had become an authority on such matters – Chaos armies were second only to those of greenskins for their reliance on the strength and personality of their leaders.

If the Chaos warrior could be taken down...

Listing wagons rose from the ferment where Felix had last spotted the champion's dark blue armour, like beached wrecks. There was no sign of him, or his coterie of icon-bearers and musicians, but Felix was certain that he was in amongst that wreckage somewhere. He looked past it to where a paltry group of spearmen or pikemen – it was too far away to tell – in Hochland colours defended the hill from what looked like a nearly endless surge of rabid beastmen. It was destined to be a last stand unless someone did something about it.

That that someone would again have to be Felix Jaeger, poet, propagandist and unlikely wanderer, struck him as sorely unfunny.

A resounding *clang* clawed Felix's full attention back to the immediate fight. A grizzly Kislevite axeman had blocked the stroke of his beastman counterpart and now tested his biceps against the beast's. Elsewhere, Felix saw another man gored by a charging beastman's horns and trampled under its hooves. A ululating goat-like cry warbled from somewhere within the crush of bodies. It was less a battle than a bar brawl, a form of close-quarters, no-holds-barred violence in which the semi-feral beasts of Chaos were eminently equipped to excel.

'Keep together,' Felix shouted, charging to the aid of the Kislevite and hacking his unsuspecting opponent down from behind. 'Don't try to take them one-on-one. Don't try to match them for strength. Stick to your friends and trust them to fight for you.'

'Jaeger!' someone nearby belted out with the patriotic fervour of a battle cry. The Kislevite took it up in his heavily accented tongue and suddenly Felix was surrounded by a coming together of men shouting his name.

A mix of anger and embarrassment gave Felix the strength to plunge Karaghul clean through a beastman's neck. The Chaos blitzkrieg through Kislev and the Empire had ground cities to rubble and brought both nations to collapse, and the men left behind were hard and coarse, dark stones sieved from the more civilised flour. For some reason they looked to Felix to be a leader, but he was just like them: a man trying to get home to his family. He hadn't saved a single one of them from Chaos. He had just brought them together and given them a direction.

Altdorf.

The painful memories associated with home, and his decision to leave it in the first place, were forced out of his mind as a powerfully built beastman in a red leather jack and a visored helmet bulled through the herd from Felix's blind side. It swept back an enormous war-axe. Felix reckoned that that had been about five minutes. He had always fancied himself an optimist. The axe-beast made it to within arm's reach when it crunched to a sudden standstill and coughed blood over the side of Felix's face.

'The manling's with me,' came a voice like an iron boot on beast-man gristle.

The beastman clawed feebly at the air as it was hoisted from the ground, Gotrek's starmetal axe still buried in the base of its spine. As if raising a fully-grown and armoured bull gor over his head was a feat he could gladly repeat all day, the Slayer spread his cut and blistered lips into a spiteful grin. Blood spotted his scalp, increasing to a patter every time the beastman flailed a hoof for his huge crest of orange hair.

'Must we stop for every mewling stray that falls into our laps?' said Gotrek. The runes of his blade glowed redly through the suspended beastman's flesh, casting a bruise-like pall of discolouration over his swollen, tattooed bulk. Purple shadows gathered within the knot of scar tissue that filled his hollow eye socket. 'I vowed to return you to the little one, manling, not every man and dwarf between Praag and Talabheim.'

Felix ground his teeth, pulled his sword back up into a guard and turned his back on the murderous dwarf. Just looking at his one-time friend made him feel sick inside. Felix could see blood on the dwarf's hands and no amount of beastmen deaths were going to wash it away. An oath tethered the Slayer to him, and this time it wasn't even his. It was dwarf stubbornness and a grossly misplaced sense of obligation rather than his own drunken stupidity that plagued him now.

'Did you see where that Chaos warrior went?' Felix replied finally, voice wire-tight.

'You are infuriating, manling. How am I to keep you safe when you charge headlong into a herd of beasts after a champion of the Dark Powers?'

'Frustrating, isn't it?'

From behind Felix's back, there was the sound of something wet being wrenched from a blade followed by a thump. 'What was that?'

'Never mind.'

Taking advantage of the death that inevitably surrounded Gotrek Gurnisson in a battle, Felix again wiped blood from his eyes and studied the knot of Hochland spears on the hill. He was convinced that the Chaos warrior had been heading for them. He was about to share his thinking with Gotrek when he heard what sounded like a child's scream from the opposite direction. He snapped around, thoughts of Kat and a diffuse paternal longing swirling through his mind before his eyes settled on a dim haze of pike shafts and powder smoke in the distance. His fingers tightened around the hilt of his sword, squeezing the golden ring he wore on his fourth finger.

He turned to Gotrek. It punched him in the gut to have to ask.

'What?'

'I think there are families back there.'

Gotrek snorted; amusement, derision, Felix could never tell and neither reflected terribly well on the dwarf.

'If you don't then I will.'

The dwarf's expression hardened. 'And let you chase after a Chaos warrior while my back is turned? On my oath, manling, I will not.'

'You know what Chaos warriors are like. He'll be onto you the moment he – Gotrek, am I boring you?'

Gotrek smothered his yawn with a hand the size of a cured ham. He shook his head blearily. If Felix didn't know better, he'd say the dwarf looked tired. The golden chain running between his nose and his ear clinked. He ran his thumb around the rim of his axe blade until a bead of blood formed against the meteoric steel. 'I know the drill, manling. Just point me at him.'

'Push,' roared Sergeant Sierck. 'Push as your bloody mothers pushed.'

With one voice, the Hochlanders echoed the defiant roar of the newcomers from the woods and pushed. Beastmen bellowed and battered at the men's shields. The animals pushed back, but slowly the discipline of the men of Hochland ground them down the hill.

Though Markus Weissman was so overwrought with terror that his arms shook, he pushed until he wept. He would have run if he could, but they were surrounded. Now there was hope, a champion, and all they had to do was fight a little harder to reach him. Even that slim hope was almost too much to bear.

Vision spotting, Markus snatched glimpses over the top of his shield. He saw the dwarf with the axe and the red-cloaked swordsman part company, almost felt the impact as the dwarf hit the mass of beastmen like a catapult stone. He was going the wrong way! Why was the dwarf heading away from them? Then Markus saw that the swordsman was still coming towards him and that the dread warrior at the base of the hill had paused to turn towards the commotion on his flank. The armoured fiend looked from Markus and the others to the dwarf. It felt as though a lead weight had been removed from his chest.

The man and the dwarf would save them after all!

Then the Chaos warrior turned back, negligently raised one night-blue gauntlet and held it high as it erupted into incandescent black flame.

Felix felt a tingle run down the nape of his neck and he shivered, almost missing a parry that allowed a beastman in clanking mail skirts to graze his arm with its sword. Felix was familiar with the uncanny blessings that the Ruinous Powers could bestow upon their favourites but such gifts tended to run towards the prosaic – tentacles, horns, bigger muscles, deadlier blades. Disquiet running through him like icemelt, Felix sold the sword-beast a feint and then opened its gut with a deft downward flick of his blade. Felix recovered his stance as the beastman fell, cracking its flat boar-like snout on the upside-down barrel of a cannon.

This part of the battlefield was littered with the detritus of what looked like an artillery train. Bronze and steel barrels lay on the ground like caskets waiting to be buried. Felix felt a stab of regret that these mighty weapons had not even had a chance to be fired before they were destroyed. If they had then this battle might have gone very differently.

Felix still couldn't see the Chaos warrior for the broken wagons that dotted the intervening space as though dropped from the sky to their destruction, but then he didn't need to. He had enough experience of sorcerers to recognise the unease gurgling mockingly in his gut. It was just like his luck to run into a Chaos warrior blessed with perhaps the one gift against which Felix had no means of defence. Felix kissed Kat's ring and prayed for a miracle.

Where was Max when Felix needed him?

Markus's guts coiled in his belly like a serpent. The hairs on the back of his hands stood on end as if it was suddenly as cold as night, and a shiver ran him through from head to toe. The Chaos warrior had become a beacon, a pillar of black flame that touched the tormented sky and washed the beastman herds below with broken shadow. Markus had never been particularly observant with his prayers, but right then, despite his gods' failure to defend his home, he didn't see any other alternatives. Hopelessly, he cast about for the hero in the red cloak. He felt an arm slot through his.

'Sigmar preserve us,' said Ernst Höller.

'Spare us,' Markus stammered.

'Stand!' yelled Sierck, sweeping his sword high through the misted breath that wreathed his torso. The temperature continued to plummet. The professional soldier's voice was taut with worry. That troubled Markus almost as much as the sorcerer himself. 'Show them Empire st–'

He never finished.

His raised sword ignited with black fire as though it had been struck by lightning. In that sudden flash, Markus saw the man's bones silhouetted against the writhing grey of muscle and flesh. The men to Sierck's immediate left and right were screaming as searing ash fell on bare flesh and set light to their clothes. One of them was clubbed down by a triumphant beastman, but all Markus could do was stare in dumb horror. A disgusting wave rippled across Sierck's charred remains. His chest began to bloat.

Markus broke from his fugue, some instinct pulling his friend, Höller, behind him as he turned his shield from the beastmen and onto his former sergeant instead. An anaemic tentacle lined with suckers and barbs punched through his wooden shield and his cured leather vest and burst from his back.

'Doomed!' Markus croaked, before an eruption of prehensile limbs tore his company apart.

An explosion tore out the top of the hill. Distance and the proximate sounds of combat rendered it hauntingly silent, and Felix watched in what felt like slow motion as the tentacled monster was sucked back into the Realm of Chaos and body parts began to fall. Felix cursed, raising an arm to shield himself from what looked like a man's lung. It splattered against his forearm. Felix felt ill. The beast-man nearest to him was neither as concerned nor as lucky and what looked like a horse's head in a horned helm crashed through the roof of its skull like a mortar shell. With a pattering of splats and bangs, the downpour intensified.

Felix screamed for the men around him to take cover and then dived between the wheels of a hobbled gun-carriage. He flinched as something heavy and best left unidentified crunched onto the boards above his head, followed by a bony skirling reminiscent of beads cut from a necklace. An unfortunate image of vertebrae crossed his mind and the urge to vomit returned in force.

What had happened to the world, he thought? After so many years of wandering, Felix had thought himself inured to horror, but this was too much. He was sick and he was tired and he just wanted it all to stop. Not for the first time he wondered if he had done the right thing by coming to these strangers' aid when they could so easily have continued on unmolested. But that wasn't the Empire he remembered and it wasn't the one he still hoped to return to. That absence had given him a romanticised view of his homeland, Felix would not argue, but he had only done what any decent human being would have done, whether they were men of Ind or the Empire.

Slowly, the drumming on the chassis above his head eased to a desultory sputter and Felix took a deep breath and crawled out from under the far side.

The apocalyptic scene that awaited would not have looked out of place on the warped plains of the Chaos Wastes.

The wreckage of wagons and Imperial war machines lay everywhere, strewn with bodies and pulverised by falling gore. Everything, even the air itself, carried a pink glaze, thickening to crimson over the hilltop itself where a faint mushroom-shaped cloud was rising. A hollow clangour of fighting still rang out sporadically between the wrecks, but it was disarmingly calm, stunned into near silence.

Flat on his belly, Felix wriggled across the blood-slicked rocks and then pushed himself to his knees. He was surrounded by bodies, most of them men, garbed in workmanlike leather and dark tabards that marked them as engineers from one of the provincial gunnery schools. Felix wasn't familiar enough with the Empire's various institutions of engineering to tell exactly which. He supposed it didn't matter. It was one dead place or another dead place.

The body immediately in front of him already looked to have been half-eaten. Entrails spilled around the man's sides from a messy wound in his gut. There was a long-barrelled pistol tucked under his belt. The man had clearly been killed before he had had a chance to draw it. Felix supposed that that was a mercy of sorts. Without thinking, he took the firearm. A year surviving in the Chaos-occupied wildernesses of Kislev and the Empire had taught him to waste not. Taken by a sudden melancholy he closed his grip around the walnut stock, felt over the rough etching on the barrel with his thumb, A maker's mark, perhaps. Felix wondered where it was. Did their city still stand? Was this gunsmith still alive? Pushing the sudden wash of hopelessness aside, he pushed the barrel under his trousers against the opposite hip to his scabbard. There was no shot or powder that Felix could see and he had neither the time nor the inclination to go rooting through the engineer's blood-drenched pockets. He rose.

His determination to kill the Chaos warrior had become all-consuming. It heated his blood like a fever. Had he had the time to consider it then that might have troubled him more than it did, but right now he needed to punish the man – the *fiend* – that could unleash devastation like this. Quelling his protesting stomach, Felix turned again to the wagon, stuck his hand over the tailboard's sticky coating, and climbed aboard.

The squat, wasted power of a mortar barrel sat over the axle, lashed down with ropes and partially covered with a canvas. Felix moved towards it, ignoring the sticky squelching noise from underfoot as he took advantage of the high ground to get his first decent look at the battlefield.

The area around the hill had been bloodily pacified. Beastmen lay around the summit in rings like trees felled by a meteor. In Felix's immediate vicinity, men that looked as bloody as corpses themselves were only just beginning to pull themselves up and blink in horror at the scene around them. Felix planted his boot on the gun barrel and swept his cloak over his shoulder. He probably cut quite the inspiring figure, but there was little else for it if he wanted to be seen.

'Find your captains and regroup by the forest,' Felix shouted, pitching his voice low to make it carry as he had learned – in another life, it sometimes felt – as a student of the dramatic arts. 'And don't forget to keep together.'

As the shell-shocked soldiers withdrew from the weapon train, Felix turned his gaze south to where the battle continued to rage.

It looked like the Hochlanders' rearguard had pulled their wagons into a defensive ring. The vehicles' high wooden sides were hung with shields and bristled with spears. Arrows and bolts hummed through the air and, intermittently, the *crack* of handgun fire rolled over the carnage like thunder. The tip of Gotrek's crest shook violently within the churn. Felix saw a unit of kossars in long open-fronted coats running in to support him with hand-axes and javelins. Felix suspected that it was an act less of courage than of self-preservation. Felix had only followed Gotrek into half of the improbable situations that he had because the alternative – the slight chance of having to face them without the Slayer beside him – was somehow even worse.

After a moment's searching he found his target. Even amongst this level of anarchy a Chaos warrior could not hide, and nor did he seem to want to. His mounted honour guard made a discordant racket of drums and gongs and booming horns. The dark champion was marching straight towards where Gotrek was fighting and Felix was tempted to let nature take its course. He gladly would have, if not for the people trapped inside that ring of wagons. The devastation that the Chaos warrior could wreak on them was too terrible to imagine and Felix couldn't trust Gotrek to care enough about their wellbeing to help them.

The same impulse that had once driven him into a zombie-infested castle on the slim possibility that Kat had still been alive within sent him leaping for the next wagon. It had lost its left rear wheel and was pitched at a sharp angle, but this time the gloopy surface worked to Felix's advantage and he kept his balance with only a token wave of his arms. He jumped down.

Immediately a beastman ran at him, intending to skewer him on its bull-like horns. Felix wrong-footed it with a deft feint and it brained itself unconscious on the wagon's tough wooden chassis. Then he sprinted for the next wagon.

This one was little more than a twisted undercarriage on wheels and Felix slid into it, slamming his mailed shoulder into its front wheel. He winced at the flowering pain from his bruised back and then, holding his sword close to his chest, peered around and over his cover's mangled iron frame.

The Chaos warrior was about twenty paces distant and moving further away. He was as tall at the shoulder as his cavalry. The fell nightshade glow of his armour gleamed between their tattooed bodies like a solitary candle being borne away into the deep wood.

There was no more cover, but Felix still didn't think much of his chances against so many formidable-looking fighters *and* a champion of the Dark Powers. If he could get in fast, if he could take the warrior by surprise...

Felix forced himself to stop thinking. Nothing good lay along those lines. He had faced the scions of ruin more than once and, but for one instance of blind luck when he and Ulrika had together defeated Aekold Helbrass, he had never come out on top.

A warrior did not rise above the competition of all his peers and survive decades or more of strife to become a champion of Chaos unless they were far more potent a force in the world than Felix Jaeger. Felix swore, nevertheless loosening his hold on his sword to something more practical than the current death grip.

He had come this far.

'Uncle!'

Felix turned towards the direction of the shout and, as always when he saw his nephew in Ulrika's ivory-white scale armour and wielding her heavy Gospodar-style cavalry sabre, he thought for a moment that he had seen a ghost. He willed his heart to steady. That was one spirit he did not wish to see again.

Gustav Jaeger crabbed alongside a wagon some way back from Felix's position and a little to the right. It was angled such that Felix could see the heavily armed and armoured former free company men filing in behind his nephew. At the front wheel, Gustav peered around before emitting a curse and yanking himself back.

'Tell me you're not thinking it.'

Felix chose not to answer. A thousand leagues of dirt had accumulated under the scales of Gustav's armour like dust under a gravedigger's nails. The black wolfskin draped over his shoulders had an arrow stuck in it that, by Felix's assessment of the enemy's armament, could only have been a stray from their own side. His long blond hair was tied in a ponytail with a black cloth. One of his hands was roughly bandaged, but he clutched his awkward weapon in a determined grip. He wasn't the same arrogant merchant's boy who had left Badenhof.

He'd earned his arrogance.

'Shouldn't you and your men be anchoring the right?' said Felix.

'It may have escaped your notice, but we don't have a right. Anyway, I assumed you'd be about to do something borderline heroic.'

Felix shook his head. Why did Gustav have to turn everything into a melodrama?

As Felix considered his options, a Kislevite man in a much-patched hemp coat adorned with ribbons and brightly-coloured buttons ran hunched along the line of soldiers with his bow held out before him. Tassels flew from both of the recurved ends. Gustav and the others shuffled back and Kolya took his place, conjuring an arrow seemingly from thin air and drawing it back on his string. His coat was unsleeved – the Empire's spring being too warm for 'civilised' men – and the rangy muscles of his bare arms pulled as taut as his bowstring. He drew a mark on the Chaos warrior's back, then relaxed and lowered his aim.

'Just shoot,' said Gustav. 'Don't milk it.'

Kolya sucked in through the gaping holes between his teeth. 'Chaos plate? At this range? If you must hunt bear with stick then stick should be very long and very sharp, yes?'

'You think all of that makes you sound clever, don't you?' said Gustav.

'Is wisdom of oblast, friend Gustav.'

'Well, I think you make them up as you go.'

'That would be more clever even, no?'

'Shouldn't you be with Gotrek?' Felix asked, interrupting their bickering, one eye on the Chaos warrior.

'It take more than few beasts to finish *Zabójka*, Empire. And if they do,' the former lancer produced a nonchalant shrug, 'then maybe he prefer I not see.'

Felix scowled. The Kislevite's professional deficiencies as a rememberer were thankfully none of his concern. He told himself that, but he couldn't help being annoyed by it on some level. Without thinking, he drew his pistol. *Very long and very sharp.* He knew from experience that Imperial science was a long way from rivalling the destructive wonders of the dwarfs, but he would still bet on a well-made pistol against even Chaos plate any day. A crying shame then that it wasn't loaded.

'Does anyone know how to use one of these things?'

'Toss it here,' said Gustav. Felix hurled it overarm and Gustav snatched it neatly out of the air with his uninjured hand.

'Where is Max?' asked Kolya as Gustav inspected the pistol's barrel and powder chamber.

A good question, thought Felix. Max had almost single-handedly blasted them all out of Praag in the most incredible display of one being's power that Felix had ever seen, but he hadn't been the same man since. He peered again over his wagon's ruined side, watching the Chaos warrior and his retinue slide ever further out of range. Max would have taken this sorcerer apart plate by plate and then blasted whatever was left inside into whatever hell he most feared.

'Here!'

Felix glanced back just as Gustav lobbed the pistol his way. The throw was long, forcing Felix out of hiding in order to catch it. He let out a relieved breath when it didn't detonate or otherwise go off in his hands. Powerful these new weapons may have been, but temperamental they certainly were. He brought the weapon up in a two-handed grip, careful to retain some looseness in his joints to adjust for recoil, and swiftly moved after the Chaos warrior. He needed to get closer.

He sighted down the barrel. His heart pounded. He had always had a good eye.

But he would only get one shot.

Corporal Herschel Mann, last officer of Hergig, brought the arrowhead base of his kite shield chopping into a wounded beastman's skull and expelled his barely contained terror in a roar. His throat was sore from breathing smoke and shouting orders. He drew up his battered shield and pounded a beat into it with the hilt of his sword. Even he could barely hear it. Gunpowder smoke clogged his nose and his ears. Inside the ring of wagons it was sulphurous and hot and packed with bodies, most of them wounded, all of them screaming.

Herschel assured himself that it was surely preferable to what lay outside.

He was a simple man, a woodcutter's son with little ambition beyond a home in the officers' district, a modest stipend for his retirement and a crop of grandchildren to see him to a fair old age. He was also, he knew, a man of limited imagination. His nobler-born superiors had often commented on it favourably, and it had served him well as city after city fell to the relentless push of Chaos. But even he couldn't help but wonder.

How could Sigmar allow this?

One of the wagons lurched as though struck by a giant's club, sending Hochland soldiers and the beastmen they fought flying from its back. Bits of wood and splinters flew in all directions and it finally dawned on Herschel that those on the other side had tired of trying to fight their way over and were going to simply tear their way through. The wagon split in half, shedding wood like horsehair from a ripped pillowcase and driving men choking to their knees.

Coughing, Herschel levelled his sword and shield. He never had started that family that he had thought so important to him, but he would lay down his life to defend his men's. Whatever was coming for them, it could not be worse than what failure would mean. The end.

A pair of beastmen charged screaming through the cloud of splinters, wide-eyed and frothing at the mouth. Before Herschel could react, a monstrous axe flashed. The first beastman toppled as its legs were carved from under it, then the second bleated in panic before that axe chopped into its back. Herschel Mann lowered his shield and stood open-mouthed as a horrific-looking dwarf stepped onto the beastman's corpse with a grisly crunch of popping vertebrae and then ruthlessly put down its disabled fellow as it struggled to crawl away. The dwarf was a lean, heaving mass of muscle, scored by scars and barbarous tattoos and hunched over the impossible weight of his axe. A frightening crest of dyed hair rose to greater than the height of a man from his shaved head.

Herschel met the dwarf's one good eye, intending to offer his heartfelt thanks and those of his men, but something caught his tongue. The dwarf's other eye was a knot of scar tissue, as though his sight had been clawed out by some unspeakable terror. It was like looking down a gun barrel, but the good eye was worse. Herschel had buried men with more human feeling in their eyes.

The dwarf hefted his axe as he surveyed the group of survivors. His bruised lips pursed in what could only be called disappointment, and then he grunted and turned back to the fight.

Felix narrowed his eyes and tried to concentrate on his aim, but the more he tried to focus, the more his mind seemed to wander.

He saw Kat and the house in Altdorf that they had shared with his brother. Felix had not been happy there, but looking back on it now he thought that perhaps he should have been. His child would be almost a year old now. He tried to imagine what she – and somehow he had decided that it was a she – would look like, but found that he could not. In his heart, he knew that Kat, Otto, Annabella, and everyone else he had left behind in Altdorf were, if not dead, then gone from his life forever. This particular Chaos warrior had nothing to do with that personally but from where Felix was standing, ankle-deep in gore and with a pistol trained on the warrior's backplate, he seemed as fitting a recipient of a little retribution as any.

A northman struck his gong with a mallet. The sound reverberated over the clash of arms, the screams. The northman's horse snorted as he yelled something that Felix was too focused to make out.

He forced his mind to clear, letting out his breath as he had watched trained handgunners, and even Kat with her bow, do before taking an important shot. Sweat pooled between the palm of his hand and the pistol's carved walnut stock. One shot. It all came down to this. Afterwards, it seemed likely that the Chaos warrior's vengeful retinue would mob him, unless Gustav's men could get to him first. He pushed the thought aside. What would come next no longer seemed to matter.

As his vision centred, the warrior's deep nightshade armour blurred to become bruised muscle. Star-bright runes and metal spines twisted to resemble crawling tattoos.

Felix hated what these times had made of him. What was worse was the certainty that it didn't have to be this way.

'Curse you, Gotrek Gurnisson.'

And then he fired.

TWO

Shadows

'Fighting again, Felix? If you're not careful someone will get hurt one of these days.'

'I'm always careful, mother,' said Felix brightly, troubled only for a brief moment by the nagging doubt that he had no earthly business here in Altdorf on this grey spring day, tossing a silver coin to the driver and then disembarking from the open-topped carriage.

He winced and held his ribs as his feet touched the cobbles. That last fight had hurt, however much he sought to pass it off as horseplay.

Strange then that he could not remember very much about it.

He seemed to recall the loud bang of a pistol, and then being mobbed by half a dozen men twice his size. He forced a smile onto his face. Whoever his latest opponent had been, he was clearly an unconscionable knave of the worst sort. Felix hoped he had given a good account for honourable conduct, but the fragmentary nature of his recollections on the subject did not fill him with confidence.

The coachman dipped his cap to Felix's generosity and with a crack of his whip sent his vehicle rolling down the – now he noticed it – oddly deserted cobbles of Befehlshaber Avenue. At any time of day it would ordinarily be filled with hawkers and merchants, its old stone frontages competing for extravagance and the attention of the well-heeled foot-traffic that passed by. But not now. Shaking off the ambiguous sense of disquiet, he turned to where his mother waited.

She stood alone at the end of the driveway, dwarfed by the looming black iron gates that stood open either side of her. Felix had the terrible suspicion that she intended to greet him thusly every time his studies at the university were suspended for the Sigmarzeit holiday. The drive behind her was dark. Felix could barely see the house at all, just a black silhouette against the sky hidden behind rank after rank of bare-clawed maples. They rustled softly, as if aggrieved by Felix's regard, jarring yet at the same recent and familiar.

They aren't here any more, spoke a voice from his subconscious that sounded remarkably familiar. It was older, authoritative in a jaded sort of way, but unmistakably his own.

The house flickered, a degraded aspect superimposing over that silhouette as the trees became bloated and heavy with fly-infested fruits. To each one, a diseased figure had been crucified and writhed in pain. The sky crackled and broke. The visage of a corpulent, pus-ridden daemon rose over the skyline, gurgling in its own degradation and pleasure. It appeared for a minute and then it was gone, and the house returned to the darkness that had possessed it before.

His mother embraced him warmly and despite his unease Felix returned the gesture as though he had not seen her in decades rather than the few short months it must have been. She kissed him on the cheek, then pulled back and rubbed the mark her lips had made on his skin with her thumb. She regarded him with a sad smile, deepening the crows' feet around her eyes. Her blonde hair had been largely banished to lie amongst the grey and tied behind her head in a bun. Felix recognised in her his own blue eyes, his strong jaw. It was odd that he hadn't noticed it before she... before what? He couldn't remember. He was struck by how frail she looked.

'*Renata*,' intoned a voice from the house that Felix both did and did not recognise. It reminded him somewhat of his father's, but it terrified him in a way that the old man never had. It was as deep as black and solemn as death. '*Leave the boy alone and return to me. You should not be out there alone.*'

'Is... everything all right?' Felix asked. He heard a *thump* as of a footstep from the driveway. The maples had drawn closer. Their branches swayed in the breeze, or at least Felix thought they were branches; every so often they appeared to be writhing human limbs, blistered with boils and wet with blood and pus. The shadows pulled tighter. He backed away. 'You do look unwell, mother. Perhaps I should take you to the–' a vision of a too-young woman lying still on a bed beneath symbols of doves and bleeding hearts filled his mind '–Shallyan temple.'

His mother sighed. 'It is too late for that, Felix. The master still has need of me, and it is best not to defy him when he is in so dark a mood.'

Now what was it about that particular choice of words that troubled him?

As Felix backed away, the iron gateposts appeared to grow, bending in at the tips to seal his mother under a huge black arch. Shadows flowed in from the driveway to fill in the outline of the arch. A likeness shivered across its form, recognisably human yet hideously vague. The trees reached their branches over the walls of his father's estate, twisting around the shadow-figure to form curving horns that extended from its daemonic head and what appeared to be wings that opened out from its back.

His mother was still visible within the moulded darkness, but contact with this figure seemed to have affected her for her appearance stuttered. At times she appeared as a tall man, garbed in flowing white robes and standing with the aid of a snake-headed staff. At others, and sometimes in the same glance, she was an Ungol wise woman, shrouded in glittering black silk with moonlight-white hair spilling from her raised hood.

'You're... not my mother,' Felix replied. 'She died.'

'Everybody dies, Felix,' the apparition answered. 'Even me. And I suspect you as well, although your fate lies shrouded in a place where even my eyes cannot see.'

Felix held out his hand for her, glancing over his shoulder for the companion that he knew should be there but wasn't. The darkness echoed his terror with laughter.

'*Everybody dies...*'

Rain splotched Felix's eyelids. He grunted, his familiar old body welcoming him back to a world of pain. The hum of flies filled his ears. The monotonous *chop* of broken wagons being reduced to portable chunks reverberated between bare rock and the encircling trees. The taste of fresh rain lay between his lips. The ground under his back was uneven and disturbingly human in its contours. Under a fusillade of cracks, pops, and coloured stars on the backs of his eyelids he shifted position. A leather-encased arm rolled out from beneath him. Felix felt queasy. It was some way from being his preferred course of action, but he opened his eyes. Gustav gummed into focus. The rain made a faint halo around the ivory-white scales of his armour. His face was smeared with blood and bore an expression of concern that swiftly disappeared when he noticed that Felix was awake.

'What happened?' said Felix.

'We returned to Altdorf, don't you remember?' said Gustav. 'Cheering crowds lined the Konigplatz waving flags and shouting your name. Castle Reikguard fired a twenty-one gun salute to honour its hero's return and a company of Bretonnian pegasus knights performed an aerial display in your honour. Emperor Karl Franz of course named you Elector of Ostermark then and there which was met with rapturous approval by all, and then we retired to the Rose and Thorn for ale and pastries. Unfortunately that was when your dwarf challenged the Emperor and Ludwig Schwarzhelm to a head-butting contest, after which things got messy. That's probably why your head hurts.'

He wished it was just his head. 'This isn't funny.'

'No, I suppose not.' Gustav took a deep breath and let it out in a sigh. He looked down at Felix's still-recumbent form. 'But duelling with a Chaos champion and his entire retinue for a good half a minute before Kolya and I pulled you out didn't do your reputation any harm. Personally, I think you have as good a call on the Ostermark runefang as anybody else right now.'

Felix growled inwardly. If he'd had it up to his neck with men who should know better referring to him as 'my lord', then he was fed up to the eyeballs of the outlandish stories of his personal heroism in the face of evil.

Yes, he had helped Gotrek hold the ford at Choika against that beastman herd while the army had crossed, but the Slayer had done the bulk of the fighting. What Felix most recalled of that day was the chill he had come down with afterwards. And yes, granted, he had personally defeated and slain the mutant ogre that had rampaged into their camp from the oblast, but the creature had been half mad from drinking the warpstone-contaminated waterways of Kislev and had been practically dead already, not that anyone seemed to want to hear that.

In response to Felix's early enquiries into the source of those tales, Gustav had impishly suggested that they might all have read Felix's book.

'Are you getting up, then, or not?' said Gustav, fingering the businesslike grip of his long Gospodar sabre and giving the twin puncture-scars on the side of his neck a habitual scratch. 'More than enough beastmen got away to cause us trouble if they decide to come back, and their champion wasn't in as bad a shape as you'd think, considering.'

Felix stiffened and tried to rise, only for a lance of molten agony to shoot up through his legs. He bit down on the urge to scream. Muscle cramp, that was all, although *all* seemed a little trite given the pain it was causing him just now. What had become of the days when he could get through a fight like the one just gone and be ready for more by the afternoon? Now it felt as though his tendons had been stiffened with steel pins and he doubted whether he could lift his sword if a dragon were to burst from the forest. He let his efforts out in a gasp of breath and slapped his thigh.

'Help me.'

Uttering some choice phrases from the lexicon of Altdorf's docks, Gustav dropped to his haunches to scoop up one of Felix's feet and then, holding the leg straight, pushed it back over Felix's body and leaned his weight against it. Felix gasped at the sudden spike of pain, but it subsided almost immediately. He felt stiff ligaments stretch and loosen and almost moaned aloud with relief.

'Do you seriously still intend to try and re-enlist when we get back to Altdorf?' said Gustav.

'They'd have to throw me into the Reiksfang to stop me.'

Then Gustav switched legs, pushing down until Felix's vision broke out in spots. Nightmare visions of his home aflame and presided over by pustulent daemons shattered in his mind as some cartilaginous blockage in his calf went *snap.*

It would be a hard journey. Every provincial back road was a highway for a Chaos army these days, and the woods were rife with beastmen and worse. Felix had led his company of survivors this far into Talabecland by avoiding even game trails where possible, but chance encounters like this one would only grow more difficult to elude now that they finally neared the Empire's heartlands. To his surprise that didn't trouble him. In truth, he was more than a little afraid at the prospect of what might be waiting for them at Altdorf. Felix had not seen a single town or village still standing since his departure from Badenhof for Kislev two years ago.

But if vengeance was what Altdorf needed then she would find Felix Jaeger able and willing.

Gustav let go of Felix's leg and stepped back. Felix sat and extended his hand for a little help and the younger man duly obliged, clasping his hand a little more firmly than was strictly necessary and pulling him up.

His nephew was all he had left now.

Whatever happened to the Empire, Felix had reached the age where it was impossible to ignore the fact that there were fewer days ahead for him than there were behind. It was Gustav's fate he worried for rather than his own these days, the sort of world that Felix could leave for him. And for Kat and their child. If they were still alive. It was all that kept him going.

Gustav supported his uncle with a loose grip at the elbow, then stepped aside, granting Felix a view of the clearing behind him.

Felix covered his mouth with his hand and almost gagged on the stench.

A freshly tilled field of death stretched out to the treeline. Pale, lean men in muddy cloaks picked through the corpses of man and beast like serfs harvesting a crop of beans. The wind sent chills rustling through the ocean of trees, bearing the rumour of thunder from the charcoal sky to the north. The cool breeze tightened the blood on Felix's face, prickling his skin like goose bumps. He drew his cloak around his chest and shivered. There was something out there: a shadow, always behind him whichever way he turned.

A faint cry from the treeline startled him from his reverie.

His sword was half-drawn from its scabbard when he spotted the kossar in loose-fitting trousers and an open-fronted coat running into the clearing. He moved with an odd, high-kneed gait, bounding from body to body, stomping through puddles and laughing with his comrades in fierce pursuit. The man held what appeared to be a beastman's beer skin high above his head as he ran. Only a Kislevite, Felix thought, relaxing his grip on his sword.

The posse ran close to where Gotrek was overseeing the dismantlement of the Hochlanders' vehicles, the Slayer rubbing his eye tiredly with his fist and bawling at each of them in turn as they passed him. With a growl of impatience, the dwarf turned his glare towards a band of Ostland woodsmen who had had the gall to look up from their work and smile as the kossars' boisterous laughter passed by. Gotrek grumbled his way between two of the woodsmen and took over, his ancient rune-axe blitzing the wagon to matchwood in the time it took the Ostlanders to whip their black cloaks up over their faces.

Felix frowned. His feelings towards his former companion were confused. They had often argued, and too much time with only their own disparate personalities for company had bred its share of conflict. And yet somehow they had always managed to avoid coming to blows or finding themselves in someone's Book of Grudges. Despite that, there had never been a time when Felix was not a little bit afraid of the Slayer. Now, Felix could barely look at the dwarf without seeing the lives he had taken and feeling more than just a little fearful. Did Gotrek hold him in higher regard than he had

Hamnir, or Snorri? Felix knew he would never dare ask, but he suspected not. He was only human – a *manling* – after all.

He would sleep easier when the Slayer's oath was fulfilled and they could again go their separate ways. Felix shook his head as he watched Gotrek stomp determinedly towards another wagon. If he had thought being oathsworn to Gotrek's quest was bad enough, then it was because he'd never thought to consider the implications of actually being the object of one of the Slayer's damned oaths.

'Lord Jaeger!'

A soldier in a piecemeal harness of rain-softened leather and steel covered by an earthy-coloured cloak made a beeline through the bodies towards Felix. From the off-white and black of his livery and the dully golden epaulet on his shoulder he'd been a sergeant in an Ostland regiment. The man removed his helmet to reveal short, weed-snaggled hair and threw a salute.

'He's not talking to me,' Gustav whispered, somewhat sharply, in Felix's ear.

'Kolya sends word that he's called off the chase on the warband,' said the Ostlander. 'He's set sentries in the woods, but he didn't want to venture too far from the main force.'

'Very good, sergeant,' said Felix, remembering to return his best imitation salute. It appeared to satisfy the Ostlander, who saluted again, even more briskly than before, and quick-marched through the puddles in the rocks to where a short column of horse- and hand-drawn wagons was just beginning to trickle into the clearing. Peasant families clung grimly to the sides or trudged alongside.

Felix gave his nephew's hand one last squeeze, then cupped the man's pearl-wet gardbrace in his hand and eased him gently away. Whatever his feelings about it, these people – desperate as they clearly were – looked up to him. They needed their hero, and for as long as the body remained willing then Felix would play that role.

'Where are you going?' said Gustav.

'To see if I can see where we are,' Felix replied, nodding towards the high hill that the poor, doomed Hochlanders had fought to the last man to hold. Unidentifiable bits of meat glistened in the rain. It looked like a butcher's cart had been struck by a mortar.

The hilltop was deserted, understandably so, but for a moment Felix thought he glimpsed a dark figure outlined in black against the grey clouds above the summit. A frisson of dread passed through him, utterly convinced for one irrational moment that the figure spied on him on behalf of the darkness he sensed from the forest. In the space of a shiver, the feeling was gone, as was the figure, and Felix wished he could say that the two had been unrelated.

But the figure had been Max Schreiber.

Cartilage crunched beneath him as Felix pushed himself to the top of the hill. Blood oozed up from underfoot. Further from the epicentre of the carnage, men and beastmen more-or-less intact lay across each other, appearing to fight each other even in dismemberment and death. Felix covered his mouth, not so much against the smell as the taste. Flies droned around him, perhaps mistaking him for a corpse – and in spirit, surrounded by so much death, he felt like one. He swatted at the buzzing pests, more out of form than the belief that anything Felix Jaeger could do here would make the slightest difference to anything.

'Are you up here, Max?' he said, uncertain why he whispered or why his heart beat so hard.

He crunched to the summit with a grimace and turned full circle. Meat glistened. The rain made dimples in puddles of blood. Trees extended out from the clearing in every direction, whispering and downcast under the rain. The Empire was rather like a dwarfhold, Felix thought. Those men fortunate enough to visit the dwarfs' ancient fastnesses would see only the glittering audience halls beyond the mountain gates, but their deeps plumbed further into the darkness than that. The Empire was the same, its deeps hidden by tangled bowers rather than by stone. It was a sprawling country and perhaps, in days before these, even a great one, but take away its roads, its boats, and the Empire became a far darker and vaster land than even Felix could have believed.

It made the deeds of Sigmar and his descendants even more inspiring. Those were heroes, living in a time of legends. Felix's own deeds felt trifling by comparison.

He peered through the falling grey sheets in the direction he thought was north. It looked like mountains on the horizon, but that couldn't be right. They were shadowing the Bechafen to Talabheim road. There were no mountains in Talabecland.

'Max?'

Relief crept guiltily into his thoughts at the realisation that the wizard was not here. He turned to leave. In the clearing below, a few hundred men and half a dozen wagons assembled. He looked to the endless tracts of forest, and then to the mist-shrouded mountains in the north. He prayed that they weren't lost.

'The End Times near, Felix.'

Felix flinched at the voice from behind him. The warmth leached from his veins and there was very little he wanted more in this world than to never have to turn around and face the man that spoke. He unclenched his fists, took a moment to steel his courage, and then turned.

The rain flattened the old wizard's hood against his face and brought a glisten to his ashen hands, exposed to the wrist where they held the simple yew staff upon which he leaned. Once of proud ivory and gold, his long magister's robes were now bleached grey like his skin. More by memory than by their faded thread Felix picked out the elaborately embroidered geomantic symbols and coiling, self-cannibalising snakes.

'I noticed,' Felix replied, intending to sound light and failing miserably. The wizard's captivity at the pleasure of the Troll King had damaged him, but his strange condition had only worsened since Praag. It troubled Felix to see the last of his old friends in such a sorry way, but Max was far beyond his – or anyone's – ability to help.

Max stared through Felix. The whites of his wide eyes were dark and their gaze clove to something distant, a realm of horror that he and he alone could see.

'The Chaos Moon cracks asunder and falls from the heavens in a firestorm of corruption and death. The Isle of the Dead unravels and mighty Ulthuan sinks to the ocean's bottom while her chill twin falters before the Handmaiden of Khorne. Old certainties fade as new gods arise and the greatest host of daemonkind since the last days of Aenarion musters in the corners of my mind. Your eyes are closed and you notice little, Felix. Oh, so little. If you saw but a fraction of what I must...'

'Neither of us are children, Max. I've walked the Great Bastion of Cathay. I've seen the old ziggurats in the Southlands jungle. I know that Chaos is everywhere. But that's why we have to fight.'

Max bowed his head. 'You do not understand at all.'

'You could have stopped this,' Felix replied after a time, looking down as he slid his foot back and forth through the gory leftovers of men and beasts. 'That sorcerer was no match for the Max I remember.'

'I thought about it.'

To Felix's own surprise, he started laughing. It was a black laugh, the sort that only a man who had administered the ultimate mercy to friends in want of a healer as skilled as Max Schreiber could give. 'I hope for all our sakes you found some answers?'

'Yes. Some. And I knew that this was too petty an engagement to account for you or for Gotrek. You have a destiny, Felix,' said Max urgently as Felix began to turn away. 'Since we first set out together to slay the dragon Skjalandir, I have believed it, and with all that remains of me I know it now. It was not chance that brought us together then and it is not hubris to turn to fate for an explanation of what brings us all together again now.'

Felix tried to hold Max's eyes but couldn't. Their gazes slid across one another, the spaces they inhabited immiscible as oil and water. Felix shivered and wiped rain from the back of his neck, chilled to the marrow by the wizard's talk and angered by how powerfully it had affected him. His destiny, such as it was, was his own and no other's. The thought that some unknowable being might have *done this to him* infuriated him more than the fundamental loss of control over his own fate that such interference implied.

'We're not all together, though, are we? Some of us aren't here.'

'Only those that needed to be.'

Felix's lips flared in sudden rage and his hand moved of its own volition to the hilt of his sword.

Snorri.

Ulrika.

How dare he!

The rain pummelled Max's hood as the wizard beheld the middle distance. With a sigh, Felix let go of his sword. It wasn't the wizard's fault. He was sick, a man with an infected wound. He had not chosen to be this way.

'You should go,' Max murmured, nodding downhill.

On the nearest patch of flat ground between the hill and the tree-line, a gang of unarmoured men, women, and even children were busily erecting an impromptu command tent over the back of an open-topped wagon. As Felix watched, Gotrek and a handful of others gravitated towards it.

'The Hochlanders' commander is the bearer of bad tidings. Your nephew has just heard, and convenes a council of war-captains.'

A prickle of unease stitched down Felix's spine. 'How can you know that?'

Max sighed. It looked as though he closed his eyes, but with grey eyes and grey skin, both concealed under a hood, it was difficult to be certain of anything. 'Some powers I abjure by choice, others force their visions through my shuttered eyes and invade my dreams.'

Felix spun around, his heart turning loops, and tried to pick out Gustav amidst the mismatched uniforms and mud paraded under the rain below. He could see a pocket of Hochlanders in their red and green, but there was no sign of his nephew.

'I would advise you to hurry,' said Max, serene as a passing breeze. 'Gotrek Gurnisson is about to be the recipient of bad news.'

Rain tapped on the leaves above the solemn bier as it traipsed southwards in unexpected defeat. Khamgiin Lastborn, the ever-changing spear of the Silver Road, tried to ignore it and lapse back into unconsciousness. The pain from the wound in his back was terrible, worse even than the ritual scarifications his father had inflicted upon him in his trials of manhood. Pain was just a feeling, a weakness like pity or affection. He told himself that, but the rain's insistent rap on his armour demanded he pay notice and take heed.

By the Dark Master of Chaos, it hurt.

He opened his eyes and blinked away the dreams of torture and sadistic, androgynous daemon-fiends. Were they dreams or were they memories? It was difficult to know; he had lived long and suffered much, both before he had donned Tzeentch's armour and after. Casting the past to the past, he took in his surroundings. Tall trees rose above him, carving up the grey light into meagre portions of light and shadow. The rain rustled lightly through their high leaves. Watching the weaving bowers shift slowly by, Khamgiin came to the realisation that he was laid out on some kind of litter, and that he was moving.

On either side of him walked his men. They marched slowly, eyes low and shoulders hunched. The tribesmen were smeared with blood, their armour scored. Four of their strongest carried him on a shield across their shoulders. Despite his size and weight and their evident weariness, they bore their burden without sufferance. Men of the tribes were not like other men. Though it was many decades since Khamgiin had ridden the steppe, battled hobgoblin and ogre and worse every day simply to live for one more day of struggle, the pride he took in his people's prowess was as strong as it had ever been.

'Temay,' he mouthed, addressing the tall warrior to his right. The man wore a coat of iron and leather scales, woven together with a backing layer of silk and worn over a sleeveless silk vest. His head was shaved but for a topknot. An elaborate tattoo of an eagle spread its wings over one cheek.

The warrior did not answer. Weakly, Khamgiin rolled his head around to the left.

'Khidu. What struck me? Was it him?'

Still no answer. The men marched on like dead men to the underworld. Khamgiin tried to remember the end of the battle, but it was a blur of screams and fire. It had been as one-sided a rout as any he had come to expect from this soft land. Except for the dwarf. Yes, he remembered something now. The dwarf had been a foe worthy of Khamgiin's gifts. Then there had been a loud bang and then... He winced as the memory brought with it an unpleasant throbbing pain in between his shoulder blades. He worked his mouth. It was as dry as the Great Steppe, but he managed to separate his lips and move his tongue.

'Was the warrior slain? Did the Dark Master make a martyr of his enemy?'

'No, Lastborn, he was not. You failed, as I foresaw that you must.'

A woman walked behind the bier, dressed and hooded in black with face downcast like a widow. From the stoop of her back and the strands of white that strayed from her hood, Khamgiin judged her to be old, but immortality tempered such assessments and her voice rang as clear as the warning call of an eagle. Something about her presence put a sepulchral chill into Khamgiin. He turned to his men, but they walked on as if they were unaware of her or of him, ghosts in each other's worlds. He clenched his eyes tight and felt for the spark of power within him. This was a dream, or perhaps a vision such as those in which Nergüi purported to see the future, brought on by blood loss and pain.

'I bested Gorgoth the Gargantuan in mortal combat that lasted eight days and nights. I broke the numberless hordes of Hobgobla Khan and brought to heel the beasts of the Shirokij. I am the Lastborn of Khagash-Fél. I do not fail.'

'The Dark Master cares not for your sacrifice. He is not appeased with oaths or with deeds. He does not desire your devotion.'

The woman nodded imperceptibly to one side.

A ghostly figure ran through the trees there. The dwarf! Khamgiin could see his bright orange crest through the moist bark. The tattoos that covered his monstrously muscular frame were a translucent blue, at times indistinguishable from the whorls and branches behind him. In silence the spectre of the dwarf ran, battling his way through enemies that Khamgiin could not see. The dwarf ran behind a tree, and for the brief duration of his passage it ceased to be a tree and was a pillar, square-sided and mighty, soaring towards a vaulted ceiling where fiery golden runes glimmered like bleeding stars. Something about them reminded Khamgiin of the histories his father had told, of when the tribes had lived under the yoke of the Chaos dwarfs of Zharr. Before he could think on it further, the pillar was a tree again and the dwarf emerged from behind it with a man in tow. It was an Empire man in a red cloak, wielding what appeared to be a powerful magical sword. Khamgiin did not recognise him, but a tingling in his wounded spine told him that he should.

'What am I seeing?'

'What I see,' the woman replied.

A chill entering his bones, Khamgiin pushed himself up onto his elbows. 'I have seen you in my dreams before. It was you who showed me the tribes riding westward to make war on the Empire. Who are you?'

The woman bowed her head slightly, bringing up her hands in the same motion to draw back her hood. Despite his own godly favour, Khamgiin gasped. Her skin was a strange mix of light and dark, like rubbed chalk. Her lips however were jet black, as were the small horns that rose through her frost-white hair. The most unnerving thing about her, however, was her eyes. Their colouration constantly shifted and changed, like a candle behind stained glass, and Khamgiin felt certain that there were prophecies reflected there that could raise a man to the heights of the gods if he could interpret them without succumbing to madness.

'A servant. I observe and follow. History will not record my name.'

Khamgiin struggled to meet her shifting gaze. With a spurt of panic he noticed that everything around her was darkening. He was still moving, but his men were gone, as was the forest. He blinked into the nothingness that surrounded him. It wasn't just a void left by the retreat of the mortal world, it was a *thing* with a cruel will and a terrible purpose of its own. He saw the silver outline of the witch before she vanished. She was haloed by something horned and dark, something vast and incalculably ancient with a capacity for hate that left the Chaos warrior quailing and small.

'A darkness closes on me,' he hissed.

The woman's voice echoed from the shadow.

'Not only on you.'

THREE

Bad Tidings

The punch hit the Hochland corporal like a swinging morning-star, and crunched knuckles into the man's breastplate almost exactly like one. The man flew back, piling through the table that had been assembled from a plank and two barrels and scattering maps like feathers from a game bird brought down with a harquebus.

'Liar!' Gotrek roared, striding through the mess to drag the semi-lucid soldier back to his feet in a fist like an iron corbel. Despite being a foot shorter than anyone present, the Slayer filled the command tent with raw muscular presence and sheer bad attitude. His bulging arm glistened wetly, rainwater having rid him of enough blood and dirt that the spiralling tattoos looked vivid enough to be freshly drawn. He glared at the man, his one good eye bloodshot red. 'You expect me to buy this tripe about gods and daemons and all the rest of it?'

Another soldier, in a red and green surcoat with torn sleeves and a shirt of mail, broke one of the empty crates that had been deployed as seating across the Slayer's back. Gotrek grunted, staggered, shrugged splinters off his shoulders and then cuffed the man unconscious. He shook the corporal in his grip.

'I can't hear you, manling.'

'Put him down, Gotrek,' Felix ordered, staggering in from the rain with cheeks red from running and sword drawn just as the Slayer drew back his fist for another punch. At the same time, a rattling series of clicks announced pistols and harquebuses being cocked and primed. A line of men in a mishmash of bastardised liveries and gear dropped to one knee, laying their firearms over the upturned seating and drawing a bead on the bristling Slayer.

'Aim,' said Gustav with incongruous levity, wearing a grim expression that was no less a smile for that. Like everyone else, he hadn't yet had a chance to change following the recent battle. His ponytail was pasted to his face with rainwater and his white plate was dashed with wet smears of red. He looked like a highwayman, fresh from the stage of a Tarradasch play and an altercation with the evils of womanly virtue and corrupt Imperial justice. He reminded Felix rather too much of Ulrika.

'You'd let him shoot me, manling?' Gotrek growled flintily, still glaring at the Hochland corporal but clearly now addressing Felix.

Don't tempt me, Felix thought, but somehow managed to grind his teeth and not speak.

Gotrek must have noticed the tightness in his jaw however, because he turned to fix Felix with a glare. Felix's fingers didn't stray from his sword. With a grunt, Gotrek let the man go. The Hochlander clattered bonelessly in amongst the scattered maps and for a moment Felix thought the Slayer intended to leave one last boot in the ribs, but then Gotrek turned and stomped to the corner of the tent without another word. There, he picked up a crate and planted himself on it, crossing his arms across his barrel chest.

Felix allowed himself to relax. The line of harquebusiers and pistoliers visibly sagged with relief. Sheathing his sword, Felix waved in the gaggle of company sergeants that had decided a tactical withdrawal to the cover of the pouring rain was preferable to crossing Gotrek Gurnisson. He shook his head wearily as men returned to reset the seating, fix the table, and sort through the maps that had fallen on the floor. A too-young lad with haunted eyes and gore-drenched woollen coveralls – two months apprenticed to a chirurgeon before the armies of the Everchosen had ground his regiment underfoot – applied a grubby cloth to the fallen man's brow.

Felix took advantage of the lull to check on the arrangements. Such as they were.

Rain drummed on the canvas sheet that had been spread between two banner poles and the rear compartment of a wagon loaded with crates, barrels and sacks, most of them empty. In its former incarnation ferrying ore of less than dwarfish quality on the Kadrin Road to the less discerning marketplaces of Osterwald, Bechafen, and Kislev City it had been the property of old Lorin Lanarksson and his son Lyndun. They sat in the unsheltered front of the cart, soaking in the misery as only two dwarfs together could. A single storm lantern swayed with the wind from a pole attached to the wagon's rear.

A gaunt-looking kossar and a bald-headed bruiser in the black and dirty off-white of Ostland each took one end of the 'table' and reset it across the two barrels. When they noticed Felix watching they threw a salute, which Felix returned with an inner sigh. The kossar sergeant made a show of assessing the table's stability with a gentle rocking before declaring it fit for the maps to be relaid.

Men in the state colours of provinces from across the Empire's north and east and with golden epaulets on the slashed shoulders of their doublets gathered around with pages of soggy parchment in hand. Each man commanded anything between five and twenty-five men, sergeants – so titled by Felix, whose patience for provincial variation in military hierarchy was thinner than the wool of his cloak – of the ad-hoc fighting companies that had tagged along on Felix and Gotrek's long westward trek.

On the table, individual charts were strategically positioned under stone paperweights so that the overlap of one fed vaguely into the next to fashion a map of the entire Empire. Areas where Chaos was known or rumoured to have conquered had been filled with pencil drawings of hideous monsters that left Felix with grave concerns as to the artist's state of mind. Even without those personal worries it made for unsettling viewing. The only parts of the map that looked healthy were to the south and then only because they did not know any better. Daemons capered around the walled symbols of Bechafen and Osterwald, filling the forested spaces of Ostland and Ostermark and nibbling at the edges of Talabheim itself. A great tentacled monstrosity reared out of the Sea of Claws as if to drag Erengrad into the water, and stick-figure longboats peopled with gibbering horrors closed on the Marienburg delta.

Felix decided that whoever was responsible should never be allowed near pencil or paper again.

'You have timing of Ursun for his seasons,' said Kolya, lounging against the wagon's tailboard as he had been throughout, chewing on a pungent blend of locally foraged herbs and tabac. 'Zabójka might have killed that man.'

'Remind me later to thank you for the help,' Felix replied.

The Kislevite pursed his lips, cocked his head slightly as though listening intently to the rain, and shrugged. 'No matter.'

The Hochlander moaned, taking a swallow of water from the cloth that the young chirurgeon squeezed into his mouth. Felix dropped down beside him.

The man had a long mane of dark hair, crushed from being all day inside a helmet. His beard was dashed with white, and cleft by a scar that cut across his left cheek from the corner of his lip. His breastplate was almost brown from mud, blood and rust, and so well beaten that in places it had more edges than a chewed coin. The vicious dent left below the collar by Gotrek's fist was hardly the worst of it. A bronze-coloured epaulet shimmered dully from the red shoulder of his padded tunic. A singular leather vambrace that was scratched almost white hung loose on one strap. He looked up vaguely at Felix and, to his minor irritation, saluted.

'Corporal Herschel Mann, my lord, Hergig city militia. At your service.'

Felix raised an eyebrow and smiled at the slumped soldier. 'At ease, corporal.'

'Aye, sir,' the man murmured.

'I apologise on behalf of my... friend,' said Felix, glancing across to Gotrek who returned the stare with diamond tips. 'I assure you he's the same with everybody.'

The man took another squeeze of water and swallowed nervously. 'Forgive me, my lord. He asked if I had news of Altdorf and I told him aye, I did. Several of the men with me were attached to Reikland regiments, garrisoned in the outlying countryside during the... fall.'

To Felix, the air suddenly felt too thick to breathe. His heart didn't seem to want to beat.

'The fall of what?' asked Gustav.

'Of Altdorf,' said Corporal Mann. 'The fall of Altdorf, my lords.'

Shouts of denial rose from the company sergeants who had not already been present to hear the news with Gotrek. Most of them had been enlisted men serving in regiments on the Empire's hinterlands or, in the case of the Kislevite contingent, beyond it. Felix doubted whether half of them had ever been to Altdorf, but that didn't matter. It was the seat of Imperial power, home to its most exalted institutions and most decorated regiments, a cultural home if not an actual one. It was unconquered and unconquerable.

It was Altdorf.

Felix stared at the shattered soldier for a long moment, not entirely comprehending. He felt the stool kicked out from under his heart, the noose tightening around his neck as it dropped. The disbelieving chorus of his men blended together into a whining note of white noise. Deep down he had suspected that even the great citadels of Reikland could not stand against the forces he had seen heading towards them. Mentally he had prepared himself for it, but to have it confirmed hit him emotionally like a kick in the gut.

Felix raised his left hand to his eyes. The lantern-light reflected from the angular edges of his ring, short-lived tears of ethereal gold. *No.*

He forced himself to swallow, and then to look up. Sound crashed back in a tumult of angry, frightened voices.

He turned a look of anguish to the corner where Gotrek sat, arms crossed and surrounded by empty chairs. There was a grimness on the dwarf's face that Felix didn't like. A blue vein bulged from his temple, and he appeared to swell as he clasped hands to his enormous biceps and stared through Felix into the rain. West – to Altdorf. Returning to Altdorf and reuniting Felix with Kat – and perhaps expunging some guilt of his own in so doing – had been Gotrek's unwavering goal for over a year. In all of Felix's own worries and doubts he'd never thought to consider how his former companion would respond to failure.

'Lies,' said Gotrek in a voice that could have ground gravel. 'He didn't tell you the rest. Said Sigmar's own second bloody coming fought and lost. And there's more too, if your head's not already too full of foolishness to hear more.' Gotrek snorted angrily. 'Gods. Manling nonsense if ever I heard it.'

'What of the Emperor?' said Gustav, lifting his voice above the clamour.

'Safe, I heard,' said Mann, relieved to have something positive to share with his rescuers. 'The old King of Bretonnia rode to his aid, and,' he glanced anxiously towards Gotrek, 'and the gods themselves.'

A few men made signs to Sigmar and Ulric across their chests. Kolya chuckled drily. 'We could use some of that, no?'

'Gods or Bretonnians?' Gustav murmured, a half-smile teasing his troubled mask.

Kolya shrugged. 'So long as they bring their horses.'

The kossar sergeant by the table trumpeted with laughter. The Ostlander across from him gave both Kislevites a damning look. They had lost their country months ago. Most of the men in the room were feeling the loss of theirs only now. Felix merely bowed his head, part of him determined never to look up again.

Altdorf had been more than just a distant symbol. It had been hope.

It had been *his* hope.

'We should head south,' said Gustav, taking a steadying breath and striding forwards to plant a finger on one of the clearer portions of the map. 'Averheim, say. It's a long way, but it should be as far from the northern and eastern prongs of the Chaos incursion. The Emperor has to rally his forces somewhere and it's as likely a place as any.'

'How far?' asked a slender, faintly well-born man in scuffed leather armour and a steel breastplate with a big dent over the right breast and a burgundy sash over the opposite shoulder.

'Where are we now, anyway?' added another man, this one in

forester's gear with an unstrung bow over his shoulder, leaning over the maps.

'We're shadowing the Talabec Road. A few days out from Talabheim.' Gotrek tightened his arms about his chest and grumbled: 'Assuming we ever move again.'

'Talabheim?' Mann started, before Gotrek guillotined whatever he had wanted to say with a glare.

The Slayer sat stubbornly, but something forlorn in the Hochlander's face made him grudgingly relent. 'Spit it out before you get a nosebleed. *Another one.*'

'Forgive me again, master dwarf, but you're nowhere Talabheim. Fortunately, for it's fallen too. You're in Hochland.'

'Bah!' said Gotrek, rising suddenly and stamping a foot upon the ground, setting his nose-chain to clinking. 'Talabecland, or I'm a treeman.'

'I saw mountains from the hill, Gotrek,' said Felix quietly. He didn't want to put himself into another argument with the Slayer, but you couldn't disagree with a mountain. And what did it matter now anyway?

Altdorf had fallen.

'There are no mountains in Talabecland, manling,' said Gotrek as if that settled it.

'My lord, if you'll forgive me?' Corporal Mann raised a hooked elbow that Felix took to pull the man up. The man stumbled against him, giving a sour hit of days-old sweat and armour grease, and then moved towards the map table. He pressed his finger into the map. The grimy digit fell on a bull-horned icon surrounded by double-ringed walls and set amidst a proliferation of barren-looking mountains.

'We were following the main road north out of Hergig to Wolfenburg and have been for about five days. As I said, Talabheim fell the autumn before last after a six-month siege. Hergig's always been off the main road and it's been a blessing of late, enough for the city to hold out until now.'

'What changed?' said Gustav.

'A warlord named–' Mann's lips contorted around the foreign name '–*Khagash-Fél*. I'm told it means "Half-Ogre" because he has the strength and stature of five men.'

'Is that all?' Gotrek grunted.

'It was he that broke the walls of Hergig,' said Mann, somewhat defensively.

'Walls of questionable standard from the outset, no doubt.'

'Sounds like mighty doom to me,' muttered Kolya, off-hand around a mouthful of half-chewed herbal sludge.

'Do you deliberately taunt me with things I cannot have, rememberer? I can have no doom. Not until the manling is safe within the walls of Altdorf and at the little one's side.'

Felix heard the incongruous sound of laughter and to his astonishment found it was his, bleak and despairing, slow as the death of his world. 'Have you heard a word anyone's been saying, Gotrek? Altdorf is gone. Kat is gone. The Empire is *gone*.' His voice rose steadily, emphasising each additional loss with a thump of his hand.

'To hold and to protect, manling,' Gotrek intoned, voice sinking to a cavernous timbre. 'To keep forever from the earth until Gazul sunders you.'

It took Felix a moment to realise that Gotrek was reciting the final lines of the oath that had made him and Kat husband and wife. They had been wed under the dim, ruby glimstones of Karak Kadrin's shrine of Grimnir and it was not lightly that a Slayer invoked the name of Gazul, guardian of the honoured dead. Bitterness rose on bubbles of laughter as Felix spread his arms, as if to encompass the blackness that enveloped them. It was getting easier. The borders of the Empire were tightening like a noose around their necks. It was all too easy to believe that the end of everything was nigh, just out there under the pouring rain.

'We're *sundered*, Gotrek. The armies of Chaos march on our roads, garrison our cities, and now Altdorf.' Felix clutched his hair, as if intending to claw out the grey. 'By any measure, we're done.'

'Coward.'

'Coward?' said Felix, fury causing his voice to climb. 'What kind of courage is it to deny what's going on out there? It's time to stop being so damned stubborn and admit it.'

'Some of us keep the oaths we make, manling.'

Felix's fist clenched, his voice dropped to a hiss. 'I always kept my oath to you.'

'Aye,' Gotrek sneered. 'To the letter.'

'And just what's that supposed to mean?'

Gotrek waved his hand with a growl and turned to Corporal Mann, who had been watching the exchange with a look of rising horror.

'Just assuming you're not conniving with dark powers, what were you hoping to find in Wolfenburg?'

'N-nothing really, master dwarf. We intended to track the main road that far and then strike out for the Middle Mountains, skirting them westward until we make it to Middenheim. Ten men could defend the Fauschlag against a thousand. Archaon's tried and failed before and with Altdorf gone, it's the last great city still standing. It's where everyone will be going now.'

Gotrek's one eye glittered dangerously, like a dwarf with an oath to keep.

'No,' said Felix, 'absolutely not. You're talking about a journey of months, if not more, and with no guarantee we'll find anything at Middenheim other than all the hordes of Archaon waiting outside.'

If we're lucky, he thought, but reminded himself of his position amongst these men and decided not to say it. 'It's madness. I for one don't see too much wrong with Gustav's plan. I've never been to Averheim. Perhaps that is where the Emperor will go. And perhaps with aid from the dwarfs too, it's near their Worlds Edge Mountain strongholds after all.'

The men murmured approvingly at that, partly – Felix suspected – because it had come from him, but also because the only dwarf most of them had ever encountered was Gotrek, and a few more of the Slayer at your back was as appealing a prospect as it would be infuriating. They weren't to know that Gotrek was exceptional, even amongst his own tenacious kind.

The Slayer emitted a disparaging snort at the idea, to which Felix was tempted to add a round of sarcastic applause.

That's how to keep up morale in the End Times.

'Why go all the way around the Middle Mountains when you can go through them?'

Lorin's whisper-thin voice drew everyone's attention towards him. The longbeard inserted his cane shakily between the floor of the cart and the upright of the tailboard. The hardwood cane was ironclad and topped with a handhold shaped in the form of a hammer, and in any other pair of hands but his might have made for a serviceable weapon. The frail old dwarf remained as broad as two men, but he was gaunt as any dwarf Felix had seen outside of the besieged dwarfhold of Karag Dum. Heavy pink bags hung from his watery eyes. A zigzagging scar ran up one fleshy cheek to his temple, the inexpert stitching and the horrendous bite that it had closed still visible. His beard had been torn from that side of his face except for a few sad little tufts. What remained was as thin and wispy as a smoke ring blown into the rain, and as if to emphasise that he had a long-stemmed wooden pipe loosely clenched between his lips. It was unfilled and unlit but both Lorin and his son had previously assured Felix that they liked to remind themselves of the taste.

The longbeard's lip ticked nervously at the attention, and he steadied himself with a firm grip on his cane. 'There are ways. Gotrek, you know that; the ancient ways of our ancestors, beyond the guile of any man or beast to find.'

'Are you talking about the Underway?' said Felix, clenching his fists to calm himself and looking determinedly away from Gotrek lest his temper explode again.

'There are no dwarfholds in those mountains, manling, so no,' said Gotrek, exasperated as though reprising a tired argument. 'And I've told you a dozen times over, Lanarksson, there's naught in those paupers' peaks but legends, tales good for nothing but drinking a dwarf's gold.'

'I speak not of minerals or gems, Gotrek, as you well know.'

'Bah!'

Felix glanced at the map. He had never been to the Middle Mountains and, if he was honest, had never felt any great yearning to. No vengeful wight haunted them and there were no rumours of robber barons lording over decrepit castles in their heights. There was simply nothing there, unless one placed value on bare rock and year-round snow. Even the Grey Mountains harboured enough base minerals to keep a handful of dwarf clans in ale, but then Felix had heard Gotrek speak about Grey dwarfs in the same disparaging tones as he did humans.

'Then just what exactly is supposed to be in those mountains?' asked Gustav.

'Fairy stories older than your Empire,' said Gotrek, then scoffed. 'Older than ours, if you're fool enough to believe them.'

Felix felt a prickle of unease run through his skin. The fractured empire of the dwarfs was said to be almost ten millennia old. Intuitively, a myth did not survive for so long unless it concealed a grain of truth and ancient dwarfish legends were exactly the sort of thing that Felix wanted to avoid. They conjured images of high ranges and vast vaulted deeps, of stone-hearted gods, and rune-weapons with the power to raze mountains and sunder continents.

Not for the first time he wished Max were here, but to Felix's mind Gotrek had no basis on which to be so diffident. Everywhere one cared to look, prophecies were being fulfilled and forgotten myths realised left, right and centre. Even while he had been in Kislev Felix had been hearing rumours Sigmar had arisen, battling the daemonic hordes in Ostermark.

But Felix had been through Ostermark. If that was the best that even Sigmar could do then Felix was at a loss who was supposed to save them now.

Gotrek stroked his beard thoughtfully. 'I say there are no dwarfholds in the mountains, but there was one once, thousands of years ago. And whatever else they may or may not harbour, there are roads through them.'

'And these roads lead to Middenheim?' said Gustav again, earning an impatient scowl from the Slayer.

'They're the secret ways of the dwarfs,' Gotrek replied. 'The manling, my rememberer and Lanarksson and Lyndun may come with me. Everyone else has been slowing us down too long already.' His gaze swept the tent without a trace of human kindness. 'You're all on your own from here on.'

A stunned hush descended on the gathering. Kolya's eyebrows arched as though he hadn't been fully paying attention until now.

'Well...' began Lorin, cheek twitching furiously however hard he tried to hold on to his cane. Its hardwood base stuttered against the tailboard. 'I'm sure that we could make an exception given the circumstances. Being the end of the world as it is, I'm positive that Grimnir would unders–'

'I should've left that Chaos hound to gnaw on your skull a little longer, Lanarksson. You've forgotten what it means to be a dwarf.'

The longbeard's lips ticked. Gotrek had always been hard, but Felix could not remember him ever being deliberately cruel. The dwarf who stood before him now was not the same one to whom Felix had once sworn an oath of friendship over a river of ale in an Altdorf tavern all those years ago. He was embittered and twisted, either by the horrors he had witnessed or those he had wrought himself, and had darkened as the world around him darkened. It was surprising to look back and realise that Gotrek had once had soft edges, but it was true: he had enjoyed good beer and good pipeweed, had on occasion been moved to make a joke and even smile at some of Felix's; he had revelled in good food and had shared every dwarf's passion for gold and old debts.

It was as if all of that had been chipped away and all that remained now was the iron core.

The Slayer.

'You would condemn these men to their fates?' said Felix, angry again before he even realised he was speaking. 'And if they insisted, what then? Would you kill them? My own nephew? Perhaps I should expect no less from a Kinslayer.'

'What did you call me?' Gotrek rumbled dangerously, squaring up to Felix.

'You heard,' Felix shouted in the Slayer's face. 'I've been hearing about superior dwarf hearing for long enough to know that.'

Some trace residue of common sense urged Felix to stop there, but he felt as if a dam had just been breached. Gotrek had killed Snorri, the best of them by any measure of common goodness. They hadn't spoken of it since Praag. Felix had tried not to think of it. Even Gustav and his men had taken the hint and pretended it had never happened – they had their own reasons to forget those events – and sometimes hours could go by in which Felix actually believed it, but then he would hear the splitting of bone in his mind and see the blood seeping through the snow between his boots and know that it had. Felix had failed to stand up to the Slayer then and every day the guilt of it gnawed at him, and he damn well wasn't going to let things go the same with Gustav, Max, or anyone else for that matter.

'You're the coward, Gotrek. You're stubborn, block-headed, and you can go and bury your head in the Middle Mountains if you want, but Gustav and I will be taking *our* men to Averheim.'

Gotrek regarded him stonily. 'You done?'

Felix let out a hot breath and nodded. '*We're* done, Gotrek. There's nothing you can say to convince me to leave all these men behind.'

'Nothing?'

'Nothing.'

'Good. We can cut straight to it then.'

There was a *smack* of impact in the centre of Felix's face and he staggered back. He heard what sounded like a pistol going off, but that might equally have been the sound of Gotrek's knuckles cracking his jaw. Disbelief swam through his mind. Gotrek had hit him. The Slayer had never hit him before. His limbs turned to jelly as still, stumbling back, he tried to draw his sword. He saw two slightly blurred Slayers crack their knuckles before being suddenly whisked away.

Felix's last thought before he hit the ground was to realise that he was falling.

He was unconscious before he had another.

FOUR

Half-Ogre

Fire spat into the rain, struggling like bound sacrifices from stakes eight feet high. Eight of them formed a ring to enclose a portion of the cobbled square. Behind that line of fire was held a dark, roaring sea of bestial heads and pointed helms, many-armed trophy poles and rippling banners. Out of the hundreds whose voices could be heard, only eight were visible from inside of the ring: two semicircles of proudly attired warriors with the courage and conviction to back one champion against another. Each held a weapon in either hand. The two combatants bore none.

Khagash-Fél paced the border of his side of the ring with his giant stride. Cracked and ancient armour hung loosely from his broad shoulders, a battered harness of black hellsteel plates, faded runes and dead-eyed daemon faces. Long shanks of sodden grey hair scrawled down both pauldrons, his grey beard reaching as far down as his faulds. He wore it in thick braids, in the manner of the dwarfish slavers that dominated the lands and culture of the eastern steppe. With his one good eye he studied his challenger. The other was lidless, milky and blind, ruined by the overlapping rings of the slave rune that branded the left side of his face. The *other* slept within its bed of flesh within his forehead, a slit of faint sapphire light bleeding onto his brow.

With the brazen arrogance of a warrior three times heavier than his opponent and all four of his supporters, Buhruk Doombull mirrored his steps. Huge, interlocking plates of spiked iron and bronze clanked as the minotaur moved and three rune-engraved skulls swung from the chain that tied them to his waist. A black iron helm with articulated cheek guards enclosed his massive head. Ruby-red eyes gleamed hungrily within. A pair of forward-curving horns barbed with steel blades thrust out from behind the cheek guards. Hot breath snorted from his snout, steaming the brass ring that pierced his nostrils, the angular Mark of Khorne reddening fleetingly as the surrounding metal cooled.

'I am Buhruk, Doombull of Kislev,' snorted the minotaur, his every word a bellow that made the braziers flicker and shake. 'His hooves are its ashes. Its blood is his blood. His herd follows Khagash-Fél for more war.' The minotaur stamped one brazen hoof, clenched every bulging muscle into a savage knot of fury and bellowed until it seemed the ground must crack. 'More war! Where are his skulls? Where is his victory?'

Khagash-Fél gave Buhruk the hard face, the impassive mask of the steppe peoples. He raised his right arm high. Rain coursed down the scarified vambrace. His hand however, like his face, was unarmoured, and he presented it to the crowd like a relic. It was blotched yellow with age, covered by bruise-like markings of faded tribal tattoos.

'I am Khagash-Fél, and you know me.' His voice was cracked like his armour, deep like the hell that awaited this world; it pushed through the hammering rain like a blade-bossed shield for all to hear and bear witness. 'With this hand did I strike down Bzharrak the Black and lead the uprising against the Gates of Zharr. It was I who broached the Mountains of Mourn and smote down Grullgor Thundergut and took his lands for our lands.' He lowered his arm and swept it around the ring, marking the shadowed faces that lay hidden beyond the torchlight. 'It was I who first brought you the power of the Greater Gods, I who won you freedom and then gave you glory. We are one people, and there will be glory untold for us in the days ahead.'

The reverential silence that followed his words was broken only by the smack of rain on stones, the hiss of tormented flames, and then by the sonorous, panting laughter of the Doombull.

'Take your weapon, Buhruk, if you believe you can find the host of Archaon quicker than I. Or leave this ring now and do not challenge me again.'

Buhruk emitted a fiery snort, then rolled his neck, the blades that tipped his horns glinting golden in the firelight. 'Half-man is small and furless. Doombull needs no weapon. But, as is tradition...'

Keeping both bead-like eyes on Khagash-Fél, the minotaur turned to his supporters.

Three were broad, heavily built beastmen wearing ill-fitting but ornate suits of lightly banded steel. Mail skirts hung to their fetlocks. Animal skin cloaks were buckled at their throats. In the dark, it would have been easy to mistake them for winged lancers of Kislev. The fourth was a Chaos warrior in brooding black plate ringed with spikes, brass etchings, and grisly trophy hooks hung with severed body parts and parchment scraps. Khagash-Fél commanded the loyalty of hundreds of such warriors and he did not know this man's name, but he remembered that he was a man of Empire stock and had been an exalted champion in his own right until Khagash-Fél had crushed him and claimed his men. The man's customs and thinking were strange to a man of the steppe.

In the Empire, it seemed, a lord expected the fealty of his warriors, who gave it without question. Amongst the tribes, a lord would buy the loyalty of the strongest warriors with gifts and glory. And what was true for men was true also for the gods, only more so.

One of the big beastmen strained to offer up a huge spiked mace and Buhruk took it, wielding it lightly in one massive fist.

A smile teased at the corners of Khagash-Fél's self-control. The hum of daemonic energy filled his gut, battle-rage coursing through his veins like the aqueducts of fire that fed the Desolation of Zharr. It was in moments such as these when one felt the interconnectedness of Chaos. A man could take pleasure from killing, from the staging of a slaughter and the revelry that followed. It was madness to hollow one's existence by denying the gifts of all the gods but one.

On his forehead, the Eye of Katchar snapped open.

A murmur of dread and awe passed through the watching warriors, stretching out towards the deep yawn of time as the world around Khagash-Fél slowed to a crawl. He could see the individual gobbets of flame that spat out from the torches, watch each drop of rain as it smashed against Buhruk's helmet into hundreds of tiny, infinitely reflective pieces. In contrast to the stalled immensity of the minotaur, the sepia-tinted shades that danced around him were a disjointed blur of action, reaction and possibility. Khagash-Fél felt his heart beat faster. Even this brief and incoherent glimpse of the future was intoxicating. The temptation was always to look a little deeper, see a little further, but with an effort of will he pulled back. To see all that the Eye would have him see was to duel with madness.

Such prophecy was the demesne of the gods alone.

Absorbing as much of the following minutes' most likely course as he could, Khagash-Fél held out his hand for a weapon. His hand moved towards the leather-scaled tribesmen as if through deep water. Of the eight weapons presented he selected an axe, and for a moment the future lost a measure of its uncertainty and became clear. Then the Eye of Katchar closed. Khagash-Fél blinked away disorientation, the feeling of *limitation* that always followed the return to the present as the world resumed its normal pace and hue.

He brought up his axe. 'I accept your challenge, Buhruk.'

The minotaur thrashed his head through the air as though fending off a daemonic possession, then issued a thunderous bellow as he dropped his horns and charged. Khagash-Fél looked up as the Doombull loomed over him, opening up his massive chest to deliver a blow from his mace intended to crush the champion's skull in one hit.

Exactly as Khagash-Fél had foreseen.

He punched the head of his axe up into the Doombull's unarmoured belly, forcing a wheeze of rotten, meaty breath from the minotaur as he dropped to one knee. Khagash-Fél side-stepped, reversed his grip on his axe and then lashed it back across the minotaur's cheek guard. Blood and metal sparks sprayed from the open face of Buhruk's helm and Khagash-Fél strode behind him, lifting his bloodied axe above his head to the rapture of the crowd.

Buhruk rose slowly and turned, wiping his bloody snout on his wrist. 'You are fool to goad the Doombull. I will break your bones and drink their juices, half-man.'

Khagash-Fél made a *come* gesture with his axe.

Nothing was as beloved by the gods as drama.

With a howl of primal rage the minotaur roared forward, frenzied strokes carving through the air like a barrage of rockets. Khagash-Fél parried and dodged, always a second ahead of every blow. Each time Buhruk paused in his assault for breath, Khagash-Fél was already exploiting the opportunity to back away, his axe throwing fresh blood from another shallow cut onto the cobbles. The howls from beyond the fire-line grew more rabid with each libation.

The Eye of Katchar could not reveal every possible outcome, but he had become adept at sifting the improbable from the most likely; particularly with a battering ram such as Buhruk Doombull.

The minotaur's torso bulged as if being squeezed from below, his mace coming down like a meteor. Khagash-Fél made to move aside, then snarled. It was time for the Doombull and his supporters to see what they challenged. His hand swung up to shield his head, the minotaur's mace hammering into his open palm and driving him down to one knee. The cobblestones beneath him shattered, blasted rock ricocheting between the two warriors' armour.

Buhruk's bellow of victory turned into a disbelieving snort as the dust settled to reveal Khagash-Fél alive and unscratched with the minotaur's mace firmly in his hand. Khagash-Fél twisted the mace-head aside and shoved Buhruk back with a kick in the gut as he rose. Khagash-Fél's heart thumped powerfully within his chest. He could almost hear the erratic *boom-boom* echoing from the underside of his breastplate. With a discipline forged over centuries into a mask of hellsteel, he maintained the hard face as he flexed his ringing fingers. Inside, he grimaced; that one he had felt.

'Your own god favours me more than he does you, Doombull. No weapon of fire or fire-born can harm me.'

The torches danced on the tumultuous roar of acclaim.

'Another!' Buhruk howled, throwing out his arm to his supporters for a weapon, any weapon.

Quicker-thinking than the beasts beside him, the black-armoured Chaos warrior snapped the steel head off his lance and threw the weapon into the ring. Buhruk caught it out of the air in his massive fist as though it were a short spear, raising it overhead for a stabbing thrust and bringing up his mace to wield both like some monstrous daemon-possessed war machine. The beastmen in the shadows bayed like starving wolves, shouting down the hiss of the tribesmen at this breach to the ancestral tradition of the challenge.

Wary now, Khagash-Fél stepped back. The Eye of Katchar had not shown him this. Tossing his axe out of the ring, he turned and yelled back to his own supporters for his more favoured weapon: 'Sönögch, a sword.'

A tall warrior in armour of metal scales and a conical leather helm with a horsehair plume moved to obey. As the sword flew from the man's hand Khagash-Fél saw that a fifth figure now stood amongst his supporters.

Everything seemed to slow down, as if the Eye of Katchar showed him his future once again.

The sword hung in midair as though trapped in crystal.

The shaman, Nergüi, was a flourish of colour beside Sönögch in his long, feather-like blue robes. Eagle feathers, animal teeth and gemstones glittered in the firelight. Dozens of bead necklaces made a frill around his throat and across his narrow shoulders. An elaborate feather headdress screened his weather-scoured features from the rain and torches. Only his piercing amber eyes shone amidst the umbral shade. For a brief moment they met Khagash-Fél's one. With a movement so subtle it failed to disturb the chimes sewn into the streaming silk 'feathers' of his robes, Nergüi shook his head.

The sword sailed with celestial slowness into the ring.

Khamgiin.

A hammering filled Khagash-Fél's head. The groan from his left gardbrace announced the swelling of his bicep as his fists clenched; fists that were turning a deep magma-red. Steam hissed from the joins in his armour where the rain struck his bare skin.

His last born was dead.

Khagash-Fél opened his mouth wide as if to cry out, but no sound issued forth but a strange, hollow buzz, that of a swarm of mad-dened wasps sealed within a jar. There was a rising pressure in his gut, like the urge to vomit only much more intense and with an irresistible will of its own behind it. Steam poured off him as, with a resounding *crack*, his jaw dislocated and stretched still wider.

His sword came towards him.

Khagash-Fél batted the blade aside to send it skittering away across the stones.

Everything snapped back into focus.

Buhruk bellowed a new challenge and raised his spear as Khagash-Fél finally released a cry of his own, a droning roar that rose from his gut, flying from his distended jaw on a torrent of bloated, pestilential flies. The Doombull swung his mace into the swarm, as effectual as a brush in holding back a wildfire, and an instant later he was engulfed in it. The minotaur screamed as if he was on fire, swinging wildly from within a chittering second skin, as he tottered forwards and then toppled. On hitting the ground his mighty frame burst apart, thick bones and armour plates piling into the cobbles and scattering putrid chitinous bodies across the ring.

Khagash-Fél sucked back a deep breath, working his jaw until he felt it click back into joint. Fury glimmered down to a cold point, the dark ember after an inferno.

'Is there another challenger?'

Men and their horses crowded the road, filling the narrow street with the creak of rain-softened bull-hide armour and drunken laughter. They cheered Khagash-Fél's victory as he and Nergüi strode past. The shaman's bone clogs clicked on the cobbles, the strips of sodden blue silk that made up his robes trailing through the excrement that ran in rivers down a drainage channel in the middle of the street. A rat the size of a fox and covered in blisters scurried from a doorway to lap at the stream. The half-timber walls that flanked the cobbled road were scratched with depictions of steppe spirits – Katchar the all-seeing eagle; Khorûne the warhorse; Nhorg the carrion crow and harbinger of pestilence; Silnaar the hound, the reveller – or the newer symbols of the Greater Gods they represented. Others had been knocked down altogether to leave piles of rubble, over which mangy children formed loose tribes to fight for the acclaim for their elders. The thatch had gone to the horses. Horse-hide tents shrugged off the rain within the ruins, drab cone-shaped structures draped with skins and furs and pegged into the rubble with bone pitons.

Even within the walls of the civilisation they had crossed mountains to level, the tribes still preferred the comfort of their tents. On another day, it would have been amusing.

Khagash-Fél walked to a stone building that had lost its front wall, roofed only by a skeletal frame of wooden beams. Rainwater sluiced through onto the men bent over their steaming anvils below. The flat notes of hammers beaten into solid iron rang out. A ribbon of sparks screamed through the open wall, stuttering, pausing, then flaring up again as a heavily tattooed smith pressed the sword in his hands to the sharpening wheel.

'How does she fare, Darhyk?'

At the deep knell of his voice, the smith looked up and grinned. His shaven head glistened with a mixture of rainwater and sweat, his dark hair worn as a topknot and looped around his neck out of the way of his craft. A brand similar to the one on Khagash-Fél's face – marking him as once the property of the steel-shops of Zharr Naggrund – had obliterated half of the man's face. His muscular torso swam with tribal tattoos as he drew the sword from the wheel and held it before his eyes. They were tightly bound with black cloth and he ran his fingers blindly down its lithe, curvaceous edge.

'She is a fine figure of a blade, warlord. What I would give to see her with my own two eyes.'

'You would not be the first. And whatever you would give, she would take from you. That and more.'

The smith sighed and lowered the gilt-edged blade to within a hair of the spinning stone wheel. Nergüi faced determinedly out into the street. His shoulders shook with yearning. 'Then she is a true lady,' said Darhyk. 'Had I been you I would have let her dance with the Doombull.'

'Ildezegtei does not lower herself to such games, and nor would she forgive the interruption to her ablutions.'

'The gods see you victorious in any case,' said Darhyk, kissing his fingertip, placing it to his heart, and then pointing it north towards the home of the Greater Gods. 'My prayers now are for your son.'

Khagash-Fél showed Darhyk a face of stone. 'The gods seldom heed my prayers, old friend. I doubt they heed yours.'

'Yes, warlord,' Darhyk replied smartly, returning the blade to the stone with a keening shriek of what sounded almost like pleasure.

'This way,' said Nergüi in a relieved murmur once they were away from the smith's workshop.

Everywhere there were warriors: singing, drinking, casting bones, feasting around great fire-pits dug out of the cobbles, and fighting, anything to make the weeks of inaction pass more swiftly as their scouts hunted for the armies of the Empire and the next phase of the war. Occasionally there were beastmen amongst them, but for all that the End Times had united them, their ancient breed and men were too different to commingle and the herds confined themselves largely to the forest outside the walls.

How Khagash-Fél had come to despise those woods.

It was foreign, unnatural terrain. At times it felt like a wall around the city, one designed to keep him and his horse warriors in rather than invaders out. Viewed from the city's tallest buildings it stretched on forever, and it felt like no surprise that even the limitless legions of Archaon could be swallowed without trace. Some days it was easy to believe that there really was nothing but the forest, that the world beyond its borders had already fallen to the Realm of Chaos and this pocket of rain-lashed stone was all that remained.

The gods had guided him this far. They had called him from battle with the forces of Greasus Goldtooth and summoned him to this strange place, and he refused to believe that even the gods would call on the mighty Khagash-Fél without good cause. If they could only send him a sign, some inkling as to what great task he had come here to perform and where it was to be done.

Instead they had taken his son from him.

And if the tribes did not leave this place for fresh conquests soon then Buhruk Doombull would not be the last champion to die by his hand.

After about half an hour of ruin and squalor, they approached a small patch of scrubby common flanked on three sides by high-walled stone buildings with mock battlements on their roofs. The Empire men – *Hochlanders* – had made a stand here, blocks of spearmen and halberdiers packing the road and the common while their feared longrifles poured down shot from the surrounding balconies. There had been straw bales here and big, circular targets erected on wooden stanchions set up on the grass. This had been a place where men practised their martial skills. But no longer. This was Nergüi's realm now, a place with one foot in the stirrup of the final ride. This was where the shamans brought the injured and the sick.

It was a place that Khagash-Fél, blessed by the gods, had had no cause to visit before now.

Hitching up his robes, Nergüi traipsed into the muddy quagmire that a succession of rain and hungry war-beasts had made of the grass. The targets and straw men were long gone, replaced by a number of interconnected tents, each large enough to incorporate several chambers within their thick hide walls. Unlike the practical tents of the warriors these were a lustrous white, cut from the carcasses of the white pegasi that dwelt amongst the highest peaks of the Mountains of Mourn and glowing from within with the burning of fragrant oils. Runic symbols and expansive, sprawling motifs had been scratched into them and glistened in the wet. Elaborate spirit catchers made of feathers and beads and lengths of white silk fluttered between the structures like moths after the illuminated hides. Wind chimes sang mournfully. Coloured flags fluttered from rings punched into their sides, all the way to their open tops where incense-scented smoke puffed into the rain.

Nergüi strode ahead into the tent complex.

Younger men in similar but less ostentatious garb to the shaman moved purposefully between covered door flaps, hurrying from shelter to shelter to protect vials of unguents and baskets of sweet-smelling herbs from the rain. A handful of hulking bray-shamans wandered between tents, sniffing at the entrances like hounds in a stranger's village. Khagash-Fél could taste the distinct, at times conflicting, strains of magic in the air. It fomented something superstitious and primal in the back of his mind, stirred by the muffled chants of shamans, the smell of incense, the eerie song of chimes.

Nergüi approached the entrance to a tent that looked little different from the others that surrounded it. A dark-antlered skull flanked by a pair of stakes formed a lintel. Each was topped with a covered brass dish filled with oil that lapped under a greenish flame. Khagash-Fél caught the scent of wild grasses and for an instant he was on the back of a horse, charging across the open steppe with the wind in his hair and just a score of men at his back. He shook off the memory. That had been centuries ago. Here amongst the trees and rain and darkness was where his present lay.

A heavy flap of tasselled silk closed the entrance. Nergüi stretched an arm through to draw a portion aside and a thick, sweaty odour pushed out. Khagash-Fél could hear a murmured chanting and the hollow wooden beat of funerary sticks from within.

The shaman waited.

Khagash-Fél steeled himself. To avoid a foe's eye was to let him know he was feared and Khagash-Fél feared nothing, without or within. One man's loss, even his, meant little in the final counting. The strong marched on, the imperfect perished. The gods remained.

He nodded once, ducking under the skull lintel and into the waiting gloom.

A warrior's name was earned, not given, and Khamgiin Lastborn had come into his by being the only one of four sons to survive his quest into the Northern Wastes to claim the notice of the gods. Now he lay in state upon a woven mat of horsehair and grass, hands crossed over his powerful, silk-shirted chest. Though lacking his father's gifts, Khamgiin had lost little of Khagash-Fél's great stature.

It was strange to see him so unadorned. A Chaos warrior's wargear was a favour from the gods and not so easily set aside, but with the passing of that favour, Khamgiin's armour had fallen away like bark from a dead tree. Now he reminded Khagash-Fél so much of the man – the boy – who a hundred years ago had mounted his sturdiest horse and ridden into the Kurgan lands to the north. It produced an odd sense of longing that he could not quite place or describe. He had been right the first time.

It was... strange.

Nergüi danced and hummed, sometimes breaking into a low chant and shaking his voluminous sleeves in the air before returning to his rhythm. Small bowls of burning oil had been positioned meaningfully around the room. They produced more smoke than light, and brass covers cut with weird and disturbing designs reduced even that liminal glow, turning the walls themselves into shifting scenes from the daemonic heart of the netherworld. The shaman's undulating hum and the ethereal rhythm of his acolytes' funerary sticks added to the unreal air.

Khagash-Fél turned back to his son. The body was scattered with black feathers. It was traditional to question the dead on the future before their cremation, for like a man on a good horse their vision went farther and with more clarity than that of men with their feet trapped on mortal ground. Intently, Khagash-Fél examined the pattern into which the feathers had fallen, but despite the foresight granted him through the Eye of Katchar he did not have the skill to interpret such prophecy. He would have to speak with Nergüi later to learn what his son had reported from his ride to his patron's domain.

'What mighty champion felled you, Khamgiin? Where are they?'

There was no answer there, and he was uncertain what had made him ask. Perhaps it was the play of light and shade across his son's face? For a moment Khamgiin's eyelids had appeared to flutter, deep black pits gaping open from an abyss. Nergüi's singsong chant sank as if into a dream, and some compulsion had Khagash-Fél kneeling at Khamgiin's side and placing his hand upon his son's. Khamgiin's hands were clammy and cool, but a throbbing ache started up just behind his forehead as soon as he touched them. Shadows flowed around Khamgiin's still face, deepening the eyes, hollowing the cheeks, parting around his lips to draw in more of the surrounding darkness like a last breath into a dead man's lungs.

Khagash-Fél resisted the urge to pull away, confronting this strangeness and the mortal fear it aroused in his heart. He tightened his grip.

'Who felled you?'

'Whom do you hope will answer, Half-Chosen?'

Khagash-Fél's grip on his son's hand stiffened. Cartilage snapped under his fingers. On the dark mask that wore Khamgiin's face there was no suggestion of pain.

'By what right do you ask?'

A pulse of agony seared through the Eye of Katchar and into his brain. Khagash-Fél grunted in pain, as though his eyes had been held open to an intense light. Or a deep, terrible darkness. The pain forced itself into an image, second-hand and blurred, tinted blue, but in it he saw Khamgiin. His son wore his gifted armour and strode through a herd of beasts towards a small knot of terrified men on a hill. They were Empire men. Hochlanders. Their spears glinted green and blue. Such men could not have bested the Lastborn. He tried to take command of the vision in his mind and move it forward, but he could not.

'What is such insight worth to you?'

A second stab of pain and the Eye inched open, stirring like a dragon disturbed from slumber. A confusion of places and people, futures and past, hit his mind at once.

A thickly-muscled dwarf Slayer tore through the mass of beastmen that sought to bring him down. His axe glowed with runes that hurt the Eye to look upon, and in a watercolour smear of pain the shapes and colours that made him ran instead to the form of an old, blond-haired swordsman in a red cloak, with a rare skill with his runic blade.

Khagash-Fél sensed a flicker of hatred for these two, of fear even. As he watched the vision ran again, the beastmen that the pair battled thinning and blurring until they became something altogether different. Something daemonic. The creatures were dark-skinned with savage, evil faces. Their limbs were multi-jointed and sawed crazily as they attacked, ending in a spread of black knife-like claws. The dwarf tore through them with an equal savagery. The man followed in his footsteps, fighting back-to-back, deeper into the underbelly of what looked like a fortress. Silvery-red runes glowered from the high basalt walls.

'Did one of these best my son?'

A chuckle oiled through the shadows. *'It is not Altdorf or Middenheim or any of the great cities of this age that will witness the Slayer's final days. Where but in the halls of the first Slayer can the last great Slayer meet his doom?'*

'This means nothing to me. The gods called me west to fight in the final war,' Khagash-Fél growled. He felt as though he were pleading, as though he knelt before one of those gods even now. His heart beat so hard it felt twice its proper size.

Khamgiin's black lips twisted into a sneer. *'One god called you, Half-Chosen. One god did not forget his mighty champion in the east, and you have a higher purpose. My purpose is the true purpose of Chaos, and few have earned the ire of Chaos as have these two fools.'* There was a blunt stab of pain in Khagash-Fél's Eye and the vision focused on the man and the dwarf, the dwarf battering through a river of daemons as the man fended off the hordes at his heels. Again Khagash-Fél had that strange sense, that door-seam glare of incandescent loathing and ungodly fear. *'His is the power to thwart the End Times themselves. He cannot be allowed to fulfil his destiny.'*

Khagash-Fél's mind reeled. Avert the End Times? Impossible! The Everchosen had arisen. The Old World stood on the brink, and Khagash-Fél had brought the tribes halfway across the globe to give it its final push. It would be his legacy, his glory. The thought of some nameless warrior – worse yet, a *dwarf* – driving back the tide of Chaos even after it had risen so high brought his blood to the boil and yellowed his vision with hellfire.

Black laughter wound its shadowy voice through Khagash-Fél's long grey hair, causing the oil bowls to flicker. '*Mighty warriors of portent and prowess have faced them and fallen, but they are not invulnerable. These are the last days. I have been shown their downfall and by my will and by my word I command it so.*'

For a moment, Khagash-Fél was too lost to rage to answer. His logical mind watched his heart and soul hurtle down into some unknowable abyss. His head felt light, his vision blurry. The shadow that sheathed his son stretched into a triumphant smile. The rage guttered and all that was left was the emptiness. This was a god, he realised, with a deep and thorough coring of his convictions. All his life, both mortal and beyond, he had auctioned his sword to the Great Powers as though they were nothing more august than distant paymasters with pockets full of silver. But the being that deigned to address him directly now did so from a position of power as inconceivable to him as his own favour was to the likes of Darhyk or Nergüi.

With an effort of will, he controlled himself. There was no trait more celebrated amongst the tribes than self-discipline. A man could be born to be swift or strong, but the conviction to face down pain, privation, or fear itself with nothing but force of will and the hard face came only from within. He was the Eagle of Mourn, the Colossus of Zhar, the greatest ever hero of the wide eastern steppe.

It would take more than a god to cow him, and this god had come to *him*.

'Who are you?'

'*You know my name. Go deep into your soul. You will find it there, etched in shadow upon the cruel heart of man.*'

Khagash-Fél did as he was bade and turned his mind's eye inwards. He sensed malignance, ambition, a shadow cast even across the ultimate darkness of time. There was a name, one he seemed intuitively to know. It was a name so ancient as to have become legend, a king amongst daemons, the first mortal ever to ascend to the second tier of godhood and become a daemon prince.

'Be'lakor.'

'I am power, I am corruption, I am the Dark Master of Chaos and the time has come for me to arise and take form again. This land shall be the cradle of a new dominion, the place and time where four will at last become five. Many of the warlords between here and the Fortress of the First Slayer are mine and will be yours to command. Others must be brought to heel.'

Khagash-Fél took what felt like the least certain breath of his life. The shadows were beginning to retreat to the corners of the room. Nergüi's somnolent chant again played at the corners of his mind. Then he smiled.

The gods had answered his plea.

He had his sign.

FIVE

No Way Back

Felix awoke from a nightmare in which something formless and dark hunted him through the forest, and though he had sought every avenue to escape, branches like claws had pulled at his hair and cloak and roots had reached out from the ground to make him stumble. With every step the forest darkened and his pursuer, though formless and unseen, drew palpably closer. For some reason, the notion of drawing his sword and facing this hidden foe had filled him with terror. So he had run, pushing through the lashing branches and into a clearing much like the one in which he had just fought. The rocky ground was littered with bodies and though he could not see their faces, he had known absolutely that here lay every man and woman he had ever known or loved. Large parts of the dream remained a frantic blur of branches, of shadows and fear, but he recalled turning up to the sky, watching as darkness rolled across it with the inevitability of a rising tide. The forest around him had sunk into blackness and from it a voice had rumbled. It had sounded like a voice, and Felix felt that it was speaking to him, but it was too vast to comprehend, too alien in its intent, and all he could grasp was the horror.

He came to bolt upright, heart pounding. He was in the back of Lanarksson's wagon. A bed had been made out in the front corner with a roll of soft fleece and partitioned from the rest of the wagon by piles of crates. An oil lantern, set to its tightest aperture, cast a mean and uncertain glow over the rough wooden surfaces. He had his sword in his hand, but the nightmare residue creeping through his chest warned him that it was already too late.

A meagre pile of his possessions had been assembled in front of an upturned box beside his bed. A sepulchral figure sat silently on the box. Felix's already frantic heart jumped. He covered his mouth to smother a cry of shock.

Unperturbed, Max Schreiber licked the tip of his finger and peeled back a page in the small leather-bound pocket book in his hand.

Felix's hand moved unconsciously to his heart where he generally kept his journal, wrapped in an oilskin between his mail shirt and his chest. The oilskin lay in the pile on the floor, on top of his neatly folded mail and cloak.

'How long have you been here, Max?' he asked, fiery lines of pain tracing along the bones of his jaw as he spoke.

Painfully, his hand felt over a wild bed of bruises towards a split lip and, above it, what felt like a roughly reset nose. *Gotrek.* Then he remembered the rest and a salty warmth stung his eyes.

It was gone. Altdorf was really gone. Kat. Otto. All of it.

He was alone.

The wagon bumped, rattling the crates and forcing a fresh groan out of Felix. They were still moving. He could see through the rope ties between the wagon's wooden sides and its tarp roof that it was dark outside. And it had stopped raining. He could hear the slushing sound as the wheels rolled through puddles and soft mud.

'Where are we?'

'You have not recorded an entry since the day you rescued me from the Troll King's gaol,' said Max absently, finger running backwards across the page, grey lips moving silently. The lantern light seemed to bend around him, leaving him grey and ill-defined, dominated by the shadow that the book cast upon his chest. It was a thing of wings, of horns, of darkness. Felix shivered and almost missed what the wizard said next.

'Why?'

Felix tenderly drew his fingers from his jaw. 'And what exactly would you have me write?'

'This is your final adventure. It should be recorded.'

'Final...?' asked Felix, chilled, though he could not say why. He knew that this would be his and Gotrek's last journey together. When they arrived in Middenheim – he could only assume that to be where the Slayer was now taking them – he doubted that either one of them would be sorry to see the back of the other. But there was something about the way Max said it. Something... terminal. 'And who would read it, Max? If Altdorf Press is still running then they're doing better than the rest of the city by all accounts.'

The wagon bumped over another rut. Water splashed.

'Where are we?' Felix asked bitterly, enunciating carefully to try and protect his jaw. 'Where did Gotrek take us? And what happened to Gustav and the others?'

It took Felix a moment to realise that Max wasn't really listening. The wizard turned another page.

'I too have trouble sleeping.'

The tangential shift had Felix blinking to keep up.

'Often in my dreams I am flying,' Max went on, insistent as a night breeze. 'I am high, riding above the clouds. The peaks of mountains rise through them like islands. I can feel the wind on my...' his hand rose hesitantly from the page to feel the edges of his hood, '...my face. Where the cloud breaks I see the world beneath me turn dark. Roads shrivel. Forests mutate before my eyes. The cities of Chaos sink into the earth. I am alone, but I hear a voice whisper to me. It is a woman's voice, and she calls to me by name, though I do not know her. She tells me that it does not have to end this way.'

'Enough, Max,' said Felix, reaching across to touch the wizard's arm. Despite his ashen, ghostly appearance, the man felt entirely normal to the touch. His once ivory-coloured robes were stiff, tailored for battle. His arm was warm.

Felix and Max had never been the closest of friends. The wizard's lecturing manner had often grated, his empiricism starkly at odds with Felix's hopelessly romantic outlook, but their philosophical differences would undoubtedly have proven fodder for endless debates in taprooms the world over had it not been for Ulrika. Even now, with hindsight and perhaps even a little wisdom, Felix found it difficult to unpick the tangle of hurt feelings, petty arguments, and jealousy that had ultimately defined his relationship with her and, as a consequence, with Max.

There was an element of masochism in dwelling on such things – such *times* – with the world the way it was, but though he lived through an age of gods and monsters Felix was, whatever that now meant, still only human.

'Always my journey ends in the same place, deep inside the ancient heart of a mountain. There is power there, power that I cannot describe, but I feel good to be there. The magic is calm, bound within rocks that have not seen change in ten thousand years. I know that I am where I am meant to be. You are there too, Felix. And the Slayer.'

'Me?'

A nod of the hood, a cold breeze that gave Felix shivers.

'I had always suspected that your steps were guided by a higher power and now I am convinced of it. They have brought you here, together, to these mountains and at this time. It is through the two of you that they will show their hand in this war.'

Felix shook his head sadly. Max was mad. He saw it now.

'I saw your death,' Max hissed.

Felix's scepticism vanished under an existential chill. 'You saw what?'

'Sometimes it is yours, sometimes Gotrek's, as if fate itself remains undecided. But for some reason I do not grieve when I see it, for I know that this is how the world will be saved.'

For what felt like a long time, Felix merely stared at his old friend. The wagon rumbled beneath them. The wizard swayed on his bench like a lonely tree in a mountain wind. Felix wanted nothing more than to tell Max that he was being ridiculous, perhaps shake some sense into the man, but for some reason he dared not. He was still a dangerously powerful wizard after all, and a broken one at that. The silence between them stretched. Felix's thoughts returned him to a prophetic dream that he himself had once had. He had been asleep at his desk in his brother's Altdorf townhouse when he had dreamt of fighting alongside Gotrek and Ulrika on the floodplains of Praag. As it ultimately turned out, it had been accurate almost blow for blow in his dreams. He had not had the time to devote much thought to it since, but now he wondered.

Had it been destiny guiding his steps as Max suggested, perhaps towards some ignoble end in the lonely heights of the Middle Mountains?

With a creak of creased leather, Max eased the pocketbook shut and held it out to Felix. No Grail Knight of Bretonnia had ever been presented with a relic invested with such portent.

'You have been through too much together for it to count for nothing now,' said Max. 'Do not leave him to face this trial alone.'

'What trial?' said Felix.

A knock startled him.

Kolya's saw-edged face appeared from behind the partitioning crates. His gaunt cheeks were drawn as though he had been up all night, and his dark hair was wet. The Kislevite took in Felix's drawn sword with a raised eyebrow.

'They say man who fights monsters in dreams need not wake up.'

'What do you want?' said Felix irritably, lowering his sword to the bedding.

'Zabójka asks for you.'

'And Gotrek always gets what he wants.'

Kolya shrugged. 'I do not care to know him as you do, but I think he is... ashamed for what happened.'

Felix snorted, then winced as pain flared in his jaw. He suspected a broken bone, but he was no expert. Max could wile away the entire day at his bedside, but a little healing magic was clearly too much to expect. He turned to the wizard but the box on which he had been sitting was empty, Felix's belongings piled neatly around it. The lantern stuttered and Felix suppressed a shudder as he dropped his gaze to the journal that had somehow found its way into his hand.

He wondered if he had woken from his nightmare at all.

Felix lowered himself from the back of the wagon, the rain-softened game trail on which they had stopped oozing sludgily underfoot. A handful of smaller wagons were strung out behind them, soldiers and camp followers clustered around for warmth and mutual protection. A thin mist wove between the dark boles of the forest, split fitfully by shafts of moonlight. Tattered shreds of cloud streamed across the face of the moon, and even though Felix could not feel the wind here amongst the trees he pulled his cloak close against it. There was a chill in the air. The treetops moaned quietly and their lower leaves shivered. Nightjars and robins cried out from the depths. Moonlight glinted back from watching eyes.

Felix took a deep breath, tasting the air. It was decidedly colder, holding to a trace of winter, and unless he was imagining things it was also a little bit thinner.

'Are we close to the Middle Mountains?'

'It always looks the same in your country. Everywhere, it is more trees.'

'You sound like Gotrek.'

The Kislevite pulled a face.

Stars blinked through breaks in the canopy. Felix tried to guess what time of night it was. He would hazard 'late' and there was something in the feel of the air, a latency, that made him think early morning. Felix's gaze lingered on the treeline. He could just walk away from this, just walk into the forest and go. His heart pulled on him to do it. He could leave Gotrek's oath and Max's prophecy right here and make his way to Middenheim alone.

'Go if you want,' said Kolya, reading his thoughts or perhaps just sharing them. 'I tell Zabójka you hit me.'

Felix shook his head. He could not leave without Gustav, who in turn would probably not leave without his men. And these soldiers needed Felix. They believed in him, for better or worse, and Felix felt that he owed them something for that. No, like it or not, he and Gotrek were stuck with one another for a little while longer yet. Max could call it fate if he liked, but Felix preferred to think of it as a painful inconvenience that could not be cast aside soon enough.

As Felix watched, sergeants sent detachments of men fanning out into the forest.

'But maybe you keep head down,' Kolya continued in the same off-hand tone. 'I shoot two beastmen scouts earlier today, and that man there?' The Kislevite pointed to a Hochland forester in green and umber as he strung his bow and disappeared into the forest. 'He claims he sees northern rider. Me? I think it is a strange horse that tries to run in a forest.'

'Take me to Gotrek,' Felix said with a sigh.

Ever since he had been a child, forced to endure weeks of darkness and strange noises at his father's lumber camps in the Drakwald, Felix had hated forests. He could not imagine what Gotrek had found in this one that was so important.

'Am I right?' said Kolya, ducking under a dripping branch and spreading his arms to encompass the tangled mass of dark, mist-wreathed trunks. 'Here, even mountains have trees.'

'The Middle Mountains were at least a week away,' said Felix, palming aside the same branch and following in the Kislevite's steps. He peered into the cloying mist, searching for the telltale glimpse of a peak. There was nothing. Damp mosses glistened silver against the north face of the trees. Grasses conferred darkly. Nascent bluebells filled the air with their scent, their flowers closed within tiny helmets, withholding their full colour against the final encroachment of spring. Life, on some level, was going on. It was actually rather dispiriting. His attention veering from the trail, Felix stamped his foot in a deep puddle, splashing freezing water into his boots and startling a small brown frog that hopped out of his path and into the undergrowth.

Kolya chuckled.

'Through all these trees? A week at least. But Zabójka took us onto Wolfenburg road, and returned to forest only when he say his secret path is near. Oh yes,' Kolya added with a tight little smile, 'the army of marauders and beasts marching north behind us on same road maybe also have something to do with it.'

Felix stopped, stunned, a wet branch swinging back to slap him in the chest.

A herd of beastmen their company could just – and he meant *just* – about handle, but a Chaos army on the march was a vastly different prospect. Felix had seen plenty of them on the roads of Ostermark when he had first crossed back into the Empire: whole regiments of Chaos warriors marching in step, the hellish banners, the bray of horns, the reek of char where daemons walked, the way the ground itself seemed to shake underfoot as broken and branded Ostermark men pushed the Chaos legions' infernal engines of war west towards Talabecland. They were memories that would stay with Felix as long as he lived. And Gotrek had seen them too.

'Did no one try to stop him?'

The Kislevite paused under the moon shadow of a wide beech tree. Were it not for his colourful patchwork coat then Felix doubted he would have been able to see the man. 'Is up to you of course, but I suggest keeping down your voice.' He nodded towards the surrounding forest. 'Not all of Chaos army stayed on road.'

Felix was uncomfortably reminded of his nightmare of being hunted through a forest that had itself been somehow complicit with his doom. Looking around him now, he could see where some of that imagery had come from. *I see your death.* He shuddered. It wasn't a pleasant comparison to draw.

'Are they following us?'

'Look at this,' said Kolya, taking a frond of something leafy and green and producing an expansive shrug. 'How is anyone to follow anything in this?'

'Kat could,' said Felix wistfully. His wife had been a true daughter of the Drakwald, and what had filled him with night terrors had been as unthreatening and common to her as a stroll down Befe-hlshaber Avenue, a gauntlet of hawkers, vendors and beggars that had in turn filled Kat with dread. Reminiscence hardened into a lump in his throat. He swallowed it with difficulty. 'She could track a single beastman several days ahead. And I once saw her shoot down a running beastman at three hundred yards by nothing but moonlight.' He shook his head, disbelieving still. 'The best shot I ever saw.'

'No offence taken,' Kolya returned. 'Is she as beautiful as she is deadly with a bow?'

'You know you've asked me this question or one like it a hundred times since we left Praag.'

'You are the poet, Lord Jaeger. Describe her to me and maybe I will not ask again.'

Felix sighed. 'She was smaller than most women, and slender, but she could move through the forest like a deer. And she had the most beautiful dark hair, except for here.' He pointed to a spot above his left eye. 'Here she had a lock of silver that shone regardless of day and night.' He ran his finger absently down the side of his face to the corner of his lip. 'And a scar here. It didn't bother her, and she knew it didn't bother me.' He smiled despite his heartache. 'I'm no oil painting myself these days. And the gods save the merchant she caught staring at it. I think I once saw her humble Gotrek with that stare of hers, though I might have been mistaken.'

'She sounds a veritable *atamanka*,' said Kolya approvingly. 'The terror of beastmen and of men's hearts in all your forests.'

'She was.'

Kolya took his employment of the past tense without comment.

Felix blinked away what might, given time and opportunity, have budded into a tear. At times like this he missed her so much that it was impossible to believe she could be gone. How could a ghost cause his heart such pain? But she was gone. A part of him wallowed in the pain, held the knife to the self-inflicted wound and demanded he suffer it. He should have been there. His presence in Altdorf would not have swayed that battle, he knew. He doubted whether even Gotrek and his axe could have made the difference, but he should have been there. The thought of Kat frightened and alone left him feeling hollow, nothing but a cold skein of unspoken grief. He wondered if it was the same guilt that drove Gotrek.

During the denouement to their disastrous last hours in Praag, Felix had learned that the Slayer had himself been on a quest in distant lands when his family had been killed by goblin raiders, and had shared his one-time comrade's grief as he had heard the part that Snorri Nosebiter had played in their deaths. And now Snorri was dead too. Felix hoped the murder of his best friend brought the Slayer comfort.

'Will you stay with Gotrek when you reach Middenheim?' Felix asked, shaking off thoughts of splitting bone and bloody snow.

'Until he falls in glorious battle against many foes.'

'And then?'

'What chance for cup of kvass in your city?'

The Kislevite slung an arm around a tree trunk that was perched on a mossy tussock of gnarled roots and earth and pulled himself up. The man turned and crouched, a grin deepening the shadows on his narrow face. Felix frowned in annoyance, though whether with Kolya or with himself he wasn't sure. Sometimes he wasn't sure what he really wanted at all. Even after everything Gotrek had done, as far as he had sunk in Felix's esteem, Felix couldn't shake the sense of *import* that he had carried through so many adventures. It wasn't just professional pride, the hours he had spent in swamps and deserts and corrupted ruins, scribbling by starlight with mortal danger always just around the corner. It went deeper than that.

It was a saga that needed its ending.

Reaching under his mail, Felix withdrew his oilcloth-wrapped pocketbook and held it up to the moonlight. 'I could give you my journal. The first entry is just after Gotrek and I departed Castle Reikguard with Kat and Snorri on the road to Karak Kadrin, but I can answer any questions you might–'

Kolya waved the offer away. Felix's grip on the book hardened.

'Gotrek deserves better.'

'If you think so, why did you leave him?'

Felix sighed, but said nothing as the Kislevite dropped a hand to draw him up onto the tussock.

He didn't have an answer for him.

Gotrek was standing in a small clearing between the wrecks of two coaches, hunched wearily over the awesome weight of his axe, glaring from one to the other. The vehicles were gaudily painted in bright, primary colours, rails and trims picked out in gold paint that shimmered in the torchlight of the men picking their way through the scattered debris. The body of the one nearest to Felix was peppered with arrows and a dark splash of blood coated the ladder to the driver's platform. The second had been turned onto its side and gutted. A lantern had been slung from its undercarriage, casting a hesitant pall that advanced a way into the forest and then retreated, over and again, like a rat around a trap. Smashed boxes littered the ground, spilling what looked like face paints and glittering costumes over the forest floor.

Travelling players, Felix thought with a familiar wrench, probably hoping for sanctuary in the mountains.

'Mutants, I think,' said Gustav, moving out from behind the

upturned wagon, flanked by a pair of heavily armoured soldiers with wary eyes and hands on their weapons' pommels. He carried a second battered lantern that lit his face eerily from below.

Felix's relief at finding his nephew alive and well threatened him with a smile, a twinge to his injured jaw bringing it out as a grimace.

'Nice to see you too, uncle.'

'What makes you think it was mutants? There's a Chaos warband hunting us, apparently.'

'Their tracks are... strange, and seem to be heading north into the mountains.'

'You found tracks?' said Kolya. 'Show me.'

Gustav nodded, spared Felix a furtive smile, and led the Kislevite back around the wagons.

Mutants ahead, a Chaos warband behind, and who knew what awaiting them in the Middle Mountains. The forces of darkness enclosed them on every side. With a glance to the solemn rank of trees, Felix loosened the collar of his cloak. For a moment he had almost felt the shadow around his neck.

'Over here, manling,' grunted Gotrek, a little less of the usual flint in his voice, and gestured behind him with a jerk of the head.

Felix pulled his fingers from his collar and straightened his back before stamping over to join him. The Slayer lowered his axe and glanced aside as he approached. If Felix didn't know better, he'd think the dwarf was actually *sorry*. His single eye was bloodshot, as if the pupil had been struck from behind with a spear. His enormous muscles trembled with the effort of keeping him upright. Sigmar, what would it take to make the dwarf sleep?

'You just decided to punch me out, then,' said Felix. 'The old dwarf ways not as secret as you thought they were?'

'There's a lot of ground between us and the mountain road yet,' Gotrek growled back, then shook his head with a clink of gold.

'I didn't wake you to argue. I have a new rememberer for that. I wanted you to see something before we head further from the Wolfenburg road.'

'About that–'

'This way, manling,' said Gotrek, lumping his axe once more to his shoulder and trudging away between the two wagons. 'Just a little further.'

Even from the overgrown outcropping that jutted from the forest to overlook the Wolfen Vale, Felix could smell the blood. A sprawling city that could only have been Wolfenburg, the capital of Ostland, blistered the earth like burnt and puckered flesh. Banners of tattered skin flew from its battlements, lit from beneath by candles of human tallow. Like a pumpkin carved into a nightmarish mask and then set around a candle, the shattered walls gleamed with thousands of individual points of light. The breaches in the city's walls had been packed with polished skulls, and her lights now shone through the eye sockets and fracture wounds of her people. The alpine wind blowing through those walls returned the dead their voice, a haunting moan that filled the sparsely forested bowl of the river valley.

The great stone bastion of the Elector's Palace stood within an inner ring of fortifications, all now half-demolished, a moat of rubble around a gutted citadel from which the fell symbols of Chaos glared out over the city. Nearby, the granite keep of the Knights of the Bull stood in a similar state of ruin. Rising between them like a judge from its promontory atop a rugged scarp was the remnants of the chapter house of the Order of the Silver Hammer. The ancestral home of the Knights of Wolfgart – the Witch Hunters, as most men knew to fear them – had been subjected to a more comprehensive pogrom of desecration. Even from afar, the deep warpstone glare emanating from the crater made Felix's stomach turn.

He had seen Kislevite *stanitsas* ransacked and burned. He had seen the gruesome tribune poles that had dotted the oblast and that even the crows dared not overfly. Every man in his company brought talk of destruction, of smashed armies and broken cities, and Felix had believed every word. But this was the first time he had seen first-hand for himself one of the great cities of the Empire in ruins.

And it wasn't over yet.

On the road before its walls, two vast armies collided. Ten thousand banners danced like daemons on hot coals. Hundreds of mounted northmen with coloured pennants streaming from their short lances ploughed through endless blocks of heavily armoured and hideously mutated infantry. Beastmen battled each other in churning whirlpools of froth and fur. Bursts of dark magic charred the air. Ogres in blasted plate mail bellowed, islands of brute power in a sea of foes. Huge, muzzled beasts sent gouts of flame rolling through the melee, immolating fighting men by the score. It was a cauldron of noise.

There wasn't an Imperial banner in sight. This was a battle between the gods of Chaos, rival champions feuding over scraps and favour. Felix turned away, sick.

'I wanted you to see this,' said Gotrek. Scrawled with tattoos of doom and dishonour and worn haggard by many months of bloodshed, the Slayer looked as much at one with his time as Felix had ever seen him. 'This is what your Empire has become now, manling. Wherever you go this is what you will find. As sure as the stones of Everpeak, Middenheim is the last city of man. That is where the little one will be waiting for you. There is nowhere else to go.'

Felix simply stared over the opposing hordes in numb horror.

There was no end to the Chaos Gods' appetite for carnage. When the Empire and her allies were broken and the world was theirs, would they then fall on each other like this until only one champion remained standing? And then what? What kind of world would one ruled by Chaos be? Felix couldn't imagine. He didn't want to.

'I think that Chaos warrior you let go has followed us here,' Gotrek muttered softly, as if sorry to intrude on Felix's thoughts.

'I didn't *let him go,*' Felix spat, still staring at the unbelievable act of violence being staged in the valley below. 'I put a bullet between his shoulders.'

'Same thing,' said Gotrek with a shrug, then nodded down. 'I recognise some of the markings on those beasts down there. If I had one I'd wager a Bugman's that they're from the same herd we fought back in the forest.'

Felix didn't bother to look for himself. Although dwarf eyes were generally not as sharp as a human's – an adaptation to low-light vision, or so Max had once explained – they had a remarkable capacity for picking out intricate detail. Felix supposed that when one got down to the mechanics of it, the inner workings of a fine dwarf-made clock or the tribal war paint on a beastman's hide were all very much the same.

'And what if they follow us onto the mountain road? They could use it to attack Middenheim.'

'Dwarfs don't build a thing for others to use, manling. Archaon himself could walk those mountains for ten thousand years and never get near those roads.'

'Fine,' Felix sighed, sickened as much by the tug of inevitability as by the rivers of blood being spilled. Watching it brought Max's words ringing between his ears: *your final adventure.* 'Fine. I'll not fight you. We'll take the dwarfs' mountain road and we'll go to Middenheim together.'

But no further, Felix thought, as the Slayer nodded wearily and turned his back on the slaughter below.

'Where are the man and the dwarf?' demanded Khagash-Fél, his voice a barely human growl, focusing the bested champion's mind with a tightening of his grip over the kneeling man's bald head. The warrior's skull creaked and he groaned in pleasure.

The champion was naked but for a pair of electrum bracers that clasped his forearms like entwined lovers and a belt to which a quartet of dazzling – now thoroughly dismembered – daemon women were chained. His superb muscular definition glistened with an oil that his pale skin seemed to exude, shining like buffed iron as mounted tribesmen thundered by with flaming arrows nocked to their bowstrings. Arrows and blades alike had glanced off the warrior's smoothly lacquered flesh. Shafts lay unbroken on the ground where he knelt, teased from the air and prostrate before his beauty. Even Khagash-Fél's own exalted daemon-blade, Ildezegtei, had caressed the champion's musculature like a doe-eyed doxy swooning over a legendary hero on the eve of battle.

The gods adored a stalemate above all other outcomes in war. What better to please an uncaring immortal than strife without end? But these were the End Times, and Khagash-Fél found his patience for such trivialities waning.

He squeezed until the champion's amaranthine eyes fluttered.

'The gods grant you great power. What do you think that they gifted to me?'

'Warlord!'

A tribesman jumped down from his horse and dropped smoothly to one knee. His bare chest was knotted with muscle, an artwork of scar lines and tribal tattoos. Concentric rings of scar tissue made a maze of one side of his face, with one lidless pearly white eye the prize at its centre, much like the slavers' brand on Khagash-Fél's own face. The warrior's head was smooth but for a long topknot, the olive-dark skin slick with blood and sweat. 'The Doombull's scouts speak of a small group of men striking north on foot into the forest.'

'And a dwarf?' Blood trickled around Khagash-Fél's cracked and yellow fingernails. Bone began to creak.

The tribesman sneered. 'No man can make sense of those beasts. I sent our own scouts ahead to see for themselves.'

'You did well...?' The champion of depravity moaned once more and with a sickening *crunch* of bone went slack. Khagash-Fél shook pinkish matter from his fingers and turned to the tribesman with a question in his voice.

'D-Darhyk, warlord. I have ridden with you for years.'

'Of course,' Khagash-Fél murmured, dismissing the already forgotten warrior from his gaze and turning to the city that its champion had called Wolfenburg.

Tribesmen galloped around the skull-studded curtain wall, waiting for the perfect moment when all four of their horse's legs were off the ground and man and mount together seemed to glide before sending shafts wrapped with burning rags arcing over the city. Speed, power, courage; the horse-archers of the tribes were without peer, as devastating as a rampaging thundertusk or a charge of the metal-shelled knights of the west. It was without surprise that Khagash-Fél watched the Chaos warriors and their Kurgan brethren retreating to their stronghold, warmed by an ember of pride in the twists of smoke that rose over its grey slate rooftops.

There had been a time when such a faultless dismantlement of a rival champion's war machine would have filled his heart with pleasure, but no longer. The Dark Master of Chaos had elevated him above such trifling affairs and he saw the conquest of this insignificant bastion of apostates and pariahs as the gods themselves must see it – a burning point on a map, one drawn on black canvas to depict an empire in shadow, a remount waiting for him on his road. He had pledged his soul to one god and there was no way back now. The dark smoke coiled like horns, reaching skyward against a backdrop of mountains.

'It is as Khamgiin Lastborn revealed to me before his final ride,' said Nergüi. The shaman sat astride his eggshell-grey mount, the frayed blue feather-strips of his robe fluttering down to its shanks. His narrow eyes peered into the smoke as though searching for a message left for them by the departed spirits of fire.

This was not destiny's fulfilment, but its opening sally. Nergüi and his old ways had taken Khagash-Fél as far as he could. Ahead there waited a new guide, one who heard the commands of the Dark Master as Nergüi had once relayed the wishes of the old steppe spirits. He felt it in his blood, saw it reflected by the Eye of Katchar into his dreams.

'Mountains,' said Khagash-Fél, the single word that his son had related through the cast of Nergüi's black feathers rumbling from his cavernous chest. That was where the Dark Master's prophet awaited him, the one who would guide him to the red-cloaked man and the Slayer. Those mountains would be where they fell. It was fated.

The champions of Be'lakor came for them.

PART TWO
DEATH TO MY ENEMIES

Late Spring 2527

SIX

Into the Middle Mountains

A trickle of stones rattled down the steep sides of the gorge. Felix retraced their descent to a formation of bare and weathered rocks, a grim knuckle of sedimentary earth slowly grinding its way through the mountainside. The surface bore a dark sheen from the previous night's rain. As Felix watched, a last desultory pebble bumped downhill. He strained his eyes. The relentless rush of the river beside them filled his head with white noise. For a second, he would have sworn there had been a human figure up there amongst the rocks.

Imagination could be a cruel thing.

With a nod of reassurance for the benefit of the soldiers around him, he forced himself to look away and trudge on with the long column of men and carts. The soldiers smiled, apparently content to take their safety at his word. Felix wished he could convince himself so easily. It felt as though he had been walking with a noose around his neck and a trapdoor beneath his feet ever since Gotrek had first led them into the pass. Not a minute went by when Felix didn't squirm with the sensation of being watched, and every watch he awoke with eyes already sore in anticipation of another day's straining on rugged-jawed ridgelines and distant shapes in the rock.

Unable to help himself, he glanced back up.

Past the rock formation the gorge rose to an ice-blistered peak, an unnamed titan of grey stone slumped under the leaden weight of the sky. The world had become a darker place since word of Altdorf's fall had reached them. It wasn't just in his mind.

The pass was tightening. The mountains crept a little nearer each day. The sense of sliding into some kind of funnel from which he could not escape was ever present. It made his muscles ache and his mind whirl and trying not to think about it only worried him more. With every ineluctable step forward the grey in the sky appeared to grow a little blacker. It was a mirror to the world for the world to see, and whenever Felix looked he saw doom closing.

And so he endeavoured not to look.

The company ate the day's meal on the march.

Black bread and nuggets of hard cheese were passed down from Lanarksson's wagon and then from hand to hand down the long, winding column of women and men. The sun was dipping behind the western peaks when Felix, walking with the middle of the column, saw his own mean ration. He chewed it slowly, making it last, as he surveyed the line of beaten men strung out ahead and ultimately winding out of sight deeper into the pass.

Quickly, as if to catch whoever might be watching in the act, he glanced again to the surrounding slopes.

There was no one there, but the sense of watchfulness remained, and Felix could not help but consider how vulnerable they were to any kind of an attack. There was little that could be done about it since the path was already barely wide enough for the wagons, but Felix couldn't help but worry. It was as if his mind had forgotten how to do anything else. He wondered if all generals felt this way, or only the reluctant ones.

It was a wonder any battles were ever won at all.

Following the food came a cupful of ale, carefully doled out for each fighting man by the most sober-looking veterans that Felix had been able to identify. They wore dark leather armour with steel plates sewn in, and pushed a handcart laden with a single small barrel. Stern soldiers with loaded crossbows guarded its progress. Complaints fell on ears that were neither deaf nor heartless, but which had heard every tear-jerking tale there was at least twice already today and umpteen times the days before. The black-capped sergeant saluted Felix, his measuring cup in hand as though offering a grim toast, and then poured him a generous measure. Without thinking about it, Felix drank his due and no more, passing the remainder back.

The Slayer ignored the ale-men as he had the passage of bread and cheese. Felix wondered how long his former companion could go without food or water. At times Gotrek muttered to himself in what sounded like strains of Khazalid, the dwarfs' well-guarded native tongue, but for most of their journey into the Middle Mountains he had been silent, glaring alternately between the valley sides and the soldiers ahead and behind. Determination alone seemed to sustain him now, but surely even the Slayer's formidable constitution would have to fail eventually.

Felix had no idea what he was going to do about it when it did.

It was a rare cloudless night, the stars shining fitfully against a sky as clear as polished glass.

A cluster of tents had been pitched against the frothing waters of the river, hugging to the scant protection afforded their flanks by a sharp curve in its course. Unfortunately, the ground further from the water was naught but solid rock and after the first unsecured tents had threatened to slide into the river the men had instead thrown down bedrolls with what amounted to a collective shrug and a thumbed nose to the harsh vagaries of fate. Felix had heard and read that generals moulded the armies they led in their own image, and he was somewhat gratified to see something of his own attitude in their response.

A handful of soldiers hauled off their boots and braved the rapids to cleanse their aching feet. Others took advantage of the respite to refill canteens or rinse their clothes, but most simply slept where they fell. There were no fires. As the night chill set in men shivered in their dreams, while those detailed to watch paced the picket of spears around the camp's perimeter rather than freeze.

Felix took his own shift on the picket in the final frigid hours before dawn, huffing mist onto his gloved hands and peering up the starlit slopes. It still felt strange to look on a night sky that did not contain Morrslieb, the fell twin of the greater moon that tonight bathed the gorge in silver. He could not say that he missed the presence of the Chaos Moon, but even as the harbinger of evil that it was, it was difficult to see its destruction as a portent for good.

He considered raising the matter with Gotrek, for the Slayer never slept these days; he sat enshrouded within his axe's ruddy aura, not so much watching as impatiently awaiting the dawn and the chance to move again. The hole in the Slayer's un-patched eye reminded Felix of howling wolves, of goblin arrows, and ultimately of Kirsten, Felix's first great love, who had died in the same attack that had claimed Gotrek's eye.

With a heart's sigh, Felix clapped his hands and stared into the night. Had he not loved and lost enough since then? He could understand as well as anyone why Gustav wore Ulrika's armour and why Kolya inked the same horse onto his bicep each morning. It was more comforting sometimes to hold on to the pain rather than let it go. He wondered if Gotrek felt the same way as, for all his race's inscrutable character, Felix had come roundabout to the conclusion that dwarfs and men were really not so dissimilar as each liked to think. They were all children of the Old Ones, if that high elf antiquarian with whom they had argued in a Marienburg tavern was to be believed. Their disagreement had later been taken outside, the scholar himself subsequently dumped unconscious into the canal, but in a way Gotrek had proven the elf correct – they did all bleed the same colour.

Felix chose not to disturb him. He felt that they had edged towards a *detente* of sorts, but it was still too difficult to talk to him. He didn't even know how he would start.

He was looking up at the sky, idly entertaining the notion of drawing his journal out from his under his shirt, when the sound of whispered voices from further along the palisade put to bed such civilised musings.

'It is said that Emperor Karl Franz, imbued with the might of Sigmar, fought three daemon princes in the battle for the Imperial Palace,' whispered one man, breath fogging around a dark silhouette sat on an upturned box behind a rank of spears. Felix recognised the rural Hochlander accent of Corporal Herschel Mann.

'Felix once struck a wounding blow upon a Bloodthirster of Khorne,' said a second, invisible man, not whispering in the conventional sense but possessed of a voice that seemed to dwell in darkness.

Felix scowled and tried not to listen. He shouldn't have been surprised to learn that Max was responsible for the stories about him circulating through the company.

His nephew would be so thrilled to learn that there wasn't a well-thumbed copy of his book hiding in someone's pack.

'Truly?' said Herschel.

'Wielding a rune-hammer that none but the heroes of the dwarfs had wielded before or since, and screaming Sigmar's name.'

Felix snorted into his collar. At least he'd remembered to include the screaming.

'I had no idea,' Herschel murmured quietly. Felix felt the man's eyes turn his way in the dark.

'There are many more tales,' said Max. 'It was Felix's own hand for instance that delivered the death blow to the corrupted dragon, Skjalandir.'

'These are days of gods and heroes,' Herschel agreed.

'And men of destiny.'

Felix rolled his eyes and tilted his head back to the stars. The stars didn't care who he'd been or what other men thought he was. They were the same here as they were over Altdorf or Middenheim, and for some reason that thought heartened him through to the dawn.

The morning began with a shower, raindrops pattering over sheets and bedrolls and rousing stiff men from their slumber. Aching in their bones, the company broke camp and resumed their march.

The Middle Mountains dragged by, vast and empty and seemingly unchanged by the days spent travelling through them, except perhaps by their creeping nearness. The clouds deepened in pitch through the day until the sky was as black as burnt wood. The air grew cold and difficult to breathe, and several soldiers complained bitterly of headaches and of nosebleeds that would not stop. Felix had walked the Worlds Edge Mountains with Gotrek and travelled the Silk Road across the Mountains of Mourn, and he was accustomed to these conditions and did his best to help the men to adapt to them – to breathe deeply, to stop by the river often and drink – but even he was starting to feel the effects of what the dwarfs disparagingly called 'altitude sickness'.

'How much further to Middenheim, do you think?' asked Felix, setting his foot heavily on the ground and turning to watch as a gang of strong but tired men got behind Lanarksson's wagon to lift its back wheel from a furrow in the track. Lorin mouthed hoarse instructions from the driver's seat.

'Assuming this goes to Middenheim at all,' muttered Gustav.

Felix thumbed his wedding ring slowly around his finger. He did not want to consider that possibility, but Gotrek's sense of direction had not proven itself to be especially reliable lately. He wondered if it could be connected in any way to what was happening to the world at large. Could the dwarf's loss of bearings be another symptom of the same malaise that afflicted Max? He couldn't answer that; these were questions beyond him and he knew it.

An apathetic cheer sounded over the roar of the water as Lorin's back wheel crashed onto solid ground and the wagon again got moving. Felix looked over it to the jagged line of peaks. He shivered.

'I can't shake the feeling we're being watched.'

'It's not just you,' said Gustav. His eyes were bloodshot and his left nostril scabbed from a recent bleed. He scratched his bandaged right hand incessantly at the puncture scars on his neck, eyes constantly on the move from peak to peak. 'I've not seen so much as a bird, but you can feel it, can't you?'

'We probably are being watched,' Gotrek's voice rumbled from up ahead. The dwarf neither turned around nor slowed his pace, but the handful of soldiers between him and Felix clutched their weapons a little more tightly and pinned their gazes to the mountainside. Felix silently cursed his callousness.

'I thought that none but a dwarf could find these roads.'

Gotrek chuckled mirthlessly. 'We are following the river, manling. A blindfolded troll could make it this far. I would have thought it obvious that we are not yet on the old dwarf roads.'

'How long until we are?'

'I don't know.' Gotrek shrugged, glaring at the shadows over the too-near horizon. 'I've never been this way before.'

'We should make a plan for if we can't find this supposed road,' Gustav murmured, eyes ahead, fingers scratching. 'I don't want to be walking through these mountains until we arrive out the other side in Nordland or starve to death. I say give him two more days to find his way, then we turn back, make for the south.'

'We'll find it,' said Felix, mustering a confidence that he did not the least bit feel and fortifying it with a smile.

Gustav scoffed but hadn't the energy to add anything further.

Felix walked on, thinking about what Gotrek had said, the nape of his neck prickling with imagined arrows.

'Beastmen!'

The cry rang out from the head of the marching column. Men and women scattered screaming in all directions, covered by the staccato *crack* of handgun fire. Puffs of powder smoke rose over the column, dispersing into the thin air as the volley echoed through the gorge.

Felix huffed a dozen strides up the side of the valley, and then spun around, waving his arms in a cutting motion across his chest. 'Stop. Cease fire.'

The spindly pair of goats that some oxygen-deprived mind had mistaken for beastmen lying in ambush loped between the rocks and bounded away. Despite two-dozen bullets being fired in their direction it didn't look as though either one of them had been hit.

'Pity,' said Gotrek, and at first Felix thought it was the lack of a herd of beastmen that was troubling him, but then the Slayer turned on Gustav and grinned nastily. 'Looks like we may starve to death yet.'

Felix pinched the bridge of his nose and took a deep breath of air that felt more watered down than the ale in a Mootland tavern. Worries burned up what little air his brain was receiving. How much ammunition did they have left? Were they being tracked by the besiegers of Wolfenburg, and if so, had they heard those shots? He forced himself to breathe. He didn't think he could take much more of this. His heart was going to give out long before Gustav's deadline to cut their losses and turn back.

Looking on the bright side, the journey had at least given him the time he needed to recover from the battle in the forest. A tension headache pulsed through his skull and the tendons in his hands were as stiff as hawsers from hovering over the hilt of his sword, but he walked like a man with joints again, which was progress of sorts. His face no longer felt sore from Gotrek's punch, though his ego was still a little bruised and, though he was a thousand leagues from a mirror, he doubted that a broken nose and a couple of cracked teeth would add anything to his looks. Not that there had been much interest in those lately. He sighed, suddenly miserable again.

So much for the bright side.

Gotrek issued a grunt and directed Felix's attention through the spreading powder plumes to the head of the column. A handful of the scouts had returned. Kolya ran ahead of them, whistling through his fingers before waving his hand above his head and then shouting enthusiastically as he gestured towards something further on. It was far too far for Felix to hear what the man said, river or no river, too far even to pick out the expression on his face; but he had neglected Gotrek's powers of hearing.

'A dwarf township,' said Gotrek, running his thumb around the rim of his blade and eyeing Gustav's back with his tongue out. 'Where we join our road.'

Lorin Lanarksson parked his wagon in what looked like a court-yard, the longbeard craning his neck around and whistling in awe as he pulled up on the reins. Petrified grass fell apart like talc as the iron-rimmed wheels rolled to a standstill on the ancient flagstones. The generally stoic mountain-bred mules snorted nerv-ously in their traces. Lyndun jumped down and tried in vain to soothe them. There was something in the air. Men filed under the weather-smoothed stonework of what a few thousand years and some imagination could render back into a gatehouse. The strains of animal distress echoed back on them from the crumbling blocks of wall that surrounded them.

Felix closed one hand over the hilt of his sword and the other around the neck of its scabbard as he looked around.

The township was little more than a few hundred ancient struc-tures huddled under the vastness of the mountain. The river ran through the edge of it, separating the courtyard and the remnants of a wall from the rest of the town, presumably as a defensive meas-ure. Several bridges, only one of which was even close to being intact, made possible the crossing. The courtyard itself was slowly filling up with men, moving with superstitious care around foun-tains that had been weathered down to pitted grey stone to which only the occasional dwarfish form could be ascribed from the cor-ner of the eye. It was unnerving, the likenesses vanishing into the stone when looked upon directly.

The mountain itself was dotted with old mine heads and fortifi-cations, all now ruined, connected by a winding causeway that ran towards a broken citadel. The fortress was embedded into the rock at the summit where it caught the last of the light as the sun dipped under the western peaks. Something metallic glinted from its battlements, but it was too far away to make it out. Felix assumed it was some defunct feature of the ancient dwarfhold and returned his attention to the causeway. He assumed that this would be the path they would be following come the morning in order to get onto the dwarf roads to Middenheim.

For some reason he found it difficult to follow the path all the way from top to bottom. There was clearly a start and clearly an end, but his eye simply couldn't seem to get from one to the other without getting lost. He wondered whether there was some manner of obfuscating runecraft at work, or merely clever design coupled with the effect of diminishing sunlight on tired eyes.

As Felix watched and worried about what the next day would bring, the men set up camp under Corporal Mann's direction. Tents were erected within the square and fires lit. A picket of spears was established, both on the sole bridge and under the jagged, mouth-like opening through which they had passed the crumbling defensive wall. A pair of men hauled a sack of oats from Lorin's wagon between them and bore it towards the river to make gruel for the camp's supper.

The clap of struck steel resounded between the maudlin stones and Felix drew a sharp breath, spinning back around and drawing Karaghul a thumb's width from its sheath.

'*Doskonale*, friend Gustav, your skills improve.'

Felix let the breath hiss out between his teeth and slid his blade back into its scabbard. He didn't know where these young men found their energy.

A ring of cheering and laughing soldiers surrounded the two men as they traded blows. Kolya danced behind a curved *ordynka* shortsword held in his weaker left hand, his right held behind his back, his colourful hemp coat jangling as he ducked and rolled. A slow altitude bleed trickled down Gustav's nose, accentuating the grim focus on his face. His longer sabre slashed purposefully through the air, excepting the odd occasion when the Kislevite fancied a cheer and raised a ringing *clang* with a parry.

'Keep your distance, Empire man. You have reach on me, use it...'

The duel continued without Felix to watch it. There was no need. Kolya was the better swordsman by a distance, perhaps better even than himself, although he liked to think that he could have taken the former lancer in a fair contest in his prime.

The softer tap of metal on stone drew his attention from the revels and towards Lorin Lanarksson who shuffled towards him, pausing occasionally to rap on a piece of masonry with the hammerhead grip of his cane.

'My great-grandfather was part of an expedition to these mountains from Karak Kadrin. He would have been younger then even than you, Herr Jaeger.' The longbeard gripped his cane and looked up to the ruins that dominated the northern skyline, his eyes wide with emotion. Torchlight stitched across the bite mark on his face. 'To think that I stand upon the very stones that he once did.'

Although on a logical level Felix had realised that there must be many dwarfs younger than his own fifty years, he nevertheless still thought of them all as wise old longbeards or great slabs of permanence like Gotrek. Felix wasn't sure whether the reminder diminished that impression or simply made him feel older and tireder than he already had just a moment before. What he could appreciate however were the timescales that the dwarf was alluding to. Four generations of that long-lived race could mean millennia. Felix had personally met dwarfs who had lived through the last Great War two centuries ago and had still been going strong.

He wondered what had happened to those dwarfs: old Borek and Prince Hargrim, or even Malakai Makaisson for that matter.

All dead, probably.

The thought depressed him, though not nearly as much as he felt it should.

Felix pressed his gloved hand to the wall as if it might let him feel the same mix of awe and wonder as it had the longbeard. He felt nothing, just a prickling down the nape of his neck as if an assassin stood behind him with a crossbow loaded and aimed. He shivered. It was nothing.

'Don't tell me. None of them came back alive.'

'Oh no, they all returned: penniless and ashamed and pitied as well-meaning fools, but alive.'

'What did they come here to find, if these peaks are as empty as everyone seems to think they are?'

The longbeard hesitated. His face ticked and he rubbed his beard with his hand to soothe it while he hurriedly located his pipe and bit on its long wooden stem. Felix heard the wood splinter and the longbeard pulled it morosely from his lips. 'I don't know how to describe it. There's no human word for it.'

'None at all?'

'It's never come up. I don't think it's ever been discussed with someone who's not a dwarf.' Lorin nibbled on the fractured pipe stem and shrugged. 'To be completely honest, Herr Jaeger, we barely talk about it amongst ourselves since so few believe that it exists at all.'

Felix sighed. Sometimes he missed Gotrek's economy of words.

'It is… Kazad Drengazi. It is a temple, and legend says that it lies somewhere within these mountains.'

Felix could not entirely say why, but he felt that those two words of Khazalid conveyed a depth of meaning that Lorin's well-intentioned explanation could not give. Before he could enquire further, Gotrek stomped over, his axe resting lightly against his shoulder. The Slayer jerked a thumb back, indicating the ruins behind him.

'What are you standing around for, manling? Do you want to find the Middenheim road or don't you?'

'Wouldn't Kolya or one of his scouts be better suited?' asked Felix, not at all sure he was keen on the idea of spending the coming night alone with Gotrek picking through some desolate ruin.

Gotrek muttered something into his beard, turning slightly as if to ensure Felix couldn't read his lips, and produced an exaggerated shrug. 'Come or don't, manling. It's your choice.'

Felix looked up at the sky, thinking of all the reasons that he absolutely shouldn't leave the camp and accompany the Slayer, then swore and strode after him.

Someone had to, he told himself. It might as well be him.

SEVEN

The Ruined Dwarfhold

Gotrek crouched before a granite block, hidden away within the corner of a ruined wall at the riverside end of a wide, empty street. Felix stood nervously at the Slayer's back, fingers fidgeting around the grip of his sword.

The buildings were constructed in what he had come to think of as the dwarfish fashion, massive blocks laid atop one another with such expertise and precision that there was no sign of mortar and, by Mannslieb's haunting light, it was next to impossible for his human eyes to discern the joins. There was an eerie stillness about this place, a graveyard serenity that the faraway murmur of the river could not detract from. It was impossible to stand here, surrounded by such age, and not wonder at the forgotten lives that had touched it. Who had they been? What had they done? Did anything of them survive in the world he knew? The romantic in him, perhaps, staring into the cosmos and praying for some sign of stability. The minds of men weren't built to consider such sweeping timescales as this, the kind that diluted the thinker's bloodline to water and eroded his most enduring legacy to dust on the wind. To stand here was to be forcibly reminded of one's place and prominence in a world already steeped in history. Felix wondered if Karl Franz or Magnus the Pious or even Sigmar himself would have felt the same way in his shoes. The thought should probably have shamed him for its boldness, but for some reason it did not.

'Do you ever feel that we're on the wrong side of history?'

'No.'

Felix smiled weakly, glancing over his shoulder to the pricks of light and occasional voices from the camp across the river. He could smell cooking oats. His stomach tightened with hunger. Some other disturbed sense made him shudder. 'Doesn't all of this make you wonder about the people who lived here? Will this be us one day? Is this what will be left of the Empire if we fail?'

'Middenheim won't look nearly so pretty in five thousand years.'

Felix examined the ruins with a new perspective. Could they really be so old? Now he was looking at them in this way, he recognised that this town had none of the features he had come to associate with dwarf settlements. There were no gyrocopter towers such as the dwarfs used for swift communications and provisioning of isolated outposts like this one. He had seen none of the great stone bastions used for housing cannons. Felix knew that the dwarfs had taught the secrets of gunpowder to men, and helped to found the engineering schools that, as much as the Colleges of Magic, had made the Empire the force it was. Felix clung sadly to that final thought.

Was.

Was it possible that there had been a time when even the dwarfs themselves had not possessed such knowledge? It seemed difficult to believe. Although it made sense intellectually, he had simply assumed that dwarfs were gifted with an inherent racial understanding of such secrets. The realisation that they had mastered them over centuries of methodical trial and error only deepened Felix's respect for their achievements.

It made him more determined than ever that something of their civilisation be spared.

With one more glance over his shoulder, he joined Gotrek in his examination of the marker stone. The granite was green with age and framed by a thicket of brambles that had pushed through the softer stones amongst which it had been set. The runes carved into it were still legible however, once Gotrek had pulled down the obscuring weeds. At least Felix hoped they were. They were just cuts in the rock to him, and had he not been here with Gotrek he probably would have dismissed them as something scratched into it by a passing bird.

'It's *klinkerhun*, manling, runescript, but very old. It's difficult to be sure but I think we're on the right track.' The dwarf looked up and peered down the street, his dark-adapted eyes piercing the gloom in a way that Felix could only envy. 'Let's head on and see if we can find another. There's dozens of old roads heading into the mountains and I don't want to be two days out before realising we're on the wrong one.'

Felix nodded his agreement as the Slayer stood up and stomped down the road. He paused to examine the runescript. There was something mournful about it, in need of remembrance. Could it really be something as simple as a road sign they were following? *Empirestrasse – Middenheim 125 miles.* The outlandish thought made Felix smile as he turned away and after his former companion.

It felt good to have a destination again. It was something to cling to, and that was hope of a kind.

Their footsteps echoed through the ruins. Gotrek was actually being cautious, Felix realised, but even so his hobnailed boots scratched at the stillness like climbing pitons on bare stone. Felix glanced over his shoulder, convinced for a moment that he had heard the footfalls of another moving in parallel through the ruins. He dismissed it as the work of his imagination. Either that or his own too-loud footsteps being rebounded back at him. His mail shirt no longer seemed entirely adequate and he drew his cloak over his shoulders, as though the ragged Sudenland wool was a welcome layer of added protection for his back.

Felix held his sword a little more closely than he had before, matching the Slayer's shorter stride so that their feet hit the road in unison. There was loneliness here of a kind he had not felt anywhere else; not in the misted swamps of Albion nor even on the lifeless sands of Nehekhara. These ruins were steeped in it, like stones in the desert that had absorbed it all day and now radiated it at night. He mentioned the feeling to Gotrek.

'Even in my people's Golden Age, when Karaz-a-Karak could put a throng of fifty thousand upon the field and not suffer one less hammer at her forges, there were naught but a few thousand here. They made a go of it, they were dwarfs, but they left in the end.'

Felix strained his eyes into the dark that filled the crumbling relics on either side, as if by willpower he could make them see as Gotrek's could. His imagination populated the shadows with goblin raiders, charging through the streets on their wolf mounts while dwarfs screamed and their city was looted and burned. But Felix couldn't see any obvious indications of battle damage. Skaven, perhaps? His heart beat a little faster at the thought of that vile, duplicitous race. He did not think himself a hateful man, or a coward, but he hated and feared the ratmen more than any other horror he had encountered. They were poisoners, saboteurs and assassins. They had murdered his father, nearly killed him more than once, and, but for a fortuitous twist of fate here and there, had very nearly brought down the Empire long before now. Even in failure they had burnt half of Nuln to the ground and destroyed the Gunnery School.

He thought back to that third set of footsteps that he had convinced himself was just his imagination.

Sigmar, he prayed tightening his grip on his sword, let it be skaven.

'What happened?' he managed to ask after a few minutes of picturing what he would do to the rat he found between him and Kat.

'Nothing "happened", manling. There was just nothing here worth staying for.'

The inherent sadness of that caused Felix's shoulders to droop and he eased his grip on his sword.

'And the temple that Lorin mentioned?'

Gotrek gave a disparaging snort. 'The witless old fool. It is not a temple. It is a fortress.'

'What does the name mean?'

Gotrek pursed his lips and considered. 'There are some words that your language does not have meanings for. Suffice to say, manling, that it does not exist or it would have been found by now. The road we look for was not built by the dwarfs that once lived here, but is one of the dozens laid by the explorers who came hunting the legend of Kazad Drengazi.'

Gotrek pointed northwards and up. Felix could see nothing, except perhaps the glint of something metallic catching the light of the stars, but took it on faith that the Slayer was indicating the citadel on the mountain. 'The last dwarfs to abandon the old dwarfhold travelled north on one such road and took it to your lands. Or what would eventually become your lands. It was they who helped the humans turn Middenheim into the fortress she is. They gave her walls, dug her mines, and even laid the designs for the funicular that serves the summit today.'

Felix's eyes widened but he said nothing. He had given up trying to comprehend the age of this place. The Fauschlag had been an unassailable stronghold long before Sigmar turned the disparate human tribes into an Empire.

'Those early miners found a labyrinth of caves and tunnels within the mountains,' Gotrek went on. 'One was extended to meet the road from here.' Gotrek snorted thoughtfully, dropping to his knees to inspect another of the roadside rune markers that Felix had not even spotted was there. 'Although I doubt Grimnir himself could tell you why.'

So that was how Gotrek planned to pass under the Chaos hordes that undoubtedly besieged the City of the White Wolf and get inside.

A gust of wind from the north carried an eerie moan through the ruins.

Dare he even hope?

'Was that wise, building a back door into your fortress, I mean? Who else might stumble onto these same roads?'

Gotrek scraped moss from the marker with his thumbnail and grunted: 'Impossible.'

Felix wished he could be so sure. Before he could open his mouth to seek further reassurance, Gotrek raised his hand for quiet and sniffed the air. Gotrek licked his finger and held it up to find the wind, turning in its direction – north, down the street – and glared into the dark. Felix bit his lip, sword raised.

'What is it?'

'Shhh. I thought I smelled something.'

The dwarf turned to Felix, who shook his head. He still had that cooked-oats smell in his nose, and he suspected that even had he not it would have been difficult to detect much beyond the gentle reek of his own unwashed clothing.

'I told you, you wanted Kolya,' he murmured. 'He's good at this sort of thing.'

The Kislevite had formerly made his living hunting monstrous game across Troll Country and the Goromadny Mountains, trading the prized carcasses with the Kurgan-speaking tribes that dwelt there. He didn't have an old man's tired eyes or aching joints, nor did he have the same need for a bedroll and a fire and a cupful of gruel that Felix did. More importantly, he was Gotrek's rememberer now, and his place was surely here. Was it the man's laxity or Gotrek's conscious choice that had Felix here in his stead?

The Slayer muttered gruffly and then fell silent, standing up and crossing over the road as if Felix hadn't opened his mouth at all.

'Over here, manling,' Gotrek's lowered voice called back from under the shadows. 'I don't think we're alone.'

Gustav Jaeger and two free company men in soiled burgundy and gold overlaid with plate armour and cloaks crouched around the footprint left in the soft mud. It was a little larger than a man's. Gustav sank his finger into the print, eyeing the rushing ribbon of pearly white froth that roared by them. He had the strange notion to taste the muck on his finger, but resisted and shook his hand dry with a scowl. He was being watched, judged, and it was making him jumpy.

'What are you thinking, friend Gustav?'

'I'm thinking I'll not be sleeping tonight.'

Kolya grinned and squatted down on the opposite side of the print, tracing it with his finger as though mentally mapping its shape. The shells and pebbles tied into his coat by coloured ribbons bounced softly off one another as he moved. The square patches of hemp that made up his clothes were grey in the dark, but no less bright by contrast to their surroundings. A freshly drawn henna in the style of a horse glittered with a faintly metallic tint from his forearm. He stood, planting his own foot into the mud beside the print and backing away to examine it.

'Larger than a man, and heavier: see how deep it is compared to mine.'

Gustav studied the print intently. He was no tracker. He had peppered Kolya and those men he was expected to lead with questions on the subject, but there was no escaping the fact that he had not travelled anywhere without the aid of a road and a hired guide until the Battle of Badenhof had forced him. His skills would never match those of other men, he knew. Men like his uncle.

Nevertheless, the print looked to him to be no more than a few hours old.

'Some sort of monster?' growled one of his men, a scarred greybeard named Sturm with a sword across his bent legs and a half-cocked pistol in hand.

'I don't know,' Kolya admitted. 'But I have seen prints like this before. On the oblast.'

The Kislevite scanned the opposite shore, drawing his bow halfway taut to sight along the shaft. The tassels attached to its recurved ends fluttered lightly in the breeze. The Middle Mountains were a long way from the northern oblast, but Gustav could see the huntsman's instinct at work.

To Gustav, the darkened ruins looked insectile, giant spiders on segmented legs of black limestone. They hugged the mountainside as though waiting to scurry down and overwhelm them.

'Do you see something?' he hissed.

Kolya lowered his bow, brow knotted in consternation. Gustav swallowed nervously. Something that Kolya couldn't spot was infinitely more worrying than anything he could.

'Double watch tonight,' said Kolya. 'Eyes on bridge, and keep distance from river.' He turned to Gustav and pursed his lips, a fatalistic shrug so subtle it didn't even disturb the shells in his coat. 'And for sake of your uncle pray that it is interested more in us than him.'

Felix covered his nose and mouth against the scent of rot. It filled the rubble-strewn portico that Gotrek had led him under, clinging to the weeds that grew up like a cocoon around the sickly green corpse that lay towards the back of the room. It was a goblin. Its foot was clamped between the jaws of a bear trap that had been hidden amongst the rubble. Judging from the state of the wretch's fingernails and the bloody scratches between its ankle and knee, Felix reasoned that it had spent a good portion of its final hours trying to claw its way free. It was dark and beginning to bloat, and what looked like tiny bite marks were evident all over its body.

Felix took a step forward, rubble crunching underfoot and sending rats squealing through the undergrowth for the far corners of the structure. His heart thumped. Edging forwards, he crouched beside the corpse. A prickly thicket of dandelions held up the goblin's body like a cushion, only its strangler's hands and arrow-shaped head hanging over the edges. Its eyes and lips had been eaten. Felix covered his mouth again and turned back to the doorway where Gotrek had remained, wedged under the doorframe, axe held lightly in one hand and scanning the opposite side of the street with his one good eye.

'I doubt this poor thing has been following anyone for at least a week.'

'Pity for a goblin, manling? For shame.'

With a sigh, Felix sheathed his sword and instead drew a short knife from a leather pocket inside his right boot. He used it to clear away some of the weeds and rot around the bear trap and frowned. Even under the merest whisper of moonlight, the sharp steel gleamed. There were no markings anywhere on it to suggest that it had ever been worked by a tool. It was, quite simply, some of the finest craftsmanship Felix had ever seen.

'Left by one of the expeditions that passed this way, no doubt,' said Gotrek, then returned his gaze to the street.

The Slayer's wariness was setting Felix on edge.

'Is there something out there?'

Gotrek grunted, noncommittal, and without turning towards him jabbed the eye of his axe up to the ceiling. From the outside, it had looked like this building had another couple of storeys, though the thought of traipsing through rats and darkness and who knew what else to find a set of stairs that might not even hold his weight was strangely unappealing.

'Why don't you go take a look, manling?' said Gotrek absently, settling in to watch. 'I'll just wait down here.'

Morzanna, prophetess of the Dark Master, had seen the moment that a dozen mutant knights in full battle regalia had piled into her chamber a hundred times, long before she finally heard the clatter of their footsteps up the stairs of the tower she had adopted as her own. The only furnishing was an unused mattress of bound straw that lay against a wall – more for the appearance of it, the acceptance of a kind gesture, than for its utility. The rest of the floor was occupied by fragments of stone that had crumbled from the ceiling. Weeds hung down, ropey creepers playing against her small, dark horns as she paced beneath them.

She walked to the window. It was wide and tall, installed for the view rather than for defence, and that was one of the reasons she had chosen it and no other had wanted it. She leaned out. The mountains were felt rather than seen, a cold breeze from a depthless void. The ruined township lay against it, a stitch in a black cloth. The stream was a thin gurgle in the distance. She frowned, then slid a few inches to the left. Here.

There came a knock at the door and she smiled brightly, Delphic fangs catching the moonlight. That had been unexpected, a nuance that prophecy could conceal.

She turned her hunched back to the window and smoothed down the glittering black silk of her dress, straightening the jet spider brooch that held it all in place. She had played the Ungol wise woman for many years, and it was a comforting guise to inhabit. It suited her. She had enjoyed the wandering, the isolation, the empty miles of oblast separating herself from the dreams of others. The fear in which even those who had ridden countless leagues to receive her wisdom had held her was something she had enjoyed less, but which she had always respected: she had earned their fear, and it had suited her too.

And even in the Empire where men would not know an Ungol from a Ropsmenn from a Gospodar, the instinct to fear a crone in black remained.

'It is open,' she answered, voice as clear as moonlight despite the age evident in her appearance.

A square-jawed warrior with a rectangular iron shield in each of his two left hands pushed through the door and stepped to one side to admit the immense armoured form of High Zarr Koenigsmann.

The one-time Grand Master of Wolfenburg's Knights of the Bull wore his stigmata with grace, but the signs of the Dark Master's favour were there. A large man, he was simply immense in the full plate and surcoat of his fallen order. But the proportions were not quite right: his huge chest and thick arms were oversized in comparison to his legs, his bovine nose was too flat and broad as though it had been squashed, and a thin down of black hair was just beginning to spread out from his beard and fringe. His fearsome bull-horned helm he held underarm.

'Did you have trouble sleeping, prophetess?' grunted the High Zarr, nodding towards the bed.

'Always, my lord,' Morzanna answered with a glassy smile.

'It sounded as though you were having a bad dream.'

Morzanna sighed. In her mind's eye she saw a dark templar, the rupture in his breastplate where it would be, the blood that would dye his white surcoat red. 'It was not mine.'

Koenigsmann grunted again, as men did in the presence of one who saw their futures more clearly than they saw their own past, taking his helm in both hands and rolling it between his palms. As he did so, the knights that prophecy had promised Morzanna piled in.

Moonlight glittered across bared blades, lifted the white from the black on the once-proud tabards of Ostland's boldest. Horned helms and fiendishly spiked knee and elbow guards tangled the slender spaces between them like branches in an ancient wood. And not all of them were components of the warriors' armour. Slathering, muscular tongues glowed with faint bioluminescence in the dark. Pincer claws clacked open and shut like the vacillations of some predatory flower. Tentacles thicker than a strong man's neck flexed and slithered across man-mountains of steel plate.

For as long as there had been men in Ostland, small bands of mutants had lived a nomadic life in the harsh isolation of the Middle Mountains. These men were not they. They had fled with their master from the doom of Wolfenburg and had forged for him an army worthy of their patron.

And where they rode, the seed and the shadow of Be'lakor had gone with them.

'The outsiders are still coming,' Koenigsmann hissed suddenly, striding past Morzanna to the window and looking out. The dark knight scowled, stiffly lowering his helm to the weathered window-ledge. The alpine wind ruffled his beard and drew goose bumps from his darkening, daemon-touched skin. 'Is it him, this mortal warrior that can strike such terror in a god's heart?'

Morzanna closed her eyes, summoning the image of a flame-crested dwarf and a handsome swordsman in a red cloak to her mind. An almost maternal warmth filled her. She did not know whether this particular vision was past, present or future, for this pair had touched her life at every stage. But for them, Morzanna would not be here at all, for she could still see the doomed world in which Morzanna the child had perished in the purging fires of Mordheim. If only the Dark Master's nemesis could see what she saw, could *know* how, through her, he had changed the world and how he would change it yet. His destiny illuminated the heavens like a star, and gods and men alike ignored it at their peril.

'He is wanderer,' she whispered, opening her eyes and banishing the vision from her mind. 'He is warrior and daemon-slayer. His fate will shape the world and others beyond it. He is to be the Dark Master's downfall.'

'And he wishes to escape this destiny?'

Morzanna parted her lips into a soft smile of devil-spined teeth. How was it that everyone bar her continually misunderstood the nature of fate? It was not an arrow that struck at random and could be avoided with luck. It was what would be. It was what had to be.

'If anyone has the power to try, it is him. If anyone has the arrogance to believe they can succeed, it is him.'

'Very well,' said Koenigsmann heavily. 'We'll take their scouts while they're separated and then hit their camp while they sleep. Spread the word.' He jabbed his finger into the double-shielded knight's breastplate. 'Command the ambush personally. The Dark Master will arise.'

'Aye, my lord,' said the knight, marching from the chamber and taking half of the warriors with him.

'Can you tell me any more of how we will triumph?' asked Koenigsmann, turning to Morzanna.

'Triumph, my lord?' Morzanna asked coldly.

In her mind she saw the ruptured breastplate. The blood on white. There was another reason she had selected this tower for her quarters despite suffering neither cold nor fatigue.

'My lord,' one of the knights muttered, a heavy-set man in a scythe-edged harness of articulated plate with a stone bull pectoral clamped over his chest. His visored helm was open to reveal yellow eyes and a thin moustache. He scratched at the side of his head, mirroring something that had appeared on Koenigsmann's.

It was a red dot, the tip of a lance of light that, from its angle, appeared to originate from a higher tower or possibly from the mountain itself.

That she did not know.

With an irritated expression, the High Zarr bent his head and swatted at the dot. His hand passed through it. The dot danced unperturbed over his temple.

'You were kind to me, High Zarr,' said Morzanna. 'You deserved a more caring master.'

The thunderous report of what sounded like a small cannon rumbled through the ruined township just as Felix threw his shoulder into the pine door for the third and final time and burst through onto a viewing platform. It looked like it had been a belfry. The walls were open on all sides except for narrow corner supports that held up a tiled roof. There was no sign of a bell, but Felix could see the stanchion where it had used to be. He imagined it being used to sound shift changes to the workers in the mines above. Or to alert them to an attack.

Felix ran to the nearest ledge and peered out.

It was like looking out to sea on a moonless night. It was just shapes, the whisper of an icy breeze, the fading echoes of a gunshot and... what was that? He held his breath and listened. Yes. He could definitely hear running feet, the clink of mail, the clap of swords in their scabbards.

He blinked hard and tried again to see. For a moment he wondered if his eyesight was finally going the way of his joints. Then he scowled and disregarded it. He doubted that a slow decline into decrepitude was something he was going to have to worry about.

Who had taken that shot?

There were a few handgunners amongst Mann's troop, but none of them carried anything big enough to make a noise like that, and all of them were back in the camp anyway. Felix's stomach dropped as the upshot of that hit him. He and Gotrek had managed to separate themselves from their own force and walk straight into a potential enemy.

He had to warn Gotrek!

He pulled back from the ledge, just as the Slayer's bellicose roar from the street below heralded the clangour of steel on steel. Felix swore. Gotrek had sent him up here on purpose to get him out of the way. He clutched his sword and turned to run back the way he had just come.

Damn that Slayer.

And damn his oath.

EIGHT

Ambushed

Felix clattered down the stairs, bouncing off the square walls of the stairwell in his haste. The steps were too broad, the angle too low, designed for bigger feet and shorter legs than his, and his descent felt more like that of a stone dropped down a well than a run. He could hear the sounds of battle from outside. The stone walls muffled parts but seemed to amplify others, filling the weed-constricted space with wild shouts that came in answer to challenges that Felix had not heard and the ring of shields struck by phantom blows.

He half fell back into the portico where he had left Gotrek and almost landed on top of a grotesque pair of warriors. One was a heavily armoured hunchback with a battleaxe in both hands and a porcine snout protruding from a closed hood. The other was a willowy fighter with purplish skin and a pair of crab-like claws in place of her hands. From the looks of shock on their inhuman faces they were as surprised to see Felix as Felix was to see them, and in the short time available to think he realised that they must have entered through the back with the idea of ambushing the Slayer in the street. And then there was no more time for thinking.

Expelling his pre-battle nerves with a shout, Felix punched his pommel stone into the hunchback's nose before the mutant could raise his axe, using the momentum of his descent to dog-pile the heavier warrior to the ground. Somewhere along the way, Felix had drawn a knife from his boot and he drove it through the mutant's throat. The hunchback gargled, arterial blood squirting over Felix's fingers. He looked up to mark the other fighter and cried out at the sight of an enormous chitinous pincer streaking for his neck.

Felix pulled back out of reach and then rolled off the dying hunchback, ripping Karaghul from its sheath as he rose. A spasm of muscle pain shot up his right side but he ignored it, raising his sword to parry as Willow Crab pounced over her stricken comrade and attacked. Shards of cherry-black chitin flew as the first claw almost punched Felix's sword from his hand. Gritting his teeth against the pain coming from all quarters of his tired old body now, Felix backed off, clasping his ringing right hand with his left to wield the Templar sword two-handed and direct the second claw-stroke into the wall above his shoulder. The hideous mutation chewed through the rock as though it were stale bread. The mutant advanced under a barrage of clacking pincers, left, right, left, like some loathsome steam-powered threshing machine given lithe flesh. Felix couldn't back away fast enough.

His heel hit something unpleasantly soft. The goblin, he realised with disgust, dodging and feinting and using every trick of footwork he knew or could devise on the spot to get out from under the mutant's claws, slashing across her ribs as he spun away and into the space he had cleared with his retreat. The mutant hissed in pain and turned after him, tongues of purple flesh licking out from the edges of the wound to pull it closed. Felix brought his sword up in resignation.

Why did the Dark Powers bestow the most powerful gifts?

The glint of something sharp caught Felix's eye amidst the weeds and rubble. Realisation hit and with an unworthy smile he positioned it between him and the advancing mutant and angled his sword into a guard.

The mutant lunged for him, her foot landing on the metallic disc that Felix had seen. There was a violent *snap* as the jaws of the second foothold trap bit shut over her ankle. She shrieked and swung a claw, dragging her mangled leg and the steel trap along behind her, either by accident or intent on positioning herself between Felix and the door to the street where Gotrek fought.

'Perish the Dark Master's downfall,' she whispered.

'Over my dead body,' said Felix. He had no idea who the Dark Master was or what interest it had in Gotrek, but right then he didn't care.

Willow Crab grinned like a death mask with far too many teeth as Felix went on the attack. Her movements were restricted by the trap that had bitten through her leg to the bone, but she was still quick. She was skilful too in a top-heavy sort of way, but Felix was better; he had been doing this longer than this woman had been alive and he knew his sword better than most men knew their wives. He scowled, Karaghul slicing through Willow Crab's belly, then her arm, then her thigh.

He knew it better than he knew *his* wife.

Tentacles of semi-regenerated flesh rippled from numerous cuts and Felix drew back for a killing thrust up through the ribcage when the thump of running feet dragged his attention back towards the staircase.

More filthy-looking mutants in slimy cloaks and scratched leather armour piled in through the same back entrance that Willow Crab and Hunchback must have used. They came with a motley parade of hatchets, spears and nets and possessed no physical armament as impressive as those he had already dealt with, but that wasn't going to matter given the sheer weight of numbers on their side. A claw snapped a hair's breadth from his ear, and Felix retreated towards the nearest corner with his sword up.

He had always expected to die this way. Spoken aloud amongst comrades and friends it sounded terribly brave and honourable, but Felix didn't feel either. In that moment, what he wanted with all his heart was to see his wife and child one more time. Just once.

Was that too much to ask this world for?

The first of the newcomers came for him, cloak billowing out beneath it with the undulations of what appeared to be squid-like tentacles in place of legs, and levelled its fisherman's spear to impale Felix like a salmon.

Felix brought his sword around instinctively to parry. The spear shaved across the blade, wood peeling from the shaft as it went, and Felix kicked the mutant in the groin. Three more spilled around the first, brandishing axes and knives. Too many. More still were streaming in through the passage that fed past the stairs.

One of the cloaked figures in particular drew Felix's attention despite the important proximity of several others. This one was tall, walking with hooded head held high with the aid of a staff gripped in two dark hands. Felix felt what little light there was in the room drawn towards that figure. The hairs in Felix's skin pulled at their roots and even his eyes seemed to want to leap out of their sockets. He would have shut them had he dared.

'Sigmar...' Felix breathed.

The shadows that cloaked the figure opened out like the sepals of a pure white rose. Long ivory robes blazed with golden runes. The simple staff writhed in the man's grip, a wraithlike serpent coiling out of the wood like a djinn from a lamp and hissing. The mutants screamed and covered their eyes, but Felix, strangely, didn't feel the intense light at all. If anything it was restorative, leaching the aches from his bones. He felt better than he had in weeks.

The wizard muttered something in an arcane tongue and moved his fingers swiftly before his eyes. Shielding her face behind one giant pincer, Willow Crab leapt for him, only for the wizard to display an open palm of brilliantly radiating fingers, a wave of light purging the shrieking mutant of her stigmata limb by limb before a second wave blasted her into incandescent motes mid-air. Before the first sparkling fleck had hit his face, the wizard had slipped into a new incantation, voice rising and hands moving furiously as tiny spheres of diamond brilliance burst out of the aethyr around him and whizzed unerringly towards their terrified targets, mowing the mutants down like weeds.

The scent of metal solder and immolated flesh filled Felix's nostrils. He ducked, several of those magical bullets shooting alarmingly close to him, but remarkably none of them struck. He watched from a crouch as the last mutant warrior scrambling over the bodies piled on the stairs took a white bolt in the back, spasmed, and then collapsed.

Felix looked over the burnt carpet of dead in shock and no little horror.

Max Schreiber faded slowly back into the afterglow of the carnage he had wrought. He pulled his hood back over his head, concealing the misting of his face and the inexorable eclipse of his eyes. Shadowy tendrils arced between his fingers and the darkening folds of his hood. He took his once again plain yew staff and leaned on it wearily.

'I wanted to tell you about a dream I had,' he said, blankly.

'You... I'm sorry, what?'

'I dreamed of a hunter,' Max went on, as if unaware of his

surroundings or the lightstorm he had just unleashed on the mutants that still sizzled around him. 'He was beset by beasts of land and air and sea. Hunter, Felix, don't you see? Hunter. Jaeger. That is the meaning of your name.'

Felix stood up slowly and took a deep breath. He reaffirmed his grip on his sword. The belfry had been cleared but he could still hear the sounds of battle outside and even Gotrek, particularly in his exhausted state, couldn't fight alone forever. He waved a hand in front of the wizard's face.

'Listen to me, Max. Do you know where you are?'

'On the path of destiny,' Max answered with a faint, chilling smile, looking through Felix's hand and deep into his eyes. 'I dreamt that I flew again, you and I seeking the ancient power of the dwarfs, but this time it was I that died. I think that maybe I have some role to play in your destiny after all.'

Felix withdrew his hand and repositioned it around his sword for a two-handed grip. When Max was like this it wasn't worth the effort of trying to talk him. 'Gotrek has a destiny, Max. I'm just me, the same old Felix. And the "hunter" thing is pretty tenuous. Kol-ya's a hunter.'

Max shrugged. 'Who?'

Shaking his head, Felix squelched through the charred gristle towards the doorway.

'Wait,' said Max, dreamily, and then with a shout: 'Felix, get back!'

Felix saw the flash of a struck match from the opposite side of the street. Not enough warning on its own, but thanks to Max's prescient shout he was already diving across the doorframe and into cover. He hit the ground flat as a torrent of shells from what must have been a larger-calibre variant of a repeater handgun blistered the ground where he had just been and chewed the stonework surrounding the doorway into an unrecognisable shape.

He breathlessly kissed his wedding ring in thanks for his life as he dragged his feet in from the doorway.

With a whine like an exhaling dragon, the storm of fire ceased. A thin drizzle of rock fell from what was left of the doorframe. Felix felt himself tense as he waited for the next barrage. He had encountered weapons like this before, but rarely, the sort of experimental ordnance that would normally be deployed only to the largest battlefields and even then under the careful stewardship of the most competent master-engineers. Felix had never faced followers of Chaos with this kind of weaponry before. It was something new.

Felix wasn't at all sure he liked it.

'Move away from the wall,' said Max, crouching down and laying a hand onto a patch of weeds that stood up between a pair of burnt, misshapen corpses. A pulse of jade light passed down the wizard's arm and into the ground.

Felix held his breath, but nothing happened. An accelerating whir from outside told him that the volleygun was about to fire again. He rolled his head back to examine the ruined stonework. It wouldn't take another salvo.

'I said move away,' said Max.

Felix could feel the ground beneath his elbows shudder as though it were being slowly wrenched apart. The stonework groaned. From the corner of his eye he saw one of the mutants rising. Felix gasped, but it wasn't the mutant: it was the weeds underneath it swelling. The same macabre scene was being enacted throughout the room, mutated corpses giving way to vigorous green growth.

Max mouthed an oaken creak of an incantation and the plants responded. The front wall turned green. Mosses and vines knotted together like green steel ringlets in a mail coat. Felix shuffled around and wriggled back, cringing from a questing root that squirmed across his thigh. Before Felix's disbelieving eyes the wall turned thicker and greener until there was not a single stone visible at all.

Over the engorged groan of growing plant life, spinning gun barrels screamed.

Felix dropped himself back to the ground and covered his face under both arms, flinching with every sap-soft *thump* that struck the living wall. After a few seconds, he uncovered his face.

A wide-leafed creeper whipped before his eyes like a lion's tail. Something thorny scratched his chin. Pale fluids dribbled down the vegetative barrier, but new growth was already healing the punctures and thickening the wall further still. He slapped at the wide leaf, staring open-mouthed around him. He had some knowledge of the nature of the aethyr, and he knew that it was divided, as the particular talents of the eight Colleges of Magic were similarly divided.

And Felix had never seen Max work magic like this.

Max rose silently, cracking the knuckles of the hand he had just used in his spell and sending what looked like bark chips sprinkling from his fingers. The grey flesh still carried a faint jade glow. 'You see now why I was loath to aid you before. Everything about this is wrong. I am a mage of the Light. Teclis himself taught the first magisters of the Colleges that man cannot master all the winds of magic. To attempt to do so is to expose one's soul to the evils of Chaos.'

Felix didn't know what to say, and right then they had greater concerns. Gotrek's battle cry filtered thickly through the pulsing vines. Metal sang. And what of Gustav and the camp, were they under attack as well? No, as harsh as it might have sounded, he would take this newly empowered Max Schreiber over the old one any day.

'Can you get us out?' he said instead, cutting to the only thing that mattered.

'Of course,' said Max, as though it were so obvious he hadn't thought to raise the matter himself.

The wizard clasped his hands tightly around his staff, his robes sinking into the surrounding shadow. Felix noticed his own fingers appearing to unravel and become one with the darkness. He could no longer feel the floor beneath him and it melted into nothing even as he watched. The putrid, nectar stink of magically invigorated plant life disappeared. If he could have filled his lungs with shadow then he would have screamed.

'Gird yourself,' said Max. 'Grey magic takes some adapting to.'

The first thing Felix became aware of again was sound. He could hear Gotrek's shouts interspersed with others, cries of anger and of pain, the clangour of weapons and the crunch of mail and meat and bone.

Then images came, seldom in alignment with what he was seeing and all the more jarring for it.

To the metallic chatter of chain guns he saw Kolya, thigh deep in rushing white water, engaged in fierce hand-to-hand combat with a pair of stout axemen in long mail shirts, round shields, and winged helms, before the darkness swept through them and they were gone.

He saw Herschel Mann marshalling a firing line of Hochland longrifles, but the voice he heard yelling was someone else's. Fire fizzed back and forth between the opposing banks of the river, a trickle versus a raging torrent.

Disembodied, Felix was helpless but to watch as a volleygun carved open Lanarksson's wagon from front axle to tailboard. Big Lyndun tumbled down the steps from the buckboard, leaking blood like a colander. Lorin emerged from beneath the canvas roof, mouthing a cry that was lost somewhere in the aethyr shade and sporting a crossbow before a bullet tore out his throat. Two more punched through his chest, and then Felix heard a snatch of the dwarf's voice before the shadows rolled in.

There was Gustav, leading a charge over the splintered remnants of a picket line and into the tight shieldwall of heavy infantry that was advancing against them over the bridge. Pistols blossomed from the front rank. He heard and saw men roar and then there was a clashing together. Gustav's Gospodar sabre flashed and then the vision was gone.

'No!' Felix shouted, though with what and to whom he was uncertain. 'Take me back to that last one. Gustav needs my help.'

Disconnected visual elements came and went. He saw a stab of orange crest, like the sail of a storm-tossed ship on a swell of armoured mutant warriors. There were ruined buildings webbed with shadow.

The darkness swirled through one and bore Felix's flailing consciousness with it. An incredibly muscular figure was crouched by a window. He had a red scarf tied around his forehead and wore a pair of bug-eyed lenses marked with cross-hairs, through which he looked down onto the scene below him. Felix couldn't say what the figure was watching. There seemed to be no spatial connection between the images he was passing through and he didn't know the layout of the township well enough to stitch them together. The marksman raised what looked like a longrifle. It had a long cylindrical barrel attached to the top of the stock and some kind of scarlet glowstone within it that sent a beam of light in the direction he aimed.

And then the darkness pulled them apart again.

There was a *crack* like a thunderbolt and a mutant warrior in thick steel plate in parti-coloured black and white went down with a steaming crater where his visor had been.

Who was attacking who?

None of this made sense.

The confusion of images and sounds and gunpowder smells arranged themselves into ordered focus. The shadows slunk back to the aethyr where as far as Felix was concerned they were henceforth invited to remain.

With one hand, Felix felt over the side of his body to ensure it was all where he had left it. A wave of dizziness passed through him as his body delivered two contradictory senses of where he was supposed to be standing right now. Despite what a large, increasingly queasy, part of him insisted, he was no longer in the belfry. In fact he could see the belfry at the far end of the street, the ruin rising out of the tangle of weeds like a memorial stone on the site of a forgotten battlefield. The street between him and it was a grinding churn of armoured warriors, twenty or so Chaos knights and half again as many corpses, converging on Gotrek and his axe.

The Slayer issued a bloodthirsty peal of thunder and drove his axe through a warrior's raised shield and deep into his groin. Blood spurted across the dwarf's beard. Slivers of splintered steel peppered his snarling face with a metallic finish. A back-slung elbow cracked the side of a warrior's helmet like an egg. A warhammer smacked against the Slayer's shoulder blade and drove him to his knees. The hammer came down to crack his skull open. Gotrek caught the haft of the descending weapon and, in a bulging display of strength, yanked the hammer from the warrior's grip and split it in half across his knee. A bare-knuckle punch as he rose sent a knight with four arms and a droning morning star in each hand crashing through two of his companions with a dented breastplate. A mutant with spines running down his ears and along the outside edges of his hands went down screaming with a shattered shin. Gotrek withdrew his boot and stamped on the knight's thigh as he decapitated him with a single blow of his axe. More came in, smothering the Slayer with sheer weight of numbers.

Gotrek was formidable, but he was only one Slayer.

Felix cursed under his breath, looking back over his shoulder to where the river was lit up with gunfire like a firework display. Breathing hard, he turned back. For better or worse Max had brought him here. Gustav and the others would have to look after themselves.

'Wait,' said Max, seizing Felix's shoulder at the most disconcerting moment possible, just before he had finalised the decision to charge and directed his muscles to see it done.

'For what?

'Do you remember poor Claudia?' said Max conversationally, his special brand of madness impervious to the grunts and the cries and the wrench of torn metal. 'I feel I understand her a little better now. The power of the Celestial is a blight that no man is equipped to bear.'

Felix shook his head as the wizard spoke, noticing as he did so that the multi-barrelled chain gun embedded in the ruins opposite the belfry was being pivoted about by its broad-shouldered crew and onto the street. They were going to gun down their own just to take out Gotrek.

'Gotrek, look out!' Felix yelled as the powerful weapon opened up, spraying the combatants with fire.

By virtue of numbers alone the mutants took the brunt, forced into an electric dance by the hail of bullets driven through them. Their thick armour offered scant protection and blood seeped through coin-sized holes front and back. Gotrek took a ding to his rune-axe that ricocheted off, leaving a black smudge on the starmetal. He roared furiously, then took a shot to the shoulder that punched him down.

Felix cried out, breaking free of Max's grip to charge forward.

The cannon wound down, but before the dazed survivors could so much as pick themselves up a roar went up from both sides of the street and dozens of stocky warriors poured out from hiding amidst the ruins. Once on the open road they formed grimly into ranks and closed on the surviving mutants – and Felix! – like the walls of some mechanical dungeon trap.

These were not at all like the mutants Felix had just been fighting. Their tough, practical mail was unembellished but for the occasional spiked iron vambrace for added brutality at close quarters. Each bore a shield carrying a uniform runic device, tightly locked with their comrade on either side. Felix could see their faces within their open helms. Their cheeks were leathery, noses squashed and red, eyes hard behind their full unkempt beards.

Dwarfs, Felix realised, dismayed. Both he and the mutants had been ambushed by dwarfs. Had they taken one look at Felix's tattered appearance and mistaken him for a mutant himself? Sigmar, he couldn't blame them.

And as for Max...

A handful of the mutant warriors rallied themselves for a counter-charge, throwing themselves onto the advancing shield-wall which seemed to essentially grind over them. The remainder, clearly brighter than the rest, broke and ran, only to be picked off one by one with well-placed shots from marksmen positioned in the neighbouring buildings.

The dwarfs held every advantage. They had numbers, enviable discipline, and their superlative night vision had enabled them to ambush the mutants at their most vulnerable moment and take them out at range as they fled piecemeal.

The last mutant went down at a sprint with a crossbow bolt protruding from his throat. He collapsed just a few yards from where Felix stood.

Gotrek's fate and what Max's magic had shown him of their camp left him under no illusion that these dwarfs were rescuers. He was the last man standing simply by virtue of the fact that he was yet to be overtly aggressive or run away. Perhaps they thought him craven enough to be questioned? There was no more to it than that.

Could these dwarfs themselves be aligned with the gods of Chaos?

Stranger things had happened in these dark times, and they would not be the first Chaos warband to fall on that of a rival.

As he watched, the dwarf formations began to break up, axemen dropping down to deliver mercy kills to the fallen knights. Felix's heart froze. Gotrek! Would these dwarfs recognise what they were doing before it was too late? Would they care?

'Wait,' he shouted, throwing down his sword and stepping over it with arms raised, halting only when a quarreller raised his crossbow to aim at Felix's chest. His skin itched as though it could already feel the bolt whizzing towards it. 'My name is Felix Jaeger,' he proclaimed in his loudest and most confident oratorical tone, uncertain what that was supposed to mean to these dwarfs, but for some reason determined to let them know it anyway.

Daring the sharpshooters' iron nerves, he brought his raised hands together over his head to tease off his left glove. Then he lifted that hand, all fingers tucked in bar the fourth to display the rune-inscribed dwarf gold that banded it.

'I swore an oath before the Slayer shrine of Karak Kadrin. I am the hammer-bearer and a daemonslayer, and on the word of a dwarf-friend, stop!'

The dwarfs slowly lowered their axes, apparently impressed enough to not kill him. They muttered to each other in Khazalid. Felix saw more than a few shrugs amongst the throng.

'Who's in charge here?' said Felix. 'Someone get him a message to stop the attack on our camp.'

More urgent muttering. The quarreller finally shouldered his weapon and Felix slowly lowered his hands, noticing as he did so the red spot that had appeared on his chest. Felix froze. The dot played over his armour for a second and then vanished.

Felix released a relieved breath, catching movement from the corner of his eye as a muscular dwarf with a bright red crest of hair rose up from behind the rough parapet of the rooftop across the street and laid his large, powerful-looking longrifle down against the stonework. The dwarf was short and immensely broad. He wore a thick leather coat with a high, fur-edged collar, which, contrary to spring cold and common sense, he wore open at the front to reveal amazingly defined muscles. Twin bandoliers containing an unusual cylindrical type of ammunition were looped over his shoulders and crossed his chest. His white beard was, most unusually for a dwarf, shaved almost to the jaw.

Felix gaped, his open mouth struggling unwittingly into a smile.

The dwarf pulled his goggles from his face, leaving them to hang by a rubber strap from his neck, and then pinched his eyes.

'Felix Jaeger. Ah wouldnae believe it if ah hidnae seen it with ma ain eyes. Whit in the world are ye daein here?'

NINE

Makaisson

Malakai Makaisson flung back the bleak iron doors of the mountaintop citadel and strode into the greeting hall of the ancient dwarfs. Felix imagined that it had been rather more welcoming in the past. Columnar stumps marked out what looked to have been a runic design, possibly with some kind of cultural or even magical significance to the ancient architects of this place, but now left Felix minding the remaining ceiling supports with an unease he was unaccustomed to in dwarf-built structures.

The walls had been constructed with defence foremost in mind and thus had been built without windows of any kind. Now, however, breaks in the stonework allowed in the night and the patch jobs courtesy of canvas and nails did a poor job of blocking out the breeze. Thick black cabling lay everywhere, running through heaps of rubble and scrambling up columns to what looked like iron gantries from which an intermittent light flickered and hummed. It was neither torchlight nor the precious glowstones that Malakai had innovatively employed in his handgun, but a cold, soulless kind of glow. The smell of oil lingered on the stones and Felix could see it on the faces of the dwarfs he saw working on the walls' repair as they turned to him with expressions of wonder. They probably hadn't been expecting company.

'It isnae any belter tae keek, but she's oors.'

Felix assumed that meant it was good. Makaisson, he had once been told, hailed from an isolated far-northern community of dwarfs in the Dwimmerdim Vale, and his unusual manner of speech took some re-acclimating to. Gotrek regarded the ceiling sourly. Felix could still see lead where the bullet had punched into the bone of Gotrek's shoulder but it had stopped bleeding and that, it seemed, was enough for him.

'Not too bad. If you like the feel of rain on your face.'

Felix thought it was the nearest thing he had seen to paradise in a long time.

Malakai Makaisson, he thought with something approaching wonder. He still couldn't believe it. What were the chances? Felix hadn't seen the Slayer-Engineer since he and Gotrek had last passed through Nuln. Malakai had been teaching at the Gunnery School at the time, although Felix had heard through his various military contacts in Altdorf, and later from Snorri, that the dwarf had returned to Karak Kadrin to play his part in the debacle that was the Sylvanian campaign. Felix had assumed him dead. Snorri had thought so. At that moment Felix was almost inclined to give in to Max's urgings and put it all down to destiny.

'I've never seen anything like this,' said Gotrek, eyeing the lighting rigs suspiciously. 'Never in all my years. If the Guild ever saw this your great-great-grandchildren would be swearing the Slayer Oath.'

'Aye, mibbe ye're right,' said Malakai, an air of melancholy settling over him as he looked over the hall that he had rebuilt. 'Ah suppose ah willnae tell 'em if ye dain't.'

Gotrek grumbled darkly, glaring at the cables as if they were snakes.

'How did you come to be in this out of the way place?' asked Max, softly insistent, gliding under the strange artificial light that could find no purchase on his skin. The wizard had been attacking Malakai with questions almost from the moment the engineer had first presented himself in the township.

Felix found his persistence unnerving, but if Malakai felt the same way then he didn't show it.

'It's a lang tale, young Schreiber, but if ye're o' a mind tae hear it...'

Felix held under the threshold as Gotrek, Max, and Malakai walked deeper into the greeting hall. He smiled. For a moment it was just like old times. Malakai Makaisson had that kind of effect, as if the end of everything was something one just had to look at in the right kind of way. But then his mind filled in for him the shades of those who were missing: one tall, blonde and achingly beautiful, the other stocky and broad with an idiot grin and a crest of multi-coloured nails.

With a sigh so deep that the thin air left him dizzy, he turned to look back the way they had come.

A scattering of torches marked the line of men, dwarfs and field guns on rickety wooden wagons as it crawled up the mountainside, throwing random pockets of illumination onto the barren rock and ruin of its surrounds. Both his men and Makaisson's appeared too tired for bitterness, just another near-tragedy to mark the passing of another day. He tried to follow the snaking trail of men back down to the township, only to be thwarted by whatever cunning design or enchantment protected the dwarfs' old paths through the Middle Mountains. The township was a black steepling in the mountains' cleft far below, visible more by the faint twinkle of the stream under the stars than by the buildings themselves. He frowned.

Was that another glint of light down there in the ruins? And another over there, further back in the pass where the mountains surrounded the river as it fled for better lands. It was probably just a few mutants that Malakai's force hadn't accounted for, but part of him wished that it was something worse. That worried him. Would this hunger for vengeance pass with the war's end or their arrival in Middenheim, or had he been irrevocably tainted by the encroachment of Chaos into the Old World? Or did the fact that his bloodlust bothered him prove that was not the case? He clung to that thought. It was comforting.

'We were being followed by a force of northmen,' said Gustav to the dwarf clansman wedged under his shoulder. His voice was breathy with altitude and his nose was bleeding again, a scarlet trickle running around his mouth, down his chin and steadily *drip-dripping* onto his armour. A ripening black eye already dominated one half of his face. His armour scales had been loosened out to ease the pressure on bruised ribs and he walked with a wince.

'Don't worry about it,' said the dwarf. He glanced up at Gustav and then looked away in embarrassment and mumbled: 'Those mutants have been trying to find their way up here for months, and the goblins before them for who knows how long. Aeons. The Wastes will freeze over before they get to the top of this mountain.'

'Dain't touch that!'

Felix turned to see Malakai Makaisson swat Gotrek's hand away from one of the cables that coiled up the nearest column.

'They're carryin' power frae the black water generators in the auld deeps. Mah ain design. Thaur waur mair important uses fur the insulation though, sae yer in fur a shock if ye tooch it.'

Gotrek scowled, but pulled his hand back just the same. It was probably only Malakai that could get away with talking to Gotrek like that.

Felix remained in the doorway just long enough to determine that Gustav, Kolya, Mann and the dwarfs' leaders had everything in hand, before hurrying on after the others. With Malakai's warning in mind he paid extra heed to where he stepped, taking care to avoid the over-floor cables where they ran through the rubble. He had had enough shocks for one day. It didn't seem very sensible to leave something so dangerous just lying around on the floor, but Felix supposed that the dwarfs were accustomed to it.

'What do you mean by more important uses?'

'Ach, ye'll see. But where wiz ah?' The thrum of some industrial process taking place in a distant quarter of the citadel began to make itself felt through the stones. They approached a stairwell leading up, and Malakai moved towards it with Max in step. 'Aye noo, and tha' was hoo auld Ironfist and ah got separated efter tha wee beasties chased us oot of Sylvania. Ah saw hoo bad things were gonnae get efter tha, sae ah and those stuck wi' me cam tae this wheesht place for a special project.'

'You should've gone back to Karak Kadrin,' said Gotrek.

'Ah hear the Slayer Hold went doon no lang after tha.'

'Aye,' Gotrek grumbled, deadly serious. 'What of it?'

Felix walked through the crumbling innards of the castle and was overcome with awe. Steam filled the corridors and walkways that Malakai led them through, hissing between the bolted sections of great rusted pipes. Every few dozen steps they passed a room filled with unusual machinery. In some pistons rose and fell as if the mountain was sucking in steam. In others, internal walls had been knocked down to create space for rank upon rank of huge, gleaming engines that put Felix in mind of some infernal printing press. A juddering conveyor carried complicated metallic components from press to press, all attended by a single dwarf who made notes in a small book. Every stone shook as if the castle was being bombarded from above and everywhere dwarfs moved about with a purpose. Felix had to remind himself that it was the middle of the night outside.

Malakai Makaisson had constructed something astounding out here in the middle of nowhere, and Felix felt an urgent need to know why. Knowing the Slayer-Engineer as Felix did, he expected it to be both wondrous and destructive.

With a warrior's eye, Felix looked about for signs of the weapons that the dwarfs were undoubtedly fashioning here to turn the tide against the hordes of Chaos, but could find nothing obvious. In what looked like finishing rooms, dwarfs in long-sleeved white overclothes blasted steel sheets with steam hoses while others buffed and polished. Machines that looked like iron-toothed mouths attached to conveyors spat nails into buckets that were then loaded onto carts for distribution.

Felix stepped to one side to allow a burly dwarf with a sweat-sodden grey beard to barrel down the narrow corridor behind a wheelbarrow filled with thick metal plates. Some quixotic type of armour perhaps? Felix could not for the life of him imagine what sort of monster Malakai intended to clad with it.

Gotrek watched the barrow rattle down the corridor, jaw clenched. Felix knew the Slayer was as curious about what Malakai was up to here as he was. He also knew that Gotrek was far too stubborn to ever ask.

'All right,' said Felix, 'we give up. What are you doing here?'

'We've all got oor ain weapons tae brin' tae these times, young Felix, and these are mine.'

'Forgive me, but they don't look much like weapons.'

'Nae the noo, laddie,' Malakai grinned, stubbing his nose with a finger as thick and browned with grease as a sausage.

Gotrek snorted, though over what, Felix wasn't minded to ask.

'It's destiny,' said Max. The steam billowed through his robes as though he had just been summoned from some black dimension. He leaned into his staff and gazed about himself with bleak-eyed wonder. 'It has to be. What else could reunite us all at such a pivotal moment in time?'

Malakai rested the muzzle of his gun on his shoulder and shrugged. 'Mibbe it is and mibbe it isnae. It disnae seem tae make a difference either way ye keek it though diz it?'

Felix shook his head ruefully. Why hadn't he thought of telling Max that?

'And anyway,' Malakai went on. 'Ah can see a few who arenae here. Did poor Snorri Nosebiter get his memory back?' He turned to Felix with a half-cocked grin. 'And how aboot yer wee lass, Ulrika?'

Felix's heart skipped a beat when he heard the question. He turned to Gotrek. Gotrek glared back. Felix's tongue felt as though it was stuck to the roof of his mouth.

'They both fell in Kislev,' said Gotrek, his one eye fixed on Felix.

'Well ahm sure it wiz a guid death. We'll drink tae Snorri's honour when this is all ower.' Malakai reached out and took Felix's shoulder in a consoling grip. It felt like being crushed under a rock, but Felix barely felt it. 'And ahm sorry aboot Ulrika, she were a braw lass wi' a guid heart.'

Felix felt Gotrek's eye on him, and looked away just as a dwarf with a screaming circular saw sheared through the neck of a silvery-white sheet of metal. 'Yes,' he answered hoarsely. 'Yes, she was.'

They passed through dozens more corridors and several further sets of stairs, always rising, until Felix was well and truly lost and desperate for a window if only to assure himself of where he was in relation to the outside. They passed taprooms in which dwarfs drank and smoked with the same dour determination with which they worked. A steam whistle wailed through the halls, making Felix jump when it first went off behind his ear.

The sound hung in the air for several seconds after the initial blast. Felix counted them, cringing a little with every added number at the thought of what dark thing might lurk in the valley and be drawn to such a din. To the dwarfs, however, it appeared to represent nothing more terrible than a shift change, workers in leather overalls covered in soot and oil and with protective gloves hanging from their wrists staggering into bunkrooms to rouse bleary-eyed comrades and slump into their still-warm beds. Watching them made Felix's eyelids feel heavy and he tried and failed to suppress a yawn.

In rooms lined with armour dummies and weapon racks dwarfs shed work gear and strapped on mail and shields, no doubt for a shift patrolling the township below or manning the citadel's walls. The dwarfs were a dying race, Felix knew, and had been for millennia. As such they had few professional soldiers, their armies comprised largely of dwarfs like these who set aside their trades in favour of axes in times of war. Even knowing that, Felix was impressed by their fortitude.

On the door of one such barracks room a large circular target had been mounted and as Felix walked by a dwarf in half-tied mail aimed a bulky crossbow towards him. Felix's heart leapt into his mouth. The dwarf was clearly blurry-eyed from over-work, or else maddened by Chaos! The dwarf pulled on the trigger and a second later the yellow ring in the centre of the target bristled with iron bolts. Steam hissed from the strange mechanism riveted to the basic crossbow chassis in place of the conventional drawstring and crank as the dwarf lowered his weapon and moved to tug his bolts out of the door. He grunted a greeting to Makaisson as they marched past.

Felix turned to glance back before they turned onto another corridor.

'What kind of weapon was that?'

'King Byrrnoth Grundadrakk of Barak Varr tasked me tae gie him a crossbow faster and better tha' them the dark elf scallies wur usin' agin his shipping. New bolts get fed intae the track frae a hopper and forced oot wi' a wee burst o' steam for a mair powerful shot.' Malakai shrugged as if he were describing the operation of hammer and nail. 'But auld Grundadrakk in his wisdom didnae like whit they cost tae build sae ah kept the few ah made for maself. Ah wonder what's left of the auld place noo?'

'Barak Varr?' said Felix and shrugged. He thought of Kolya's map, the great empty swathe south of the Talabec and west of the Middle Mountains.

'She is beset, but stands, the last stone on the path to the Everpeak,' said Max quietly, eyes averted. 'Vermin rule in her deep places, and like rotten grain from a breached drum they spill from their conquests in Hirn, Izor, Eight Peaks and Azul.'

For a minute everyone walked in silence.

Felix turned to Gotrek. He had learned from Snorri that the two dwarfs had used to live in a hill town – much like the ancient township they had just passed through – under the protection of Karaz-a-Karak, the Everpeak as men knew the capital of the ancient dwarf realm. In a sense Gotrek was learning of the plight of his home much as Felix had just days before. The Slayer stared grimly ahead as if it meant nothing. And perhaps it didn't, Felix thought with a sigh. Then Malakai sucked in through his teeth and spat on the ground.

'Well tha doesnae sound tae guid, diz it?'

'No,' Felix agreed, meaning to say something more but unable to find the words for it.

'If you go in for that sort of talk,' Gotrek muttered.

The corridor came to an end in what looked like a vast feasting hall. Great ceiling arches soared above them, carved into the likeness of longbeard dwarfs striking together tankards of ale over the centre of the hall where they met. Each was a work of art and that they had endured the millennia in such a recognisable state did credit to the dwarfs that had poured such loving labour into their artifice. Scores of low slung tables filled the tiniest portion of the room, leaving the rest to cracked tiles and more of that black cabling that seemed as pernicious in this castle as weeds. A handful of dwarfs in armour sat at just one of them, picking at the thin-looking vegetables that wallowed in gravy in their trenchers. Felix felt his mouth water and heard his stomach growl. He thought of the empty crates and sacks in his company's wagons and looked about himself with fresh wonder and – almost – hope.

There must be hundreds of dwarfs here. Far from enough to win the war, but enough to make a difference if used wisely; enough to *hurt* the enemy, to let the Dark Gods know that there were still those that fought them. Whatever Gotrek's misgivings about Malakai Makaisson's intentions, Felix felt sure that the ancients who had once lived here would have approved. It had to be something truly remarkable to warrant such an expenditure of resources and the dedication of so many.

Malakai's footsteps echoed from the grandiose beams as the Slayer-Engineer strode towards a large set of double doors at the far end of the hall and flung them wide.

Cold mountain air rushed through. It carried the scent of engine grease and oil and the barely discernible hum of some kind of idling engine. Felix stepped out into the night. The wind, reminded of its strength so high above the world, tore between the castle's battlements and riffled through Felix's hair and cloak. With one hand positioned for safety on the pitted basalt of the rampart beside him, he restrained his hair with the other. Gotrek peered over the side and spat down. He watched it fall for a long time, and then grunted with what sounded like approval.

The castle's uppermost fortifications had been filled with a forest of metal girders, made into a towering scaffold by horizontal and diagonal beams and ringed with walkways and ladders and dangling ropes. Steel-wound hawsers the thickness of Felix's arm fed through massive brass rings that had been unceremoniously bolted into the ramparts and swept up to some mysterious point in the sky. They bobbed up and down, as though attached to a ship that rolled with the waves. Beside Felix, Max however was looking up, his dark eyes alive with visions of destiny. Felix joined him, feeling his excitement rise as the blinking spots overhead that he had initially mistaken for stars turned out to be a string of guide lights employing the same arcane technology with which Makaisson had illuminated his castle. A shape emerged from the darkness as Felix's eyes adapted to it – a huge, gleaming curve like the underbelly of a whale. Cold light glinted from the riveted metal hanging beneath it.

Felix was lost for words.

They could do it. They could reach Middenheim. They could do anything.

'Aye,' said Malakai Makaisson, arriving in between Felix and Max and winding both men with a firm clap on the back. 'Did ye miss her?'

The children of the tribes ran amongst the beaten Middle Mountains fighters, laughing and squealing as they pulled faces, danced around discarded blades, and kicked at men's shins. It was an old game. Khagash-Fél, as old as the tribes themselves, remembered when he had run amongst captured warriors of the Yusak to prove to his father that their enemies did not frighten him. That had been more than a lifetime ago. Gods had been and passed since then.

Reining in his enormous black warhorse, Khagash-Fél dismounted. His boots hit the ground with a thump of meteoric iron. A frightened murmur passed amongst the mutant warriors as they saw him approach. They had dwelt here too long, hidden in these mountains and deaf to the Dark Master's call. They were Empire men and thus born with water in their bones. They had forgotten how it felt to look upon a true champion of Chaos and know terror.

'Who leads you?' he intoned.

Silence.

One-by-one, Khagash-Fél cracked the knuckles of his hand. At least one man moaned. The tribe's outriders had herded up just under forty of the mewling chattel. Those few in whom the Dark Master's blessing was most evident were picketed here on the stone ground by the river at the town's entrance, surrounded by a ring of tribesmen and beasts. The rest he could still hear screaming as they were fed into the great cauldron that had been set up in the valley beyond the walls, to be boiled alive in the traditional manner reserved for the blood enemies of the tribes.

Khagash-Fél was pleased to hear the old ways being upheld in the midst of such upheaval.

He approached the man who had made a sound. Self-evidently he was weak of heart and likely also of body and spirit. The man had been divested of his helm, revealing a wide mouth filled with poisonous-green teeth. His beard flexed unnaturally of its own volition and his pale, westerner's skin was slippery with sweat. Khagash-Fél ground his teeth at the stench of urine rising from the man's faulds. The man condemned himself still further with a whimper.

'Who leads you?'

'He is dead, O mighty one, slain in battle with the dwarfs and their allies.'

Khagash-Fél glanced to the castle that sat atop the mountain to his left. There was a road leading from it to the town but as hard as he focused on it, he could not force his eyes to track it all the way down. Mentally, he bade the Eye of Katchar to open and reveal the path's true course to him, but it was a gift of the gods and not his to command, and it remained stubbornly shut.

'Then who now leads you?'

The weakling warrior glanced for support to his comrades, who, showing equal sallowness of spirit, averted their faces. He opened his mouth and stuttered, then screamed as Khagash-Fél stooped down to grab him by the throat and drag him two feet off the ground.

And now the man fought: too little, too late. The mutant kicked out at full stretch to dink his toe on the warlord's breastplate, working his large mouth for a bite on the tattooed skin around his neck. Khagash-Fél tightened his grip until the man's eyes bugged out of his face and his lips drained of colour.

'Had I and my people not come here, to whom would you have turned?'

The man opened his mouth and stared, perhaps seeing the great eagle come to snatch away the soul of the craven and bear it to its damnation. The creak of cartilage echoed up from his constricting throat.

'Who?'

A frightened murmur passed through the watching captives, maybe seeing their own fate in the warrior's slow death. All except one. His eyes narrowed. A slender old crone observed the scurrying children with an awkward look of affection. She was draped in black silks, ice-white hair pierced by dark horns. As if only then noticing his presence, she drew her attention from the children to regard him. Her skin was a chalky black. Her eyes shimmered like scrying pools.

Khagash-Fél felt a thrill of recognition, of destinies coming together in the time and manner that they must.

His guide.

His prophet.

Watching proceedings from the bare back of his grey horse, Nergüi traced a ward against evil through the air. Strips of blue silk danced across the pony's muzzle. The chimes sewn into his robes tinkled in warning. 'She is a witch, warlord, and a potent one. Be wary when you question her, and kill her swiftly afterwards.'

The woman smiled, baring teeth like tiny knives. Nergüi's browned face contorted in anger and he held out a hand to his acolytes for his staff. One of them had handed the eagle-feathered rod to him before Khagash-Fél could raise a hand for peace.

'Do you not fear death?' he asked. 'Or do you think perhaps that I will not turn my blade on a woman?'

'Everyone fears death, Half-Ogre, but I know that you cannot kill me.'

'She is a prophetess,' hissed someone from amongst the gathered tribesmen before Khagash-Fél could glare into them his will for silence.

Nergüi raised his staff until it was held vertical. He began to shake it rhythmically up and down, so that the glass-eyed beads threaded through its feathers shook. In time, he pounded on his chest with an open palm. Khagash-Fél recognised the chant as one of dispelling, but it felt suddenly childish when brought before the god-touched prophetess, so composed in her own power that she did not even look at the tribes' shaman as he spoke.

'Do you claim that you can see your own death?' said Nergüi.

'Can you not?'

The shaman laughed, grinning to his acolytes and the warriors around him who had ridden with him over countless leagues and many years and who now laughed with him. 'Perhaps these Greater Gods have something finer in store for me.'

The woman glanced at Khagash-Fél. The corner of her lips curled. Prismatic fragments of something terribly profound glittered across her eyes. Khagash-Fél found himself absorbed. There was truth there, he could feel it, as only one great power could recognise in another. And she saw something similar in him, he knew. He regarded her in a wholly different light. He had lost four sons. It had been many centuries, but he would need more if he was to found a dynasty to rule the Dark Master's empire.

'Perhaps they do indeed,' she answered, sharp as a crystal blade.

Unbeknownst to the men around him, Nergüi had stopped laughing. He rattled his staff fiercely. 'Your foresight did not serve your former master, witch.'

For a moment, the seeress looked sad. 'It is not prophecy that I give you but the future as it can only be. If all men were blessed equally by fate then none would be happier about it than I.'

'And what do you see, prophetess?' said Khagash-Fél eagerly.

'Your people believe the dead see things that the living do not. You are right. Long ago I died, or should have but for the blind heroism of a man centuries unborn, and now I see as the living cannot. I see the end of things, and a future, a world on which the doom of great warriors will touch.'

'Are all your visions so opaque?' Nergüi sneered.

'I see you in battle with the hero you seek,' she said, ignoring the shaman and addressing Khagash-Fél, then turning to point a clawed finger to the old castle on the mountain. 'There. A battle to the death.'

Khagash-Fél grinned.

'Good luck,' said Nergüi, lowering his staff. 'The tribes know well the magic of the dwarfs and their black kin. These are hidden ways. There is no way to that castle.'

The prophetess turned back to Khagash-Fél. 'The one you hunt is marked by destiny. The fates of worlds still unborn converge upon him. His doom draws near and his passage is as the setting of the moon to my eyes. I am Morzanna, prophetess of the Dark Master, and this one once saved my life.' She extended her small, clawed hand and, despite Nergüi's warning hiss, Khagash-Fél dropped the now-limp corpse in his grip and took it, swallowing it in his ogreish palm.

'Come, Half-Ogre. Allow me to guide you to your destiny.'

TEN

Unstoppable

'You're a genius,' Felix breathed, craning his neck as far back as it would go and gawping at the dark behemoth that strained on its hawsers like a harpooned whale.

It was an airship!

The darkness gave Felix only the vague impression of sleek contours, an outline defined by the glow of guide lights, but he could say without fear of contradiction that this new airship was every bit as immense as the first. It would be a squeeze, but Felix saw no reason why it couldn't carry all of Malakai's dwarfs and all of Felix's men wherever they needed to go. Already the possibilities were racing through his mind. Flying to Middenheim was just the beginning. They could drop bombs on the Chaos hordes as they attempted to scale the Fauschlag. Utilising the airship's phenomenal speed and range they could ferry in supplies from all over the world, or scour the land for survivors, unifying the Empire again in its common struggle. As history now remembered Magnus the Pious and Praag, perhaps children two centuries hence would learn the names of Malakai

Makaisson and Middenheim. It was only one airship, but the implications were endless.

The guide lights glinted from the steel rims of glass portholes and from the barrels of organ guns and the blades of rotors. They turned dreamily, and it was these that were responsible for the quiet drone that Felix could hear against the wind. Looking closer, Felix could see that there were gaps in the bodywork of the fragile metal vehicle that dangled from the gasbag. The airship was unfinished, but it looked wondrous enough for Felix.

'You rebuilt the *Spirit of Grungni*.'

'Ah called her *Unstoppable*,' said Malakai, stomping across the blustery rampart to the side of the great steel tower where a mechanism of wheels and cables had been bolted to the scaffold, adjoining what looked like a pair of parallel vertical rails that headed straight up. Malakai stood beside the contraption and put his hands on his hips. The wind bent his crest at the roots and ruffled his collar. 'It's whit ah always wanted tae call the last yin, and noo there's naebody tae say otherwise.' He patted the scaffold. 'This yin's all mine.'

'There're holes in it,' said Gotrek.

'She isnae ready yit is she, ye big wazzock.'

'How did you get enough liftgas to fill the gasbag?' Felix cut in before Gotrek could respond with anything even more insulting. 'You told me before that it was difficult to find. You'd built a whole town to manufacture the stuff.'

'Ye're right, laddie, and tha's a sensible question.' Malakai glared pointedly at Gotrek who snorted and turned his back to go and pace the ramparts. 'The auld mines all ower this place were filled wi the stuff. We joost pumped it oot.'

'And what about fuel?' said Gotrek. The dwarf paced with arms crossed, gripping his swollen biceps, but his one eye glittered with an excitement that Felix suspected he could not entertain until every possible flaw had been gone over and cast aside. 'There's nothing in these mountains and never has been. No gold, no iron, and no coal either.'

'Everything we used cam wi us frae Sylvania, but ye're right, there isnae much black water in the tank. Enough tae fly us tae Karaz-a-Karak in a guid wind.'

'That's where you're going?' said Felix, feeling much of his excitement ebb away. He'd been foolish to think that Malakai would want to fly his airship north when he could take it home to aid his own people. No doubt the dwarfs stood a better chance anyway. If anything had a right to describe itself as impregnable then the Everpeak was it.

For a moment Felix considered asking Malakai to take them all with him. It would undoubtedly be safer there than Middenheim ever could be, but more than that there was the prospect of skaven to fight if Max's reports were to be believed. There was a debt of blood still owed there.

He sighed and let the bloodlust go. There was no point to it. If he found the rat that murdered his father, then what would change? No, he knew where he had to go and had been resigned to walking it before this.

As soon as he arrived at that decision breathing felt a little easier, as if a pressing weight had been removed from his shoulders.

He felt as though he had been tested somehow and had passed.

'That's where he *was* going,' said Gotrek, turning to face the engineer. He tightened his grip on his biceps until the muscles of his chest and neck bulged. The bullet wound in his shoulder oozed. 'Now he's going to Middenheim.'

'We can fight aboot it when she's guid to go,' said Malakai, meeting the other Slayer's bleak stare without blinking. 'It's joost a waste o' breath until she is.'

The engineer reached behind him and pulled on a lever that was part of the mechanism at his back. As he did, there was a hiss of vented steam from the top of the scaffold and then a metallic wail as a small iron cage came hurtling down the vertical tracks. Just before it looked as if it were going to shatter on the roof of the castle it slowed, issuing what sounded like a sigh, and then bumped home with a clumsy kiss of metal upon stone. Steam rushed out from the braking mechanism, flooding Makaisson to the knees as he pulled open the metal door, turned to Felix, and beamed.

'Ah ken ye'd want tae see her. Fur auld time's sake.'

Felix didn't know what to say. Seeing the airship was like being reunited with an old friend, every bit as exhilarating as finding Malakai himself alive and well; more so, in fact, he was ashamed to admit. Taking his gawping silence as assent, Malakai turned to Max, who nodded once, and then to Gotrek who grunted and shook his head.

'It looks the same as the last one. I think I'll go and see what my so-called rememberer is up to.' The Slayer touched his damaged shoulder and drew in a sharp breath. 'Maybe I'll see about this too,' he added grudgingly.

'Sorry aboot tha',' said Makaisson, sounding almost genuinely contrite.

Gotrek bared his yellowed teeth. 'Next time, aim a little lower.'

'You should get some rest,' said Felix, promising himself that he'd curl up somewhere too just as soon as he'd had one glimpse inside of the airship. 'I can't remember the last time I saw you close your eye.'

'Plenty of time for that, manling,' Gotrek muttered wearily as he turned away. 'Plenty of time.'

The elevator cage was, mercifully, much slower on the ascent than it had been on the way down. Felix wondered whether some technical marvel instructed it when passengers were aboard and to adjust its speed accordingly, but opted to save his questions in favour of clutching the bars of the cage as his stomach dropped through his feet and the ramparts of the castle disappeared below. The metal girders of the scaffold flitted by, the cage shuddering as it climbed higher. Felix tightened his grip until his knuckles were white.

'Exhilarating,' said Max, in a cold tone that didn't know the meaning of the word.

'Ye git bored o' it,' Malakai shouted over the wind that the climbing elevator sucked in and down.

Felix disagreed, and heartily so. He had travelled in similar devices to this one, both above ground and under it where such technology was commonplace in the mines of the dwarfs, and however he picked through the gamut of feelings rifling through his innards 'boredom' was conspicuous by its absence. Felix clung to the sides and watched the airship bloat as he was drawn nearer, the metal gondola that hung beneath the gasbag flashing faster and faster between various bars and stanchions until the elevator cage arrived at the top of the scaffold for an unimpeded view of Malakai Makaisson's awesome invention.

There was a squeal of brakes and Felix's view was filled with steam that gouted from a whirring array of wheels at the terminus of the tracks as well as from the elevator itself. Felix's heart lurched as the elevator slowed. He shivered in the cloud of condensing steam as the cage arrived in its housing with a – he supposed – reassuring *bang* and Malakai drew back the door, this time on the opposite side of the cage to the one they had entered, opening onto the scaffold.

Felix was the last out, stepping onto a timber gangplank that wobbled dangerously underfoot and immediately regretting looking down. His stomach turned a somersault and he had to fight the urge to fold down to his knees, grip the gangplank, and never ever let go. He had been higher, he knew. He had sailed higher than mountains in the *Spirit of Grungni*, but there was something about seeing that distance quite clearly beneath your feet that made it seem a great deal higher. And besides, he thought queasily, trying to remember which side of the scaffold faced the roof of the castle and which a drop over the parapet – this whole castle was built onto a mountaintop.

Willing his stomach to settle and his arms and legs to stop shaking, Felix followed after Malakai and Max to the edge of the scaffold where another sickeningly slender length of wood ran to an open door in the gondola's side. The plank was secured at each end with brass rings that rolled around the stanchion as the airship shifted in the wind. He supposed that looked vaguely sturdy. He watched as Malakai bounded across like a goat. The gangplank wobbled alarmingly under the dwarf's bulk, but not enough to dissuade Max from gliding across after him. Felix took a deep breath and this time remembered not to look down, holding out his arms for balance as he practically ran across and jumped into Malakai's arms.

'Welcome aboord,' Malakai yelled as Felix stepped reverently onto the iron deck and looked around at the small boarding chamber.

A single white light shone from a fixed point in the ceiling, illuminating metal rivets and the edges of plates. It was all so well polished that Felix could see his blurred reflection in them. He scratched his greying beard ruefully, turning a full circle before coming to the circular door-hatch that led into the interior of the gondola. It was solid steel and, unlike an ordinary door, was opened by rotating a wheel mechanism in the centre and then waiting for the locks to release. Felix didn't understand the logic behind the design but the dwarfs had similar systems aboard their submersibles as well, so he assumed it served some purpose for dwarfs were nothing if not pragmatic.

With a glance at Malakai for permission, Felix took the wheel in his hands. His heart was hammering. He ran his hands around the smooth curve of the metal. For a moment, he felt as if he could turn this wheel, stand back, and find Ulrika and Snorri and everyone else waiting for him on the other side. He smiled. And then he, Gotrek and Snorri would escape below for a good hard drinking session before the ship got under way. He sighed, a lump in his throat. He would never have thought, living through those terrible adventures, that those would be the best days of his life. What he would give now for one more argument with Ulrika, or a hung-over Snorri Nosebiter as the greatest of his problems. He was surprised to find himself even missing Gotrek. The Slayer was still around, of course, but what Felix found himself yearning for was his *friend*.

Malakai reached around him, and gave the wheel a gentle downwards tug to set it spinning. 'A wee bit stiff for human hands,' he said, with an understanding squeeze of Felix's shoulder. Malakai was remarkably empathetic for a Slayer.

'Yes. A little. No doubt I'll get used to it.'

'Sae, whit dae ye both want tae see first?'

The dwarfs' infirmary was the busiest part of the castle, playing host to a steady stream of minor injuries from the battle as well as the cuts, scalds, and bruises that seemed an everyday part of life for the workers here. Behind a partially screened off corner, a craggy-faced elder with his long grey beard held in a net chewed on the stem of an unlit pipe and concentrated on sewing shut a nasty-looking cut on a warrior's arm. A younger dwarf watched over his shoulder, on hand with a damp cloth and a half-empty jug of ale and prepared to deploy either one. Elsewhere, dwarfs in bloodstained leather aprons and gloves hurried about bearing trays of what looked like instruments of torture. One particularly grim-looking dwarf threw a bucket of sickly red water over a drain in the floor. Men moaned. Some lay unconscious on tables. Dwarfs sat stoically upright on benches or else stood, suffering their injuries as only dwarfs could.

Allowing the cruel alchemy by which crippled men were transformed back into soldiers to proceed around the table at which he sat, Gustav slowly unwound the foetid bandage from his hand. It felt like grinding one's fist into a bruise. A sour milk smell emerged as it unravelled. He probably should have changed the bandage sooner, but what did he know, he wasn't a healer, and it wasn't as if clean cloth had been spilling from their empty grain sacks. He reassured himself that nothing dead ever smelled that bad.

'The Dushyka wise woman said always to do it quickly,' said Kolya, leaning onto the low table over a plate of something indescribable in gravy and a mug of something worse.

'I bet that's what all the ladies told you,' Gustav replied, forcing a smirk.

Kolya grinned, massaging his ribs – bruised, but luckily not broken following a battering by a dwarf's shield – then shuffled uncomfortably on his bench. It had been made to seat a body half his height and with a backside twice the girth of his. 'I know seven languages, friend Gustav. There are many peoples beyond the northern face of the Goromadny, and I have almost as many wives there.' He settled and shrugged. 'Winters are long on the frozen sea, no?'

'You married more than once?' said Gustav, not in the least bit shocked by anything this northern savage might do. The man spoke Kurgan and, insofar as Gustav cared to differentiate, was practically Kurgan himself. He remembered that the Kislevite had been a winged lancer in his old life, as well as a hunter. He thought of the pictures of proud riders in gorgeous mail accoutred with amber and jet, cloaked in animal skins with coloured pennants flying from their lances amidst the famous feathered wings on their backs. It was difficult to reconcile that image with the hemp-clad ruffian that Gustav had grudgingly come to know.

'Wife is not horse,' said Kolya with a shrug.

'Does that mean something?'

'If you are Kislevite.'

The final layer of bandaging came away stickily, flesh clinging to the final strip of cloth as Gustav peeled it back. His nose wrinkled in protest and he grimaced as he attempted to flex his fingers. His hand was still red raw, the skin mottled with partially healed blisters. After everything he had gone through in Kislev, outliving even the accursed vampiric beauty who still haunted the beating of his heart, to be laid low by a misfiring pistol was a cruel fate.

Kolya pushed his bowl across the table towards Gustav. 'The dwarf who gave it me said it was fortifying.' He mimed a spoon-to-the-mouth motion. 'Eat.'

Gustav examined the thick stew, trying to identify the misshapen lumps that floated in it like dead bodies in the Aver. He turned to the dwarf beside him who, with his arm in a sling, had his bowl to his lips and was slurping with gusto. Seeing Gustav's regard, the dwarf set down his bowl and clapped his lips.

'Tastes like chicken.'

'I'll take your word for it,' Gustav said, pushing the bowl back towards Kolya.

The Kislevite stuck his finger in it for a taste, then shrugged and picked up his spoon. 'Makes man wish for cup of kvass to sear taste buds, no?'

Ignoring him, Gustav again tried to force his fingers to clench.

Blisters popped and dead skin pulled as far as it would stretch until the pain became too great and he had to relax. He wondered if he would ever wield a sword properly again.

'My uncle used the exact same gunpowder as I did. Why am I the one with the ruined hand?'

'Do you wish you had both been hurt?' said Kolya.

'Of course not.'

The Kislevite shrugged and thumbed something gristly from the corner of his lip. 'Is of no matter. Do you think I do not wish ill on that axe-wielding zabójka of a dwarf?'

'That's different. Following Gotrek's like being chained to a hippogriff.'

'You are on a fast horse to nowhere, friend Gustav. Some men ride with reins and stirrups, but us?' He raised his spoon in a toast. 'We hold on and pray to Ursun we do not fall, and hope our destiny follows in the path of others more gifted.'

'I'm not following anyone,' Gustav muttered, willing his fingers to curl as if that alone would prove him correct. 'Unlike you, I can leave whenever I want.'

'Then leave.'

Gustav opened his mouth, but then hesitated. He could abandon his uncle's path, of course he could, but what would he do then if he did? He had discussed the idea of making for Averheim with several of the company sergeants – it made sense to have a contingency – but that had been before they'd marched several days in the wrong direction with a Chaos warband on their tail. It still made sense to him as a destination, the largest city of the south and presumably well away from the Chaos forces that marched from the north and the east. He knew that a lot of the men thought in private as he did, but they were too wedded to the growing heroic legend of Felix Jaeger to leave him, and Gustav didn't fancy braving the Empire's wilds alone. But he told himself that he could leave if he chose to.

Kolya's grin was more insulting than anything he could possibly say.

Gustav was facing the door behind the Kislevite's back as Gotrek stomped into the infirmary. The Slayer grunted something in Dwarfish to an orderly who checked him at the doorway, then pushed the dwarf gently but very firmly to one side so he could scan the room with his one bulldog eye. Gustav found himself sitting a little straighter as the Slayer started towards them.

'Is not so bad,' Kolya went on, oblivious. 'At least your hippogriff does not talk tiresomely of doom, then kill his best friend as he killed mine and decide that what he really wanted all along is to walk all the way to Altdorf.'

Gustav's eyes widened as the Slayer loomed over Kolya's back. His bullet-drilled shoulders were almost three times as broad as the Kislevite's. His frayed crest brushed the ceiling. His good eye, bloodshot and bleary as it was, bored into the back of Kolya's head.

Kolya swivelled nonchalantly around. Something with the fur still on bobbed in his spoon. He directed a wink at Gustav and grinned. 'Not that I am ungrateful, of course. For all of those years that I spent with the freedom of the plains did I wish to see the endless forests of our eternal ally.'

Gustav was astounded that the Slayer did not simply plough his fist into Kolya's face right there. He hadn't known the dwarf as long as either Felix or Kolya had, but he'd read his uncle's books. He'd kept that fact to himself, but he had.

'I see you're keeping yourself idle,' Gotrek growled with the faintest slur of either mild drunkenness or the most extraordinary tiredness.

Kolya shuffled along a few inches and pushed his ale cup back across the table for the Slayer, but Gotrek remained standing, like some chipped and pitted statue.

'What do you know about machines, manling?'

'Little,' said Kolya, smile fading into seriousness. 'Some men of the rota bore harquebuses, but I not like to depend on thing I cannot fix myself or rebuild if I must.'

Gustav recoiled as the dwarf's stare turned on him. 'Me? Nothing.'

With a grunt of expected disappointment, Gotrek looked down the table. 'Who's the senior engineer here?'

The dwarf sitting next to Gustav set down his bowl and dabbed his beard on the edge of his sling. 'And who are you, son of Grimnir?'

'A good pair of hands, that's who. I'll spend a day or a week in this castle if it means shortening our journey to Middenheim by as much, but Makaisson's soft and this lot look lazy.' He stared the broken-armed dwarf down. 'They'll not idle an hour longer than they must if I can help it.'

'Were you an engineer, then?' mumbled the dwarf.

'What do you mean, *were*?' said Gotrek, threateningly.

'Nothing, nothing,' said the dwarf, appealing with his eyes for help from Gustav and Kolya and finding nothing going. 'I'm sure we could put you to work somewhere.'

'Now,' Gotrek growled, menacing the injured dwarf to his feet. Then Gotrek took Kolya by the scruff of the neck and hoisted him up from under the table as easily as a large man would lift a puppy. 'To work, manling. If you can pick up a spoon you can pick up a paint brush. Do you want to see Middenheim or not?'

Gustav hurriedly drew himself up.

His hand suddenly felt a whole lot better.

Over the next few hours, Felix walked the steel hallways of his youth, a journey as dizzying in its way as the wildest elevator ride ever could be. Everything was as he remembered it. He could have followed the layout of the corridors in his sleep. Every bolt and rivet had a memory attached. Each room that they passed brought a flood of long forgotten images and feelings. That wasn't to say that the interior of the airship was exactly the same as it had been. Huge sections of it were clearly unfinished. Some corridors were little more than swamps of loose cabling that spilled from unplated walls. Others lay in darkness with copper fronds splaying from holes in the ceiling. But his mind seemed more than willing to skip over such minor discrepancies.

Malakai took them first to the bridge. Felix brushed his fingers over the dials, gauges and brass-knobbed levers that lined the walls, threw himself into the leather embrace of the command chair and swivelled it around, then bounced to his feet again to grasp the huge nautical steering wheel and gaze through the view screen at the rugged peaks visible in outline against the black sky. Max merely looked, taking in everything at a glance, lost in some inscrutable reverie of his own.

They toured the engine deck. Black-faced engineers moved around as if Malakai and the others were not there at all, communicating with each other by sign under the din of huge horizontal pistons sliding in and out of thick metal jackets, the chug of steam boilers and the relentless thrum of the engines. The decking trembled underfoot and Felix could almost see the air vibrating between the walls. Jabbing his thumb back the way they had come, Malakai took them onwards.

A sweep of the lower decks took in the airship's observation turrets. While Max waited in the hallway, Felix pushed his head into the bubble of each one and inhaled deeply the scent of metal polish and grease. Within each of them was an organ gun set up on a gimbal-mounted platform that allowed the weapon to swivel a short distance in any direction by the use of foot pedals. He smiled sadly, hearing in his mind the rapid-fire *boom* of dozens of these turrets as a vast red dragon swooped alongside to rake its claws through the steel and hawsers of the gondola. He held the walls and eyed the ceiling as Malakai took them aft, half expecting to feel the hull judder.

The rear of the gondola was given over to a hangar spanning several decks in height and filled with partially dismantled gyrocopters in bays marked out with strips of a strange glow-in-the-dark metal. Felix shook his head, marvelling as he never ceased to do at the ingenuity and cunning of the dwarfs. With the bays so marked, the dwarf pilots would be able to find their vehicles instantly, even in total darkness. These gyrocopters however had a distinctly cannibalised look, and Felix assumed they had given of themselves for the greater good of the airship. He patted the cool fuselage of one as they left, appreciating its sacrifice.

They passed the mess hall, bolted-down tables and chairs peopled by carousing ghosts. Felix thought he saw his old quarters. It was difficult to be certain, as spartan and unfinished as it looked, but he recalled that there had been only three single quarters on the airship and he convinced himself that this one had been his. He lingered at the doorway, remembering the times that he and Ulrika had shared within those walls, before Malakai called him away.

Max stood hunched against his staff under the low ceiling of the corridor beside a metal ladder as Malakai reached up to wheel open the ceiling hatch above it. It was one of several that led through the labyrinth of crawlways between the gas-filled cells that filled the gasbag and allowed the airship to fly. At the very top would be the cupola, a metal dorsal spine that ran the length of the gasbag and was flanked by a – as Felix recalled – wholly inadequate handrail.

'How long before it's ready to fly?' Max asked as Malakai spun the wheel and threw open the hatch. A marshy smell drifted down into the corridor. Felix knew that liftgas was, of course, lighter than air and so presumed it to be some impurity that the hard-pressed dwarfs had been unable to fully remove. Felix hoped it wouldn't affect how she flew.

'Difficult tae say,' said Malakai, clapping grease from his palms and then sticking his thumbs under his belt. His brutish features furrowed, as if giving the question its full due. 'Therr's a few kinks that still need tae be worked oot.'

'Kinks?' said Felix.

'Aye. Ah may have bin exaggeratin' joost a wee bit when ah said we had fuel enough tae reach Karaz-a-Karak.'

'And what about Middenheim?'

Malakai shrugged his enormous shoulders. 'Joost a wee hop ower the mountain. But ah think ah can squeeze a wee bit moor oot o' these engines, joost a matter o' flyin' high enough. Ye can gan faster fur less at higher altitood where the air is thinner. It's ower ye're heads ahm sure, but the problem then is ye cannae see where ye're gaun and ye're flyin' on instruments.'

'And why is that a problem?' said Felix.

'Another kink. Ah cannae get the blasted compass to work, and if the compass willnae tell ye where ye're gaun then ye huv to descend tae take bearings and ye're back tae where ye started.'

'Is it a problem with the compass? Have you tried another one?'

'Aye, Master Jaeger,' said Malakai with an exasperated sigh. 'Ah tried another yin.'

'It's the polar vortex,' said Max softly, barely audible above the hum of the deckplates resonating with the engines. 'It's unstable, throwing out far more raw magic into the world than it should as the Chaos Wastes expand and great sorcerers pull it every which

way. I can see it all around me, and I suspect that's what under-
lies your problem as well.'

Felix considered the implications of that and found that they
were too large for him even to fully comprehend. Ocean-going
trade would undoubtedly become next to impossible, with devastating implications for cities like Altdorf and Marienburg. It
took him a moment to remember that both of those places had
already been destroyed. It was pointless to try and guess what
would happen after the war was won. First it had to *be* won and
that had never looked less likely. He wondered if this strange
magical dysfunction of the airship's navigational instruments
could in some way be responsible for the difficulties that Gotrek
had had finding his way through the Empire. He voiced his question out loud.

'Aye, mibbe. Put a dwarf's feet on the ground and he'll almost
always ken where he is. We donae think aboot it tae be honest.'

'Several races possess seemingly innate abilities that are supra-
natural in origin,' said Max. 'Greenskins would be a case in point.'

'We'll finish our tour oop top shall we?' said Malakai, grabbing a
rung and hauling his bulk up the ladder before Max could run on
into any further detail.

Felix had remembered correctly – the handrail that encircled the
dorsal spine was a heavy-duty iron bar that looked like it could
stand up to the charge of an Imperial steam tank, but had unfortunately been positioned at a height only halfway up his thighs.
Felix couldn't help but imagine how easy it would be to tip over
and fall a long, long, *long* way to the ground. The wind didn't help
matters. It was incredibly strong at this altitude and Felix had to
spread his feet along the corrugated metal walkway and bend into
it to avoid being blown over. He imagined there was nothing but

the wind between him and the Realm of Chaos and the thought of that left him queasier than any amount of vertigo.

He looked up from the latticework iron sheets that interlocked to make up the dorsal spine and saw Max and Malakai standing at the forward edge of the walkway. Max's robes blustered in the wind but the wizard himself seemed otherwise unmoved by it, as if the wind blew through him to interfere only with the clothes he wore. Malakai's crest pulled all over the place and his long coat snapped like a dog that had been left in a cage. The engineer did up the coat's front buttons and pulled down his goggles. Felix noticed that they had tiny cross-hairs inscribed on the lenses. Then Felix also noticed something else.

It was dawn.

The vast inverted bowl of the sky was a spectrum of colour running from deep black overhead through shades of purple and ever-lightening blues to a crisp morning white as Felix lowered his gaze to where the mountain peaks bit into the sky. So much for sleep, he thought with belated tiredness. He'd completely lost track of time in all the excitement after the ambush in the township. Bent against the wind, he joined the others at what felt to him a safe distance from the edge. As the sun rose nearer to the horizon, the darkness on the easternmost mountaintops became shadows that lengthened and narrowed before disappearing altogether as the summits were flooded with gold.

Beside him, he heard Max sigh. Felix had felt so confined within the pass, and before that in the forest, that it came as a shock to learn that the world was still out there.

Who would have thought that in a world riven by Chaos, such beauty could still exist above its clouds?

Felix swept his gaze across the enfolding dawn, and on every mountain that he looked at he saw evidence of re-wilded roads and

ancient structures. They were small things, little more than moun-
taineers' lodges and certainly nothing on the scale of the dwarfhold
he was standing over, but they seemed to be dotted throughout the
Middle Mountains. What could have brought such lasting indus-
try to a mountain range that everyone seemed to agree possessed
nothing of value but the glory of its sunrise?

'What are all these buildings?' he asked Malakai, sweeping his
arm across the horizon. 'Were they part of this dwarfhold at one
time?'

'Nae, Felix, this place wiz never sae grand. Those roads wur built
by adventurers that came after, lookin' fur Kazad Drengazi here in
the mountains.'

Felix felt his skin prickle and it had little to do with the wind. He
pulled his cloak over his chest regardless. 'Gotrek mentioned that
place. He said that it doesn't exist.'

'He's nae fool when he nae wants to be yin. He's right. It's naught
but a bairn's story.'

'Tell me more,' said Max in an urgent whisper that set Felix immediately back on edge. The wizard rested on his staff, the wind
whipping through the hem of his robes, as he looked out. Then
he raised one hand, palm out to the sun, bowed his head and
appeared to close his eyes. He stood like that for a moment. 'Something is out there. I hear it calling, but... not to me.'

Malakai stuck out his lower lip and turned to Felix with eyebrows
raised, apparently impressed or, if he was thinking what Felix was
thinking, chilled to his core. 'Then ye're already closer tae findin'
the danged place than anyain's come sae fur.'

'*Kazad* is the Khazalid noun for "fortress", is that not so?'

'Aye. Though ah'd ask how ye ken that.'

Max let the question ghost through him as though it didn't exist.
'And *Drengazi*?'

Malakai hesitated, and Felix understood why. The dwarfs were as protective of their language as they were of any of their secrets. Felix was a dwarf-friend, had been Gotrek's shadow for over twenty years, off and on, and had been privileged to visit several of their greatest cities and even he could barely string together a sentence in the elder tongue.

'Tell me,' Max pressed, insistent as the wind.

'Ah'm nae keepin' secrets, laddie, even though they're mine tae keep. It's joost there's nae guid translation fur it. It means *Slayer*, but even tha' isnae quite right. It's the yin Slayer. It's all Slayers.' Malakai shook his head. 'Like ah said, there just isnae a right fit fur it.'

The Fortress of the First Slayer, thought Felix. Why did that have such an ominous ring of inevitability to it? Even as he considered its meaning, the shadows that the dawn had just banished seemed to be creeping back, resembling the claws of some black horror scraping across the mountains' sides.

'And what is it?' Max asked.

'What dae ye lads ken aboot Grimnir's quest?'

Felix shook his head without turning away from his mountain view. Grimnir was said to be the first of the Slayers, the warrior god of the dwarfs who long before the dawn of man had sought to end forever the threat of Chaos by marching into the Wastes and sealing the Chaos Gate on the blade of his axe. It didn't seem to have worked.

'He left his people to journey alone into the Chaos Wastes,' said Max. 'As I understand it he intended to destroy the polar warp gates, to rid the world of magic and slay the Chaos Gods. Of course he didn't succeed, and some speculate that he is trapped somewhere outside of time in the Realm of Chaos, locked in eternal war against the daemons of Chaos, much as Caledor Dragontamer and the great elf mages of the same era were trapped upon the Isle of the Dead.'

'Ah wouldnae gae as far as tha', but aye, if ye like. He gie'd one o' his two mighty axes tae his son, Morgrim, and then went north. But naebody knows hoo far south the Wastes stretched in yon days, nor whit road north Grimnir took. Except Morgrim. And he ne'er spoke a word.'

'So what you're saying,' Felix began cautiously, thinking that he understood and not liking where it was heading, 'is that Grimnir himself might have once passed this way, thousands of years ago on his way to fight the Chaos Gods.'

'Some dwarfs think sae,' said Malakai with a shrug.

'I know so,' said Max with a conviction so absolute that if he demanded the sky turn red then Felix would have half expected it to do so. 'It is here and there is a power in it. It calls to Grimnir's heir for a resolution. The confluence of destiny has called us here together. I have never been more certain of anything.'

'Tha's the legend,' said Malakai, a little more cagily than he had begun, unnerved himself by the wizard's words and manner. 'It's said a great power is held there, waitin' fur Grimnir's heir tae use in the last Great War.'

'You're thinking it's Gotrek, aren't you?' Felix said, turning back to Max and shivering. The wizard was scanning the horizon with the intensity of a hawk, his flat grey eyes like coins dropped in a well too deep and dark to grant wishes.

'Everyone kens tha' Grimnir's heir is Thorgrim Grudgebearer, the High King. He has Morgrim's axe. Unless ye've stowed him in yin o' yer carts then ah reckon he's in the Everpeak aboot noo.'

'We will see,' Max murmured, possibly to himself.

Felix stepped back from the ledge, arms around his chest as he backed away, and shivered as he turned around and walked the few dozen strides to the opposite edge of the cupola overlooking the approach to the castle. It didn't help. Felix doubted whether anywhere in view of where he stood now would be far enough to escape the creeping chill of destiny that had wormed its way into his mind with the wizard's portentous words. How many tales of Sigmar's return, Valaya's fall, and the death of the elven forest did Felix need to hear before he could start to accept such insane suggestions without resistance?

Could Gotrek really be Grimnir's heir?

If what Malakai said was correct then no, but dwarfs were always so rigid in their interpretation of such things and perhaps the legend – the prophecy? – was intended to be read figuratively.

No.

They weren't here to find this Kazad Drengazi, they were going to Middenheim, and Felix doubted that even the Vengeful Ancestor himself would be able to change Gotrek's mind about it.

Felix winced as a spear of light from the castle's rune-hidden approach temporarily blinded him in one eye. He bent onto one knee and held the handrail as he peered down onto the mountain trail. He saw what looked like a string of glittering specks making its way towards the castle. He watched for a moment more, his heart seeming to slow as a handful of the nearest dots resolved into helms, spear points and banner poles. An army was coming. But surely that was impossible. Still gripping the handrail, he snapped his head around.

'Does this airship have any way of warning the castle of an attack?'

'Ah keep tellin' ye, there's nae Chaos army tha' can get oop yon road.'

'Purely speculatively,' said Felix.

'Well, aye, there's nae point wastin' a guid vantage like this. There's a steam horn tae alert the brig o' danger, but the workers doon below will all ken whit it means.'

'Good,' said Felix, turning back to the vertiginous view and tightening his grip. 'I have a terrible feeling that you might want to use that.'

ELEVEN

Last Dawn

Khagash-Fél sat high on his Chaos steed and regarded the citadel that the Dark Master would have him conquer. The ancient
stone ruin capped the mountaintop like a skull on a shaman's
staff. Tiered battlements rose in broken procession towards the
summit from which that strange metallic contraption floated like a
cloud, glittering in the morning sun. He watched as lookouts with
dew in their beards raised heavy, lensed devices to their eyes and
peered back towards him, shouting words he could not hear in a
language he did not understand. Khagash-Fél ignored them and
turned to the gate.

It was an imposing, albeit rusted construct of iron that he knew
from experience would be solid all the way through rather than
plated oak. The gate was further reinforced with horizontal bars,
bearing great spikes long enough to foul a battering ram or impale
a minotaur and inscribed with runes of protection and power.

In the shadow of the gate was a small courtyard, ringed with
weathered statues and large enough only for a few score men or
a handful of small war machines. A deep crevasse surrounded

the courtyard like a moat, spanned by a simple iron bridge that was little more than a flat length of metal with a handrail. There was not even a mechanism by which to raise it in case of attack. A small advantage. Before reaching even that choke point however, an army would be forced into almost single file by the narrowing causeway that wound sharply and steeply through the sheer walls of the mountain – and all while arrows and bolts and the gods alone knew what else hailed down from those battlements above.

In the Chaos Wastes, war was unlimited by scale or variety, but for men of the steppe, a fortification meant a hill too steep or rugged for a charging horse or at most a wooden palisade. The tribes' experience of siege warfare came largely from folk memory, their grandfathers' tales of once-in-a-generation campaigns against the Ogre Kingdoms or the great ziggurats of the Chaos dwarfs.

He raised his fist to signal a halt as he considered.

At his command the tribes gathered under their banners into hundred-strong units, his zarrs showing sufficient wit and experience to order their men into narrow-fronted units of four or five that would, at a push, be able to scale the final stretch of trail. Here and there, men in conical steel helmets with elaborately quilted brims delivered speeches that were greeted with roars and beaten shields. The ordered formations allowed more men to squeeze up, bringing dozens of banners and thousands of men into view between the mountains, but Khagash-Fél knew without having to see the thousands more hidden by the winding trail that the call to order would be passed down to them in moments. The air might be thin and the climes alien, but the endurance and courage of his people would see them conquer the edges of the earth and beyond.

The beastmen were another matter. They milled in the narrow gaps between the formations, stamping their hooves, bellowing challenges to the dwarfs and to each other. Gongs were clashed and great bells tolled, fetishes rattled and bones were cast as bray-shamans decked out in their most lavish hide robes presided over a dawn chorus of harsh animal cries and colour.

Khagash-Fél had already decided who would be first onto the bridge. He doubted whether he could restrain them for much longer if he wished to in any case.

'Have you ever seen warriors as disciplined as my people?' he said, calling back to the god-touched prophetess, Morzanna, who rode a pale steppe pony amongst his chosen warriors a respectful distance behind him. 'They fight and live in *arbans* of ten men. Each of those will come together in battle under the banner of their *zuuns* of a hundred, and the *minghaans* of a thousand.' He drew in a deep breath, proudly gesturing to the banner pole fixed to his backplate. 'None before I had united the tribes to command a *tumen* of tens of thousands.'

'The Chaos Gods abhor order in all its vagaries and forms,' said Morzanna, examining the zuuns, islands of armoured discipline in a rebellious sea of beasts, as if uncertain whether she preferred to sink or swim. 'Do you not find it strange that they demand it of their armies, that they should elevate champions capable of instilling it with an iron hand? If the map of our destinies is already drawn, then what place is there for Chaos?'

Khagash-Fél touched the lidded Eye on his forehead softly. He had some understanding of what it meant to see the future. It elevated a man, even as it changed him. He dismounted and closed his hand over the hilt of his sword, Ildezegtei, wrapped in the softest leather and the most sumptuous silks at his waist. He bared an inch of steel, enough to summon moans of wonder and lust from his chosen.

'I was a mortal man, brash and headstrong, leader of an arban of brothers and blood-kith, when the Chaos dwarfs tricked me into an ambush and took us.' He laid a finger across the concentric rings of scar tissue that covered the left side of his face. 'On that day I swore to never again lead men to defeat and since that day I never have. With the blessing of Khorne did I walk unharmed across the river of fire to my freedom, and with this blade and the gifts of the Greater Gods did I unite my people and claim my vengeance. Tell me where the Dark Master's rival lurks, Morzanna, and I will crush his skull in my bare hands as I once did to my captor.'

'I cannot tell you where he is. Only where he will face you.'

'How convenient,' muttered Nergüi from his own position further back amongst the chosen.

'Can you shatter the dwarfs' doors with your sorcery?' said Khagash-Fél, determined to give Morzanna the opportunity to prove her powers, and by extension those of the Dark Master, to men like Nergüi who struggled to cope with the pace of change. First the Greater Gods, then the Dark Master; what next?

Morzanna closed her eyes and bowed her head in the direction of the castle. The dwarfs there unhurriedly armed and armoured themselves as artillery pieces were pushed into position. 'I cannot,' she said after a moment had lapsed, opening her eyes and facing Khagash-Fél without apology. 'I sense the presence of a powerful wizard here. He works against me.'

'More powerful than you?' asked Nergüi with a smirk.

'Perhaps.' She bared her teeth in a sharp smile. 'I guarantee however that *he* will not interfere with *you* either.'

'She leads you down a black path, warlord,' said Nergüi, turning to Khagash-Fél and shaking his staff at the heavens. The shaman was magnificent in his bright, feathered headdress and flowing regalia. He glinted and chimed in the sunlight as though passing spirits alighted upon him to whisper their counsel. Seldom before now had Khagash-Fél doubted that they did. 'She has guided us onto the dwarfs' secret roads and for that I will offer her and her patron praise, but we can use these roads to strike at the city the westerners call Middenheim. It is what brought us here, warlord. We can add the tribes to the might of Archaon and you will rise to be the strongest of his right hands.'

Something in Khagash-Fél flared in anger at the mention of that particular name. Who was Archaon to him? He was a name, a myth borne east by Dolgan warbands. He was nothing but a pretender to the Everchosen Crown. He did not know where this knowledge came from but he *knew* it; there was none other than Be'lakor with the right and power to call Khagash-Fél his servant.

'Tell me where, Morzanna.'

The prophetess extended a clawed finger and pointed to the bridge.

Khagash-Fél nodded as he spun around and strode for the causeway, just as a mighty wail went up from the flying vessel moored at the castle's summit. The beastmen roared, taking it as a signal, and surged for the gate as one.

The dwarfs' last dawn was here.

Gotrek pulled his good eye from the rent in the greeting hall wall that he had been sizing up for repair and turned to where Gustav, Kolya, and a handful of other men waited with tools and wooden boards held underarm. The duty foreman eyed them distrustfully through deep-set eyes, thick arms wrapped around a step-ladder as though expecting one of the men to make off with it. The deep thunderblast of the steam horn reverberated between the standing columns, shaking dust off the gantries and causing the lighting to stutter even more than before.

'Doesn't look like that many.'

Gustav cocked his head towards the gate and listened to the

animal cries and stamping hooves. It sounded like hundreds, and he wished now that he'd followed Kolya's example and kept his weapon with him, but the dwarfs had all assured him that their fortress was secure and like a fool too tired to make his own mind up he'd taken them at their word. He'd sworn never to put himself at the mercy of another's judgement and yet here he was, back in the daemon's nest. Ignoring the dwarf master-builder's protestations, Gustav strode for his own section of wall and ripped its temporary canvas patch clear. What he saw made him gasp.

Hundreds of beastmen were swarming up the causeway towards the bridge, but worse even than that was the figure that strode amongst them.

Clad in a leering harness of battle-scarred black plate, his bare head towered over the tallest beastmen. Long grey hair hung across his broad shoulders and a braided grey beard lay like a tabard over his breastplate. His face was craggy and tattooed and looked to have been the focus of some insane artistry to leave it hellishly scarred. Blue light seeped under the lid of a third eye upon his forehead. In his hand he wielded a double-edged greatsword that looked to have been edged and fullered in gold. It sang a death song that was, like war itself, sickening to contemplate and behold and yet at the same time exhilarating beyond compare. The curve of its blade, the way it found the light, called to Gustav's heart. He moaned softly. It would be an experience of surpassing wonder to see that blade closer to, to feel it enter his torso and slide through his guts as it sang that elegy for him and him alone.

Gotrek's strong hand on his shoulder squeezed the alien feeling out of him.

'Nothing to see there, manling.'

'I...' Gustav shook his head as the sudden lust that had moved him ebbed away to be replaced by the lingering taste in the mind of something foul. 'I think you're right. Sigmar, it's the same war-band we saw outside Wolfenburg. They've followed. I thought you said it was impossible.'

'It is,' Gotrek answered flatly.

'Do you know what the wise woman says about things thought impossible?' said Kolya before Gustav and Gotrek's combined glares convinced him to shut his mouth.

'Will they be able to find their way to Middenheim from here?' Gustav yelled, some abiding insanity almost driving him to take the Slayer by the throat and shake an answer out of him.

'Not if they're all dead.'

Gustav retreated open-mouthed from the Slayer's slack-jawed, boneheaded lunacy and turned for support to Kolya and the others just as the foreman and most of the other dwarfs in the hall were starting to run for the stairs up. A disbelieving laugh burst its way out of him.

'So much for dwarf courage.'

The Slayer's open palm struck him like a shovel. For a split second Gustav blacked out, coming around to see the ceiling spinning as he stumbled back into a man's arms. His head filled with bells. A tooth dropped onto his tongue and he bent forwards to let it run out on a trickle of bloody drool.

'If you were meant to be clever, manling, the gods would've made you a whiny little elf. Be thankful I owe your uncle a debt.' Gotrek indicated the departing dwarfs with a dip of his crest and a grunt. 'They've gone to evacuate what secrets they can, and sabotage that which they can't,' he said, not exactly inspiring Gustav with confidence in their chances. Then he pointed to a tanned Kislevite with the salted look of a seaman, an Erengrad docker perhaps, garbed in a sleeveless wool shirt and brown breeches held up by a rope belt. 'You look like you want to see out the day. Get up those columns and start pulling that rigging down. It'll hold up better than the cow-skin they've got flapping over the holes in the wall at the moment.'

The man nodded and got to work as Gotrek set about distributing tools and duties and then sent men dashing to the walls bearing wooden planks and salvaged iron plates. As each lighting rig came down the hall grew dimmer, illuminated predominantly now by the sunlight spearing through the breaches. And then even that was diminished little by little as men covered them with iron, found holes and began to hammer.

'Are you mad?' Gustav wailed. 'We won't be able to see.'

Gotrek grinned. His yellow teeth gleamed until the last big hole was covered and the glow from the dwarf's rune-axe turned his face red.

'You'll see well enough when the wall comes down. Until then there's nothing to look at.'

From the cupola of *Unstoppable* the assembled multitudes of Chaos looked almost like a single monstrous entity. Men were indistinguishable from beasts, and the tongue of bodies extending along the causeway put Felix in mind of the curious ant-eating creature that he had once marvelled at in the jungles of Ind. The thought that he and his friends were the ants in this scenario was not at all reassuring. The wind whistled in Felix's ears, a thin mockery of the tumult that ensued below him. But even from this altitude, Felix could pick out the grey-haired giant in hulking Chaos armour that strode ahead of his hordes. With a crushing certainty Felix knew that this was the champion named Half-Ogre that Mann had spoken of and that Felix and Gotrek had spied in battle outside Wolfenburg.

The champion had been following them. But why? For what possible reason?

'Malakai, I'm so sorry,' Felix began, but the engineer had already dropped his backside onto the lip of the open hatch down and had his strong hands on the metal to feed himself in.

'Did ye gi' 'em a map? Then it isnae yer doin'. C'mon noo.'

Makaisson set his hands and feet onto the outside of the ladder's siderails and slid down into the gasbag. Felix ran for the hatch. The fortress was undermanned and ruined, but it was still a formidable proposition and any position held by Malakai Makaisson would not crack readily. He could still help Gustav and Gotrek if he hurried. He slid his legs into the hatch until his feet hit the rungs, then sought out Max. His throat tightened in fear.

A shadow closed about the wizard like a fist although Max, with a terrible effort that was writ into his face, held it at bay with a light that he appeared to force through the pores of his skin.

'Go, Felix,' said Max, clutching his staff and groaning as he dredged more and brighter light until he glowed like a lightning rod in a storm.

The shadow menaced and swirled, formless by its very nature, yet possessed of a substance of will that Felix felt in his soul that he recognised, some shared darkness in the common nature of man. He saw the hint of wings, the spectre of a horned, crowned head. Felix's limbs felt dead. A paralysing terror filled him and made him want to do nothing more than scream and jump into the hatch after Malakai, and in the same mental breath mocked his singular failure to muster even that much courage. It was unnatural to feel such potent dread, he knew, but that knowledge made it no less debilitating. It was the same shadow that had hung on his shoulder since his first return to the Empire. It had stalked him through the Great Forest, closed over the Middle Mountains like a net, and now it was here.

'Go!'

Max's yell dragged Felix out of his stupor, though whether it was the work of the wizard's voice or the purifying rays that shone through the daemonic mist that enveloped him Felix could not be sure. 'There is a powerful sorceress down there. She is attempting to summon a daemon.' The wizard groaned, a pulse of white light driving back the struggling daemon another inch. 'Go and find Gotrek. Help him. Find Kazad Drengazi. You can do nothing for me here.'

For a moment, Felix still couldn't move. Light and dark churned over one another before his eyes. He gripped the hilt of his sword and then let it go.

Max was right.

He wasn't a wizard or a scholar – this was not a battle he was equipped to fight.

'Don't die, Max,' he shouted, as he slid into the shaft, for some inexplicable reason closed the hatch after him, and then slid down after Makaisson.

The first rocket corkscrewed out from the battlements on a geyser of black smoke before exploding against the mountainside. Rubble rained down onto the causeway and the beastmen charging up it, the near miss goading them to ever greater urgency as they raced for the bridge. The dwarf gunners made minute adjustments for range, declination and speed and waited as the beastmen roared onto the final ascent. The order to fire boomed from the ramparts like a handgun volley.

Khagash-Fél watched from their rear ranks as the front of the castle went up like a powder keg stuffed with Cathayan fireworks. Rockets hissed skyward trailing multicoloured plumes of smoke. Mortar rounds screamed like the damned. Gatling cannons chattered. Lead bullets tore beastmen to shreds by the dozen, firing lines tracking back and forth across the narrow rank even as the explosive munitions streaking down from above pulverised the path and reduced the piled corpses to ash. Khagash-Fél strode through it, his eye on the bridge. A mortar shell detonated in midair, showering him with gobbets of fire. All around him, beastmen lowed in agony and rolled amongst the corpses of their brethren as their fur burned away to muscle and bone. Khagash-Fél's flesh turned red and molten where the fiery substance burned. No weapon of fire or born of fire could harm him. Such was the Blood God's gift to him. A cannon added its own deep voice. Khagash-Fél felt the thin air breathe in as the lead shot sailed past him and crashed through the packed ranks of beastmen behind him.

He emerged from the firestorm glowing hot. His armour steamed. The runes that marked it shone a fierce gold and the dead-eyed daemon faces that decorated the ancient plates appeared to come alive and writhe in torment on the fire. He saw one of the dwarf gunners point at him and yell and angle his weapon downwards. Not to Khagash-Fél, he realised, but a point further up the trail.

The bridge.

The dwarfs meant to deny him the bridge and the battle promised him in prophecy.

Anger flooded his belly. He felt his stomach bloat and the furious beat of tiny wings against the underside of his throat. His vision reddened as he fixed his gaze on the dwarf and his craven engine of death. Nurgle had filled his gut with his ravenous children and Khorne had remade him in fire, but the Dark Master had shown him something greater, the uniting power of a pariah.

Khagash-Fél retched as if he was about to be sick, flies filling his throat and swarming into his nose and mouth. As each plague-mottled insect passed his lips it ignited with the fury of a god scorned and struck towards the battlements. Thousands of tiny explosions rippled across the front of the castle, triggering secondary detonations as the maddened insects bored into powder kegs. An engineer ran the full length of the ramparts, fumbling with his ammunition belt before it exploded, throwing his remains over a cannon and igniting it, the resulting blast flipping the war machine onto its back and flaying its crew with fire. The last explosion drove a great crack through the wall of the castle from the cannon batteries on the uppermost ramparts down to the gate itself, practically splitting the old dwarfhold in two.

Injured dwarfs cried out in pain and horror. Fires crackled behind savage breaches in the wall.

Crunching on the handful of flies still trapped between his teeth and swallowing them, Khagash-Fél brandished Ildezegtei to the crippled fortress and its defenders. With the exultant roar of his beastmen filling one ear and the blessings of the Dark Master in the other, he took the last steps towards his destiny.

Gustav Jaeger coughed on the tidal wave of dust that the rupture in the ceiling brought down into the greeting hall. Columns that had been teetering since before the dawn of man came crashing down. Distant explosions resounded through the stonework, men and dwarfs armoured in rock dust adding a paltry rejoinder as they returned fire from gaping breaches with pistols and crossbows. Having experienced merely second-hand the fate of the dwarfs' artillery, Gustav almost wished they wouldn't bother.

At least Gotrek's punch had dazed him enough to deaden the worst of the impacts.

He stumbled towards the gate. The damage done to the surrounding wall had buckled its frame and left it hanging on its hinges. He moved with the vague idea of bracing it with something, although he had no good idea how or with what. He certainly wasn't strong enough to move even the smallest chunk of the debris that littered the hall and would have been unable to identify the tool for doing so if it were presented to him. He sought out Gotrek, spotting the dwarf under a cloud of dust by the damaged gate.

He had never understood his uncle's fondness for this particular Slayer. His race was as alien as any other, and few amongst those other races that Gustav had encountered were more terrifying in their strangeness than Gotrek Gurnisson. Shrouded by the smoke of war, he looked like a barbarian of the Unberogen days, a mass of muscle girded for battle in woad. But Gustav doubted whether any warrior-king of Sigmar's blood had been as broad of shoulder or thick of neck as Gotrek. He was inhuman. His axe highlighted the muscular distinction in blood red. Gustav had never seen it glow so brightly. The light smeared through the murk and pooled within the runic engravings in the gate.

'Back to the airship, manling, and make sure your uncle is on it when it leaves. And tell Makaisson if I see him flying anywhere but north to Middenheim then I'll be coming for him next.'

'We'll all go,' Gustav yelled, trying not sound as relieved by the task as he felt.

'No time,' Gotrek returned, turning around and kicking the broken gate out onto a scene of ash and thunder. Smoke lay over the courtyard and hung above its statues like laurels. Animal screams echoed between them. The bridge was black and hazed, but Gustav saw the infernal outline of something large and hot approaching from its far side. 'The bridge is narrower than the gate. I'll hold them there.'

The Slayer glanced over his shoulder, silhouetted in fire as Gustav instinctively backed away from the approach of whatever daemonic being threw out that glare.

'Tell the little one that this was for her this time, not for me. Promise on your oath that you'll tell her that.'

Felix landed in the metal hallway to find Malakai Makaisson halfway down the corridor waiting for him. The thrum of the engines had increased to a level that Felix could feel vibrating through the iron rungs of the ladder in his hands, the rattling of bulkheads only serving to heighten the engineer's agitation.

'What kept ye?' Makaisson barked, then snapped up a hand. 'Ne'er mind. There isnae time tae hear it. Ah huv tae to git tae the engine room tae coax this bucket o' spare parts tae fly without comin' apart from under oor feet. Ye ah need on the brig. Ye dae remember how tae fly this thing, ah hope?'

'Fly? Fly where? We have to get down there.'

'Ah'd expect nae less o' ye, but ah heard there wiz nae oath between ye noo.'

Felix gripped the ladder's siderail. Perhaps he had allowed Max to get inside his head, but his relationship with Gotrek had become less and less about that decades-old oath. Perhaps for Gotrek that was what still mattered, but if Felix was honest with himself then that was not the reason he had followed the Slayer for as long as he had. It had been an adventure at first and that had been reason enough, but somewhere along the way he had come to remain because he had felt that he should.

He knew exactly when he had come to that belief, too – he had been here aboard the old *Spirit of Grungni*, coming circuitously but inevitably to the decision to join Gotrek's quest into the Chaos Wastes, easily the most dangerous realm in this world. And why? He had been told it was his own decision, that no oath bound him to follow, and yet he had done so, because he had felt the hand of destiny on the Slayer's path. He still felt that he had earned his own chance at happiness, and Kat certainly had, but if he was offered the opportunity to leave the Slayer and this life again he was not sure what he would do. The world seemed to have other plans for them all.

Max was right. Felix didn't like to believe it, but he was right.

'Come on,' said Malakai, glancing over his shoulder and then starting back towards Felix as though intending to drag him to the bridge. 'There's nae way back, laddie. The tower will be filled wi' parts coomin' up and engineers gaun doon. Ah willnae let some Chaos beastie get a hold o' ma airship. I'd destroy her first. Gotrek wiz an engineer, he'd agree wi' me.'

Felix groaned. No way down. The bridge. Why did that niggle at something in Felix's mind?

Like a bolt to the back of the head it came to him. He opened his mouth to say something, then decided there was no time for it, and was spinning on his heel before his lips clamped shut and running down the corridor, with his scabbard whipping at his heels and Makaisson yelling after him.

'Where are ye gaun? The brig's the other way. Felix!'

The engineer's cries disappeared around a bend as Felix pushed his old legs for one last sprint, taking turns without needing to think about them as though he had lived aboard the *Unstoppable* all his life. The engines chuntered and groaned. The decking rattled like the armour of a charging horse.

Every so often after running past dozens of empty doorways, he passed a room where dwarf engineers worked frantically, sometimes with only their feet exposed beneath huge pieces of machinery. Felix saw shock on their faces at seeing a human running about on their airship in the instant before they flashed out of view and he ran on. Any moment, he half expected to hear a challenge or feel a crossbow bolt in the back. None came. Either the dwarfs were simply too busy, or bad news like Felix Jaeger moved as quickly through a dwarf host as it did amongst men.

At the end of a short corridor, he hurtled through an open doorway and onto a gantry overlooking a large hangar.

The gyrocopter hangar.

He slammed into the handrail, causing the whole structure to shake alarmingly, then pulled himself left for one more short run to the ladder. He staggered up to it, wheezing, and folded over the handrail. It was the air. He couldn't seem to catch enough of it. Oh yes, and he had skipped a night's sleep, hadn't eaten since Shallya alone remembered when, and should have had enough of this sort of thing twenty years ago. But apart from that...

He took a deep breath and swung himself over the ladder. As Malakai had done before him, he positioned his hands against the outside of the siderails as though they were the wheels of a mine cart on their track, then took his feet off the rung and slid to the bottom level of the hangar.

Allowing his racing heart the moment it needed, he looked around. In agreement with his earlier assessment, the eight or nine gyrocopters within the luminously marked bays looked to have been functionally if not completely disassembled. Steel plates had been removed from the vehicles' fuselages, likely for use on *Unstoppable*, revealing the engines' gleaming innards. At least half of them were missing rotors and the one nearest to Felix had even had the pilot's seat stripped from the cockpit along with most of the controls. It seemed hopeless to expect to find anything in here that would fly, but Felix knew dwarfs too well for that. They were a pragmatic people and if there was a reason for carrying a flight of gyrocopters in the first place, then Makaisson and his engineers would want to keep at least one operational against such an eventuality.

He grinned when he found it and would have beat the air with his fist and whooped in jubilation had he the energy. The gyrocopter was parked in the bay nearest to the aft doors and furthest from the walkway, hence the reason that Felix had not spotted it immediately. Its nose section was embossed with the snarling visage of a god that Felix presumed to be Grimnir depicted in brass. The blades of its main rotor hung limp. The flying machine was secured to the deck by a series of leather straps looped between its landing skids and the mooring rings bolted to the floor. The ground within the marked bay looked as though it had been recently swept, and the fuselage smelled freshly oiled and polished and felt smooth to the touch.

With the growing fear that he would actually have to go through with what he had been thinking, Felix moved around the gyrocopter, unfastening the straps so that they hung slack over its skids, and then climbed into the cockpit.

The leather seat softened around his weight as Felix scanned the controls. He had never flown one of these things himself, but he must have seen it done dozens of times. It had not looked that difficult when the earnest young scholar Varek Forkbeard had first talked him through the terrifying complexity of onboard gauges, dials, and controls, but now it felt as if they were multiplying before his very eyes. He closed his eyes and tried to relax into it. Most of them didn't matter. If the vehicle was low on fuel then he would find out soon enough and there was very little he could do about it anyway.

Between his awkwardly bent knees was a leather-bound stick. This controlled the angle of the main rotor to give movement either left, right, forward, or back. There was also a trigger just above the grip that controlled the gyrocopter's main armament, the narrow-muzzled steam cannon that projected from the brass figurehead's mouth. Felix had no idea whether it would fire if he pressed it and decided that he should probably leave it alone. With his left hand he located the other stick just outside his leg. He squeezed it as he concentrated, playing with the foot pedals that responded by pulling the tailfin left or right depending on which pedal he pushed. It was a profoundly terrifying sensation. Carefully, he let go of the left-hand stick. Yes, he remembered now, that one was responsible for lift.

Now he just needed to figure out how to start it.

Oddly enough, when he had flown in these machines before it had always been in some kind of a hurry.

He ran his finger over the control panel, trying to ignore the nagging voice that demanded he start pushing likely looking buttons and instead to remember what Varek had taught him. There! His finger hovered over a blue button marked with a strange rune and positioned between two glass-fronted gauges. It looked familiar, and it felt like the right position for it.

He hesitated a moment, then pushed it and held it pressed. A rapid string of clicks sounded from behind the control panel and the entire gyrocopter juddered into life as its fuel ignited. The assorted dials arrowed into the red and then slid back into more equitable zones. Felix's heart reluctantly climbed down from his mouth. What maniac had designed them to do that? With a slow but rising rhythm of *whumps* the rotor blades began to turn. Felix hurriedly set about strapping himself in, only to glance up and realise in a moment of horror that he had neglected to open the hangar door.

Ducking low in his seat to avoid the whirring blades despite the fact that they were a good distance above his head, he cast about for the mechanism to open the outer door. He found it – or at least what looked like it – further back against the forward bulkhead.

It was a slanted metal bench inset with knobs and dials and the wall behind it was hung with netting, presumably for whoever was working at that station to hold onto if necessary.

Abandoning the gyrocopter, he ran towards the control station.

Amongst the assorted gauges there was one large lever with a pair of angry-looking red runes displayed beneath it. Felix looked at the hangar door and then back to the lever. It had to be it. It had to be. With a prayer to whatever god looked after men this far above the ground, he took it in both hands and pulled it.

There was a meaty *clank*, then another, the sound of a chain being paid out somewhere beneath the deck, and the door began to open.

Black smoke boiled in and with it came screams. At the same time, *Unstoppable* groaned like an old soldier in pain, the drone of her engines blasting through the open doors.

The unpiloted gyrocopter had risen to almost head height, and Felix huffed back aft, grabbed a hold of its teasingly swaying landing skids with a running jump and hauled himself back into the cockpit. He took one of the seat straps, then cast it aside in favour of the control sticks, pushing down the left-hand stick to arrest the gyrocopter's climb. His stomach leapt and then bottomed out and Felix feared for a moment that he was definitely going to be sick, but then the craft appeared to stabilise itself.

The gyrocopter hovered, yawing truculently in every direction despite his ashen-faced intent to keep it still. He took a deep breath. He could do this. It really wasn't so hard.

Easing the main stick down caused the gyrocopter to tilt forward and shoot through the hangar doors like a crossbow bolt.

Acrid smoke whipped across Felix's face and he looked down to see the dwarfhold broken up and lit by hellish fires. Dwarfs in armour emerged onto the top battlement of the castle bearing crates full of scorched equipment, jostling with the scores already waiting for the elevator at the foot of the metal tower. True to Makaisson's word the elevator was steaming down from the airship with a complement of engineers crammed inside. More waited at the top. A handful of dwarfs with bulging backpacks scaled the tower's ladders like ants climbing up a tree. Felix picked out the taller figure of Gustav amidst their number and felt a surge of relief that his nephew was far from the fierce fighting at the castle's gates. The feeling didn't last long.

Screaming, Felix grappled the gyrocopter over a raised corner turret and then plunged into a stomach-lurching turn that sent the flying machine chopping into the thick smoke that pumped out of the front of the castle.

The gyrocopter rattled under the pressures of conflicting air currents and his own inexpert handling as he struggled to bring it down. Part of him desperately wanted to slow down, but the louder and terrifyingly cogent part told him that the one thing he wanted to be inside even less than this gyrocopter was a stalled gyrocopter plummeting towards the ground. He held steady on the stick and in fewer heartbeats than Felix dared to count he was through the smoke cloud and soaring over the causeway.

Rabid beastmen swarmed up the trail and behind them came northmen in unusual conical helms and eastern-style armour. They advanced with a discipline that an Imperial force of half the size would have been proud to achieve: armoured infantry pushing up behind the beastman screen, followed by what looked even from Felix's rare vantage to be a numberless horde of mounted bowmen.

An arrow thumped against the underside of the fuselage and another whistled past his eyes to be carved into splinters by the gyrocopter's rotor blades. The gyrocopter's armour was thickest on its underside – that being the conventional direction of attack – but the mere fact that the northmen's weapons were able to strike him at all at this range and speed disinclined him towards taking chances with their capabilities.

Felix brought the nose around to the left and then swung back to the right to double back and descend.

He was getting the hang of this now. It was simply a matter of looking far enough ahead that he could ease the flying machine along its course without needing to resort to rash tugs on the stick. The dusty smog rising from the causeway below him made that difficult, but with a little concentration not impossible.

After a few seconds he realised that he must have passed within range of the citadel's guns. The cloud he was struggling to see through was rising from what was left of the road. The mountain face it wound through had been blasted away and the rubble piled onto the road. Bits of beastman poked through the rocks, serving as handholds to their monstrous kin as they clambered over, determined as ever to close with their enemy.

The gyrocopter whirred over the scree pile and into view of the castle. Its gate was wide open and the wall breached in numerous places, but Felix could still see men and dwarfs firing from within. The courtyard however was empty except for statues and Felix soon saw why.

Gotrek and the huge Chaos warrior blocked the bridge with a battle of such ferocious intensity that it made the spinning blades of his flying machine appear sluggish by comparison. The Slayer's axe left ruddy streaks in the air behind it, its runes glowing hot enough to burn, only for the long, undulating blade of the Chaos warrior to sashay across every blow and beneath every guard. Felix couldn't say how the warrior was doing it, but every time it looked as though Gotrek was about to land a telling blow the Chaos warrior would inexplicably alter his approach, closing the opening and sending another stroke carving across the Slayer's arms, wrists, and chest. Gotrek bled like a gutted sow. And with the regularity of a beating heart a pulse of blue light washed out from the startling eye on the champion's forehead to cleanse the air of its rune-cut scars.

Gotrek angrily waved Felix off as the gyrocopter swept over the dwarf's head and around.

Felix could see that the beastmen too were standing off, unwilling to interfere in their champion's battle or simply too afraid to do so, and for that Felix didn't blame them. The defenders on the other side of the bridge were not nearly so shy, firing from the cover of the castle with pistols and bows and pitching dozens of beastmen into the chasm to their distant dooms. Bullets rattled off the Chaos warrior's broad shoulders like coins flung at a steam tank. Felix even saw one mark a direct hit on the champion's fiery red cheek only to ricochet off in a welter of sparks and shave the side of Gotrek's scalp. Gotrek roared, blisters popping up across his head, and struck a wild, upward-arcing blow with his axe.

A pulse of sapphire bathed the Half-Ogre's face and time seemed to hold its breath.

Felix watched as the Half-Ogre managed to twist, pull himself out of the way, and then slam his elbow joint into the back of Gotrek's neck as the Slayer stumbled across his body. The Chaos warrior then avoided Gotrek's backswing as if he had read the dwarf's mind, and in the same fluid motion hauled Gotrek back across him by the roots of his crest and punched the hilt of his sword into the Slayer's nose. Blood spattered the warrior's bare fist, where it boiled. Gotrek staggered and yelled like a drunk, the Chaos warrior shoving him back and hitting him again, hard enough this time to snap the Slayer's face around and lump him to the ground.

Could Max have been wrong after all? Was Felix witnessing

Gotrek's long overdue doom at last? The Half-Ogre looked up and smirked as Felix bore down. Felix saw something in his eyes: a kind of recognition, anticipation even.

Without thinking about what he was doing, Felix pushed down the stick to accelerate and squeezed on the trigger as though he meant to crush the stick in his bare hands and tear it from the gyro-copter's cockpit. His concerns over the weapon's functionality were erased in a jet of superheated steam that hissed above Gotrek's recumbent form and struck the Chaos champion's armoured torso. The warrior and the bridge behind him disappeared under a wave of steam, the beastmen on the far side screaming in agony as the blast from the steam cannon boiled them alive. Felix held the trigger down until the gyrocopter had swept over the bridge again and was banking back around.

Steam lifted from the iron bridge to reveal several blistered bodies. The Chaos warrior stood amongst them with cracked armour and furnace-red skin, turning towards Felix and raising a hand as if to beckon him down. Behind him, Gotrek sat up unsteadily, brushed a hand through his scorched crest and spat a gobbet of blood off the side of the bridge. Felix swore. It looked like he was going to have to land. He would have to...

The bewildering array of controls before him expanded to fill his view. He regarded it with a sinking feeling.

Ah, spoke the dry voice of his subconscious, *we appear to have uncovered a fundamental gap in our knowledge of gyrocopter operation.*

Teeth gritted, he angled the gyrocopter's nose down until the muzzle of the steam cannon was centred on the Half-Ogre's chest. The Chaos warrior spread his arms as if inviting another try. The champion had been able to predict and counter Gotrek's every move, but now he just stood there as Felix's flying machine powered towards him. Gotrek roared for Felix to turn aside and then, when it dawned on the Slayer what Felix was planning, grabbed his axe off the ground and ran for the courtyard. He threw himself to the ground and covered his head under his arms. The Chaos warrior merely grinned.

Felix could only assume that this course was too mad even for one touched by the Dark Powers to imagine.

Counting his luck that he'd been too distracted with steering to properly strap himself in, Felix waited until the last moment and then leapt from the cockpit.

Felix's flying body barrelled over the warrior's head. The champion roared in disbelief for the second before the gyrocopter crashed through him, driving him down into the bridge like a nail struck by a hammer. The gyrocopter's fuselage crumpled as it ground into the iron edifice, rotor blades shearing off one by one. The ancient structure squealed under the punishment. Felix hit the ground, intending to roll, but instead landing on his back and bouncing clear as the vehicle's fuel tank exploded, swallowing the bridge in a massive fireball.

Felix kept his head buried as bits of metal peppered his mail, uncovering his face only as the fireball roared itself out to reveal a mangled ruin of blasted iron in its wake. Its final scream ringing in his ears, Felix staggered up and moved towards the torn mess that projected from the near side of the chasm. Beastmen raged impotently on the opposite side, a kaleidoscope of animal faces and whining noise. Felix blinked and covered his ears but neither seemed to help. He swayed on his feet. That calm, forever helpful inner voice advised him that he had probably taken a blow to the head and should sit down.

He groaned. Slim chance of that.

A tattooed hand clung to a spear of metal. The flesh looked

ancient, splotched with liver spots and faded ink, but a gnarled old oak had never held the earth between its roots more tightly. The warrior was still alive! Where did the Chaos Gods find these champions? The man's feet kicked over an abyss. The strands of his long grey mane tapered and burned.

The bridge creaked alarmingly as Felix stepped onto it and drew his sword.

'Your doom is foretold,' the warrior snarled, swinging his free hand for a better hold that wasn't there. His face was one of cold contempt, but his accent was familiar, similar to those of the barbarous horse tribes that plagued the steppe between the Worlds Edge and the Mountains of Mourn. Felix had been given cause to rue their horsemanship and suicidal bravery more than once during his near-fatal journey to the lands of the Far East. 'The Dark Master will allow only one victor here.'

'If I had a penny for every doom I'd been promised then I'd be High King of the dwarfs by now.' Gotrek stomped carelessly onto the bridge stump. There was a juddering squeal and the Chaos warrior's handhold pitched him ever further towards oblivion. Gotrek raised his axe two-handed over the warrior's wrist.

'I am a favourite of the gods, painted one. No weapon touched by fire in its making can harm me.'

'Is that right?' Gotrek brought his enormous axe to his one good eye as though considering testing the champion's words, then stamped his heel onto the warrior's fingers.

Bones crunched, but no pain showed on the warrior's face, just a flicker of defiance in his human, seeing eye as Gotrek ground his foot forward and kicked out, pushing the Chaos warrior's broken hand out into empty air. The man flailed in hard-faced silence, a fierce lament going up from the beastmen as they rushed like stampeding cattle for the ledge to watch their champion fall, but not once did the warrior scream. Felix held the man's gaze, then watched him disappear.

Several seconds later, a final *bang* from the bottom of the gorge startled him from his vigil.

Gotrek put a heavy hand on his shoulder. Felix suspected it was less about offering comfort than it was borrowing a little support. The Slayer's jaw was blue, his face was bleeding, and Felix didn't like to think how close his former companion had just been to death. If he had been a minute slower in coming to Gotrek's aid, if he had acted differently in just the slightest way, then it would probably be the both of them down there at the foot of the mountain now. The very idea offended him in a way he could not adequately explain even to himself.

It was a feeling.

The Slayer's doom was coming, of that Felix had never been more certain, but whenever and however it came he was convinced that it would be an act that shaped the outcome of the End Times.

For good or ill.

Gotrek found strength to hawk up a gobbet of phlegm and send it arcing across the chasm towards the beastmen stranded on the far side. It fell well short, but it seemed to give the dwarf some pleasure.

'If Makaisson should ask,' he said, the burning wreckage that lay strewn all over the courtyard glittering in his one good eye, 'we'll tell him it was an accident.'

Khagash-Fél lay broken on the rocks. Beastmen, beaten into still, submissive shapes, were draped over the mountainside, their bloodied bodies glittering with bits of metal in the narrow shaft of light. The break in the chasm, coming far above after what looked like leagues of sheer, mountainous black, looked like a mouth and

Khagash-Fél felt as though he had been swallowed by some mythical beast.

How could this have happened?

He was the Fire of Zharr, the Eagle of Mourn, the Plague of Yusak and the Delighter in Blood. He had slaughtered daemons and champions by the hundred over decades he had long lost count of. The Dark Master had chosen him for the destruction of his enemy; his prophetess had guided his sword. He bared his teeth, conquering the weakness that would have him scream at the broken bones that simple action upset, and tried to rise.

He would not fail!

'Be still, Half-Ogre, your servitude is done.'

Morzanna crouched over him. Her claws pushed lightly upon his breastplate like a child seeking to hold down a bull. With a coarse groan, Khagash-Fél dropped back onto his bier of rocks. He tightened his eyes for a moment and snarled.

'You saw this. You knew how this battle would end and you let me fight anyway. Why?'

The prophetess smiled sadly. Her eyes glittered softly under the distant light. 'When you understand that, you will know what it means to tie your destiny to one as mighty as Be'lakor's.'

Khagash-Fél tilted his head back to face the light. As a youth, he had once scaled a mountain this high and almost as steep to raid an eagle's nest for an egg to present to his father. Even then his feats had been legend. It was an almost impossible climb up. Or down.

'You are not here,' he said simply.

'Your mind dreams the ultimate dream, Terror of the East, but I am here with you.' The woman spoke with a genuine sorrow. 'Such is my gift.'

'I will not beg for my life.'

'You are brave. You deserved a more caring master.'

The woman glanced to the deep shadows where beastmen lay like basking birds on the rocks. A figure whispered out of the darkness. His feathered robes fluttered and chimed in a breeze that Khagash-Fél could not feel. His bone clogs struck the earth with a rhythm eerily reminiscent of the one played on funerary sticks for the passing of Khamgiin Lastborn.

'You gave your life for the Dark Master,' said Nergüi, headdress rustling as he crouched. His weathered face was wide with awe. 'All the tribes speak of your sacrifice. They will serve to the last man. As will I. Forgive me, warlord, that I did not see until now.'

'No,' Khagash-Fél snarled, for the first time in his life seeing with the clarity of a dead man. He had been used until he was useless, and now it was the turn of his people. 'Take my sword. Lead the people to Middenheim and the horde of Archaon as you asked of me. The tribes are not the Dark Master's to destroy.'

Ignoring him, Nergüi rose and turned to face Morzanna. The shaman bowed his head and handed her his staff. Glass beads and bright blue feathers abased themselves around its eagle-skull tip as she wrapped her claws around it.

'Obey me!'

'You are speaking to a ghost, Half-Ogre. He cannot heed you.'

With that, Morzanna whipped her claws across the shaman's throat. Air escaped in a hiss, bubbling through the rush of blood that, despite his words of consent, Nergüi sought instinctively to staunch. His dimming eyes found those of his warlord. Blood spurted between his fingers as he tried to work his tongue, but somehow Khagash-Fél heard every word.

'*You did this.*'

The blood on Morzanna's hands was turning black and rising off her like smoke. A similar substance was gushing out of Nergüi's throat and mouth, enwrapping his body like a shroud and lifting it off the ground on huge, bat-like wings. The deep laughter of the blackest of gods rippled through the hardening cloud.

'The airship of the dwarfs is swift,' said Morzanna, voice strained with the effort of channelling the primeval horror she would unleash upon the world. 'But the wrath of Be'lakor has no limit.'

TWELVE

Flight

The wide leather chair aboard the bridge of *Unstoppable* was more comfortable than any bed Felix had ever lain in. At least it certainly felt like it just then. The vibrations of the deckplate seemed to massage the aches from his body. The low hum of the engines was a lullaby. The way whips of cloud struck across the forward window felt like the airborne equivalent of drawing a blanket over one's head. Even the bickering of the dwarfs felt soothing in its familiarity.

'This isn't the way to Middenheim,' said Gotrek, standing directly in front of the window with his arms across his chest and glaring belligerently into the clouds.

'That's cause we're gaun tae Karaz-a-Karak,' Makaisson snapped back. He had his coat buckled and the fur-lined collar pulled up. His goggles had been pulled down over his eyes and he gripped the wheel with thick, fingerless leather gloves, standing on tip-toes in order to see over Gotrek's shoulders.

What they both hoped to see through such thick grey cloud Felix couldn't imagine.

'You didn't have enough fuel to reach the Worlds Edge Mountains and you certainly don't now you've got a belly full of men to weigh you down.'

'At least ah huv yin less gyrocopter tae worry aboot,' said Makaisson with a sideways tilt of that fierce, goggled head towards Felix. 'But if ye can git us tae Middenheim withoot a compass then ahm all ears.'

Gotrek snorted. 'I am a compass.'

'Ah know ye think sae, but ye really arnae.'

Sensing an argument with no quick resolution and that Felix could not seem to trouble himself with the outcome of, he moved his gaze over *Unstoppable*'s bridge. Dwarf engineers moved purposefully between stations, arguing quietly in Khazalid. One had a section of deckplate off and appeared to be applying solder to the steering shaft even as Malakai flew. Dwarfs were never the most extroverted with their emotions, but they all looked worried to Felix.

'How are you feeling?' said Max. The wizard stood over him, unhooded. Bone-grey flecks silvered his hair and beard. His colourless flesh creased with concern.

'I should ask you that.'

'I was a wizard of the Light,' asked Max, smiling for the first time in an age. 'That was not the first daemon I have been called upon to banish, although it was certainly the strongest. I am fine, Felix, as I see you are. I suggest you get some rest now while you are still able.'

Felix rubbed his eyes and yawned. 'Gustav and the other men? Did they make it aboard?'

'Yes. Malakai was ready to leave them behind, but by destroying the bridge you bought time to evacuate the fortress. You're a hero.'

'You get used to it,' Felix muttered drowsily.

'Felix.'

'Mmmm?'

'It's coming together, don't you see? Do you remember the dream I told you about in which I was flying?'

It took Felix a moment to respond. His lids hung heavily over his eyes and his own body felt like a ponderous, distant thing. 'Didn't we all die in that dream?'

He was asleep before Max could answer.

Tall, slender pines rose out of the snow like the bars of a cage. A broken wind plucked the strings of the spiders' webs that hung between the boles, trapped dew dazzling like jewels with reflected light. Felix's presence here in this boreal wood disorientated him only for a moment, then he drew his cloak tightly about himself and blew on his gloved hands. A red squirrel bound in a silk cocoon hung from a branch, turning gently in the breeze. Felix's breath misted in front of him, decorating the lattice of delicate webs strung up across the trail. His hand strayed to the hilt of his sword. The forest was dark and eerily quiet. The only sound to intrude upon it was the crunch of snow under his boots, and those of his companion.

'Hurry along there, young Felix. Snorri thinks he saw something up ahead and he doesn't want it to get away.'

'What are we looking for?'

The hugely muscled dwarf turned around and shrugged. He was bigger even than Gotrek, a little shorter but broader at the shoulder with arms thick enough to grapple down a charging bull in each hand. Tattoos covered his bulk. His short beard was dyed red, but in place of a Slayer crest a line of nails with colourfully painted heads had been hammered into his skull. He pawed at his cauliflower ear, abashed.

'Snorri was hoping you remembered. His head feels funny.'

Felix's breath caught as he noticed the horrible red scar that split the middle of the Slayer's forehead from the bridge of his nose to the base of his crest of nails. It looked like someone had hewn into his skull with an axe.

For a moment, Felix had the sickening memory of Snorri Nose-biter on his knees, staring up with a face flooded with tears to the starmetal axe coming for his shame.

This is the Shirokij, came a lilting female voice in his mind. *Your path was laid here.*

Felix shook off the feeling with a shiver as Snorri shrugged and carried on.

The Trollslayer hefted his axe and hammer and peered into the trees. Felix drew his sword as silently as he could. He glanced up, convinced he had heard a faint chittering from that direction. The branches swayed, flecking his bare cheeks with snowflakes. A bird, he thought, though he could not remember seeing one.

'Did you hear something?'

Snorri turned his open face upwards and gave a whoop of joy. A second later a huge dusky-shelled monstrosity was dropping from the canopy, pinning the dwarf to the ground under its mass. Its eight fur-frilled legs were segmented and encased in dark red chitin. Enormous black eyes glared at Felix from an armoured polyp of clacking fangs that dripped with digestive venom.

'Help Snorri, Felix, its feet tickle,' came Snorri's muffled yell, followed by a crunch as of a hammer bashing through the giant spider's chitinous underbelly. The spider squealed and scurried sideways, a treacle-like spatter dappling the ground beneath it. Snorri ran after it with his axe raised only to be thrown into a tree by a swinging foreleg. Loose snow dolloped from the branches to bury him to the elbows.

Felix raised his sword as the spider scuttled around on the spot to face him. It hissed, mouthparts scissoring menacingly. He glanced sideways at Snorri, the old dwarf whistling the tune to a dwarf mining song as he dug himself free. Felix rolled his eyes in disbelief, wondering what it was about this situation and this idiot Slayer that made his heart ache the way it did.

Through breaks in the trees he saw more giant spiders scuttling towards them with a hideous clicking sound. Felix spun around. They were coming from every direction. Desperately, he looked around for a more defensible spot.

'Snorri, what's that?'

Felix pointed into the woods. Just visible in the gloom, its mossy outline swallowed up by the forest, was a cottage. Its wattled pine walls were dingy, its roughly thatched roof pierced in several places by the branches of the forest canopy and tangled with glittering silver webs.

'This way, Snorri. We can hold them off in there!'

Before Felix realised what he was doing, he was barging past his spluttering companion and into the trees. A spiked-shelled horror lunged from the undergrowth and he veered to put a sturdy pine between them, lashing out on instinct at another as it came scrambling down the trunk and sending a chip of chitin flying from its mandibles as he ducked beneath it and ran on. From the unsubtle roars and the splintering of chitin, he gathered that Snorri was crashing after him.

With an inchoate cry of his own, Felix charged into the clearing. And then stopped.

There had been dozens of spiders here. Where were they?

Heart hammering, he lowered his sword in confusion and looked over the dismal cottage that stood alone now in the silence of the wood. Warmth leached from his chest and he shivered as though a ghost had just passed through him.

He turned around, dizzied by a wave of relief as he spotted Snorri. The bodies of dozens of giant spiders lay amongst the boles of the trees and scattered like tree stumps over the clearing, upturned with their legs curled over their bellies. The Trollslayer swayed on his feet and chuckled. His body was riddled with bites and pinkish froth was coming out of his mouth. He spotted Felix and made a gurgling sound, shaping to throw his hammer at him only to accidentally toss it behind his back and fall into a giggling heap on the ground.

Felix tried to go to him but the air around him was suddenly too dense to move through, like something from a nightmare, blurring the trees and the cottage until all he could see was Snorri and the woman who settled over him in a rustle of black skirts.

She put her hand around Snorri's throat, dribble running through the dwarf's beard and over her fingers before she removed her hand and took his giant palm instead, scratching her nails along the palm lines and uttering a singsong chant. Felix felt the hairs on his arms stand on end and a shiver run through him. He recognised the voice as the one which had spoken to him just moments earlier. The woman was working magic.

'You should have died today, Snorri Nosebiter, but I will not allow it. You slaughtered my guardians, you intruded on my seclusion. And you imperil my very soul should my master find what I do to you now.' She hissed, a strange kind of smile on her lips as a nail dug a new branching line into his palm and drew a trickle of blood. An arc of something magical flared from the droplet and crackled over her knuckles. 'The doom you seek shall elude you until the day that I decree. It will not come for many years, long enough for you to suffer. And when you are whole again, when those you most love surround you again, then you shall have a death that brings you nothing but pain. This is your curse,' she smiled sadly. 'A gift worthy of a Slayer. You will have the mightiest doom.'

Felix watched transfixed as the woman redrew the palm lines in blood. She looked up from the moaning dwarf, treating Felix to a conspiratorial smile as the power to rewrite destiny flashed in her lavender-pale eyes.

Her appearance was painfully familiar to him and yet wrong in every measurable way. Her back was bent, her hands unsteady as if from a wasting frailty at odds with the force crackling from too-long, almost claw-like nails. Her grey hair was tied back with a pin. Her face was kindly but sad. She was clothed in layered skirts of black silk decorated with coloured shards of chitin and glass beads. It was his mother, Renata, but it wasn't. The voice and the eyes were both wrong, as were the strange clothes. His mother had always hated black; the only time Felix had seen her wear it had been for her journey to the Garden of Morr.

'This is the second time you've tried to appear to me as my mother. Why?'

'I never had a mother,' the old woman replied, skin darkening and hair growing paler as she spoke. 'But I had a father who loved me more than the world. I remember being surrounded by people who cared for me.' She looked at Felix strangely, colours lapping at the purple of her eyes until Felix could no longer be certain what colour they were. Small horns began to push through hair that was now completely white and shone like the face of the moon. 'I have felt the kindness of strangers and have tried, in my own way, to show the same to others.'

A final burst of power blasted Snorri's hand from the woman's clutches. It lay steaming in the snow, the dwarf mercifully unconscious with a look of vacant dread scrawled across his features.

Revulsion filled Felix like bile from a ruptured gut. Was it even possible for a mortal being to possess such world-changing power? This woman had altered Snorri's fate. Whatever doom he might have had she had taken from him to instead see his life end underneath Gotrek's axe. His mind reeled with the implications. If Gotrek was merely responding to the tugged strings of this old hag's web, then was he still culpable for his friend's death? Felix shook his head sharply. Gotrek had still been the one with a choice to make. No hand but his had struck the final blow.

'I would hate to be the beneficiary of your *un*kindness.'

'Your friend, Max, always believed that you were being guided by a greater power.' She spread her hands demurely. Each finger ended with a sharp black claw. 'He is powerful and wise, and your meetings with him over the years have been more than fortuitous.'

Felix's brow knotted as he fought to order his thoughts. 'You were the sorceress that Max spoke of back at the dwarfhold. Why would you "help" with one hand and then loose a daemon on us with the other?'

'Have you not at times sympathised with some of those your companion is compelled to slay? But it is not sympathy. I do what I must for whom I must, for even my master cannot see as clearly as I do. I have watched over you for a long time, Felix, guided you through the choices you must make and the allies you would need come the final hour. It was my magic that staved off old age long enough for you to reach it, and my summons in your dreams that called you back from the Far East in time to shape it. Your friend's death was necessary, as was the manner of it. It tethered Gotrek to you in a bond of grief, and only together can you achieve what I alone know that you must.'

'You had no right,' Felix breathed, his thoughts swirling over every loss and tragedy in his life, seeing them for the first time through the retrospective prism of fate – as this strange seeress might have seen them since before he was even born.

Had Kirsten, his first great love, died in a goblin raid because he would in a heartbeat have left the Slayer to be with her? Was it more than mere serendipity that had brought Felix into possession of Karaghul, a weapon that had saved his life on countless occasions, and then seen the Templar order to whom it rightfully belonged crushed under a beastman invasion? Felix clenched his teeth. How very convenient. Had it even been this woman's urgings that had led Ulrika into damnation, simply so that she might one day decades hence reunite him with Gotrek?

His hands bunched into fists, arms shaking with emotion. There were tears in his eyes as he spoke. 'How dare you? You're talking about my life as if I was just a character in a play, in your play, but it's *my* life. Those weren't your decisions to make.'

'You and I both walk in the shadow of others, beings of great destiny, and we both must do things we abhor to see those destinies realised.'

She gestured to Snorri's recumbent form as if to demonstrate her point and Felix gasped at the discovery that the body was no longer Snorri's. His beard was longer and darkly red, his one eye rolled up into its socket. Blood speckled his tattoos and formed a spreading pool under his enormous chest. Felix stared at the dwarf's face, praying – despite the visceral certainty that it was hopeless – to see breath dimple the blood in which lay his nose and his limp, hanging mouth. Felix put his hand over his mouth to keep from being sick. Without the slightest transition to alert Felix to the change, the body had become Gotrek's.

The Slayer was dead.

'Why are you showing me this?'

'It is not for me to decide what you see,' the woman answered, seemingly perplexed that Felix would even ask. 'It is your future, not mine.'

'This is not my future,' said Felix, unable to remove his eyes from the body. Gotrek's chest had been torn open, savaged as if by a wild animal or a daemonic creature. It would have taken a monster of extraordinary strength and power to inflict such injuries on Gotrek. Felix felt as though that should probably alleviate his pain, but it didn't. 'I won't allow it.'

'You are powerless against the opponent that awaits you in Kazad Drengazi, Felix, and Gotrek's passing will be the doom of this world.' She crouched beside the fallen Slayer and passed her hand across his face, closing the lid of his unseeing eye. Then she looked up at Felix. 'But it may be enough to save the next.'

Felix shivered and closed his eyes, hoping this woman and her visions would disappear and he would wake up – it was clear now that this was a bad dream of some prophetic sort – and find himself again on the bridge of *Unstoppable* with Gotrek alive and well beside him.

'Some are tied to their fates,' the seeress went on. 'Beings like Gotrek are rocks, immovable, stepping stones towards a certain future, but you...'

She rose, turned and spread her arms, tilting her head back to gaze towards a vaulted ceiling where golden-red runes glimmered like fireflies on a hot night by the banks of the Aver. There was no sign that there had ever been a forest. The floor was tiled with slabs of white stone, each one marked in the centre by a vengeful-looking rune. It was dwarf-made, but more ancient than any dwarfhold he had ever seen. A terrible power dwelt here; even through the filter of another's vision he could feel it in every rock and rune.

'This will happen because I have seen it. What comes after is yours to claim.'

'What does that mean?'

'It means you have a choice to make, Felix Jaeger. Will you stand by the Slayer to the end, knowing that it will mean his death, or will you leave him here in the Fortress of the First Slayer–' She pointed to Gotrek where he lay '–and let the slim hope of a better future die with him?'

'I–'

The woman looked up sharply and bared teeth like tiny daggers in a snarl. 'It is time for you to go. Awaken. Warn your companions if you are able.'

'What is it?' said Felix, the fear of whatever could make an individual of this seeress's obvious power nervous enough to penetrate the swirl of questions that filled his mind. 'I don't even know where the place you're talking about is!'

The golden runes glimmered to darkness. Shadows closed around the great pillars of stone. There was a form to them of sorts, like being captured inside a pair of gigantic black wings.

'Wake up, Felix. He is coming for you.'

Felix groaned as he opened his eyes. It had become something of a habit, a pre-emptive measure ingrained over the last few months into his subconscious, but there didn't appear to be anything particularly untoward awaiting him on *Unstoppable*'s bridge.

The first thing that struck him was the quiet.

Most of the engineers who had been bustling between the stations had since departed, to leave the handful who now operated the various ancillary bridge functions that Felix had never quite managed to understand. They stood at their posts in silence, moving only occasionally to adjust a dial or flick a switch. The engines hummed on a low, resonant register. Max stood by the entrance hatch, leaning against the circular frame with his arms loosely crossed and staring into space. Gotrek sat in another of the swivelling command chairs on the opposite side of the bridge to Felix, tending to his wounds and trying to pull what looked like glass splinters from his knuckles with his teeth. Malakai Makaisson stood in brooding silence at the helm, goggles hanging around his neck, staring determinedly forward and making minute adjustments to their heading with slight turns of the wheel.

That was when Felix noticed how dark it had become, the bridge lit by a cool unnatural light that gleamed from pinprick sources that ran in tracks along the bulkheads, deck, and ceiling. At first Felix thought that he had slept away the entire day and that *Unstoppable* now flew through the night, thus explaining the absence of the other engineers to some well-earned rest, but then he noticed the real cause. The clouds they were flying under were as black as pitched oak, tendrilous strands whipping past the view screen as the airship ploughed through.

A feeling of unease sat in Felix's belly. He peered through the window. The peaks of the mountains were jagged, uneven teeth in the darkened landscape, like a great maw opening up to snatch them from the sky.

'What's happening?' he asked.

Malakai turned around at his question and gave him a serious look, as if to make sure he wasn't joking. Felix noticed that the goggles resting on his chest were smashed, owing to an incident that was probably not wholly unrelated to that responsible for the thick black eye he now wore instead, underscored by a half-moon gash that roughly traced the original position of his goggles. From across the room came a slurping sound as Gotrek sucked in and spat out a piece of glass. The engineer glared at Felix sulkily. 'We're gaun to Middenheim.'

Felix glanced to where Max stood, but the wizard appeared to have no complaints over the course or destination. Felix wished he could be reassured by the wizard's ambivalence.

'Just a spot of rain, manling. It rains a lot up here in the north, if I remember.' Gotrek heaved himself up out of his chair and came stomping across to where Felix sat, nervously twitching his swivel chair from side to side. Suddenly conscious of it, he stopped. Gotrek grunted and wrapped his arms about his chest. Dark clouds and a palpable sense of chill whistled past the glass behind him. 'You sleep like a halfling. Middenheim can't be more than a few hours from here and I was worried I wouldn't be able to wake you when we arrived.'

'It's good to see you alive,' said Felix without thinking.

Gotrek's eye narrowed. 'Why? Should I not be?'

A vision of the Slayer dead – no, ripped apart – at Felix's feet returned to him and his mouth suddenly felt too dry for him to speak. He thought about what the seeress had told him about Gotrek's doom, about how it would be the doom of the world itself. She hadn't been the first to prophesy that the Slayer's demise would be the downfall of others, but this had been the most forthright and forbidding such warning he had yet been given. Perhaps it was the times. It was too easy to give credence to portents of doom when the world was already in flames.

He managed to pull his thoughts from those images, watching them run like panicked horses for the familiar ground of Kat and his daughter. In his mind now, they stood not in Otto's Altdorf townhouse but on the walls of the Fauschlag, waiting if not for him then for some other kind of end. He liked to think that the ease with which he saw them there, this infant he had never seen in a city they had never visited, meant that there could be some truth to it.

That was all he wanted. With all his heart, that was all he had ever wanted. Part of him would let the Slayer find his doom, and even join him in it, if it meant that his daughter might have a future free of war.

Realising that he had been silent too long, Felix masked his disquiet behind an unconvincing smile. 'Alive and well, I meant. After a fight like that.'

Gotrek's lips pursed in thought, but he said nothing. Felix noticed the tired red glaze in the dwarf's eye. The Slayer's stamina was extraordinary, but his continuing refusal to rest was madness even by his standards.

'Is there something you want to talk about?' Max asked softly from his position by the hatch.

Felix shivered as if a cold beam had just been shone on his back, looking up and then quickly drawing his gaze back without meeting the wizard's eye.

To Gotrek alone he might have been moved to confess the seeress's prophecy, but not Max. The wizard thought of little but the Slayer's destiny. Had Felix told him what he had been shown then Max would no doubt have insisted again on seeking out the mythical power of Kazad Drengazi and facing whatever fell guardian awaited Gotrek there, regardless of what the fallout for the rest of the world might be.

Well, Felix planned to prove the seeress wrong.

She could have told him that Grimnir's legendary fortress was home to a thousand doughty warriors and the Ancestor God himself, and Felix would still not like the price. Middenheim was hours away, and for the first time in an age Felix and Gotrek were of one mind.

'Whit on Grimnir's axe is tha'?' Malakai shouted, taking the wheel in his immensely strong grip and staring dead ahead through the forward window.

A frisson of dread jerked Felix out of his chair like an electric shock and he moved to stand beside the engineer. Gotrek joined him. Max bowed his head to his staff and muttered a string of words under his breath that made Felix's skin tingle.

Felix looked through the thick glass of the window, his eyes widening as if forcing him to behold the monstrous black tear that seemed to be ripping open the sky in their path. In its dark core, Felix could feel the cold depths of eternity. Shreds of cloud streamed around its borders, taking on a protean show of colour reminiscent of those that the winds of magic could, when in full force, create in the northern skies. The effects it was producing on the surrounding sky were already causing the deck of the bridge to tremble. And it was getting wider.

'What is it?' Felix yelled back, countering the sudden weakness in his knees with a steadying hand on the engineer's broad shoulders.

'Damned if ah ken.'

'It's an opening to the Realm of Chaos,' said Gotrek. 'I've seen it before. Once.'

'Can we avoid it if we turn around?' said Felix.

'There's nae enough fuel, laddie. If we dae tha' we may as well joost land right here.'

Felix felt the hand of destiny tightening its grip. Which was the right course and which was wrong? How was he to know? He turned to Max, but the wizard had yet to re-open his eyes, the occasional turbulence shaking him against his staff.

'Hawd on!' Malakai roared, pushing forward the first of the row of levers by his right hand and then gripping the wheel as though he never intended to release it again. The drone of the engines ramped to a higher pitch and Felix felt a force driving him back towards the aft bulkhead. The clouds hit the window with greater speed and power and the vortex swelled before them like a pit of despair.

Felix was convinced that Malakai Makaisson had decided to fulfil his own Slayer Oath right then in a blaze of pointless glory after all.

'Huv ye ever ridden ower a tidal wave in a steam ship?'

Felix's expression of horror indicated that he had not and prayed never to.

'Turn awa' and it'll keel ye ower. Ye huv tae gae at it full ahead and hope tae all yer gods ye punch oot the other side.' The engineer wrenched his hand from the wheel to grab the chain that swayed in the turbulence above him and haul down on it.

Steam screamed from whistles on every deck, billowing from vents and portholes like smoke from the jaws of a dragon as *Unstoppable* surged full steam ahead into the heart of darkness.

As Felix watched, utterly helpless to affect his fate, a school of dark shapes began to arrow from the rift. They appeared tiny, but as they flew closer Felix realised that to be an illusion peddled to him by distance and the awesome scale of the vortex itself. They were flat-bodied, glassine flesh of boundless black, ray-like wings rippling on unseen currents as they swept *en masse* towards the airship. As the forerunners angled past the nose of the vessel they revealed hideous arrow-shaped mouths filled with sharp teeth and flanked by flat, dark eyes.

Malakai leaned forward to catch a glimpse of the daemons clawing over the gasbag above them and scowled, his guttural curse drowned out by a burst of cannon fire as the first engineers finally reached the organ gun turrets and opened up on the swarm.

Explosive bursts painted the dark skies with devastation, shredding the screaming rays to a daemonic essence that dispersed into the clouds like vapour. *Unstoppable*'s firepower was immense, it was a fortress in the skies, but the enemy were too numerous and more just kept on pouring out of the rift however many the gunners could banish back to the Realm of Chaos.

An impact to the side of the gondola flung Felix sideways and would have surely sent him rolling across the deck had he not had a firm grip of Makaisson's shoulder. A painful squeal ground through the bulkhead and Felix's mind kindly bequeathed him images of foul daemonic things raking across the bows of the gondola. He swallowed hard and tightened his grip, uncomfortably reminded that the armoured vehicle in which they travelled was kept airborne by little more than the few dozen cables that connected them to the gasbag.

Felix clutched the hilt of his sword in horror.

That was what they intended to do. The daemons meant to destroy the gasbag and drop them all to break on the mountain! A section of armour plate spun down from above and cracked against the view screen.

'Malakai!'

'Aye, ah see 'em, the sleekit divils.'

Felix drew his sword a thumb's width from his scabbard. He wasn't nearly as helpless as being on this airship made him feel. He could still fight, and he would rather fall under a tide of claws than plummet to his doom trapped inside this iron box. He turned to Gotrek. The Slayer nodded grimly.

'We'll make it, manling. Just one last fight.'

Then Max's eyes snapped open. The wizard emitted a strange sound that seemed to come from the very base of his throat and placed his hand on the bulkhead. A flash of pure white light passed from his palm and into the metal, and a moment later discharged from the outer hull in a crackling arc that purged the vicinity of the daemonic and blackened the view screen with the vaporous effluvium of their annihilation.

Felix almost smiled. If Max could keep them off the body of the airship then they might just be able to ride out whatever it was that had been opened in their path.

'They will keep on coming until I am too exhausted to stop them,' said Max, a mild tremor of exertion in his voice. 'Gotrek is correct. Within that rift lies the Realm of Chaos. These are not greenskins or skaven. There will be no end to them until it is closed.'

'Close it, then,' Gotrek growled.

'Believe it or not, that is actually what I had in mind.'

'What's it doing in the middle of the Empire?' said Felix.

'The encroachment of the Chaos Wastes makes such things possible,' said Max, one hand stuck to the wall and one on his staff as the turbulence shook him. 'Even so it would demand a sorcerer of tremendous power to open something like this, several sorcerers most likely.'

Felix thought of the seeress who had come to him in his dream. Did she possess the sort of power Max was talking about? It was frightening to imagine but after what he had seen of her it was impossible to consider anything else. He wished he could decide which side she was on.

'Why?'

'To keep us from Kazad Drengazi.'

Gotrek growled angrily. 'How many times and in how many different ways do I have to tell people we're going to Middenheim? Manling!'

Felix drew his sword the rest of the way.

'Let's go draw them a map.'

'Wait,' said Max. 'Sealing the rift will require all of my concentration. I won't be able to aid you–' The wizard hissed and scrunched up his face as though he had just tasted something sour. 'Something comes. Something... dark.'

'They're all dark!' Gotrek roared, as Felix turned to the shattered view screen and gave a small moan of horror.

Something vast had emerged from the rift, surrounded by a billowing school of lesser daemons, and sending out a bow wave of abyssal dread that rocked Felix to the deepest and most securely held quarters of his soul. It was the same terror that he had felt before on the cupola before Max had distracted its attention from him, but exponentially worse. Its sleek, powerful black form was a nightmare cut in volcanic glass. Its horns were an endless curve of damnation and despair. The daemon prince dipped and soared, bat-wings beating, revelling in the power of flight and the dark delight of simply *being*.

The cannonade faltered as the dread prince flew nearer, and there was some slim satisfaction in knowing that the dwarf crew suffered the creature's aura as sorely as Felix did himself. With a pitted, obsidian-black sword the length of a Reiksguard's lance the daemon levelled its challenge to those watching from the bridge, then tucked in its wings and barrel-rolled under the steaming airship.

Felix didn't need to hear the words spoken to know that the daemon had been calling out Gotrek and no one else.

'He's gawn for the aft hangar,' said Makaisson, craning his neck awkwardly to peer under the cracks in the view screen to the simple setup of mirrors that granted a partial view around the top and sides of the gondola. Then he turned to Felix. 'Tha's whcre maist o' yer lot are stayin'. Ah think young Gustav is doon there.'

The life drained from Felix's face. 'Gotrek–'

'Clear the birds from the roof, manling. If the big one wants a taste of my axe then he'll get it.'

Felix nodded reluctantly. 'No finding a doom now.'

'I'm no longer seeking a doom, manling, as you should well know.'

'You know how these things creep up on you when you stop looking.'

A slow grin spread across the Slayer's brutal features. He spat on his hand and thrust it out. 'No enemy shall have my shame before we both stand upon the pinnacle of Middenheim. You already have my oath, but I will swear on it again.'

Felix hesitated. That oath had been the cause of almost as much trouble and grief as the one that Felix had made long ago, but for some reason, with their long-sought goal perhaps hours away, the past didn't seem to matter.

At least not that part of it.

He took the Slayer's ham-sized fist in his own calloused hand. 'I remember a good tavern from our last visit there. You and Snorri were sleeping off a hangover at the time, and I always wanted to go back.'

For the first time Gotrek showed no anger at the mention of that name. He shook Felix's hand solemnly. The oath was made.

Now all they had to do was keep it.

THIRTEEN

Be'lakor

Felix and Gotrek parted ways at the mid-section maintenance hatch without so much as a best-of-luck. Gotrek bombed on down the hallway, axe held firmly in both hands. Felix rolled his eyes, reached up to spin open the hatch to the gasbag, and then took a rung of the ladder in his left hand. As he did so, a terrific scraping sound passed through the body of the ship. Felix grimaced, more than half expecting to see a murderous black sword perforating the hull or some winged horror scratching through the bulkhead. His ring finger rattled against the iron rung. It was a similar mix of apprehension and dread to when he had been caught below decks of the Bretonnian merchantman *Cecilie* when storms had driven the Aarvik-bound vessel over the rocks that lurked beneath the Manannspoort Sea. It was the same kind of helplessness, the knowledge that there was likely very little that he could do to influence his fate.

It seemed to be a recurrent theme of late.

The ever-present rumble of *Unstoppable*'s powerful engines dropped in register. The low drone made Felix's teeth hum. The sense of strain was palpable, every surface shuddering with effort as though the airship had somehow become snared on something. What they could possibly have struck up here Felix didn't want to imagine. He thought of the rift, the one thing he had been trying not to think about since leaving the bridge.

Were they too late? Could they have hit it already?

Felix couldn't even begin to imagine what it would feel like to crash an airship through a vortex to the Realm of Chaos and if he was completely honest then he was hoping to live a little longer without having to find out. Just as it had been aboard that ill-fated Norscan adventure however, Felix could see no better alternative than simply getting on with things and trying not to think about it.

No sooner had he come to that decision than the disarming sensation of gravity altering its angle of attack tipped him off balance and almost pitched him down the aft hallway. He rolled on his ankles. The whole ship lurched backwards. In panic, Felix clanged his sword-hand against the ladder's siderail and held on tight to the rung as his feet were suddenly pulled from under him and his stomach dropped through them down the now steeply-angled hall. The engines strained mightily.

The daemon prince was dragging down the airship. It was actually pulling down the entire airship!

Felix walked himself hand-over-hand towards the safer confines of the maintenance shaft as the deck continued to tilt and his legs swung loosely beneath him.

He hoped that Gotrek had closed some hatches behind him.

It was a long way down to the hangar deck otherwise.

Pieces of junk machinery rolled across the tilting deck of the hangar, piling into the aft bulkhead as a force strong enough to buckle its thick iron doors tightened its grip on the outer hull and heaved. Men and women were dragged from their nightmares to claw at the deck and scream. Gustav Jaeger's heart muscles resonated with sympathetic horror. He inserted his fingers deeper into the holes in the metal deck and snatched at the scarred hand of a bald man in an unbuckled red and green tabard as he tumbled past. The sudden, fierce grip on his burnt hand caused his vision to waver and he almost passed out from the pain, but from somewhere he found the grit to clench his teeth and hold on.

One minute he'd been laying bedrolls and distributing what blankets they'd managed to salvage from the dwarfhold amongst the soldiers and families camped here in the hangar, and the next his world had been turned literally on its side.

The doors gave a wrenching sound of steel being forcibly separated from steel, and a huge serrated black blade split the inch-thick bulkhead like old wood. A shriek of ice-cold black wind raced through the breach.

The Hochlander in Gustav's grip screamed a garble of panicked gibberish and began to struggle. Gustav's face turned purple with agony. He couldn't hold on much longer. Pain caused his own grip on the deckplate to slip, and with a despairing cry Gustav threw the man off. The soldier tumbled away, thumping bodily over the nose of a gyrocopter and then rolling limply towards the doors.

There, the infernal sword proceeded to carve through the bulkhead like a butcher's knife through ribs, opening a long horizontal incision through which streamed a dark, misted chill and a primal dread. Metal screeched as the blade was twisted ninety degrees, carving upwards as easily as it had cut across. After cutting a track almost twelve feet long the sword squealed around again to make a third cut, parallel to the first. Gustav clung to the deck, numbed by a combination of cold and horror, almost grateful to the throbbing in his injured hand for the affirmation that despite what he was witnessing he remained a living, feeling, human man. The blade carved down to meet its original incision, completing a perfect rectangle.

Gustav felt the temperature drop by several degrees. The back of his skull throbbed as though the bone were being pried open from within. His wounds ached as if the stitching on all of them had simultaneously come undone. Dark magic. He had gone his entire life without needing to learn what it felt like, but after his experiences in occupied Kislev it felt as horribly familiar as a recurring nightmare.

An explosion of onyx flame blasted in the bulkhead's eviscerated section.

It thumped to the deck and more frigid air washed in after it to reveal a shape that someone without conception of scale or the ability to feel the grip of fear might describe as man-like. The air froze in Gustav's chest and for what felt like a fatal span of time he couldn't breathe. In that moment, Gustav understood that everything he had experienced in Kislev and before was nothing. He could fight well enough to get by, the sense of entitlement that came with his upbringing seemed to translate well into a knack for leadership, and he knew how to carry through a plan.

But he was not his uncle.

He did not have what it took to fight a greater daemon – the might of the Chaos Gods made flesh.

Its clawed feet tolled on the deck like the call of midnight. Shadows scrapped around its ankles, benighted children squalling for the approval of their dark master. The daemon drew itself to its full height, lifting back its horned head and beating out its leathery black wings. The daemon was as lithe as a panther, and though its musculature was harder than stone it had a smooth, ephemeral quality akin to smoked glass. An eight-pointed star, the symbol of Undivided Chaos, shone like a crack in the void from its broad chest. It clenched its fists, muscle gliding across muscle, glorying in its own dark skin. Gustav quailed, enraptured, as the gaze of the demi-god passed briefly over him. Its eyes were a bottomless black, an eternal shadow into which a man might fall, forever fall, and never, ever reach their darkest point.

He had barely even noticed that the deck had levelled out and he was lying flat once again.

'Away. Back from doors. *Zbiec!*'

Kolya ran against the flow of bodies with his bow unslung and in hand, the deck levelling out beneath him now that the airship's engines were no longer fighting against the might of a daemon prince. He nocked an arrow to his string and in the same unbroken action fired. The shaft disintegrated before it came within six inches of the daemon's chest.

'*Świnia!*'

The Kislevite pulled another arrow from his quiver, then threw it aside with a fresh curse and unhitched a hatchet from his belt. He tossed it into the air and caught its haft as it spun, casting aside his bow and drawing a short, curving sabre from the fur-lined scabbard at his hip. His freshly drawn hennaed forearm glittered with a faintly metallic tint as he carved a blinding sigil of practice strokes into the air. Gustav would always think of Kolya as a bowman, but he had heard his uncle describe the one-time winged lancer as something of a gourmand with weapons.

Felix may not have realised it, but coming from him that was high praise indeed.

The gaunt-faced northman's courage was infectious, and from it Gustav managed to draw the strength to stand and draw his own, longer, cavalryman's sabre. Despite everything she had put him through, he longed to have Ulrika at his side again to wield that weapon now.

'Does the oblast have a clever saying for this?' Gustav shouted, praying by volume alone to erase the quaver that the daemon had set in his voice.

'It does not,' said Kolya with a faint smile and a shrug. 'For my life I cannot think why.'

The daemon ignored the two men utterly, looking over their heads and past those screaming for the hatchway into the corridor. It grinned like a shark and unfurled its wings, shadows bunching beneath them like extensions of its own awesome muscles, and then launched itself into the air. Gustav gasped and lowered his sword, tilted his neck back and turned to follow its short arc to where it pounded into the metal deck like a warpstone meteor. Nearby men and women were tossed from their feet by the shock that rattled through the walls and floor. The daemon ignored them, insects too small and harmless to be worth the tiny effort of being swatted.

'You ever have feeling we are not important, friend Gustav?'

'Only every day.'

An angry red glow bathed the far wall, a stark relief to outline the daemon's limpid black.

The daemon prince laughed coldly, ominous as black ice on a frozen lake. 'You defeated a worthy pawn in Khagash-Fél, son of Gurni, but now you stand before a king.'

Gotrek stood framed by the hatchway that led out of the hangar into the hall, bruised and battered, but a rock in the stream of panicked men and women running past him for the hallway. He thrust his jaw belligerently towards the towering daemon prince. His axe glowed painfully bright in one massive hand, enough to force the dwarf's eyelid down to a sliver; the other he held in a *back* gesture towards Gustav and Kolya.

'Yes,' said the daemon prince. 'There will be no human to save your skin this time.'

Gotrek growled and brought up his axe.

'Run, Gustav,' Kolya murmured, pointing with his axe to the pair of metal ladders leading up to the walkways above.

Escape by the main hatchway meant braving the daemon prince, but there were doors onto other decks up there. Gustav had explored them thoroughly when the dwarf crewman assigned to the human survivors had brought them down here. He didn't like to go anywhere with his eyes closed. Not again.

'Aren't you coming too?'

The gaunt-faced man shrugged and turned towards the main hatchway. 'Man owes you horse, what do you do?'

'I don't know!' Gustav shouted after him. 'I never know what the hell you're saying!'

Kolya turned his face half around and grinned. Gustav felt a terrible wrenching in his heart, as though it yearned to stay. As if it knew that this would be the last time it would beat in this intolerable man's company.

'You and the dwarf deserve each other,' said Gustav.

'Terrible thing to say,' Kolya tutted. 'Do I ever say you deserve your uncle?'

With a low growl, the daemon prince rose to his full height. He exuded a nimbus of shadow. The iron bulkheads began to creak as if being drawn inwards by an invisible force. Gotrek's axe brightened sharply, enough to force the Slayer himself to look away from it with a grunt.

'Your enemies in the Realm of Chaos are legion, Slayer. Did you believe that an immortal would forgive?'

The daemon prince brought up his huge black blade, except that it was no longer the same sword. In a sense it was, but at the same time it was also quite clearly a vicious-looking brass axe with a jagged edge. In the other hand, the daemon prince cracked a whip that had definitely not been there before. In a subtle realignment of muscle and flesh, the daemon prince began to change. His face elongated into a bestial snout. A fiery red liquid that looked something like blood drooled between his teeth. His dark skin reddened, thickening muscle crunching his once-regal stance into a savage hunch that threatened awesome violence. The foot that stepped out from the caul of shadows was hoofed and shod in brass.

A shiver entered into Gustav's bones, bringing a tingle to his muscles and to his sword arm in particular, a strange amalgam of supernatural terror and the urge to quench that terror in the blood of friend and foe alike.

'Eternity is mine and I will feast upon your brain yet, Daemonslayer,' said the transformed daemon, its voice a brazen battle horn, the vengefulness and hate it bellowed tempered by the cool original that still wove through it. 'All hail Be'lakor for granting me the gift of vengeance.'

Without waiting on an explanation, Gustav spun for the ladders and ran as though the pits of damnation were opening up beneath him.

Felix poked his head through the already open hatch onto the dorsal spine. Mayhem on an otherworldly scale flooded his senses from above, below and all around. Daemon-rays knifed through streaking cloud, wails peeling from their hideous arrowhead mouths. Soldiers in Hochland colours were spread out along the walkway, stabbing wildly up with their halberds as rays swept in, wings rippling and whip tails lashing. The wind tore up snatches of shouted commands from an officer, lost somewhere amongst the unit of bowmen at the handrail. The archers fought against the fearsome wind to steady their bows long enough to aim and fire. A pool of blood spread from the corpse of a dwarf engineer, slumped headless in the throne of the nearest organ gun turret.

The sense of altitude and of velocity was incredible. The wind was a cold black hand pushing Felix back into the shaft. He fought against it, golden-grey hair thrashing about him as he planted his sword flat onto the walkway and drew himself out. The force of the wind on his cloak almost pulled him over the side, and Felix put his hand to the clasp at his collar, his first instinct to unfasten it and let it go to oblivion without him. He dropped his hand, instead wrapping the hem once about his waist and tucking the loose end into his trews. Sentiment would allow no less.

This tatty scrap of Sudenland wool had kept him warm on his very first adventure, years before he had had cause to rue the name Gotrek Gurnisson. And Sudenland didn't even *exist* any more, a small fact that always made him marvel at and bemoan his age, depending on his mood. Right now, he did the latter, but there was fight in this sentimental old fool yet.

Keeping low, he ran to join the Hochland halberdiers fighting beside the handrail.

'Praise the gods,' yelled Corporal Mann. His voice was hoarse from shouting, grey eyes wide with a terror his mind couldn't fully process. Behind him, the rift had widened to consume all but a blazing corona of sky. Felix tried not to look directly at it. There was horror enough for any man with the dark-bodied daemons continuing to stream from its black horizon. 'We're holding them off,' Mann went on, 'but there are more underneath out of sight of our bows.'

'They're attacking the gasbag, and the hawsers that hold it to the gondola,' Felix shouted back.

'What does that mean?'

For a moment, Felix was about to describe to the corporal in some detail exactly what that meant, but on this occasion his mind moved quicker than his tongue. What benefit would that knowledge bring either of them?

'Try not to think about it.'

Weaving through the halberdiers and between a pair of archers in mid-draw, Felix gripped the handrail and looked over the side. A sickening vertigo rushed up to greet him and he swiftly removed his eyes from the bottomless whirlpool of cloud and focused on the gasbag. Thick nets hung down from the handrail. Felix had seen dwarf engineers clamber over them like goats over a mountain trail to conduct field repairs on battle damage – after the dragon incident for instance – and remembered being rather impressed by the dexterity and balance of so rugged a race. He also recalled being quite happy to remain up here with his hands just where they were on the handrail, thank you very much.

He swallowed the knot of fear, reaching over for a handful of the coarse black rope and giving it an experimental tug. It was strong. He'd been afraid of that.

'We have to go down.'

Mann laughed nervously. Then stopped and looked down. The wheels turned. 'No...'

'We're finished if we don't,' said Felix, knotting his arm up to the elbow in netting and bellying backwards over the handrail. The whole thing had a perilous amount of give, swaying alarmingly both as he slid his feet into the net and in reaction to the wind.

He took a deep breath, resolved still to at least resemble the hero that these frightened men needed him to be, and glanced up. Corporal Mann and his men were dropping their halberds to draw their katzbalger swords and follow him over the handrail. Felix felt the netting quiver against him. He found a wan smile, a warm feeling prickling into the edges of his nerves. As if being seen to be fearless and actually being it were not so dissimilar after all.

The gasbag was too large to defend in its entirety, but then they didn't have to protect it all.

Malakai had once explained that even with half the liftgas cells destroyed the airship would still fly, and that were she to lose any more then she would simply sink gradually to the ground. Unless they were all to burst at once, of course, an event that the engineer had repeatedly assured him was impossible. All they needed to win was time, enough for Max to seal the rift.

And preferably before they sank deep enough, gradually or otherwise, to crash into the Middle Mountains.

Kolya had been four years old when he had first taken a life. The trap he had stolen from his father's gear had broken the marmot's back and sprayed its blood over the frost that clung to the young grass. In the years since, he had almost convinced himself of the lie that he had not known it was bad luck to hunt the animals in spring when mothers foraged for the hungry young in their burrows, but he had known. Of course he had known. Since he had been old enough to tell a polecat from a plover he had understood the rhythm of the seasons. His father had taught him and his half-brother that. But he had been hungry, for acclaim and for the experience.

He had wanted to know what it felt like to kill.

The Bloodthirster of Khorne brought all those feelings back to him as if he were shivering on the oblast again: the exhilaration, the thrill, the power, the enduring, simple pleasure of watching the frost turn red. Kolya recognised the greater daemon on an instinctual level. There had been a bond of sorts between them since that late spring day when he had first taken a life and found that he enjoyed it.

The daemon thrashed its bestial face, appearing to strain against its own crimson musculature, then let loose a savage bellow and launched itself at the Slayer.

What followed was too quick for Kolya's eye to keep track of. Gotrek and the daemon collided in a storm of blows that, for the brief fiery moment that it lasted, filled the empty hangar with the ring of steel. The combatants rebounded from one another. Gotrek staggered aside, bleeding from fresh claw marks all over his arms and chest as well as a deep gash across his forehead. He held his head at an angle to direct the trickle of blood towards his gaping eye socket. Kolya was astonished that the dwarf was even still standing after such a punishing experience. However, the Bloodthirster too carried a mean dent in its bronze breastplate. Several grazes in its ruddy flesh sputtered with hellfire, granting fleeting glimpses of something black and inviolate beneath.

'You're not the same daemon I fought,' Gotrek rasped. 'You smell as bad but that one at least gave me a decent fight.'

'But it is, Slayer. Be'lakor calls and we, the banished and the abandoned, heed the Dark Master's summons. After my destruction I might have been condemned for another thousand years, but now I am free. The power of your own Slayer Fortress is what freed me. Think on that. And when Be'lakor possesses it then I will be the mightiest general in his army.'

'If I hear one more word about that place...'

'You cannot escape your doom, Slayer.'

'I certainly can't escape hearing about it,' Gotrek growled.

Silently, Kolya worked his way behind the greater daemon's back, readying his hatchet and marking a target in an unarmoured slit between the base of the monster's enormous bat-like wings. He didn't doubt that its flesh would prove as tough or tougher than whatever metallic Chaos-substance it wore for armour, but he would take what advantage he could. Having witnessed its opening sally, he doubted he would get another opportunity.

He pounced, but at the last second before his axe struck the daemon beat its wings, buffeting him with a glancing blow that knocked the axe from his hand and sent him sprawling across the deck. He made to push himself up with his now free hand, only for his wrist to erupt in pain. Screaming, he flopped back to the deck. He rolled onto his back and sat, cosseting his broken arm to his chest with a grimace.

Ursun's teeth, the daemon was as strong as it was fast. He had underestimated Gotrek's toughness, though he suspected that the great bear himself walked lightly around that one.

Gotrek took advantage of the momentary distraction to sink his axe into the back of the daemon's leg. The Bloodthirster bellowed in agony. Starmetal runes sizzled like branding irons, illuminating in deep crimson a look of grim satisfaction as the Slayer wrenched his axe back and swung again with a blow intended to sever the monster's spine.

This time the Bloodthirster's axe was there to meet it, the mighty weapons clashing together in a peal of blood and thunder.

Flame dribbling from the tear in its thigh, the daemon unleashed a barrage of frenzied blows that would have demolished a building, sending the dwarf reeling. The Bloodthirster mercilessly pressed its attack. The stamp of its brazen hooves sent tremors through the deckplates. Its wrathful roar shook the uppermost gantries as its axe and whip made a ruin of everything within reach. The damage those two weapons wrought was incredible and yet implausibly Gotrek remained on his feet, just about, knocking aside the daemon's axe with his own and stumbling back under a crack of the Bloodthirster's whip. The whip snapped around the siderail of one of the metal ladders to the next deck and with a savage howl of rage the daemon yanked back. The ladder gave a squeal of resistance before it tore away from its fastenings and crashed over the Slayer's back.

The dwarf went under with a grunt that was as much sheer exhaustion as pain, and in a blink of motion the Bloodthirster was there beside him. It cupped the Slayer's scalp in one mighty hand and bent the dwarf's neck back to lift his face off the deck. Kolya did not think that anything would prevent the daemon from doing exactly as it had promised it would – cracking Gotrek's skull like an egg and consuming his brain.

Then an odd shadow passed across the daemon's face and it let the Slayer drop, gnashing its teeth like a dog denied a bone. It withdrew to wrap itself up in its wings and snarl in frustration.

'No,' it said, its voice growing measured to once again become that of Be'lakor the daemon prince. 'Your doom is to be at the hands of one mightier even than I.'

'I will accept no doom,' Gotrek grunted, levering the huge ladder aside and pushing himself back up to his feet. He hefted his axe, almost unbalancing himself with the weight of it, and stuck out his jaw. 'Not until I feel the stones of Middenheim beneath my feet.'

Be'lakor chuckled blackly. Bands of darkness swirled out from his folded wings to enshroud his body, reducing the daemon prince to a shadow and a breeze. A cyclopean golden eye pulsed from the cloud. The laughter turned hateful and dispersed, but the voice purred from all around.

'It will be exquisite.'

Gotrek slashed his axe through the cloying gloam. 'You're not the first to make such an empty promise.'

'Empty?'

Gotrek spun around and raised his axe with a snarl.

From the shadows behind him emerged a new figure, taller than either Be'lakor or the Bloodthirster but supple as a willow sapling. A slender loincloth hung between its long, cream thighs. It wound a lock of dazzlingly multi-coloured hair around one finger as it gazed in hunger and adoration at the Slayer. In two more hands it held a long, undulating blade that put Kolya in mind of a woman's tongue. The fourth ended in an elegant pincer claw that clicked with an aching melody. Its beauty resisted definition of male or female, man or beast. It was at once everything Kolya could imagine or yearn for in his darkest fantasies. From the divine to the infernal, it whispered of ripeness, readiness, of promises awaiting fulfilment.

'Nothing in this world of delights is *empty*, precious Slayer. It was not my fate to fight you when last we met and it is still not. That is to be the pleasure of another, he who stands above us all.'

'Swill-spitting hell-spawn,' Gotrek roared, swinging back his axe and barrelling towards the daemonic beauty.

The daemon yawned as though bored, covering its mouth with one delicately-fingered hand before waving it dismissively towards the Slayer. A thunderclap went off under the dwarf's chest, blasting him from his feet and sending him careening into the last of the ladders. The iron frame buckled around him and then rolled him out onto the deckplate like kneaded bread onto a board.

He showed no immediate inclination to rise.

Ignored for now, Kolya hurried to the dwarf's side. He crouched amidst the metallic debris and offered his uninjured hand. Gotrek stared at it as if mentally fixing its position relative to his nose, but then the haze cleared from his eye and he glanced up at Kolya.

'This is the day you've been waiting for, rememberer. Why would you help me now?'

Kolya met the dwarf's gaze. It was all he dreamed about, that gaze, coming for him through a crowd of Kurgan, even as Kolya feathered the dwarf's breast with arrow after arrow, loosing faster than any man could outside of a dream but never fast enough. He would see the blood of Boris Makosky, of his beloved Kasztanka, and some nights would bring him further slaughter as his doomed effort to flee that gaze moved him to the tirsa of Talicznia where Marzena, the wise woman, and his half-brother Stefan burned.

Zabójka he had named him, and he had vowed to watch the murderer die.

He sucked in his gaunt cheeks, feeling on them the gaps in his mouth where the dwarf had kicked out half of the teeth on the right-hand side of his face, and shrugged. Call it a feeling. Humanity, maybe.

'Some things more important than promises made in blood, more important even than horses.'

'Aye,' said Gotrek, his one eye appearing to turn inward. 'Aye, some things maybe.'

'Beautiful sentiments,' said Be'lakor, himself once again, darkness falling from his muscular forearm like the folds of a cloak as he raised a claw to point at the man and the dwarf. 'Ten millennia hence, I will bid the daemon-spawn that rule this world in my stead to recite them in your memory.'

A sizzling bolt of dark magic leapt from the daemon prince's claw-tip and struck Kolya in the chest. His limbs spasmed as he was plucked from the ground and flung back. Steam rose from his hemp coat, the smell of burnt fur and feathers. Arcs of charge washed across him. He moaned in pain, tried to get up, but found he was incapable of doing anything more than twitch.

Gotrek rose and turned, thumping his chest with a vengeful roar. 'Fight me, lurker. I promise you'll not get a better chance to finish me, in Kazad Drengazi or anywhere else.'

'I have seen Morzanna's prophecy, Slayer, and I know that you have witnessed it as well. She does not sleep, but through her do the doomed dream of prophecy and death. That has always been her special gift.'

Gotrek cast his gaze down, fingers tightening around the haft of his axe. A growl started deep within his chest. 'You followed me all this way. And for what? This play fight?'

'You?' Be'lakor crossed his arms across the whispering silver sigil on his chest and chuckled deeply. 'Whatever made you believe that I cared about *you*?'

The daemon prince gestured towards the forward bulkhead. The temperature plunged. Breath turned to mist inside Kolya's throat. Frost stitched across the metal as, with a calamitous groan, the hatchway onto the corridor crunched slowly closed. Together with the broken ladders, Kolya realised that Be'lakor had effectively cut the hangar deck off from the rest of the airship. The daemon prince himself was already beginning to fade, extremities shining off into the aethyr, but not so much that he could not raise an incorporeal hand, summoning a discus of angry black energy that buzzed above his open palm like a steam-driven wood-saw.

'But I would hate to leave without a parting gift, so please, accept this with my compliments.'

The daemon prince dropped his arm and threw the moment before he disappeared.

Kolya watched the discus come for him with a detached sense of sorrow. He had always believed that he would outlive the Slayer's mad quest, maybe return to what was left of Dushyka and search for his brother, but he still could not move a finger. He grimaced. No matter. His ears filled with a furious roar that might have been Gotrek's, and then Kolya heard and saw no more. There was a sudden heat, a crashing cold, a singular moment of incandescent pain that lasted an eternity before it was spent.

Then silence.

And Kolya's war was over.

* * *

'Dae ye almost huv it?' bellowed Malakai Makaisson. His immense biceps strained at the wheel. All the colours of the aethyr flickered across the single lens of his goggles, now strapped determinedly over his face, flat reflections of the High magic that throbbed from Max Schreiber's staff.

'Just a little longer,' Max replied tightly.

'Ah know ye dain't tell me how tae fly mah airship, but it's lookin' joost a wee bit hairy oot there.'

Max grunted, nodding his understanding of the situation, bending every last ounce of will that he possessed to the task of sealing the rift. He was a magister of the Light College; he had memorised by rote a hundred banishments and counter-spells long before he had been allowed to glimpse the second level of the great – now lost – pyramid of Light. The principal underlying each of them was the same; some manner of repetitive cant that freed and focused the mind on that which disturbed the natural order. Daemonic possession, restless shades, portals into strange dimensions both natural and fabricated, Max had faced them all, but this was different.

The power pouring out of the rift was breathtaking. The scale of it went beyond human comprehension. The tear filled the sky as if it meant to encircle the airship whole to swallow it in one calamitous bite. The colours that had streamed from its periphery were no longer visible. All that remained was blackness. It was not empty, though, far from it. Max could feel the malice seeping from that opening. There was something in there, a mind that Max could feel in the same way as he could feel fire on his skin as he burned or water in his lungs as he drowned, but whose reasoning was just as impossible for a mortal man to discern. It was the complexity of the universe, and its simplicity. It hated Max both as a representative of the mortal races but also as the man and individual that it recognised as Max Schreiber. That the Chaos Gods should reserve even a miniscule fraction of their enmity for him alone was at once chilling and strangely exhilarating.

Max shook his head. His thoughts were wandering, driven apart like sheep harried by wolves. There was too much random magic coming out of the rift. It was impossible to focus, and that made his mind easy prey. Had he a circle of acolytes to fortify his mind it might have been different, but he was the only wizard of any kind on board, and several successive attempts to make do alone had left his mind reeling and the taste of burnt copper in his mouth.

That left the brute force approach.

Reluctantly, he rallied his mind within the walls of his own head and concentrated upon his own power. Without needing to explore its limits, he knew that it was greater than it had ever been. The discoveries he had made in Praag, the... *things* he had done, had changed him and he could not say that it was all for the better. That alone was reason enough to doubt whether he should use these powers to their fullest, but it was not the only one. The End Times had upended many established truths, but there were many that still held. There were still dark things lurking beyond the veil of the aethyr, and it remained unwise to announce oneself to that realm with a reckless show of power.

Yet he could not escape the conclusion that he had the power that he needed, precisely where he needed it. He had had dreams of prophecy, and he knew that Felix and Gotrek had greater destinies than being swallowed by the Realm of Chaos.

Malakai grunted as the light from Max's staff redoubled in intensity.

'Dae ye huv tae dae it sae brightly? Ahm tryin' to see where ahm gawn.'

Max's mind wrinkled from the sour note in the aethyr like

parchment from a candle flame. It was the daemon prince that he had felt before, but his presence was much more powerful now that he had returned to his native plane. A vile name curdled the substance of the aethyr. It was one Max was horribly familiar with from his long studies into the nature of Chaos. The deeds attached to it were legendary, and in truth he had considered it no more than a story, a heroic epic told amongst the champions of the Dark Powers.

And yet here he was. The first. The Dark Master of Chaos.

Be'lakor.

The daemon had not returned to the aethyr. He was passing through it, hunting for something. For *someone*. For...

Max's grip tightened around his staff.

'Oh no.'

A ripple of unease passed through Felix. It felt as though the clouds had parted to reveal a glimpse of his own tombstone. It had come from nowhere, and was not a helpful feeling to harbour when one was hanging by a rope miles above the ground. Felix slashed Karaghul behind him, opening a diving ray from mouth to tailfin. It veered off with a shriek, but the clouds boiled with more. Schools of the daemonic creatures strafed the soldiers spread out through the netting. Others fixed their horrible flat bodies to the gasbag, squirming like hellish leeches to work at the metal with their teeth. The airship alternately rumbled and groaned.

He and Corporal Mann had fought for every rung and hold to reach the midline of the gasbag, where the outward slope steepened into a short vertical drop that then swept back in towards the gasbag's belly. The trick, Felix knew, was never to look down, but that bridge had been crossed and burned behind him some time ago and it was with a rather blithesome refusal to obey his own good sense that he looked down.

For a moment the clouds thinned sufficiently for Felix to see the great steel hawsers that swept down into the distance. They creaked like old bones clad in iron rust, audible even over the wind and the howling of daemons. Beneath them, like a wreck dredged from the ocean's bottom, rode the gondola of *Unstoppable*. A damp powder fizzle of small-arms fire crackled from ladders and portholes into the swarm of flying daemons. The precariousness of their situation was terrifying to see. Felix knew that if those daemons were to succeed in separating the gondola from the gasbag then, without its engines and supplies, he would be just as doomed as Malakai and the rest of the airship's crew.

As he watched, however, the rays broke off from their assault and turned as one in a new direction. His direction.

Felix gaped at the big black mass coming his way until the cloud blew back in and obscured them. The small company of men must have drawn them away. It was better than having them attack the gasbag, he supposed, but the sheer number of them made a mockery of his bold intentions of holding them off for even just a few minutes.

Felix's thoughts ran circles around each other in his head. Should they stay a little longer, occupy the daemons for as long as they could, or return to the dorsal spine while they still had a remote chance of doing so? Yelling words of encouragement to the men around him, he quickly looked around to judge how much longer they could usefully fight. Everywhere, the men of Hochland were beset, hanging by arms hooked through the netting and flailing about them with their swords. The first of the incoming wave of rays broke the clouds below and Felix made up his mind.

'Up! Everybody back up to the top.'

Felix clung to the shaking net until he was certain that nobody had remained behind to be the hero. He glanced between his feet and cursed in confusion.

The daemons hadn't altered their course at all. They weren't being drawn by the force of Hochlanders.

They were coming for him!

'What are you waiting for, my lord?' shouted Herschel Mann, fighting his way back down flanked by a pair of his soldiers and making short and unfussy work of holding the daemons at bay with the superior length of his officer's longsword.

Felix took another look down. His heart seemed to slow to a crawl. They were good men, deserving of at least a chance to survive. In the circumstances, the errant 'my lord' didn't grate quite the way it used to. 'Go on ahead. I'll be right behind you.'

'The men would never forgive me if I left you behind.'

'You're not. I'm just giving you a head start.'

Felix lurched his sword around to swipe at the first bullet nose to scream up from the clouds under his feet. The daemon wrung its flat body around the tired stroke and lashed its tail across his back. His mail absorbed most of the force from the blow, but the mail ringlets biting through his undershirt to impose another line of bruises made him cry out in pain. On reflex he pulled himself tighter to the gasbag, swinging out again and missing again, but this time the daemon issued a panicked shriek that, but for the absence of a wound, almost convinced Felix he'd hit it. With a ripple of rubbery wings, the daemon peeled off, the masses coming in behind following it in unbroken formation.

The unexpected reprieve made Felix laugh.

'Humorous is it not, Felix Jaeger, these quirks of fate?'

Felix gasped at the thin, chilly air. His gaze shot up. Above him like a monolith carved in obsidian to an ancient god was the daemon prince. His wings beat slowly, deliberately, shadowing Felix's racing heart. Dark clouds brushed his muscular frame.

'Laugh on, mortal,' said the daemon prince, raising his monstrous sword over Felix like an executioner. 'Only in a world where the gods make games of destiny and men bay like wolves beneath the Chaos Moon can one so feeble be prophesied as the downfall of one so mighty.'

Felix brought up Karaghul as the daemon prince cut down, but the black blade struck not at Felix himself but at the netting that he clung to. The ropes severed without resistance, snapping one by one until there was nothing to hold up that which remained. The netting dropped away. Felix clung on in blind terror as the gasbag's riveted shell shot by. Something still attached caught. The loose end of the net whipped out from the hull, the change of direction drastic and, at such speed, snapping the rope through Felix's despairing fingers and flinging him out into the clouds.

FOURTEEN

The Sacrifice

Felix's arms and legs whirled as he plummeted. His cloak pulled free from his breeches and tore around him in a roar. The air rushed by too fast for him to draw breath. He was going to die. The thought raced around and around in his brain, growing ever shriller as his heart beat faster and faster. It hurt, as though it were being squeezed, and Felix wondered whether it would be the ground or his own terror that killed him first. He was going to die! Futile as the tiny spark of rational thought still extant inside his mind knew the struggle to be, he clawed through the clouds. It was like trying to catch the wind. His despairing scream was lost to the gale in his ears, the blistering comet tail of his cloak.

The clouds began to thicken as he fell deeper, darkening, and so frantic was Felix's mind that it took him a moment to realise that his first impression was literal.

The clouds were actually getting *thicker*.

Gelatinous threads of shadow and something insubstantial that Felix could neither see nor fully touch streamed through his fingers, sticking to his skin for the briefest of moments before they snapped. He was falling into a web of shadow. And he was slowing! The shadow rose up to envelop him, sticking to his arms and legs, covering his eyes and filling his mouth with urgent threads of darkness. Panic filled him. He scratched the strands from his body even as he continued to fall, an instinctive aversion to the touch of Chaos overriding even his sense of self-preservation.

'Don't struggle, Felix.'

The voice came from the shadow itself and hence from all around, resonating with something deep within Felix's mind that wished for nothing other than to obey. It was calming, darkly familiar, but something about it made Felix fight it all the harder. He'd seen with his own eyes that there were worse fates in life than death.

A ripple passed through the clouds, the tremor of a struggling insect in a god-spider's web, and Felix felt something look up and take note. He sensed the spider. A surge of force, tinged with impatience, filled the air around him with strands. It had tried to be gentle, now it was taking him whether he liked it or not.

A crushing weight closed over his chest, but before he had time to register it the sensation had passed, the web of shadow seeming to pass through his skin and out the other side of his body as though he wasn't fully there. He shivered but not, he realised, with cold because to his surprise it no longer was. Nor was he falling. In fact if anything the clouds were rising up *through* him, and stealing a part of him away with them.

His thoughts no longer seemed to be all in one place. His body, as discovered by that shadow, no longer seemed to exist at all.

Through a ghostly skein of grey he saw Gotrek. The Slayer's mouth was open in a silent roar, his shoulder dropped like a battering ram as he charged a blocked hatchway. He saw Gustav, grainy and hollow, fleeing through deserted hallways. Lights glimmered, bedimmed, then changed, becoming instead the dials and gauges of *Unstoppable*'s bridge. Malakai Makaisson battled against the riptides from the Chaos rift, shades of eternity and damnation visible in black through the view screen.

Again the view faded to grey and Felix was pulled away. He possessed thought but no will, a strip of cloud at the mercy of the winds. Panic seemed as alien now as his own physical body, and freed of it he recognised the same spell that Max had used to extract them from the besieged belfry in the old dwarf township. Max had saved him. Now he was able to think clearly he could feel his friend all around him, but he also realised that they were not alone in the shadows. There was another, a stronger wind, pulling them both away from the others and back above the airship's dorsal spine once again. Clouds flashed by with ferocious speed, obscuring the form in their midst.

'*You would seek to defy me with shadow, wizard? I am the lord of shadow. I am the black beyond the stars.*'

For a moment, Felix felt himself pulled in two different directions. It began with a tingling in extremities he could still not yet see. He felt cold again, and the wind roared through his ears. Then there was a jolt, a wave of compression that rolled across every surface of his body as the shadows were torn away and his consciousness, bound up once again in meat and pain, was slammed face-down onto a frozen metal walkway.

His fingers crawled over the metal, feeling every weld and rivet as though it were a mountain of ice. His mind spun, confused, translocated. His skin felt as though it belonged to another man half his size. The thin, frosty air curdled in his lungs. His throat clenched, his belly tightened, and he vomited onto the walkway. Shivering like a man pulled from freezing water, Felix twitched onto his side and gasped.

Herschel Mann lay facing him, flat on his side as was Felix, eyes wide. Still. Dead. Shadow coiled around the Hochlander's face, bleeding from his glassy, horror-filled eyes like tears.

Felix cried out, rolling the other way and sitting up.

Bodies lay everywhere along the airship's iron spine, cloud blowing between them so that they resembled barrows, dark humps that concealed dead men rising in eerie monument from the mist.

'This is the mortal prophesied as my downfall?' The daemon prince's laughter rumbled over the dead like thunder as he descended, landing lightly in the running cloud on the walkway. He sneered at Felix. His wings folded in behind his back as he drew up his sword, opening his vast chest and the eight-pointed star of Chaos that glowed silver in the dark. 'I will not permit it. Not in my world.'

'This world is not yours,' Max answered, tiredly but firmly. The wizard's robes were frayed, as though he had been involved in a struggle that Felix had not been conscious of. They fluttered about him in the wind, exposing a grey-veined hand as the wizard moved to wipe a rivulet of gruelish blood from his nostril. 'As long as I live it will not be.'

'I was the champion of the Lord of Magic before your civilisation was born. I am Be'lakor. What are you to me, *wizard?*'

Max rubbed the unpleasantly dark liquid from his nose between thumb and forefinger, and with the other hand tightened his grip on his staff. Its head began to glow white. 'An agent of destiny.'

'Where I darken the sky, destiny withers. I have already dealt with the Slayer.'

Felix recalled the image of Gotrek that Max's shadow magic had shown him, trapped somewhere within the gondola of *Unstoppable* but alive. Dealt with perhaps, but not defeated.

'I believe you will find me an opponent of a different order,' said Max levelly. 'If you wish to harm Felix then you must do so through me. And I promise you, when I am finished you will be cast so deeply into the Realm of Chaos that the sun will be old and red by the time you set foot on this world again.'

The wizard's conviction caused the mighty daemon prince to hesitate, but only for a moment before he relaxed and began to chuckle, a blade of mirthless malevolence with which he stirred the winds of magic. Max bent into the sudden wind, robes pulling against him in the vortex of dark magic that swirled around Be'lakor. His staff glowed like a lantern in a storm. He raised it high, then struck it down against the walkway, discharging a sphere of electric white force just as Be'lakor unleashed a rolling torrent of black flame towards him.

Felix shook off the residual disorientation left over from his rescue to roll clear and bury his face under his arms.

The explosion shook the entire superstructure of the gasbag.

Felix uncovered enough of one eye to witness a catherine wheel of coloured fire spinning out around the wizard and his barrier of light. Without pause, Max responded with a powerful conjuration of his own. A white sphere circumferenced with hissing serpents appeared before him and shot forwards, spitting bolts of lightning before Be'lakor split it asunder with a word. With a grasping gesture, the daemon prince brought the stuff of the aethyr rushing to him, and with a snarl of disdain sent it spraying from his extended hand to erupt against Max's barrier in a pillar of hellfire.

Faster than the untutored eye could follow, Max Schreiber and Be'lakor bombarded each other with spells of ever increasing potency and pyroclastic fury.

Magic missiles fizzed and whined, glowing trails left in the air to be obliterated by the concussive blast fronts of explosions. Summoned beings rose briefly from the ferment only to be banished or simply torn apart by the crossfire. Shields both Light and Dark crackled in opposition. Commanding the heavens to his will Be'lakor reached skywards to call down a shower of warpstone meteors, each one detonating a hundred feet above the airship against an incandescent rainbow cast from Max's fingertips.

Felix held grimly on, helpless to affect this duel, as the airship shuddered.

The air itself seemed to be beaten out of shape by the magical onslaught. Like a warped mirror in a house of horrors, the damaged air distorted both light and sound. Felix could hear what sounded like screams, interspersed with bursts of wild laughter that dribbled through the clouds like poison. Wiping the taste of sick from his lips, he steeled his courage and rose to his feet. The walkway shuddered and Felix widened his stance to compensate. He could feel an intense pressure on the back of his skull, a migraine thump that drew his gaze to the body of Herschel Mann.

The shadows coiling around the man's body made his late comrade appear to twitch. And again, a flex of the fingers against the metal beneath his body. Felix's heart hammered a warning. It was more than just his imagination. A sudden movement from behind spun him around.

One of the Hochlanders rose from the walkway as if repelled by some dark magnetism, his limp body angling to plant feet onto the metal. His mouth hung open, his eyes wide and staring and filmed with shadow. The man took a staggering step forwards and emitted an endlessly echoing groan. Another step, more assured, and an eye blinked open on his cheek. Felix moaned in horror. Daemons. He didn't have enough knowledge of the subject to say whether it was the unleashed magic of two such mighty spellcasters that was drawing them or whether it was the proximity of the rift. He supposed it didn't matter.

Felix backed away from the possessed man until his thigh pressed against the handrail. Wiping ice-cold sweat from his palms onto his trews, he reaffirmed his grip on his sword. He tried to focus on Be'lakor but the daemon prince had become almost transparent, as much a part of the distortion cloud that surrounded him as a discrete entity in his own right. Max however looked little better. He clung two-handed to his staff as though it were a rooted tree and he was caught in a hurricane. His eyes and mouth were rimmed with brackish blood and he slumped a little lower with every assault that pounded into his barrier.

With a crunch of broken bones, Herschel Mann lurched upright.

The dead man drew a shuddering breath. His chest swelled, pushing out his red-and-green livery until it tore. The skin beneath was black and hard. Darkening arms stretched, a succession of *cracks* as new joints were broken into lengthening bones or old ones twisted to unpleasant angles. His face flattened, his chest broadening to swallow it up.

Felix lowered his sword, too sickened to maintain his guard. Was this what the Chaos Gods had in store for the world? Was this to be the fate of Gustav, Kat, and everyone else that survived these final days if they failed? Defiance rekindled the fight in his heart and he raised his sword, turning again to Max. He wouldn't let his friend fall while he stood idle. Not like Snorri.

Not again!

He hacked through Mann's grasping arm at the second of his elbows, then smashed his pommel into the possessed's maw as he charged past. He managed only a handful of strides before the force of magic sent him reeling back, his clothes steaming. It was not a physical barrier as such, but it was like trying to run into a fire. He gave a despairing yell, then clutched his sword for strength and summoned his willpower for another attempt. Max turned to face him.

'Go to Kazad Drengazi, Felix. Fulfil your destiny and the Slayer's. It is more important than my life.'

'No. How many have to die before it becomes important? How many is too many?'

A light brighter than anything Felix had ever seen or could have imagined existing in a world that contained such darkness blazed through the wizard's skin, and in the second before Felix was forced to look away he could not see a shred of shade on him. His eyes were summer-blue, his long hair and scholarly brow brushed with white. He was numinous and Felix ached to see the man beneath the shadow once more.

He was Max Schreiber, as Felix would always remember him.

'Both eyes open, Felix.'

A wave of radiance washed out from the wizard, purifying the possessed where they stood and rolling out towards Be'lakor, stripping the daemon prince of his wards before breaking over his infernal form. Be'lakor roared in pain and fury, the black substance of his being going up in smoke. The sky pinwheeled in response and Felix flung his hand to the handrail to keep from pitching over the side. The rift stuttered in a state of flux, at times there and at others nothing but a grey sky.

'You cannot stop me, mortal,' bellowed Be'lakor. 'Even the gods cannot stop me.'

The daemon prince brought together what remained of his burning hands and Felix felt him summoning power.

He screamed a warning, just as the circular hatch leading down into the gasbag flung back to reveal Gotrek Gurnisson's fiery orange crest. The Slayer took in the situation at a glance, slamming his axe down onto the walkway and adding his own booming voice to Felix's.

'I dreamt this,' said Max, smiling feebly, sagging against his staff.

There was an implosion, a drawing in of light and sound to a dark point ravaged by white fire. The daemon prince burned away, his essence unravelling into the aethyr with a final thunderclap of spite that crumpled the walkway where he had been standing and sent a shockwave rolling out towards Max Schreiber.

'No!' roared Felix and Gotrek together.

Max didn't even have the energy left to react. The wave struck him full in the chest and blasted him clear over the side of the gasbag.

Felix seized the handrail and had to consciously hold on to keep himself from diving after his friend. *Come back,* he urged, praying that Max could somehow hear his thoughts and find the strength. He stared into the clouds, willing for the disturbance that would let him know Max was alive. There was nothing.

Max had saved him. He had held nothing back for himself.

Felix's eyes burned but nothing would come out. How long he waited, watching the clouds rush by beneath him, he could not say.

Come back.

How many was too many? How many friends could he lose before he found himself no different to Gotrek?

The Slayer joined him at the edge. His huge fist swallowed the handrail. His one eye found Felix's. It was set hard, a diamond in stone. His battered and war-weary features parted for a wordless snarl. Felix nodded, squeezing the handrail until his hand was numb from frost and his knuckles white. For once he and the Slayer were in agreement.

They were going to Kazad Drengazi.

Nergüi's cold, dead face darkened with a scowl. The tribesmen waiting nearby to participate in the shaman's final rites recoiled from the unexpected show of animation, a fearful murmur of leather scales and dark silk. His feather headdress hissed betrayal. The spirits whose charms he wore sewn into his gown lay silent. The gash across his throat sneered at the feeble trappings of an ignorant life.

'*You are my hands and eyes in this mortal world,*' the shadows around the shaman's mouth hissed. '*But blind is what you are, crippled, weak. You could have warned me that the wizard wielded such power. He almost succeeded in destroying me.*'

'I did what I could, Dark Master,' said Morzanna, smothering the faintest, strangest impulse to smile. She could not say that a part of her was not glad that Felix and his companion were still alive, and not simply because fate had demanded that it be so.

'*Do not say it, Morzanna. Men are slaves to their destiny, gods forge it. The Slayer will fall as you have foretold he will, and then I will deal with the human myself.*'

Morzanna nodded, but the daemon prince was wrong.

Even gods had their paths to follow.

'*What are you waiting for?*' The shadows knotted and coiled around the shaman's body like tensing muscles, rippling suddenly outwards like a snap of wings. '*You have seen the path and you know what you must do now.*'

Morzanna nodded her understanding as the shadows dispersed and Nergüi became a dead man once again.

An awed murmur passed through the rank upon rank of sun-browned and leather-scaled warriors that filled the mountain causeway. They undulated over rocket-blown craters, horsehair plumes rippling like the yellow grasses of the steppe. Bowmen in armour of stiffened horsehide crouched in silence across the steep, rocky roadside. Even the horses seemed to catch the mood, scratching skittishly at the road.

Morzanna licked dry lips. All eyes were on her.

Command was not something to which she was accustomed,

respect was not a thing she had ever sought after or craved. Hers was to guide and to follow, and in truth she had little care for the company of others. Indeed, she had never felt as at peace as she had during her self-imposed hermitage in the Shirokij with her spiders; hidden from the dreams of others, at least for a time, while destiny slumbered.

She ran her claws down the hard wood of her eagle-skull staff. Feathers flew. Chimes tinkled softly in the breeze. The cool wind was biting on the face and sharp on her nose and tongue. She had heard it said that the tribes could move an army faster than any other. There was a saying amongst them that Katchar's all-seeing eye would tire and look away before their horses stopped running. The men liked to say that they could cross mountains, rivers, and even oceans and be ready to fight at the end.

A boast, but there was truth to be found there.

At least she hoped so. They had no airship to call upon and a lot of ground to catch up.

'Ready your men and your beasts,' she said to nobody in particular, neither knowing nor caring who amongst the remaining men now took charge of such things.

She extended a short dark claw towards the abandoned keep of the dwarfs. Her eyes narrowed. There was a road there, phasing in and out of her sight. She could not quite keep it in view, but that did not matter. She knew it was there.

The road to Kazad Drengazi.

And the fate of the world.

The idling engines produced a somnolent hum. Even the lighting on the bridge was subdued, reduced to a handful of glowing dials and the feeble sunlight. Clouds brushed the view screen like a mourning veil. Malakai Makaisson had shut down everything that could be shut down in order to save power. The battle had exhausted most of their fuel, and the destruction of the hangar deck had – by accident or intent – robbed them of what little the dwarfs had held in reserve.

Makaisson himself stood with both hands on the wheel, either unaware or not caring that the engines were powered down and the steering locks engaged. He wore his shattered one-lensed goggles and stared through the window into the cloud. Gotrek sat slumped in a swivel chair, to all outward appearances asleep, his brutalised physique swaying with the gentle movements of the ship. Gustav paced back and forth under the view screen, cursing under his breath and scratching at the scabs of his injured hand. Occasionally the young man would flinch, whenever a darker strip of cloud flicked across the view screen or a crosswind caused the deckplate to judder, then redouble his scratching and resume his pacing.

All of them kept to their own thoughts, plagued by their own daemons.

It was Malakai who broke the observance of silence, thumping the wheel and issuing a violent curse as the iron-bound oak splintered. 'Ah cannae believe Max is deid. Ah thought he'd ootlive us all and tha's sayin' somethin' of a human even if it's comin' frae a Slayer.' The engineer drew his knuckles out of the wheel and grunted miserably. He looked around the depopulated deck. Most of the surviving engineers were busy in the engine room or still compiling damage reports. Or tending to the dead. 'There's nae many left o' the auld crew, is there?'

Felix sighed, sat in a chair of his own. He didn't feel up to speaking yet. He shook his head. No. No, there wasn't. He turned to Gotrek.

Even with his one eye closed the Slayer looked utterly haggard. Felix had seen his companion more severely beaten than this. After the battle with the Bloodthirster in Karag Dum the Slayer had barely been able to walk unaided. But even then, having triumphed over the mightiest doom he would see in many years, Felix had not seen him so crushed in spirit. Were Felix feeling cynical, he might have been tempted to ascribe the Slayer's mood to Malakai's earlier admission that they no longer had fuel enough to clear the Middle Mountains to reach Middenheim. But that was unfair. This went deeper. If the wound were a physical one it would have gouged the bone.

To Felix's surprise – and his shame for doubting it – Gotrek actually did care about his friends, these short-lived humans with their strange, flighty concerns who had become so important in his life.

Opening that door shone a light onto another that Felix had sought after for a long time. Gotrek had been cold towards Felix since their reunion in Praag and he had often wondered – bitterly at times – what he could have done to earn the antipathy of a dwarf with such honest blood on his hands. The Slayer resented Felix's decision to leave him and return to the Empire with his new wife, he knew, but he had always believed that was because he had unwittingly reneged on some unspoken dwarf tradition of comradeship.

He had been half right. He saw that now.

Perhaps, once, it had been about the oath, about Slayer and rememberer, but that had been decades ago. How many opportunities had he been given to leave before and not taken them? Could he count them on one hand? Somewhere along the way they had become friends, possibly the only friend each of them had, and Gotrek had fully expected him to remain even without the formal obligation of the oath.

But Felix had left.

He felt sick.

'Ah say we wheel her aboot and gae back tae ma auld keep.'

Makaisson thumped his palm meaningfully and growled. 'Ah owe a world full o' hurt tae tha' daemon and whoever summoned the blasted thing ontae ma airship.'

Felix recalled the power that Be'lakor had unleashed against the airship, unleashed against *him*, and shook his head grimly. Never before had he had cause to doubt Malakai Makaisson's ability to deliver on an oath of vengeance.

'Kazad Drengazi,' Gotrek grunted as though muttering the name in his sleep, but though his one eye remained closed there was clearly still no rest to be had for him here.

Felix turned to Gustav.

His nephew was still pacing, but he pulled up with a scowl as if feeling the weight of attention on him and thrust his hands into his pockets. 'Kazad Drengazi, agreed. For Kolya, in case anyone's forgotten him.'

'A dwarf forgets nothing,' Gotrek snapped.

'Sometimes he just seems to.'

'Sometimes I forget where I stick my axe.'

'Don't argue,' said Felix weakly. He felt decidedly fragile, as though something precious inside him teetered and would surely shatter under one more harsh word. 'Just don't.'

Gotrek subsided back into his armchair. Gustav's face tightened with anger and he returned to pacing the bridge.

'Kazad Drengazi's what the daemon wants,' said Gotrek. 'It said as much to me itself. There's a power there, or so the legend says. If you're strong enough to take it.'

'If ye're worthy o' it,' Makaisson corrected him.

'What do you plan on doing with that power once you have it?' Gustav muttered, still pacing.

Gotrek watched the young man back and forth, yellowed teeth bared. 'I don't care, so long as the daemon doesn't get it.'

'We'll use it,' said Felix, pulling his face up out of his hands and meeting the eyes of all his surviving friends in turn. Gotrek he saved until last. 'Be'lakor said I'm destined to be his downfall. Those were his exact words to me before Max...' He shook his head, shivered it off. 'So we'll do what Max asked me to do. We'll beat the daemon to Kazad Drengazi, take whatever's there for us to take, and return with it to Middenheim. On foot if we have to. And we'll save the damned world if it kills us.'

'Joost tha'?' said Malakai, raising a limp smile from Gustav.

'The little one's lost, manling,' said Gotrek. The Slayer averted his eye and clenched his thighs, broken fingernails digging through his trews and into the flesh. As if to distract himself from a greater pain. 'I know that. I've known that since we heard the news of Altdorf. I just didn't want to believe it.'

'I think I've known it since Praag,' Felix sighed.

Gotrek grunted, scratched his nose self-consciously and sniffed. 'Middenheim it is then. It sounds like a plan.'

'Ah daen't mean to rain on anyin's parade, but huv either o' ye gied any thought at all tae how ye're gaunny find a place that hasnae been found in ten thousand years o' lookin'?'

Felix thought about this for a moment, then sank back into despondency. He'd forgotten about that. Max had been so certain about where they had to go that he'd assumed it would be obvious. He smiled self-pityingly. Give him a dragon in a cave or a vampire in his castle and he and Gotrek were in their element. They worked well together when things were straightforward and down the years neither one had exactly covered themselves in glory when it came to thinking things through. He recalled the view of the Middle Mountains that he had had from Makaisson's keep: the outposts, the roads, each one a stitch in a vast tapestry sewn together over the millennia. If the dogged determination of all those generations of dwarfs had failed to locate the Fortress of the First Slayer then what hope did he have?

What did Felix have that they hadn't?

A gentle bout of turbulence disturbed him from his thoughts.

What did *he* have?

He blinked, taking in the glowing dials arrayed around him as though seeing them for the first time. He looked up to stare open-mouthed at the clouds buffeting the view screen. Sigmar, he'd been so blind.

'What?' said Gustav.

'Malakai, how high can this ship go?'

'Until the air gets tae thin tae hold her. It's nae like floating a boat. It's complicated.'

Felix grinned, clapping the perplexed engineer on the shoulder and resisting the urge to hug him. The Middle Mountains' ancient dwarfs had striven for centuries, but they'd not had the genius of Malakai Makaisson on their side.

They had not had an airship!

'Take us up,' Felix shouted, too filled with excitement, the certainty that he was *right*, to control his voice. He climbed stiffly out of his chair. 'Up above the clouds. As high as she'll go.'

Unstoppable broke the surface of the cloud like a whale emerging from the ocean for air. Watery white cloud streamed down her gleaming hull, her mighty tail propellers frothing it up behind her as she climbed into open sky. It was not the blue that Felix had become accustomed to looking up to from the ground. It was a thin purple, a gauze through which Felix could see the black of space and the glitter of stars. It was hauntingly beautiful.

Felix pressed his face to the cool glass of the circular viewport by the airlock hatch. Cloud stretched for untold leagues in every direction, broken here and there by mountain peaks that rose from the surface like volcanic isles. The sun was a golden rune, shining from the purpure of the sky. The magical glow glittered from the mountaintops. One of them glittered back.

Felix gaped in wonder.

It was a citadel in the sky, its monolithic gates of iron-banded oak surrounded not by water or a ditch but by a moat of white cloud. Walls of a pale, luminous stone climbed towards the summit, rising with each successive ring as though the still-growing mountain had pushed up through the foundations of the ancient fortification. There the bright sunlight reflected dazzlingly from leaded windows and runic engravings, the stern face of Grimnir shining from the walls of buildings in hues of gold, silver and brass. The entire edifice looked as old as the stars, and yet there was an immaculate quality to it as though it had waited empty all these millennia for the tread of mortal feet.

Kazad Drengazi. The Fortress of the First Slayer. It had to be.

Had dwarfs once dwelt in this unlikely place, Felix wondered, or had the entire fortification been called to the mountaintop at the command of their god of war?

That there was something down there, Felix had no doubt. He could feel its power tingling under his skin. And what had the seeress said to him in his dream?

You are powerless against the opponent that awaits you in Kazad Drengazi, Felix, and Gotrek's passing will be the doom of this world.

He gave an involuntary shudder.

But it may be enough to save the next.

Gotrek watched from the neighbouring porthole, strangely subdued. The half-circle of admitted light cut his face in two, giving his bruised jaw a coppery complexion. Felix agonised over what to tell his companion about the seeress's warning, if anything, but the certainty that it would be a pointless waste of breath bade him keep his dreams to himself. The Slayer was going to Kazad Drengazi now regardless of what awaited him there or anything that Felix might say.

And not alone.

Felix had pledged his companion no new oath. It was unnecessary. They both knew that he would follow the Slayer to the end.

The engines growled hungrily, rattling the bulkheads as Malakai Makaisson guided them in.

'You asked me once why I do not sleep, manling,' said Gotrek, nodding towards the fortress as it slid beneath them. 'This is why. When I do I dream always of this place. I die here.' He turned from the porthole. The metallic glow that the window shone onto his face imposed a stark, disturbing resemblance to the effigies of Grimnir in the citadel below. 'And it is not a good death.'

PART THREE

HE THAT TAKES MY LIFE

Early Summer 2527

FIFTEEN

Kazad Drengazi

Felix dropped the final couple of feet between the bottom rung of the rope ladder and the smooth white flagstones. His first act on setting foot within the ancient stronghold of the First Slayer was to execute a dramatic shiver. The air on the mountaintop was cold and thin. Either on their own would have been sufficient to account for the tingling in Felix's fingertips and the blueness in his lips.

Breathe slowly, he reminded himself, hugging his chest under his cloak, *slowly and deeply.*

Gotrek was already down, swinging his axe in practice strokes as he paced out the wide plaza. It was encircled by marble statues that appeared to show various aspects of Grimnir. He was vengeance, war, honour, dishonour; in some instances he had one axe, in others two. Occasionally he was depicted dealing death with his huge hands and with daemonic gristle in his bared teeth.

On one side, a set of wide, shallow steps led up to an imposing structure fronted by square-sided stone columns. Simply by virtue of its position at the highest and most central point within the fortress, it was evidently a building of significance. Ornate entablature depicted scenes of battle, apparently the same battle, advancing through time as the eye followed from left to right before circling around the building to commence again. Unending. Felix immediately considered it to be a temple. On the opposite side a corresponding set of steps led down towards a rune-reinforced wooden gate. The plaza was set high enough that Felix could see over the inner wall, through the sparse forest of turrets and towers to the cloud sea beyond.

A breathtaking sense of loneliness pervaded the place, not that of an old man or a friendless warrior, to which Felix could relate, but that of a being that by its nature had no equal. The very stones that he stood upon now had once felt the tread of a god. It was an awesome, humbling feeling, and one that Felix would hesitate to call pleasant. He remembered when he and his father and brother had taken to the streets to witness the coronation of Karl Franz. He had caught a glimpse of Sigmar's mighty hammer, Ghal Maraz, during its presentation to the new Emperor and the feeling he had now was similar to what he had experienced at that moment.

Insignificance, but married to a counterintuitive sense of collective importance, a physical connection to something ancient and powerful.

With an effort, he pulled his thoughts away from the divine and looked up.

The sleek mass of *Unstoppable* hung conspicuously against the violet sky, an uncanny combination of sun and starlight glittering from her gun-turrets. This wasn't the first time that Felix had experienced such altitudes. There were peaks in the Worlds Edge Mountains which – as any dwarf would tell anyone – made all others resemble bumps in the ground, but he had never seen a sky like this. It was more than just altitude.

Some other force was at work here to thin the barriers between worlds.

Malakai Makaisson was halfway down the swaying rope ladder, laden with enough of an arsenal to take the peak by force twice over if he had to. The longrifle that Felix had experienced the business end of during their accidental encounter in the Middle Mountains was slung over one shoulder. With the other elbow, Makaisson pinned an enormous multi-barrelled, crank-operated handcannon to his side. A satchel that the engineer had rather gleefully informed him was filled with bombs bounced against his back. A brace of heavily modified pistols was buckled at his hip and a small axe hung from his belt by a thong.

Felix didn't want to meet the thing that would warrant the axe.

Following some distance above the engineer came Gustav Jaeger, climbing cautiously in full armour, the wind pulling plaintively at his ponytail and wolfskin cloak. Behind him came a string of frighteningly well-outfitted and intense-looking men. When the last of Gustav's company had their boots on the ground, Makaisson tugged twice on the ladder, then threw a salute with the barrel of his longrifle towards *Unstoppable*'s prow.

The airship pulled slowly up and away. The stony emptiness of abandonment crawled up in its place.

'Over here, manling.'

Felix turned towards his companion's voice and gave a start. His hand dropped to his sword hilt as one by one the soldiers looked around and cried out in alarm. Makaisson swung up his longrifle, only to turn it down into the ground with an exclamation of what sounded like surprise.

Facing Gotrek was another dwarf, although quite possibly the strangest-looking one that Felix had ever seen. Blue, red and purple spiral tattoos covered his bald head and a row of metal rings pierced his jaw in place of a beard. He was wearing what looked like a toga, but which clinked as he slipped out from between the line of statues into the plaza. Closer inspection revealed it to be a weave of bronze ringlets rather than cloth. Gotrek held his axe up warningly. The strange dwarf halted and stared, apparently fixated upon Gotrek's weapon. He pointed at it.

'*Ahz.*'

Felix turned, bemused, to Gotrek who shook his head.

'It's not Khazalid, manling. Or no strain of it that I'm familiar with.'

'I didn't realise there were dialects of Dwarfish.'

Gotrek snorted, not taking his eye off the stranger. 'You've never been to Kraka Drak, have you?'

'He said *axe*,' said Makaisson, haltingly. 'Ah think.'

'*Ahz!*' the stranger repeated.

'Aye, very clever,' Gotrek grumbled, tightening his grip and drawing his weapon nearer to his chest as though anyone could be fool enough to try and take it from him.

'You can understand him,' Felix murmured to Makaisson from the corner of his mouth.

'Ah wouldnae say tha' exactly, but ma hame is a bit oot o' the wye too and it sounds a wee bit similar.'

'I thought that dwarfs didn't change like that,' said Gustav.

'They don't,' said Gotrek flintily. 'That should tell you how long they've been cut off up here.'

'They–'

Felix looked up to note that, as they had been talking, more monkish dwarfs had shuffled into view. At least a dozen, but no more than twenty. Fewer than there were statues. Gotrek's ears were, of course, sharper than his and the Slayer had likely marked their approach some time ago. Felix wished that he could be reassured by his companion's diffident attitude to finding himself surrounded in a strange citadel by an even stranger force of dwarfs.

A place, lest he forget, that they had both been told would be the Slayer's doom.

The newcomers closed in with a metallic shuffle, murmuring, pointing at Gotrek and also occasionally at Makaisson, often with some kind of whispered argument involved.

'Everyone lower their weapons,' said Felix, raising his hand slowly from his scabbard and trusting to Gustav and his nervous men to do the same. The last thing anyone needed right now was a sweaty finger on a pistol trigger.

Makaisson held his longrifle across his thighs. He turned slowly about, pausing to listen to snippets of conversation before moving on. His face was a grimace of concentration. 'They're all sayin' somethin' tae dae wi' a prophecy. Somethin' aboot their ancestors' lang wait. And Grimnir.' He cocked his head intently and turned halfway around. 'And the End Times.' His grimace tightened still further, then he shook his head. 'Ack, ah cannae follow it all. Ah wish they'd all stoap whisperin.'

Gustav nudged Felix in the ribs and nodded urgently towards the temple.

A powerfully built dwarf was descending the steps. He was massively broad. A bronze breastplate shaped into an impossibly well-defined musculature was strapped over his ringmail toga. A purple cloak hung from his shoulders. The elaborate tattoos on his bare head depicted an epic struggle between dwarf and daemon. The dwarf in particular was remarkably well rendered, and *his* tattoos showed a near-identical scene: the battle continuing, as in the temple entablature, seemingly without end. In one bear-paw of a hand the newcomer held up an axe that could have been an exact replica of Gotrek's own. Strapped to his back and covered by his cloak but for the handle and the rim of the blade was another, equally large, that could have been its twin. Even Felix could see that these were both lesser blades. Masterfully forged though they undoubtedly were, they were weapons of common steel rather than the starmetal that had gone into the making of Gotrek's mighty axe. The runes engraved into them seemed to be symbolic, ceremonial maybe, rather than brutally functional.

The whispers ceased as the dwarf – some kind of an abbot, perhaps – reached the bottom step. There he stopped, shoulders back and axe upheld as though it were the personal standard of an emperor, appraising the company of men and dwarfs with eyes like pommel stones.

'*Khzurk a garak. Uruk ak a Grimnir.*'

Gotrek swore. Like Felix, he had been under the unfair expectation that the leader of these dwarfs would speak in a form they could all understand.

'He welcomes Grimnir's heir tae his fortress,' Makaisson translated after a moment's thought. 'And he wants tae ken which o' us it is.'

Felix glanced between Gotrek and Malakai. The two Slayers traded looks and Makaisson chuckled.

'Ye dinnae actually think it's me dae ye?'

With a shrug, hard face as emotive as fresh-hewn stone, Gotrek strode towards the abbot. There was an excited whisper of approval from the watching dwarfs that made the hairs on the nape of Felix's neck prickle. He couldn't help but feel that there was more going on here than a few poorly translated words of archaic Khazalid could convey. Without thinking about what he was doing, Felix drew his sword and fell into step behind his companion.

'*Rhingul!*' barked the abbot, throwing up his free hand to bar Felix's approach with a dark-haired fist the size of a paving slab. '*Kilza al elgrhaza ak hukan za!*'

Despite the intensity of the dwarf's words, Makaisson grinned broadly. He began to chuckle.

'What did he say?' Felix hissed.

'He said the elf will huv tae wait here.'

'*Elf?*'

Gotrek growled, unamused. 'These dwarfs must have been up here since the passing of Grimnir. When their ancestors built this fortress, manling, Sigmar's twenty-times great-grandfather was living in a cave on some elf princeling's estate.'

Felix had thought his mind had acclimated to the scales of time he had had to deal with of late, but still relentless reminders of how ancient this place was made his head spin. These dwarfs had been standing vigil on this spot all this time. They pre-dated the Empire and like true dwarfs they had outlasted its fall.

All for this moment.

For Gotrek.

For a moment Felix feared he actually was going to pass out. *Breathe,* he reminded himself again. He wished with every aching fibre of his heart that Max could have been here to see this moment. The wizard had been right. By every god there had ever been, he had been right.

Gotrek made a series of pointed gestures with his axe and grunted something in his gravelly native vernacular that clearly put across the point that this 'elf' went where Gotrek said he went. The stern-faced abbot managed to look genuinely taken aback for a moment, then bowed and stepped aside. His brother monks hurried forward with a rustle of bronze to form a procession to line the route to the temple.

No question then where they were heading.

The most ominous-looking building in the entire fortress.

Felix turned back momentarily to clasp his nephew's arm in his.

It was a warrior's shake, hand to elbow, unsentimental, but both men seemed to find it a little difficult to let go.

'We'll hold the fort until you get back,' said Gustav, his lightness only exposing the cracks in his voice. He waved towards the cloud sea. 'You know, just in case.'

'We'll be back before you realise we're gone,' Felix returned.

He couldn't say why, but he knew that neither one of them believed him.

The inside of the temple was too large to be accounted for by its external dimensions. Hundreds of huge pillars as broad as oak trees ran in rows in every direction. The only light source was the angular, axe-stroke runes that glowered from the square sides of the columns and the hazy, uncertain walls. Trying to look at the walls made Felix's eyes water and his mind want to fold inside out. The floor appeared to curve slightly upwards as it approached them, as if at some unimaginably distant point left would overlap with right, the ceiling becoming a floor, and so on for infinity. Felix put a hand over his eyes and followed the Slayer. Their footsteps echoed around him.

'*Gharaz uk azaki*,' said the abbot gravely, sweeping his arms around the surreal environment and clearly under the misimpression that he was imparting something of dire import. Felix wished they had brought Makaisson with them, but the monks had seemed quite reluctant to let even Felix pass the threshold. It had taken another round of elaborately articulated threats from Gotrek on his behalf to prevent the monks from taking his weapon at the door.

'*Zhorl*,' said the abbot, apparently satisfied and turning to walk back the way they had come.

Felix watched him go for a moment, then sighed nervously and looked around. There didn't seem to be any other way out. His skin felt hot and he pulled at the collar of his cloak. 'Are you sure you don't understand any of what he just said?'

'Are you sure you don't speak Arabyan?'

Felix bit his lip and glanced back. The doors ground shut, coming together with a resounding knell. There was the sound of locks being turned and bolts being drawn. Felix was half-expecting to hear heavy objects being piled up against the door and actually felt a little disappointed when it didn't happen.

'That sounds ominous.'

'You worry too much, manling.' The Slayer gave his surroundings a hard look, as if to subjugate them into more solid form with dwarfish opprobrium alone. His lips drew back to expose a snarl of yellow, broken teeth. 'Come out, whatever you are. My axe thirsts.'

Felix tensed on instinct.

The Slayer's booming shout resounded between the pillars, but rather than fade away it grew louder, echoes overlaying, strengthening, feeding itself until it became something greater. The pillars thrummed a basso vibration, as if the infinite dimensions of this temple had been designed to serve as the voice box of a titanic mountain god.

'WHY HAVE YOU COME HERE, SLAYER?'

Felix clamped his hands to his ears and screamed, his legs buckling under the auditory assault. The voice was not communicating in any language that he understood, and yet every word was delivered firmly and defiantly into his brain.

Gotrek stuck his finger in his ear and wiggled it about, then stuck out his jaw and shouted back: 'I heard there was something here worth having, though I'm yet to see it.'

'AND YOU BELIEVE YOURSELF WORTHY OF THE BIRTHRIGHT OF GRIMNIR'S HEIR?'

'Are you saying I'm not?'

A low rumble reverberated through the floor, setting Felix's organs to quivering like jelly. He had the horrible feeling that it was laughter.

'YOU ARE FAMILIAR WITH THE SLAYER OATH.'

'Of course I am,' Gotrek grunted, running a meaty palm through his crest with a leer. 'This isn't for show.'

'RECITE IT TO ME.'

Gotrek ground his teeth, the thick muscles of his neck bulging. He threw a cornered beast look towards Felix.

Felix hesitantly uncovered his ears. 'What's the matter? You do know it, don't you?'

'Of course I know it,' Gotrek snapped, making Felix wince. His one-eyed gaze swept the columns, a caged bear hunting its tormentor. His voice sank to a low growl. 'But I've never said it aloud before.'

Again that subterranean rumble greeted the Slayer's remark. The red-gold rune-glow grew marginally brighter. 'NEITHER DID I.'

'And who are you, mountain?' Gotrek demanded, eye narrowing.

The laughter sank into the stones, the voice rebuilding like a clap of thunder. 'RECITE IT TO ME.'

Gotrek snarled dangerously, raising his axe as if to lash out at the first thing that came within reach, then suddenly lowered his arms and bellowed at the top of his lungs: 'I am a dwarf! My honour is my life and without it I am nothing. I shall become a Slayer. I shall seek redemption in the eyes of my ancestors. I shall become as death to my enemies.' Gotrek clenched his fists over his axe and stared challengingly into the rune-lit temple. 'Until I face he that takes my life and my shame.'

Felix listened with increasing discomfort as the Slayer spoke, aware that he was a party to something intensely personal, and likely something that no human before him had ever heard. At the same time, he sensed a shift in the flows of power that ran through the temple, like water being siphoned off from some mighty dam.

For what purpose, Felix could only guess at.

The rune-light flickered.

'And you expect to find such a one here, my son?'

Felix spun around, startled. The voice this time did not boom from every quarter, but instead emerged from the throat of a very ordinary-looking dwarf who had appeared behind them. His overalls were workmanlike and his big hands calloused and stained with grease. His dark brown beard petered down to his thick waist, his hair cropped roughly close into a bowl shape as if to make a better fit for a miner's helmet. The hue of his eyes however, the set of his nose, the angle of his jaw, all reminded Felix of Gotrek.

The Slayer twisted his head half around, his deep growl catching halfway up his throat.

'Do you know him?' Felix asked.

'Gurni Gurnisson,' said Gotrek sullenly. 'My father.'

'That's your father?'

'Don't be daft, manling. Of course it's not my bloody father.'

Stung, Felix clamped his mouth shut and backed away from the two dwarfs. Or the dwarf and the... apparition? Avatar? If he was honest, Felix had no idea what stood in front of him right now. He had even less idea about what it wanted.

'But I am, Gotrek,' said Gurni, a terrible sadness breaching the stoicism in his eyes. 'Denied the Ancestors' Hall by your disgrace, doomed to wander this world as a revenant shade. But you are my blood and this place will be the death of you if you continue. I beg you, please, turn back before it is too late.'

Gotrek shook his head, his own expression a granite mask set into a permanent scowl. 'I am no longer your son. I have forsaken my home, my family, my name. Only a worthy doom will return them to me.'

'And if you fall in dishonour, what of me? There will be no other. You are the last of the line of Gurni.'

Gotrek looked to his axe and glowered. Felix thought he knew what the Slayer saw there. Snorri Nosebiter had described to him the scene that the goblin raiders had left of his home, of his wife and daughter.

'Don't I know it,' said Gotrek.

'What then of your king?' asked Gurni, taking a step forward and raising his voice to shout. 'The hold of your ancestors is beset on all sides and will soon fall. You are but one dwarf, I know, and maybe even your axe would make no difference, but your place is there.'

'I have no place until I lie in the ground,' said Gotrek. He glanced sidelong towards Felix, lips curling up into a harsh smile. 'And I'm sick of wandering about.'

Felix grinned despite himself. He did vaguely recall saying something like that about Middenheim prior to his encounter with Gotrek's fist. His thoughts turned to Malakai Makaisson and the engineer's own desire to return to Karaz-a-Karak to fight for his High King. Was this a test of some sort, to challenge a Slayer's resolve to forsake hearth and home, everything that made a dwarf what they were, in service to some ascetic brand of honour? Had Makaisson been here in Gotrek's place would that test have been failed? Felix hoped he wouldn't have to find out what would happen should whatever force guarded this temple be dissatisfied with the Slayer's answers.

'Death is a gift, I am told. But who receives it, and what value does it hold to one who gives of it so freely? How much more precious then is life?'

As the apparition of Gurni spoke, Felix again felt power being subtly diverted, the runes guttering and hazing as he looked around to see what was going to be sent to test them next. Seeing nothing, Felix returned his attention to Gotrek and Gurni.

The only thing that had changed was Gurni himself.

The apparition was blurring into the rune-light, not disappearing but changing, growing. His fading body stretched to become taller, tanned flesh folding back into dried meat and yellow bone that was then covered once again by manifesting plates of crimson steel.

'BE DEATH TO YOUR ENEMIES, GOTREK SON OF GURNI. IT IS A WEAPON OF THE GODS THAT YOU WIELD. IT DOES OFFENCE TO ITS FIRST MASTER THAT A VICTIM SHOULD ESCAPE ITS WRATH.'

The phantom solidified into its new form and Felix's mouth hung open in horrified recognition.

The warrior was enormous, half again as big as Felix, who was amongst the tallest of men, and as broad as the Troll King of Praag. His armour was embossed with writhing sigils of slaughter and death, and hung with living skulls that wailed their torment even as blood filled their mouths and seeped from their empty sockets. It smeared the warrior's gauntlets and every rivet and seam of his armour. The dead champion didn't speak, but red witchlight pulsed from the open face of his bone-horned helm. It was a foe Felix remembered too well, one he still sometimes saw before waking up to sheets doused in icy sweat and a full moon in the sky.

Krell!

Felix brought his sword up into a guard position and moved into position to protect Gotrek's vulnerable left side, only for the Slayer to warn him off.

'Back, manling. This one has to be mine.'

The mountain thundered its approval. 'A SLAYER IS ALWAYS ALONE. HE IS DEATH, AND IN THE FINAL COUNTING ALL DIE ALONE.'

Felix tightened his grip on his sword but withdrew, bound by duty and friendship to stand back and watch. Krell spun his enormous axe menacingly, a blade as black as plague and just as lethal. Gotrek brought up his own deadly weapon, the two fighters circling, trading feints faster than the human eye could follow, testing each other's guard with blows that left Felix's hands ringing just for having seen them. Krell had been a champion of Khorne before his death and subsequent resurrection. The God-King Sigmar himself had once fought him.

And he was one of the few to have crossed blades with Gotrek and walked away.

'Gotrek. Left.'

The Slayer bashed aside the wight-lord's axe and unleashed a flurry of blows that drove the champion of death back. A mortal adversary would have been torn apart by such an onslaught, but Krell was tireless, skilful and uncannily swift for so large a being, and he was Gotrek's equal in strength. Felix could see no weakness in the wight's technique, and more than once his heart leapt into his mouth as a counter-stroke scythed towards Gotrek only for the dwarf to somehow pull himself out of the way at the last moment.

Felix let out the breath that had been building pressure inside his chest.

The merest graze of Krell's obsidian blade could kill, and Felix could only assume that this simulacral version was similarly imbued. Felix had seen first-hand the slow, lingering demise that weapon had almost inflicted upon Gotrek once before.

The Slayer had claimed that his death here would not be a good one.

Had this been what he meant? Was Krell destined to finish the task he had so nearly completed at Castle Reikguard? Felix scowled, loyalty to the Slayer and all that that meant warring with what he thought he recognised as common human goodness.

He hadn't come through all of this to watch Gotrek fall to a spectre from their past.

The Slayer threw a stroke across Krell's middle, but simply from the fact that Felix was able to see it from beginning to end he could tell that it was laboured. The wight angled his body under the blow, swinging his axe overhead and launching it one-handed towards Gotrek's face, forcing the Slayer for the first time onto the back foot. He retreated, breathing hard, his axe moving so fast that it looked almost like a shield as Krell hammered down blow after blow. His bare torso glistened with sweat.

Gotrek had gone into this contest wounded and it was beginning to tell.

The dwarf drove all his flagging strength into a decapitating blow, dispatching it at Krell's neck with a gravelly roar. The wight dropped silently to one knee, driving a blood-soaked couter into Gotrek's stomach at the same moment that the Slayer's axe cracked against a pillar. Gotrek's axe sprang from his grip and he stumbled back, clutching his stomach muscles and wheezing.

Krell advanced. The champion's grin was fixed but Felix sensed triumph in the glow of his eyes. And more than triumph: vengeance, blood for his vile god. If it was not the real Krell then it was a terrifyingly close approximation. The wight swung up his axe for an executioner's stroke as Felix raised his sword and tensed for a suicidal dive forward.

'I don't need your help, manling,' Gotrek bellowed, dropping his shoulder and ploughing under Krell's guard into the wight's waist.

A hiss of dead air escaped Krell's teeth as the Slayer's low-centred, bulldog-like power carried the wight back and smashed him up against a pillar.

Stone crunched. Cracks spidered out through the luminous rock. Krell brought the haft of his axe down on Gotrek's shoulder, but though it drew blood there was no force behind it. His poleyn slammed into Gotrek's muscle-slabbed chest, but the Slayer shrugged off the blow with a grunt, denting the wight's breastplate with a punch. Dust crumbled around him. Krell seized Gotrek's fist in his, then the other, driving his knee into the Slayer's chest like a piston as Gotrek emitted a furious roar and smacked his forehead into the wight's face.

The impact beat Krell's skull against the pillar, a thin crack splitting through the bone from the back of his head over to his left orbit. Gotrek staggered back, an ugly skull-shaped red welt from the wight's chin-guard on his brow, then shook it off to haul the undead champion out of the pillar.

Dust fell over them both.

Clenching his teeth the Slayer heaved the enormous warrior up over his head, then flipped him over from front to back and slammed him into the ground.

Metal crunched, ancient bones ground together and snapped. The magic that animated the champion flickered, dazed, as Gotrek's fist descended like a bomb from an airship, shattering the vertebrae of Krell's neck and burying dwarf knuckles in the flagstones.

With the toes of his boot, Gotrek slid Krell's axe from the wight's dead grip and kicked it away. It slid across the stone floor, clattering off between the pillars long after the axe itself had vanished. Krell's body vanished soon after, disappearing between blinks.

'The real one was tougher,' said Gotrek, rattling down a deep breath and then spitting on the ground where the wight had lain.

'WAS HE, OR HAVE YOU GROWN STRONGER? IN PREPARATION PERHAPS FOR A MEETING WITH ONE FAR GREATER?'

'Bring it to me, then!' Gotrek roared, scooping up his axe and clutching it in both hands, bulging like a clenched bicep as he glared one-eyed into the emptiness of rune-lit stone. 'I thought you wanted to challenge me. Well, look at me, mountain. I stand unchallenged!'

'PATIENCE, SLAYER.'

Felix gasped as the Slayer vanished before his eyes.

He opened his mouth to cry out to the dwarf, but in the time between thinking and breathing the entire temple too had followed Gotrek into oblivion. Darkness enveloped him, lightless, shapeless, devoid even of the sensation of stone beneath his feet and air on his face. Realisation hit like a cold wave and he did scream then, or at least he thought he did, but either he had been struck deaf or there was no air for him to hear it. He didn't know which was worse.

It wasn't the Slayer who had been cast into oblivion.

It was him.

Light guttered fitfully from a torch set into an iron bracket in the stone wall and slowly dispelling the darkness. Felix studied it for a moment, disorientated, his hands padding absently over his body as if to reassure themselves they were not alone. His heart fluttered like a butterfly trapped in a lantern. The flame wobbled on its stand, light and dark rippling out from it across the room. It looked real. The warmth of it and the crackle of wood was real. Hand on his aching, stubbornly trembling chest, Felix looked over the room that the light revealed.

It was of a hard grey stone like granite, curved along one wall, with an arrow-slit window indicating that he was in some sort of fortified tower. A strange, gale-force roar sounded from outside. A full helm, the visor drawn back, and a breastplate hung from a dummy beside the window. A sheathed sword with a hilt studded with semi-precious stones was looped over a door peg. A pile of folded clothes – tabard, trews, a sash to be worn over the breast-plate, all in the blue with yellow trimming of Middenland – lay on a chest.

Next to the armour dummy was a writing desk similar to the one that Felix had once had in the study of his brother's Altdorf town-house. It was piled with sheaves of paper. Felix spread them out across the table. Real enough. They were requisition orders, watch rotations, troop dispositions, the sort of military bureaucracy that most soldiers would never dream existed but without which the Empire would surely collapse in a day.

He set them down and looked out of the window.

The roar of tens of thousands of abhumans rose to assail his ears. The pointed glimmer of as many sources of light again brought tears to his eyes. He could see that the tower he was in was one of several overlooking the unscalable walls of a mighty mountain-top citadel. It was not Kazad Drengazi. It was Imperial soldiery on the walls, and the ground, seething with monstrous forms all bearing torches and flaming arrows, was all too visible. Arrows fizzed between the walls and the winged beasts and daemons that harried the garrison, the heavier munitions of ballistae and small-calibre cannons pounding the air with thumps and blistering whines. As Felix watched, a plume of flame rolled from the forked tongue of a two-headed dragon and blasted a ballista tower to ruin. Rock and bodies blackened inside their armour tumbled onto the mountain-side. Felix shifted his view down.

A column of vile war machines rolled up the narrow causeway to the city's gate. They did so under their own malodorous power, the fuming, twisting hunger of bound daemons driving batter-ing rams and siege-ballistae over ground too treacherous for any beast of burden. Bloody steam hissed from the flared mouths of cannons, bony pitons stabbing into the rock to lock the weapons steady as great bronze barrels angled themselves upwards to fire.

Middenheim. This was Middenheim.

Was this a dream world constructed by the guardian of the mountain, or like Krell before it was it somehow more?

'How is Gotrek being tested by this?' Felix murmured to himself.

'It is your turn, Herr Jaeger.'

The voice had come from behind him and Felix spun around.

At the back of the room was a small table upon which a chess board was set. There was a game under way that looked to be four or five moves in. Behind it were two albino men in sorcerers' garb, one seated and one standing. An aura of incredible power shimmered around them both. The seated man was clad in black and leaned idly against a staff of ebony and silver as he examined the board. The tall, vulpine sorcerer standing beside him was robed instead in gold and held a glittering runestaff in gilt claws.

Felix backed away.

The mountain guardian was dredging his own mind for the enemies to destroy him!

Goldenrod beckoned to the empty chair on Felix's side of the board, but also, Felix felt, to the world beyond. As if answering the sorcerer's call there was a digestive rumble from the causeway below, followed by a slimy *boom* and the crunch of wood. The gate. The tower shook under the impact, causing the chess set to rattle and toppling the remaining white castle. Blackstaff reached across the board to reposition it, his finger lingering on the piece like an execution stayed.

'The turn is yours.'

SIXTEEN

Katerina

'Sit down, Herr Jaeger,' said Goldenrod in a high-pitched voice, gesturing to the empty chair. 'Kelmain and I have been forced to concede that it is pointless to continue to play one another when neither of us is the clear superior.'

'It was becoming an ever more tedious challenge to keep score,' the black-robed wizard, Kelmain, agreed.

'Where does it stand, brother?'

'I fear I forget.'

Goldenrod nodded portentously, turning a cunning look onto Felix. 'I am keen to see the outcome of this game. Your opening gambit demonstrates a keen and, if you'll pardon the observation, unconventional mind.'

Felix stared in confusion at the chequerboard. He backed away, shaking his head slowly, until he hit the door.

'This isn't real. I don't even know how to play this game.'

'What is real?' said Kelmain with a shrug.

'Is a dream real?' added Goldenrod. 'What about a vision, a prophecy?'

'What makes them real?' Kelmain cut in, seamlessly carrying his brother's line. 'Is it us? The way we interpret and act upon that which we see? Would we have acted differently had we not seen at all?'

'Are you saying this is really Middenheim?' said Felix, reaching back with his left hand to the wood of the door and running the palm of his right along the rough-set stones. He shot a glance towards the window, a narrow aperture through to a void of sulphur smoke and screams.

Not narrow enough.

'He's not really so bright after all, is he, Lhoigor?' said Kelmain, disappointed.

'His mind is so... binary.'

Felix's gaze was still on the window. The smell of burning filled his lungs now. He could feel it permeate through his chest. The screams were distant, almost ethereal, but impossible to distance himself from, like a haunting in a lost love's home.

'Is Kat here?' Felix asked sharply. 'Did she survive the fall of Altdorf and make it here before the siege?'

'If this is not real then we are essentially conjurations of your own mind and powerless to aid you beyond what you are able to offer yourself,' said Kelmain.

'And if it is real,' Lhoigor hissed, baring yellow-bright fangs as he leaned forward into his golden staff, 'then what makes you think that we would?'

'You killed our pawn Arek Daemonclaw. And Skjalandir.' Kelmain produced a self-deprecating smile. 'And us.'

'So you see,' said Lhoigor, fangs disappearing behind a smile as he once again indicated the chair and bade Felix sit. 'It does not matter whether this is *real* or not. The end consequence is the same.'

'But if you will play a game or two, then maybe we can give you a hint.'

'No,' said Felix, heart pounding with a desperate logic of its own. If Kat was here he'd find her. Real or not he'd find her. And his child...

He choked.

He would see his child.

Kelmain emitted a rasping sigh, scratching his cheek as though politely informing Felix he had something in his eye, and looked askance to his brother. 'I wonder if Archaon plays.'

Either one of these men could incinerate him with a word, but Felix no longer cared. His own life hadn't bothered him terribly for some time now, and now his family might actually be within his grasp it concerned him even less.

He turned to face the door, his hand closing over the brass handle and pushing it down.

'We have played with destiny and been burned,' called Lhoigor, his voice suddenly swollen with melancholy, bitter with wasted might. 'Seldom is there but one right path, and the obvious choice is rarely the best. No door is opened without consequence.'

But Felix wasn't listening.

He opened the door.

Frightened-looking men in the colours of city and state mustered in the courtyard before the east gatehouse; blue and gold, white and blue, rivers churning before the dam broke and spat them all out to the sea. Smoke poured over the walls. Concussive blasts rolled through the air, not a heard sound so much as a wave that rippled banners and spooked horses. Teams of artillerymen in crimped black livery yelled obscure, technical-sounding instructions to one another as they heaved a pair of helblaster volleyguns into positions of enfilade either side of the gate. Unhelmed and grey-maned knights drew into a line, a bulwark of steel and horseflesh that spanned the main road onto Neumarkt, their broad armoured shoulders level with the guttering of the boarded-up commission offices. Their muscular mounts snorted at those hurrying by, wolf-faced champrons snarling, unsettled by the struck match smell that pervaded the air. Every few seconds a resounding blow crashed against the gates. Drums, horns, whistles and pipes added to the thunder of beasts and guns. Rattling and barking, a battered old steam tank chugged into the courtyard and whistled to a stop.

Felix waded into the commotion as though he'd just taken a blow to the head.

He had no memory of crossing the threshold of that door, nor of heading down any stairs. And yet here he was.

'Herr Jaeger. Great Sigmar, is that you?'

Striding through the crowd came a tall knight in brilliant silver plate, covered by a tabard emblazoned with a fiery heart and a scabbarded broadsword clapping at his thigh. Felix turned to greet the man but before he could so much as open his mouth the knight threw his arms around Felix's back. There was a loud *clang* as the man's breastplate embraced Felix's mail shirt and Felix staggered back, only to be checked by the strong arms knotted behind his back. Felix coughed politely, inhaling a sour hit of armour grease and sweat. The man pulled away, powerful gauntleted hands clasped to Felix's shoulders, and grinned.

'Aldred?'

The Templar knight produced a short bow.

Aldred Keppler – or the Fellblade – had been the prior owner of Felix's sword, Karaghul, but the man had fallen to a Chaos troll in the dank ruins of Karak Eight Peaks. This couldn't be real. It couldn't... Could it? Felix wasn't sure any more. The Templar looked, sounded, and – Shallya's mercy – smelled real, and the way Felix's heart responded to the reappearance of an old and valued comrade was entirely real enough.

Felix clasped Aldred's hand between both of his. 'It's good to see you again.'

'You carried my weapon with you,' Aldred shrugged. 'It did my work in the world. That had been enough until now. Now everything changes.'

There was something about the Templar's words, or perhaps the wearied manner in which he said them, that jarred with Felix as wrong. He tried to shake the feeling off.

'I need your help, old friend. I'm looking for a woman. Katerina Jaeger, my wife, perhaps you've seen her. She's–' Felix held an upturned hand approximately level with his chest, then smiled as an image of her leapt fully formed into his mind. 'She's about this tall, dark hair with a lock of silver on the left side. Probably the most beautiful of the refugees from Altdorf.'

Aldred's expression turned stern and Felix's heart lurched over a precipice.

'There are refugees from Altdorf, aren't there?'

'There are thousands of women in this city, and children. What do you think will happen when that which hungers beyond the gate breaks through?'

Something struck the gates with a titanic crash. Wood crunched and split and iron bent, the gates splitting down the join to reveal a hideous daemon-headed ram. Liquid fire drooled from its brazen snout where it hissed against the flagstones. Cries for courage rang through the courtyard. Orders were bellowed, the names of Ulric and Sigmar thrown freely, men herded into ranks like sheep by dogs as the gate was breached again, the locking bar shattering with a *crack* and flames racing up the broken back of the gate itself.

A command was given. It sounded over the din like 'Fire!'

Arrows whistled from the windows and balconies of the disused commission offices. Most thudded into the burning wood of the gates, a handful pattering indifferently from the daemon-infused brass of the battering ram.

A woman's voice called words of encouragement from a bow militia, spread along a rooftop opposite to Felix as a missile screen for a ballista embedded within a fascine of straw bales and brushwood. Whilst the weapon crew conducted frantic last-minute checks on their machine, the archers had readied and aimed and awaited the order to fire. It came courtesy of their female officer and a sheet of arrows hissed down a half-second ahead of the next fastest detachment.

Felix kept his eyes on the woman as she dropped to one knee behind the rough, recently added battlement and reached back over her head to pull an arrow from her quiver. The shaft slid out and onto her bowstring and in one seamless motion she rose again. She was a head shorter than the smallest man in her command, and slender as an arrow. A padded gambeson jacket puffed out her chest. Her forearms and thighs were clad in light single-piece leather plates. Her short dark hair brushed her narrow shoulders, all except for the single white lock that hung errantly over her left eye. Disregarding it, she drew a bead on the breached gate. Firelight glinted from the weighty ring of dwarf gold worn on her left-hand thumb, tight against the bowstave.

Kat.

'Since the elder days has the enemy been withheld, never vanquished, but always denied.' Aldred's voice grew heavier as he spoke, his appearance shifting into a semblance of someone Felix felt he ought to know without actually appearing to change at all. And when Felix blinked, it was undeniably Aldred and surely had been all along. The Templar drew his sword and pointed back to the gates. Kurgan axes chewed through the cinders. Middenheimer spears and halberds fell back behind their volleyguns. Another sheet of arrows rained down. 'With naught but constant courage and iron in our souls have we prevailed. Now the wolves howl at the gates of your world and men like you must stand up, prove yourselves worthy, and cast the daemons back.'

Felix backed away, taken aback by the Templar's sudden and uncharacteristic intensity. 'Aldred?'

The Templar nodded to something over Felix's head, and Felix turned about just as a trio of burly Trollslayers waded through the crowded Neumarkt street in search of the coming battle. Wielding a pair of axes was the ugliest dwarf that Felix had seen in an achingly long time. His squashed nose was graced with a hairy wart at the tip and gold rings jangled from his big ears. Hurrying behind him was a slighter, younger dwarf garbed in furs, his recently shaven head speckled with orange stubble. And the third...

Felix felt his tender heart break into jagged pieces.

'Snorri thinks Felix has the right idea leaving,' said Snorri Nose-biter happily, a stupid smile on his stupid, mashed-up face. 'Why let them all come in here when we can fight them in the gate?'

'Felix has decided not to do battle with us,' said Aldred. 'He is going instead to find a woman.'

Bjorni Bjornisson's ugly face split into a lewd grin and he jabbed Ulli several times in the ribs, making an approving growl, until the younger dwarf blushed furiously and backed out of reach.

'Snorri... doesn't understand. Do you not want to fight with Snorri again, young Felix? It'll be a good one. Snorri saw the... the...' his face scrunched up in concerted thought, '*Ever-Chosen* from the walls.'

'He didn't look so tough,' Ulli declared loudly, still blushing and apparently startling himself with his own volume. He glared reproachfully at the other two Slayers.

A lump formed in Felix's throat. He had borne the guilt of his own inaction over Snorri's death over months and leagues and part of him did yearn to stand by him now. Aldred glared at him expectantly. Nor had Felix forgotten the promise he had made to the Templar's order – to wield their blade with honour, to combat evil wherever it surfaced.

He turned to look across the street to the rooftop. His heart grounded him to the spot like an anchor, but he knew where he had to go.

'Forgive me, Snorri,' he managed to choke, dragging himself away from the forlorn-looking Slayer and his companions and plunging into the crowd.

A fountain dimpled the surface of an ornamental pond, the centrepiece of a small cobbled garden surrounded on all sides by the high grey walls of Middenheim's old town. Red roses and scented honeysuckle clambered over the stonework towards the square of sky. It was red like a sailor's warning, filled with the *crump* of cannon fire and the screams of running battles. The cries weren't entirely human, and ran from the sky like wet paint down a wall. The sky stuttered, the clouds curdling by in slow motion as Felix watched, before suddenly racing. His heart hammered, disorientated and afraid.

What was happening to him? Where was he? And what had happened to Kat?

He returned his attention to the garden with the idea of getting his bearings and trying to find his way back to Neumarkt, and noticed that there was a figure seated on the lip of the pond, garbed in thigh-length armour of pearl-white lamellar plates. *Gustav*. His nephew was seated side-on, with one slender leg crossed under him and his face turned away from Felix to the fountain. His nephew ran his fingers – almost like claws – through the pond. A crowd of subdued, mournful-looking children surrounded him, their broken reflections looking up through crying eyes from the water of the pool. It was only then Felix noticed that the armoured figure cast no reflection. A sepulchral chill entered his bones.

No. Not Gustav.

The woman turned as though alerted to his presence by his beating heart and gave a predatory smile. Her short hair was as white as ash, her skin as pale as human bone. To the silvery scar across her left temple, she had added another that cut cleanly across her throat. One glance was all it took for his hands to relive the jolt they had felt as his blade had met her neck. In his mind he heard the thump of her severed head striking the stone of the Troll King's dungeon.

'Ulrika, I–'

The vampire cut him off with a throat-cutting gesture that made Felix's own throat tighten as surely as if she'd put her hand against it and squeezed. 'You are looking for Katerina,' she said, reading his mind as succinctly as she could his heart. 'How disappointing. How very predictable.'

Felix cast his gaze from the vampire to the clouds that boiled overhead, tinted red and backlit with silver. He shuddered. 'Please. The east gate's been breached. If you know where she–'

Swift as a snuffed candle's transition from light to dark, Ulrika's smile turned bestial. She snatched one of the children who sobbed around her, hoisted the young girl, who gave a piteous squeal for help, and then plunged her into the pond. Felix cried out in dismay and without once thinking about how he intended to outmuscle her ran in to pull the girl from Ulrika's clutches. The vampire shrugged him off as though he were no more than a child himself. Felix reeled back, his sword sliding from its scabbard as he recovered his footing.

'Do you know what torment awaits the souls of vampires when they finally die, Felix?' said Ulrika, water splashing her breast-plate as the girl under her grip thrashed. Sobs rose from the other children, but none of them tried to escape. It was as if they were resigned to this, or they knew there was nothing better to escape to. 'I do.'

'Ulrika, stop!'

'This is a test, a challenge. The wolves are at the gate and they are hungry, and if they are not stopped they will surely consume us all. Not all of them wear daemons' faces, manling, and if you do not kill me then I *will* kill you.'

Felix lowered his sword a fraction. 'Manling?'

With a snarl, Ulrika pushed the now still child to the bottom of the pond and sprang up, flinging out wet hands that ended in cruel bone claws. Startled by the lightning movement, Felix backed up. The vampire grinned, blurring left as Felix went right, then right as Felix brought his sword *en garde* and tried to back away, box-ing him in until his back hit a trellis and red petals fluttered down to his shoulders. The vampire's movements were dizzying, as jar-ringly unnatural as the racing sky or the screams that sounded from all around. She came on, wolfen teeth bared in a hungry snarl.

Pulling at his cloak with a curse Felix tore the mistreated garment from the rose thorns in which it was snared and rolled along the wall, just as Ulrika's fist smashed through wood, vines and stone where he had just been. Felix bounced himself from the wall and whipped around. Blood ran down his face from several small cuts. Rose thorns. There were more scratches on his hands and thorns still caught in his clothing.

Ulrika drew her arm out of the wall. Her nostrils flared at the scent of fresh blood. 'I do not recall you being this squeamish in Praag, lover. You have already killed me once. Why hold back now?'

Hissing like a cat, she threw herself at Felix, already raking for his face with her claws. Felix's sword flew up on instinct, thunking against the vampire's bone claws and diverting their thrust down his mail sleeve, but not before the sheer force of the blow had driven him back. Metal ringlets cascaded from his arm and crunched underfoot as he gave ground and parried for all he was worth. For the few seconds that he could maintain such intensity his sword seemed to be everywhere, his eyes somehow managing to keep his sword arm apprised of Ulrika's movements without the knowledge or intervention of his brain. His muscles burned. Sweat mingled with the blood that ran in runnels through the creases in his face. The vampire flowed around his blade as though the paleness of her skin betrayed her nature as a being of quicksilver, one second flowing around a breathlessly executed *schrankhut* guard and the next appearing *inside* his defence and launching a punch to his solar plexus that almost tore his body in two.

The air rushed out of his lungs as he flew back, crashing over the low seat of the ornamental pond and rolling into the water.

His vision turned murky, all diffracted jewels of light and bubbles of air. The roar of the fountain filled his ears. The instinct was to take a breath, but he resisted even as his empty lungs screamed at him, long enough to order his arms and legs beneath him and lift his head from the surface of the pond. He gasped great lungfuls of the floral-scented air. Water streamed down his cheeks and matted his hair. The fountain pummelled his back and effectively blinded him with spray. He folded over with a moan, his arms crossed around his bruised sternum.

That had hurt.

This was real!

The watery screen parted to admit Ulrika, the vampire pouncing through the spray to land astride him and drive him back under the water. The last thing Felix heard before his ears were again filled with beaten water were the screams of children. Ulrika held him under for a moment, then dragged him out, choking and gasping with his hair stuck to the inside of his mouth.

'Do you wish you had not killed me, my love? Do you resist what must be done because you know now how much it will hurt you?'

Felix wanted to answer, but couldn't. He hadn't the breath.

'In the Troll Country there was a saying: it is better to regret what you have done than what you have not. And there is so much I regret not doing to you.' She opened her fanged mouth wide and leaned in.

Felix opened his mouth for an airless scream and struggled, splashing water, but only managed to drive himself deeper under as the vampire leaned over him. The water closed over his eyes, distorting Ulrika's face and the words she spoke to him as the pressure built inside his chest.

'The fates of worlds lie in your hands, Felix. You have the power to save them, but not like this.'

Felix came up gasping for air, scratching over his throat at hands that were no longer there. Nor was he sat in a pond but on uneven cobblestones, in the middle of a street that heaved with fighting men. He looked up, wondering where he was now, rubbing the still-bruised skin of his throat. Tattered banners flew between the leaning tenements: lions, eagles, and griffons rampant showing their colours, torn but defiant in the face of the enemy. Forests of spears and halberds shivered over the advance of thousands of steel-clad infantrymen. Arrows darkened the sky. Handguns and field artillery made a constant rumble akin to being behind a waterfall, through which men and other, more bestial things hollered and screamed.

Around the spot where Felix sat, leather thigh and shin pieces creaked with strain. A company of crossbowmen stood in reserve, watching the battle, waiting for their colours to appear on the signal pole of the mounted vexillary who galloped up and down behind the front line displaying Emperor Karl Franz's colours. The air was sour with sweat and spilled beer, soiled leathers and unwashed men, the true flavours of war for which the bitterness of spilt blood was merely a condiment.

With a groan Felix got up and beat down his wet clothes. Then he looked around, eyes crossing at the strange realisation that while he was quite definitely on a narrow Middenheim street he was also *quite definitely* on a small hill overlooking a rolling battlefield filled with many tens of thousands of men. The scale of the deployment was staggering, and for a long time it was all Felix could do to join the crossbow auxiliaries he stood with and stare. There was no way that Middenheim could support so many troops. He doubted whether even *Unstoppable* could move enough gear and supplies to the summit of the Fauschlag to keep them.

Felix tried to focus on the street beneath the army. It looked like a merchant district – all houses with decorative windows, the offices of conveyancers and commissioners and the ostentatiously per-manent stone frontages of banks. It had all been stretched out somehow, thinned just beyond the point of opacity to encompass the immense hosts arrayed against each other from opposite sides of the street.

The massed regiments of the Empire held the centre of the line. Tens of thousands of infantrymen stood marshalled in proud bat-tle order, awaiting the bugle to advance and relieve their kinsmen in the raging melee that dominated the battlefield between the two hosts. The proud colours of the ten provinces were emblazoned from surcoats and standards across a dozen leagues of unbroken

files. Knights from more noble orders than Felix could name can-
tered their bulky armoured steeds between the blocks of state
troops, pennons snapping from the raised tips of their lances as
they rode into an evil wind. The rear ranks bristled with ordnance.
Their flanks were ridden on the one side by the shining knights
of Bretonnia with their intricately fashioned armour and brightly
caparisoned destriers, and on the other by the hemp-clad horse
nomads of Kislev. Some instinctive understanding told Felix that
he was witnessing the last ride of two once-proud martial nations.

Allies since the age of Sigmar, a smaller force of dwarfs anchored
the Imperial position with guns and gromril. Resolute blocks of
heavy infantry in flowing mail and winged, visored helms picked
out with gemstones and gold presented a wall of shields around
a core of artillery and missile troops. The distances involved were
great, but Felix thought he recognised their leader. Draped in a
cloak of dragon scales and wearing his orange-dyed hair in a fierce
crest, there could be no mistaking Ungrim Ironfist, the Slayer-King
of Karak Kadrin. The dwarf king led from the heart of his shield
wall, hacking open wave after wave of beastmen and Chaos warriors, enveloped in a strange aura of flame.

Looking beyond the dwarf position things became... strange.

Random visions? Prophecy?

It was too outlandish to be a dream.

Crowding the ghostly cobblestones beside their – ostensibly –
mortal enemies was a raucous host ten times more numerous
than that of the Empire and the dwarfs combined. The greenskins
filled the air with noise. Hulking leather-skinned brutes beat on
man-skin drums. Prancing goblins wearing nothing but piercings
and glitter played manic tunes on bone pipes and led their followers in shrill, exuberant chants. Every second that Felix watched,
thousands of crooked arrows whooshed from goblin bows. Rickety

trebuchets flung boulders high into the air while impatient lines of goblins with spiked helms and hand-sewn wings waited for their turn to be catapulted across the battlefield. Felix picked out the greenskins' commander where the fighting was fiercest and the monstrous champions of Chaos pushed hardest: an immense, one-eyed black orc, all welded iron plate and dark green muscle, wading into the Chaos ranks with saliva drooling from his tusks and every appearance of a brutally straightforward joy. The war-boss's host was clearly far beyond his ability to fully control, bits of it charging forward and withdrawing again almost at random; a tattered sleeve at the edge of a fine mail coat, flapping neverthe-less in the face of a common enemy.

Dumbstruck by this improbable alliance, Felix turned back to the Empire force and beyond it to the opposite flank where – if that were possible – something even stranger lined up in order of battle.

A gleaming spearline of tall elven warriors held a tide of maraud-ers at bay, handling their long weapons with a graceful, almost elegant ruthlessness. Their presence alone was not so strange. There was precedent for the armies of men and elves coming together in times of great strife, but what *was* strange was the sheer diversity of elven forces that had been deployed to the same field together. Lean, knife-chinned warriors in leather kheitans and sur-coats of nightshade purple shared ranks with princely spearmen in silver-blue scales, and with others that shunned armour altogether, lightly tanned and garbed in jerkins of autumnal leaves. Longbows and reaper crossbows spoke the common language of death in a single chorus. Felix didn't know what could have reunited such a bitterly divided race, but as he watched an enormous black dragon swooped over the elven lines, bearing with it an iron-clad elf lord and a streaming wake of shadow.

Felix felt out the dragonhead hilt of his sword, but the weapon didn't stir. It was possible that the beast was too far away to arouse the blade's killing instinct, or perhaps all of this was less real to Karaghul than it was to him.

Just at that moment, he wished he could share some of its steel ambivalence.

Because there, at the far end of the battle-line, under the stretched mirage of a vintner's awning, there hovered an entity more puissant and terrifying than anything the massed legions of Chaos could conjure. Through a pall of unnatural darkness strode a skull-faced titan, suspended above earth that atrophied under his step by a buffer of dark magic, an unconscious manifestation of a power too absolute for even that dread figure to fully contain. That being's battlefield was a lifeless wasteland that none other shared, for whenever even the mightiest champions of Chaos rode against him, men fell and rose again to swell his unliving legions. A name, an imprecation familiar to every passing student of the forbidden, trembled blindly into Felix's hindbrain and screamed.

Nagash.

'What's happening here?'

'The inevitable,' said a dry, subtly condescending voice from the spot beside him in the ranks. In defiance of logical reason and everything he remembered seeing around him a moment before, an elf mage now stood there amongst the crossbowmen. This one Felix knew personally. He was tall as all elves were but extraordinarily thin and pale, with skin that was almost translucent on the bone. His face was narrow and haughty, his almond-shaped eyes crystal pale and almost cruel. Teclis, High Loremaster of the White Tower of Ulthuan. The mage shrugged. 'The singularity. The end of everything that has come before.'

Felix listened with half an ear, eyes wide to the carnage all around him. A unit of Chaos warriors whose armour wept blood marched behind a screen of thrashing spawn into the roaring teeth of the Empire guns. A squadron of elf knights in fluted, scythe-edged armour and mounted on reptilian steeds fled from a fierce melee involving warriors of at least seven different races only to be over-run and pulled down by a pack of baying daemon hounds. Even the skies were not spared. Magic crackled through the clouds, pegasus knights and elven hawk-riders arrowing through the arcing spell effects to engage the enemy's flyers. The din was overwhelming, a demoralising weapon in its own right. Everywhere there was some-thing happening, something dying horribly and noisily. It was too much to take in as a whole.

'What happened to Middenheim? Where's Kat?'

'You have a strange set of priorities given the circumstances. If you could only imagine what I have given for the cause, if there was a way to make you fathom the depths of my sacrifice, then perhaps you would understand.'

'Is this about what happened to Ulthuan?'

The elf produced a disparaging sneer. 'You still don't understand.'

A resigned murmur passed through the crossbowmen, the clatter of gear, the near-audible clenching of teeth and hardening of hearts. A new sequence of flags had been lofted onto the vexillary's sig-nal pole: a plain white flag bearing the symbol of a crossbow, then two fluttering triangles beneath it, blue and white for Middenheim.

'Orders are: advance!' the unit sergeant yelled, then put a whistle to his mouth and sounded the march. The crossbowmen started forward and Felix, caught in the momentum of events he could neither comprehend nor control, moved with them.

He looked in the direction they were headed and clutched his sword in fear.

Without any formal warning of the emergence of so gross an anomaly, a vast silver portal now swirled over the centre of the

Chaos legions. Distortions in the aethyr arced around its aureole, spreading out to become tears, claw-rents in reality as Felix in his limited way understood it. Through those tears a shadow bled through. Watching it was somehow more horrifying than anything he had yet seen on this battlefield.

It was sitting in the hold of a ship and watching salt water pour in. It was standing in line for the noose. It was the same shadow that had stalked him through the Great Forest and the Middle Mountains and had almost been his doom but for Max Schreiber. It was death.

It was inevitability.

'What am I looking at?'

'Time is much like war. Aeon-long stretches of nothing, or what I came to consider nothing, but always moving forward, always going *here.*'

'I don't understand.'

'He's saying you have a choice to make, Felix.' The cloaked seeress from his dream marched at his other hand, the pair of elf and mutant apparently perfectly innocuous within a marching file of Middenheimer crossbows. 'To save a world or not?'

'What kind of a choice is that?'

'Not the one you think it is,' the seeress replied sadly.

'Who are you?' Felix shouted over the pound of boots and the blister-roar of gun-fire. 'Whose side are you on, anyway?'

Teclis laughed bitterly. 'She is here with you, isn't she?'

The elf pointed his moon-tipped staff towards the massed enemy formations. Felix looked as directed. For a moment he didn't see, the enemy were simply too numerous to pick out one from the horde, but then he glimpsed the shaggy grey giant in battered plate that rose head and shoulders above the melee. Khagash-Fél hacked down orcs and men from horseback, his massive warhorse champing shoulder-to-shoulder with that of another mighty war-lord. His blued armour was fantastically ornate and blazed with mystic runes that made him shimmer like a mirage. Arek Daemon-claw tore through all that opposed him with axe and lance. Felix quailed to see the two warriors side by side, and fighting in concert they appeared unstoppable.

They were also not alone.

Everywhere Felix looked he saw old enemies fighting to undo the world that he had hoped to leave for his children. The great red dragon Skjalandir soared over the battlefield as though it owned it, torrents of flame roasting through the eagle- and hawk-riders that buzzed around its bulk like insects. The necromancer, Heinrich Kemmler, skulked behind the lines, raising a regiment of zombie warriors here, dismantling a lesser spellcaster's bone construct there. From atop a horned bell that was mounted on a kind of chariot, and pushed into battle by a tide of red-armoured skaven elites, Grey Seer Thanquol chittered commands. The ratman sorcerer squealed in delight as the iron-shod wheels of his chariot ground over orcs and goblins, intoxicated by the volume of warp-stone he had consumed and gleefully vaporising those that tried to flee with bolts of warp-lightning from his claws.

Without realising it, Felix's thumb had moved from his sword-grip to the ring on his finger, feeling over the indents made by the dwarf runes that banded it. There were so many things he had never said to her. He would have given his right arm just for the chance to say goodbye, would gladly have offered his life if it meant he could hold her once more. He was being a foolish and sentimental old man, he knew, and worse, the romantic he'd always feared he was. This wasn't real. Kat wasn't real.

The tramp of feet bore Felix on: the tick of a clock, the running of sand, of blood. The Middenheimers' armour shimmered under the portal's radiance, each man a ripple in a pool, reflecting the moonlight. Felix wondered what other worlds and strange horrors lay beyond it, then decided that he really didn't want to know. He didn't want anyone to have to learn.

Because it was real.

'I have a choice to make? Then take me back to Gotrek so I can put an end to this. That's what everyone wants. One last adventure. Isn't that the way this is supposed to be?'

The sorcerer and the seeress shared a weighted look.

He closed his eyes and bent his mind towards his will.

'Take me back.'

A hot wind blew cinders in Felix's face. He opened his eyes.

He was back in Neumarkt, but this time overlooking it from the fortified rooftop on which he'd previously spotted Kat. The wooden wreckage of a ballista crunched underfoot as he moved to the edge. The merlons wore blackened, tormented silhouettes of men and women, immortalising the moment they were burned alive. Felix could taste bile in his mouth. It was as if this position had been hit with a fireball.

He placed his hands onto the heat-deformed crenellations and leaned out.

The gates were smashed, the stones around them continuing to smoulder. Islands of flame dotted the courtyard, like candles in a mausoleum, burning for the dead that littered the space. Fire reflected off broken windows, from ruptured breastplates and split helms, from fallen blades, from the tiniest morsel of bare steel on the arrowheads protruding from dead men's backs. Felix felt his eyes weaken in the dancing light. His vision blurred.

Was this one last cruel test, to gauge his reaction to the reality of what the forces of Chaos would leave behind?

Felix pinched the tears from his eyes and sniffed. 'I'm sorry, Kat. I never should have left you in the first place. I should have died by your side defending Altdorf.'

'And who would that have helped, exactly?'

Felix's fingers almost bored into the stonework. That voice. His heart sang, but part of him wouldn't allow it to believe. He kept his eyes on the pyres. 'I don't see that it would have done too much harm either. In fact from where I'm standing, I don't think it would have made any difference at all.'

'You saved Max.'

'He might still be alive if I hadn't.'

'I doubt he saw it like that.'

Felix sighed and hung his head. Then he turned around.

Kat stood in front of him. Her hair had been badly roughed up, the silver lock over her left eye stained red. Her leather armour and fabric pads were scorched and several pieces were missing. There was no sign of any other survivors.

'Are you really Kat?' he asked, looking her up and down and wondering why he had to do something as stupid as ask that question. 'You're not about to tell me I have a great and terrible destiny?'

'You do have a destiny, Felix,' said Kat, taking his hand in hers and looking up into his eyes. 'And it doesn't involve me. But I don't regret being touched by it, even if it was only for a little while.'

Felix smiled through his tears, holding her hand tightly and pulling her to him as though the beating of his heart against her chest would make her real. Suddenly all of the things he had wanted to do or say boiled down to nothing.

This was enough. This moment.

Kat moved closer until they touched hip to hip, nothing but a fiercely clenched hand between them. She smiled shyly and turned her body against his, revealing a woollen sling nestled between her quiver and the padded back of her gambeson. From within, a pair of crystal-bright blue eyes peered curiously out from a pudgy face topped with a sprinkling of white-blonde hair. Felix had no experience in these things, but he guessed that the baby must have been just under a year old. The child babbled brightly and smiled as Felix smiled, reaching out with a small hand to grasp his cheek.

It actually rather hurt, but Felix didn't care. His heart had melted and turned to gold.

'My daughter...'

'Rosa Jaeger,' said Kat softly, voice fading as the world around them returned belatedly to darkness. 'Say hello to your father.'

SEVENTEEN

The First Slayer

Felix came to, his eyes welcoming back the red-gold pulse of rune-light with a smile so bittersweet that it ached all the way to the pit of his stomach. It had all been a fantasy, a trial devised by some uncaring rune-guardian, but in his heart it felt real. He had been there for his wife when it mattered. He had been with her at the death.

He had seen his child.

To hell with destiny. He closed his eyes again, to hold on to the ache for just one moment more.

'Get up, manling. It gets worse.'

Felix buried his face in his palms and groaned as he sat up, then dragged his hands down his cheeks as if they might collapse into despair without bracing.

The Slayer stood with his axe head on the ground and his scratched hands overlaying one another over the haft. His fingers rhythmically flexed and clenched, a tic that in anyone else Felix would have described as nervous. His one eye swept over a patch of ground in front of his feet, his lips muttering quietly as though he were in deep, meditative prayer.

Felix glanced over Gotrek's shoulder. His hands slid away from his face, no longer supported by his hanging jaw. Now he understood.

Behind Gotrek there loomed another Slayer, but one so truly massive that he made Gotrek look frail by comparison. He was a head taller, the extra height accentuated by a blade of bright red hair, and with muscle enough packed into his awesome frame to wrestle down a mountain. Looking at him Felix was aware of a sense of *density*, as if more had gone into his being than should have been possible given the size, impressive as it was, of his body. He wore heavy leather boots and a kilt of iron plates sewn together with bronze rings. Other than that and a few spiked piercings along one side of his neck and the adjoining shoulder, the dwarf went bare-skinned. Tattoos crisscrossed his body, but in contrast to the intricate designs inked onto Gotrek's skin these were atavistic, branching blue lines that traced an endless spiral around his muscular frame.

The big Slayer set an enormous rune-axe against his shoulder and studied Felix with eyes of an eternal, ever-wrathful blue. Felix could have lost himself in that gaze.

The gaze of a god.

Felix glanced nervously at his companion. 'Is that...?'

'Aye, manling,' said Gotrek gruffly. 'This time it really is.'

Horsemen careened down the mountain slope, setting off a miniature avalanche of ice and scree. The earth was never deep this high in the mountains and the thin crust of topsoil concealed a hard layer of permafrost. The air was semi-frozen, thin enough to make filling one's lungs in one breath a challenge. The tribesmen seemed to revel in it, throwing ice almost playfully from their ponies' fetlocks, drawing down the fur-lined leather flaps of their helms and grinning, grizzled brown faces glowing with body warmth.

A posse of red-faced and hard-breathing riders reined in as they

thundered towards Morzanna. Their animals snorted gamely, paw-
ing at the frost. Morzanna shook scattered ice from her sleeves and
smiled, using Nergüi's eagle staff as a walking pole to climb the rest
of the way to meet them. Khagash-Fél had been right to be proud
of his people. Their fearlessness and tenacity was matched only by
their enthusiasm. And it was infectious.

Despite the fate she had always known awaited her in the Slayer
Fortress.

'Temugan claims to have seen the skyship as it entered the clouds,
prophetess. There.' The rider who spoke, a sunken-cheeked warrior
with a broad grin and fiery yellow eyes, creaked about in the saddle and pointed up to the sky. The wind riffled through the long
sleeves of his black silk vest, worn as an underlayer to a sleeveless
shirt of lamellar leather scales. 'He marked the spot and has not
removed his eyes from it in six hours.'

'Have you found a way up?'

'There is none to be found, prophetess,' the rider declared, delivering what he must have known was crushing news and doing so
without even the recognition that he should be fearful.

Men did things differently on the eastern steppe.

'Leave me, I must think on this. And tell Temugan he may rest
his eyes.'

'You are kind and powerful, mighty prophetess,' cried the horse-
man, already chivvying his mount around and galloping off with
his arban. The men rode to join the host of fur-swaddled tribesmen that mustered in the high valley. Several dark lines laced the
mountains to the south, more of Khagash-Fél's vast host filing in
through the dozens of unwarded roads and goat trails their scouts
had been able to uncover.

'I do try to be, when I can,' Morzanna murmured after they had
gone, speaking to the frigid air.

'*Your enduring capacity for compassion provides me an eternal wellspring of succour, my child,*' the air answered back. '*How it pleases me to experience your broken heart and dashed dreams over and over again.*'

'I do not dream.'

Laughter's echo rang in her ears. '*I trust that you are ready for the end?*'

Morzanna looked up the craggy, barren scarp that stoic Temugan had marked, her gaze following the incline until rock faded into cloud and ultimately disappeared altogether. There was a fortress up there. She could feel the power emanating from it, but even with that to aid her she doubted whether she had the ability to transport more than just herself over so great a distance by magical means. And any fortress of dwarf-make – particularly this one – would have potent runic wards woven into its design to prevent just that kind of solitary raid. It worked both ways, of course, and this particular citadel had been constructed as much with the aim of trapping things within as presenting a defence against those without.

She bared her fangs. It might as well have been on the moon.

'There is always a way. There must be, for I have seen myself there, as I have seen you. I need time to consider it. There are limits to my skill, Dark Master.'

'*For you, perhaps, but not for me, not here. Here the fabric of the mundane is pierced by the divine. Can you feel it, Morzanna? The End Times begin now, and neither earth nor sky shall ever be as they were again.*'

A ripple of power passed through the air, an in-breath that broke over the hollow silhouette of a bat-winged demi-god. The Dark Master was revealed for the briefest of moments before folding back under the surface layers of reality. As with the mountain topsoil, the boundaries between planes were thin here, worn fine enough by the waxing of Chaos that Be'lakor was almost capable of manifesting his own form.

The origins of Be'lakor's curse of immateriality pre-dated the written word, at least in human culture – but she had seen pictographic slabs buried in prehistoric ruins under the frigid marshes of Albion that alluded to a Dark Master, and read texts unearthed from the elven ruin of Oreagar that purported to be the translation of a proto-Khemrian oral myth, of a champion of such malevolent ambition that he was stripped of his physical form by his god.

Tzeentch himself had done this and now, one layer at a time, Be'lakor was undoing it.

A greater demonstration of her master's power she did not need, but from the rumble shaking the permafrost beneath her feet she feared she was about to receive one.

This one wasn't for her. This was for the world.

The ground had begun to shake, stones running downslope until, as the force of the quake intensified, great boulders were torn from the mountainside and sent crashing down. The sound of several thousand men crying out in unison momentarily overwhelmed even the shaking earth. Morzanna turned towards the muster ground, looking on in mortification as one of the mountains, across which columns of men were still marching, shook itself apart. Millions of tons of rock collapsed in on itself as though its foundation had just been ripped away. Men were still screaming, but it was no longer possible to hear them over the crash of rock. Another mountain split up the middle and fell apart, town-sized slabs of earth tumbling away. Morzanna stood speechless.

To whom did one pray when gods walked amongst you?

The ground lurched, almost hurling Morzanna from her feet. Her slight build spared her. Hundred of tribesmen and horses were less fortunate, tossed aside as another peak at the far south end of the valley vented the phenomenal internal strain with a magmic eruption that blasted its summit apart. Morzanna dropped, sinking her claws down to the permafrost and feeling the ground's tormented shudder. It bucked, throwing Morzanna up and then rising up to meet her. She slammed back down, still rooted by her claws, and then looked up.

The Kazad Drengazi mountain was falling away before her eyes, but it wasn't collapsing.

The valley was rising.

She had heard of cabals of the ancient Slann conducting such earth-shaping rituals, but never had she believed that any individual alive today could perform them. Be'lakor's power waxed with the onset of the End Times, and with his proximity to the daemon gate locked away within the Slayer Fortress he was close to the godhood he had long craved. And he was getting closer.

'*Your only task is the Slayer-Monks,*' said Be'lakor, his voice the roar of upthrusting rock. '*Theirs is the power to summon the wrath of Grimnir, and that is an encounter I am not ready for.*'

The screams of ten thousand pierced the clouds as the valley floor drove them higher, the laughter of black gods welcoming their terrified souls to the heavens.

'*Yet.*'

'Grimnir,' Felix breathed, gazing up into the lean, brutal face of the dwarf who looked down on him in return with something between godly indifference and outright hostility. 'But he's a... isn't he a...?'

'Those are the times you are living in, manling,' Grimnir answered gravely, his voice a rumble redolent of war-wagons heading into hostile mountains, the rising clamour of a call to vengeance.

Felix simply stared.

He had been hearing tales of Sigmar's second coming since before his departure from Altdorf and, in truth, had not given them great credence. Even after all he had seen it seemed unlikely. If the gods cared enough to intercede in their faithful's affairs then why wait until things were as bad as this? But it was one thing to hear a story of a distant war in a foreign province from a bar-fly who had himself seen neither; it was quite another to find oneself within the undeniable aura of the divine. He gazed up, certain that his body was shrinking or that the ground was drawing him under.

'You don't sound much like I'd imagine a god talking,' said Felix, gawking like a country maid before a civic parade of Reiksguard Knights in shining armour.

'Nothing's forever, lad. I wasn't always thus, and perhaps I won't always be.'

With that the Vengeful Ancestor dismissed him and turned to Gotrek.

'You're a true Slayer, Gotrek, a credit to my name. Ten millennia ago I left a mighty power here – and a burden – waiting for my heir in the End Times. You've proven yourself well worthy of it, and capable of bearing it.'

Gotrek bared a grin. Felix couldn't blame the dwarf for being pleased. It wasn't everyday one came in for personal praise from their god.

'Grimnir...' Felix absently repeated.

Ignoring him, the Ancestor raised an arm like a felled and muscularly carved oak and pointed through the lines of pillars to the door that the Slayer-Abbot had initially led them through. 'The Realm of Chaos. It's not a place you can describe to one who's never seen it. What lies beyond that door I've fought the last ten thousand years to keep out. But these are the End Times and my strength wanes. And you've my leave to pass, son of Gurni.'

'Isn't that the way out?' Felix hissed, leaning in towards Gotrek.

'This is Grimnir's path, manling,' Gotrek muttered, looking almost embarrassed to be explaining this in the Ancestor's presence. 'There is no way out from here.'

'Oh,' said Felix, sitting with his arms around his knees while he processed that small but, on reflection, rather pertinent piece of information. 'But... the abbot left. And they locked it, didn't they?'

Gotrek shook his head, despairing of manling simple-mindedness.

Well, no matter, as Kolya would undoubtedly have said had he been here. It wasn't as if there was much left for any man where they had come from. He thought of his wife and daughter. He had been prepared to offer his life for a glimpse of them and whether out of compassion or cruelty he had been granted it. If they did still live, and if there was anything he could sacrifice to buy them one more hour of freedom, of happiness, or even simply of life then Felix would give it in a heartbeat.

'Pick yourself up,' said Gotrek. 'We've not found what we came for yet.'

'Not him,' Grimnir rumbled as Felix leaned into his haunches as a preliminary to the ever-worsening task of standing up. 'You proved yourself worthy, Gotrek. He did not. He's sentimental. He doesn't understand the scale of this war, the sacrifices that must be made.'

'He's a dwarf-friend and a rememberer,' said Gotrek. 'That's all you need to know.'

Grimnir's eyes flared, his upper body somehow swelling even further as the Ancestor closed both hands around the haft of his axe. A rumble passed through the pillars like vibrations through the skin of a drum, disturbing the rune-light. Felix swallowed, feeling abysmally small. The mountain itself seemed to tremble around him.

'You would argue? With me?'

Gotrek glanced at Felix, then set his jaw. Blood trickled from unhealed cuts as he squared his shoulders to his Ancestor. 'On this? Aye, I would.'

'For once in your life, Gotrek, be sensible. It's *Grimnir* for pity's sake.' Suddenly, the only thought in Felix's head was the words that the mutant seeress had spoken to him in his dream.

You are powerless against the opponent that awaits you in Kazad Drengazi, Felix, and Gotrek's passing will be the doom of this world.

This was the place, and something frantic in the back of Felix's brain told him that it was mere minutes from the time. Urgency filling his veins with fire, he got up to stand at his companion's side. 'It's all right. I'll wait here for you, or find another way out if I can.'

'No one calls my rememberer unworthy. He as good as says it of me as well.'

With a chuckle that could have cracked an anvil, Grimnir stomped a few paces back and raised his axe. 'Then come, Gotrek Gurnisson. Bloody your axe if you can.'

Gotrek readied his axe, tension singing from every sinew, his one eye sparkling with the ruddy gold of rune-light. If Felix didn't know better, he'd think that a part of the Slayer was secretly pleased that it had come to this. What greater challenge of his prowess could there be? What greater doom?

But it may be enough to save the next.

That was what the seeress had said next, but what did that even mean?

'Stop this,' Felix shouted, no longer caring that he spoke out of turn before a god. 'You'll die here if you don't.'

Gotrek ignored him completely and Grimnir merely laughed.

'A true Slayer is more than just the manner of his doom or the measure of his disgrace. He is an aspect of me. His sacrifice is an echo of my purpose. And you are a true Slayer, Gotrek, perhaps the last great Slayer.'

As if that were a challenge that he could not allow to go unanswered, Gotrek launched himself at the Ancestor with a roar. Too quick for a dwarf of his physicality and power, Grimnir slid aside, his axe licking out with seeming nonchalance but with sufficient force to beat aside Gotrek's blade and send the Slayer spinning off-balance. Gotrek adjusted quickly, swapped his axe out of his ringing hand, growled to mask his surprise, and came again.

What exactly happened next, Felix couldn't say for certain.

Grimnir unleashed a blizzard of blows that Gotrek must have somehow managed to parry simply because he remained standing throughout. Felix could not imagine how the Slayer managed it. At times it was as if the Ancestor possessed eight arms, and watching them as they went about the business for which Grimnir was lauded was like trying to track the wings of a dragonfly in flight. The entire fight lasted perhaps ten seconds from first blow to last. Felix couldn't be sure. His mind had slowed to a crawl, numbed by the speed and fury expended before his eyes.

But what happened after, Felix felt he had always known.

He was watching prophecy unfold.

The Vengeful Ancestor swept his starmetal blade across Gotrek's body and then held it there, high, head bowed. Everything seemed to stop. Felix's heart lurched between beats. He saw the blood glisten on the rim of Grimnir's raised blade.

Then with a painful, physical sensation of acceleration, time resumed.

Gotrek was torn from his feet and spun half around. There was no resistance, no effort to regain his feet and fight again. The Slayer slapped to the ground like a side of red meat. His axe clanged down behind him with a funereal knell. The dwarf lay on his side. Blood speckled his tattoos and formed a spreading pool under his savaged chest. Felix stared at his friend's face in horror. Perhaps it was this place, this palace of vengeance, or perhaps it was the company, but Felix could feel his pulse hammer behind his ears and he felt the terrible urge to empty his lungs, beat his chest and rage at the utter, *utter* stupidity of the universe.

This was one too many.

Gotrek Gurnisson was dead.

EIGHTEEN

Last Stand

The valley floor rose above the outer wall of Kazad Drengazi like the mighty crest of a wave. It even caught the sun like one, foaming as it did with the steel glint of marauder mail and weapons. Gustav Jaeger gaped as the impossible was redefined before his disbelieving eyes. Off to the left, across the cloud sea, a mountain crumbled in slow motion, sinking straight down under the surface. The very earth beneath them seemed to be shaking itself apart. His lamellar plate rattled violently as he gripped the crenellations of the citadel's innermost defensive ring. Dwarfs in ringmail togas dashed past in both directions, yelling their own special gibberish despite the fact that no one could hear a thing over the birthing roar of a new mountain and what felt like the death rattle of the old.

The growing mountain rose higher, blotting out the sun over the citadel's gatehouse and casting a long shadow over a swathe of the lower wards. More Slayer-Monks ran from the creeping shadow like ants from rising floodwaters, bearing nothing but their odd clothes and their weapons and fleeing for the next level of fortifications. Gustav could feel his bones vibrating against each other.

He ground his teeth but they chattered anyway. The rising mountain leaned in and slowly, inevitably, like a hewn oak, it began to topple towards the gatehouse.

Gustav mewled something prayer-like, throwing himself down to hug the solid marble crenel as the fantastical tonnage of rock crashed over the gatehouse, flattening it as though it were made of sand and obliterating the curtain wall utterly. The ancient stonework of the inner ring sanded his cheek as it shook.

Compacted rock piled into the citadel, layering strata and substrata and a hot metamorphic core as the sheer weight and pressure caused parts of the avalanche to glow red and vent steam. The surface layer rushed forward, like a breaking wave racing up a beach, demolishing walls and buildings alike as it went.

Tiny by comparison were the men and horses that rode the wave. Gustav fancied they were screaming but of course it was impossible to hear. Hundreds were thrown off and crushed, but there were more than enough left behind to overwhelm the score or so dwarfs that haunted this deceivingly mighty citadel.

The rock wave ploughed down the second curtain wall, exhausting the last of its momentum to spill over into the grand, empty streets that lay beyond. For a moment there was calm, the universe taking a breath to realign itself to the new arrangement. Rubbled buildings settled. Loose rock tumbled back downhill.

Then there was a cry, exuberant and shrill, and a horde of terrified-looking marauders surged through the breaches and into the citadel's second level. Horsemen spurred ahead, galloping uphill towards the next gate and loosing arrows at the barest hint of a dwarf.

Gustav lifted himself from the crenel, watching as a group of Slayer-Monks wielding a combination of axes and flails, hammers and maces, each with a weapon in either hand, charged from a ruined building and mowed through the flank of a marauder column. Their ferocity was tremendous and Gustav clenched his fist and gave a small cheer as he saw one amongst their number hammer down the ebony-armoured Chaos warrior that had been leading the marauders' advance. Even as he allowed himself to imagine that the monks' efforts might buy the defenders of the third wall a few minutes, a skirmishing line of horsemen thundered behind the infantry column, firing at the gallop and riddling the brave dwarfs with murderously accurate bow-fire.

The resistance crushed, the marauders roared and marched on.

A loud *bang* from immediately by his left ear startled Gustav from the nightmarish scene. He turned, a sulphurous pillow of smoke smothering him for a moment and then wafting by. Malakai Makaisson dropped his longrifle to the crenel and reloaded, shouting something incomprehensible to the Slayer-Abbot who stood beside him with his twin axes crossed over his chest as he did so.

'*Orzhuk akaz uruk. Glihmhad hugorl al ikrim,*' the abbot growled back.

'It's rude to talk in a language we can't all understand,' Gustav shouted, a little hysterical and not at all sure he shouldn't be.

The engineer hefted his loaded longrifle and swung it around as if to take a pot-shot at *Unstoppable*, floating like a silver cloud above their heads. His red glimstone sight played across the airship's prow until the aiming dot found the splintered view screen for the bridge. There, Makaisson waved his hand through the beam in a sequence of sharp cuts and brief pauses, dots and dashes.

'Ah was joost askin' him if he minds havin' a wee bit o' his castle bloon up,' Makaisson explained.

'Blown up?'

'Joost a wee bit.'

'And?'

Makaisson grinned, returning his signalling hand to his gun barrel and shouldering the weapon.

'Ah told 'em he disnae.'

The Slayer was dead.

Those four words struck at Felix's mind like a chisel to a gravestone. The Slayer was dead. A tide of images ran through his brain. Faces. Places. The exotic lands they had seen together, the enemies they had battled side by side, the friends they had made. And those they had lost. He remembered a lot of drinking, a good deal of arguing, and an almost endless amount of travelling, often while cold, wet, hungry and on foot, but for some reason the memory of those forgotten hours in Gotrek's company almost made him smile but for the burning grief that had his muscles seized.

The temple chamber rumbled, as if under some kind of bombardment, but Felix didn't care.

The Slayer was dead.

Again the words of the seeress's prophecy came to him, circling around his mind like taunts however much he tried to ignore them or forcibly throw them out. His mental flailing only left him vulnerable when something he had thought safely forgotten took the opportunity to strike. The mutant seeress had not been the first to prophesy the Slayer's doom. It had been several years ago, during their escape from a black ark of the dark elves, when a greater daemon of the Prince of Pain had fled from Gotrek with the chilling message: '*One greater than I is to die killing you.*'

The Slayer was dead.

This was it then, the moment, the gimbal upon which the layers of prophecy and fate tilted in balance.

All Felix could think of was how stupid it was, how utterly vain and pointless a death. He wondered what he was supposed to do now. Was he doomed to waste away to eventual insanity in this antechamber? For all the daemons, mutants and mad priests who had jostled to give their pfennig's worth on the Slayer's doom, none of them had had much to say about Felix's: only the seeress's cryptic assertion that he had a choice to make.

He couldn't take his eyes from his companion's body. They stung. It was as though they were attached – melted, welded – and he couldn't move them.

He knew what he had to do.

It was the only thing a friend and a rememberer could do for a Slayer. This was a hall of vengeance, and the daemon's prophecy was only half fulfilled.

Felix turned on the spot and looked up, only becoming aware that his sword was in his hand and positioned into a guard when he heard Grimnir's chuckle. It was a mirthless, mocking sound, that of a corpse being dragged across gravel.

'You would fight me too, manling? And how much better than your companion do you think you would fare?'

Felix ground his teeth, but refused to lower his guard. 'Does it matter? I've nothing left.'

With a snarl the Vengeful Ancestor surged forward, axe raised high. Felix tensed behind his blade, but held his ground. He knew that it was a hopeless, a futile gesture to avenge a futile death. Grimnir's mighty axe would cleave through his own pitifully enchanted blade like a wafer. In a second from now he would be dead and he doubted that Gustav or Malakai would be around for long enough to miss him, much less mourn him. The mad thought then arose that he might as well use that second to attack. He was as good as dead anyway, so why not use that last hot beat of life to inflict upon this stone-hearted god at least one moment of the hurt Felix felt now, after he was gone.

Felix shifted position, lowering his hilt and angling the sword point up and out. Kolya had once described to him how men hunted wild boar. The beast was goaded into a charge, crashing through the woods towards the cordon of hunters that waited with spears. There was little skill, just courage, the will to stand before a charging beast, nothing between you and your ending but a point of metal.

The Ancestor loomed over him, less a boar than a savage bear, mighty chest opening up and rippling with muscle for a rending downstroke.

Felix roared and stabbed up with his sword.

Grimnir pulled out of his attack at the last minute, batting away Felix's sword with a negligent wave of his enormous axe. Then, to Felix's astonishment – and no little annoyance – the Ancestor started to laugh. He lowered his axe and put his hands on his hips, waves of mirth shaking his stone barrel chest. Felix glared, eyes stinging, as he worked life into the numbed fingers around the grip of his sword. That single parry had deadened them.

'What's the matter?' said Felix, the hoarseness in his throat lending his voice a bravado he didn't feel. He had been expecting to be dead by now, and the terror of what he had just tried to do was only now beginning to circulate through his system. 'Are you worried I'll stain your axe?'

The Ancestor's laughter settled into a low chuckle, a giant hand separating from his hip to wipe what looked like a golden tear from his eye. 'Clearly I've been stuck too long in the Realm of Chaos, for never would I have expected to find such courage in one of the younger races. Tell me, manling, are all your kind as you are?'

'I don't think I'm anything particularly special.'

Grimnir again threatened to break into a laugh, but managed to restrain himself. Felix glared angrily. The Slayer was dead, and now his killer laughed.

'What would any man do to avenge a friend?' Felix returned with a snarl.

'Your body is frail, manling, but your heart's in the place it ought to be, I'll grant you that.' The Ancestor sighed, huge chest heaving as he lowered his axe to the ground with a clang. The runes that adorned its killing edge faded, as though attuned somehow to the ebb and rise of its master's wrath. 'Maybe you aren't worthy, but it's not as though I have another ten thousand years to wait for one who is. Dwarfs are ever practical, and perhaps you are worthy *enough*.'

Grimnir knelt in the pool of blood beside Gotrek's body and laid one massive hand over the Slayer's face. So large was it that it obscured Gotrek's entire head and part of his crest. Felix started forward with a warning growl and raised his sword again.

'Leave him alone. Haven't you done enough?'

The Ancestor warned him back with a look. It was not a threatening one, but nevertheless it commanded obedience and Felix found his sword lowering. Grimnir hadn't moved.

'What are you doing?'

'Hush, manling, and be patient.'

A golden-red light shone through the join between Gotrek's cheek and the palm of his Ancestor, expanding to envelop the Slayer's head and then his entire body in an auric cocoon of energy. Felix grunted in pain and raised a hand to shield his eyes, but even as he did so the brilliance began to recede and he warily repositioned the hand around his sword.

Grimnir rose, a bloody imprint on his knees, and nodded towards Gotrek. Felix turned away his blade and looked.

There was a rasping intake of breath that filled the Slayer's chest, and then a fit of coughing, as a man dying of thirst might drink too much and splutter. Gotrek sat upright, hacking and heaving. His own blood glistened on the stones around him but the wounds on his body were healed. With one harsh valedictory cough, Gotrek took a breath and swallowed it. He looked around, confused.

Felix gasped, hand to his mouth. 'Gotrek, your eye.'

The Slayer clapped his hand to his good eye, and then like a blind man muddling in the dark worked his fingers towards the other, which had for twenty years been an empty socket.

Until now.

'What in Gr–' Gotrek glanced up at his benefactor and grumbled something under his breath. 'What's going on?'

'Arise, Slayer,' said Grimnir, extending a helping hand. 'In this place there is always more killing to be done.'

Gotrek clasped the Ancestor's arm and allowed himself to be hauled up. He clenched his fists, swung a practice roundhouse and grunted satisfaction at his healed muscles, then turned with his 'good' eye scrunched tight and stared at Felix to test the acuity of the other which the power of Grimnir had restored to him.

That and more.

The Slayer was alive!

Felix couldn't speak for the exuberance bubbling up beneath his breast.

'You're skilful and uncommonly strong, Slayer,' said Grimnir, nodding appreciatively to Gotrek's axe as the dwarf bent to collect it from the ground. 'Bearing my axe for so many years has toughened you, but you're aware that its most powerful enchantments lie dormant.'

'You speak of the Rune of Unbinding. Aye, King Thangrim of Karag Dum spoke of it, but with the passing of his Runelord so too went the craft to awaken it.'

Grimnir smiled. Felix thought it a uniquely terrifying expression.

The Ancestor held out his hand. 'Pass it here.'

Gotrek hesitated a moment – understandably so, considering – then mouthed a curse and slapped the weapon down into Grimnir's waiting palm.

The Ancestor's fingers closed around the haft, his other hand moving to cover the flat blade. He uttered a word that Felix didn't catch, whispered it to the meteoric steel through his fingers, then swept his hand aside to reveal a fiercely glowing runic mark square in the centre of the blade that Felix would swear on the very existence of the Empire had not been there before. Felix could feel the power pulsing from it. It was cleansing, like slipping into a hot bath after months of mud and road. The magic inherent in this strange place receded from its proximity, the pillars wavering yet becoming somehow *more* solid. The walls too appeared less distant than they had, standing more-or-less as Felix would have placed them according to the temple's outward appearance.

'The Rune of Unbinding was crafted to slay the Chaos Gods,' said Grimnir, returning the reawakened axe to Gotrek's grip. 'You'll find it useful.'

'You should have taken it with you in the first place.'

'Originally I'd planned to. But strong as I felt, I knew there was a chance I'd fail. And if I did then I needed there to be something of me left behind for my heir to follow in my steps. My avatar in the End Times.'

Gotrek snorted derisively.

'Moan all you want, but there it is.' Then, Grimnir presented to Gotrek his own axe. It was similarly massive and with the same extra-earthly metal employed in its making. The runes that emblazoned its surface were similar, but even to Felix's eye noticeably different. 'The End Times these are, and it's right that both of my axes should be borne together again by my heir.'

Gotrek examined the weapon and shook his head sternly. 'I'm

no thief. This is the axe of Thorgrim Grudgebearer, the weapon of my High King.'

'It is Morgrim's axe, the weapon of my son, and it is mine to give.'

'How did it get here?' Felix chimed in, his voice sounding terribly light and obtrusive after the rumbling discourse of the two dwarfs. He cleared his throat and unconsciously dropped an octave. 'Is it an illusion like the one of Middenheim?'

'That was no illusion, manling, and neither is this.'

Gotrek nodded his understanding, his voice when it came as hard and sharp as a flint. 'Then the High King has fallen. Azamar, the ever-rune, has been broken and the kingdom of the dwarfs is no more.'

'Not quite yet as you might reckon it, but it will. The numberless hordes of Grey Seer Thanquol, and one you've not encountered named the Headtaker, yet besiege it. Its doom, however,' said Grimnir, pushing the axe into Gotrek's unprotesting grasp, 'is as written as yours.'

'Can it not be saved?' Felix asked, aghast.

If the Everpeak could be toppled then what hope was left for the lands of men?

Grimnir turned a questioning look on Gotrek. If the Slayer seemed at all perturbed by the slow extermination of his people, then he didn't show it. He gave his two god-like axes a practice swing and grinned horribly.

'No more tests. I know where my doom lies. Come, manling.'

That last was called over the Slayer's shoulder as he turned towards the doorway.

'One last warning,' Grimnir called after him. 'That door has stood unopened, guarded by my monks and I for ten millennia. Opening it will weaken the wards that surround this place, make an opening for anyone else that might be waiting for it. That daemon prince that spared you aboard your ship, for instance; he assaults Kazad Drengazi even now.'

Felix cast a despairing look to the door. The knowledge that it no longer led back to the fortress and the men he had left there only increased the impotence of his agony.

Gustav.

'Can't you stop him?' he asked of the Ancestor.

'Not once the way is broken. I am but an echo of Grimnir. In truth, I wait for you at your destination.'

'Let the daemon come,' said Gotrek.

'Be'lakor is almost as old as I. He'll be at his strongest where you're headed, the very threshold of the Realm of Chaos, and you'll never get there before he does.'

'Let him,' Felix echoed, explaining as Gotrek glanced back in surprise: 'If he follows us then Gustav and Malakai might have a chance.'

Grimnir smiled and gestured to the door.

'Sentimental, aye, but brave. May it keep you strong where you go, manling.'

A thunderous report boomed out from *Unstoppable*'s ventral batteries and a blaze of organ-gun fire ripped into the ruins of the lower wards, churning up men and rubble and screaming horses with supremely indifferent firepower. Gustav's company, spread out along the wall amongst the monks, gave a ragged cheer and let off a salvo of their own. A short burst of cracks and pops from their more conventional arms sounded like a five-gun salute as the airship yawed to port, bearing away from the temple complex and over the lower wards, maintaining the same punishing rate of fire as it went.

The disciplined marauder formations broke up as individual men went to ground. A handful reappeared atop roofs or high towers to fire at the airship's gleaming metal belly, but the distances were deceptive and their arrows fell way short.

A steam horn sounded from above *Unstoppable*'s bridge, a signal of some kind, and a moment later her belly opened. The gondola's underside, something Gustav had considered to be riveted steel as solid as the rest of the hull, turned out instead to be comprised of a series of large hatches concealing some kind of ballast tank. Now those hatches swung out and a stream of dark cylindrical objects dropped in weighted silence to the streets below.

Bombs.

Gustav had read about this in Felix's book. Just one more thing he hadn't believed. He hugged the crenel again and braced himself.

Parallel tracks of increasingly violent explosions stamped a path across the lower wards of the citadel, throwing up sky-high pillars of smoke and burning debris as they went. Gustav stared in awe of the airship's power. Who needed an ancient dwarfish prophecy when they wielded something like this?

This, here, would be the salvation of the Empire – Malakai Makai-sson and the aptly named *Unstoppable*!

Already half of the lower wards were on fire, the flames sickly and dark in the thin air, and everything not already flattened teetered on the brink of collapse. Ventral and broadside cannons continuing to pound what little remained upright, the airship began the tortuous process of coming about for a second pass.

'Nae Chaos-lovin' wazzock messes wi' ma airship.'

Gustav smiled, but then, for no good reason he could perceive, shivered. A murmur passed through the Slayer-Monks and he could tell he was not alone. The temperature, already well south of freezing, plunged even further despite the fires. Gustav felt the air in his mouth begin to crystallise. A nascent headache started to thump at the back of his brain.

'Dark mage!' he yelled.

A black shape thrashed within the flames, like some giant sea monster tearing free of a net. Gustav's free company peppered the emanant beast with shot, but nothing made a mark. Makaisson brought up his longrifle with a grunt. A red dot flashed over the emerging shape of a huge, horned head. The high-powered weapon fired with a deafening *boom* and Gustav gripped the wall in anticipation, only to watch the shell ricochet off the daemon prince's forehead.

Gustav moaned. 'Be'lakor. I thought Max banished him.'

Makaisson swore and reloaded. 'Hawd the wall, laddie. It's joost yin wee daemon.'

Be'lakor burst through the flames, fire licking about his volcanic form as he threw back his wings. A sudden gale arose from nowhere to fill them and shoot the daemon prince into the sky. Gunshots flashed across his frame as he briefly soared towards the fortified gatehouse of the third wall. There, he tucked in his wings and dived.

A Slayer-Monk with a double-bladed quarterstaff hurled himself from the parapet as the daemon prince crashed through the wall of the keep like a cannonball. The fortification slowly began to collapse in on itself. The dwarf clutched his quarterstaff, legs pumping furiously as he dropped, his wall crumbling away behind him even as he did. A deep roar echoed from under the rubble of the keep and for one implosive instant the world was bleached of colour. A shockwave rippled from the epicentre, so fast that everything in the vicinity was caught in a wave of vibrating force. Then the keep cracked open like an egg, a purple fire spearing through the cracks and annihilating everything nearby in a blast of dark magic. The monk was incinerated, just a fraction of a second before the keep and a huge stretch of wall was transformed into a glass-lined crater.

Be'lakor strode through, wings upraised like a halo of black.

'Alright, sae it's a big daemon.'

'*Sihrak. Sihrak Grimnir ha!*'

One of the Slayer-Monks on the inner wall was remonstrating with his abbot, others joining in on both sides to raise what sounded like a heated argument. Gustav turned to Malakai.

'Ah gather yon abbot has the power tae call doon the wrath o' Grimnir if he wishes tae.'

'Why the hell doesn't he?'

Malakai cocked his ear to the arguing monks for a moment, then turned back to Gustav. 'He says oor fate lies wi' Grimnir's heir noo.' He listened a bit more as the abbot continued to remonstrate with his monks. 'And his rememberer.'

Gustav puffed out his cheeks and readied his sword. It looked like he was going to need it after all.

'Tale of my life.'

The doorway to the Realm of Chaos parted before Gotrek's boot, splintering up the middle like so much kindling. What was left flew apart under the attention of Gotrek's axes. It wasn't strictly necessary, but the Slayer seemed to enjoy it, an almost childlike glee at the power in his hands shining from his eyes. Felix dimly recalled a similar feeling when, as a boy, he had held a real steel blade for the first time. He smiled ruefully. *Dimly.* He followed in behind the Slayer, moving warily, his own enchanted blade held ready to fend off any ambusher that might have been drawn to such ill-advised destruction so early on in their journey.

'I have to accustom myself to the balance, manling,' Gotrek explained, still grinning, wood splinters in his beard.

'Of course you do,' Felix murmured.

A great colonnaded hall with a vaulted ceiling stretched out before them. Ceiling glimstones cast out feral shadows to lurk behind great arches that were carved into the likenesses of daemons and the Slayer that grappled them where they met. From the centre of every flagstone a red rune glowed, thousands of them together creating the unpleasant sense of the floor being covered in a carpet of fire. Felix could even smell burning too, a brimstone odour that was rising from somewhere deeper in the temple. He cast his eyes nervously over the sweeping architecture. The halls rang with the clangour of unseen axes. Daemonic screams and dwarfish cries echoed from the ceiling and walls. The columns ran with the faces of the damned.

These were not the Wastes such as they had once overflown en route to Karag Dum, nor more recently trekked through the hinterlands of on their return from Kislev.

This was an antechamber to the Realm of Chaos – the warped realm of the gods themselves.

This was where Grimnir had passed from the Old World and into the domain of the gods. This was where he had made his beachhead, fortified it with rune and stone, and by his own eternal battle and the vigilance of his followers it had stood, an island fort in an endless void of entropy, unchanged in ten thousand years.

It was astounding.

Movement from the corner of Felix's eye drew his gaze to one of the distant columns. A one-eyed creature of pus and hanging entrails dribbled out of hiding. Another scuttled after it from behind the next pillar along, a fat eyeball from which splayed a mad array of limbs, pincers, tendrils and flesh-whips, oozing stacks stuffed with the harvested eyes of humans and other mortal races swaying above it. Felix tightened his grip on his sword. A hungry moan rasped through the echoing hall. Daemons of every insane imagining of form and substance shuffled, hopped, slithered, oozed and quite literally crawled out of the woodwork, drawn by the scent of the mortal. Gotrek contemptuously hacked a rotting sword-daemon apart, and kicked its dissolving remains clear. A rustle of wings called Felix's attention to the ceiling.

He swallowed hard.

They were deserters, Felix realised, survivors of an eternal war. As Felix understood it, it was Grimnir's personal struggle that held the footsoldiers of the Chaos Gods at bay. These pitiful monstrosities here were those weak and insignificant enough to have escaped Grimnir's axe and fled into this pocket realm between their world and what Felix thought of as the real one. Weak to Grimnir, perhaps, but daemons regardless and more than enough to give Felix pause for thought. He reckoned he could take two or three – assuming he could get them one at a time – but there were already more of them in sight than that.

As a first estimate, one admittedly arrived at under duress: a lot more.

'Behind me,' said Gotrek, spinning his two axes before him and blending a feather-robed daemonette without breaking stride. Daemons gibbered and shrieked and Gotrek and his flashing rune-axes waded in with a roar. 'Keep close, manling. We don't stop until the end.'

Morzanna died here.

She had lived this moment every day of her life, had felt the heat of the fire on her skin as she had when the Pious burned her home, had heard the screams, the war-cries in a language that she had not until these last few days been able to recognise. She recognised the crumbling of the structures around her as they surrendered to the relentless shelling from above. In her mind and in her spirit she had experienced the might of the one she would call master, watched through her own future eyes as he demolished a building with a swipe of his arm and then pointed towards the final gate.

Power lensed down to a sharp black point at the tip of the dae-mon prince's claw. Morzanna felt malice rise up out of the earth at his beckoning, ripping around his form like black lace in a whirl-wind. Lancing through it came a beam of darkness, laced with purples and blues and shooting towards the gate. Screaming men and dwarfs flung themselves clear moments before the bastion erupted in a geyser of glassed stone and warped metal.

Frantic shouts rang down from the walls, a desultory volley of gunfire from the handful of defenders that weren't abandoning it for a last stand within the courtyard. Bullets beat against Be'lakor's god-like frame, ricochets crunching through corner walls or punch-ing horsemen from the saddle. The tribesmen galloped around the hulking daemon prince, loosing a storm of arrows on the run as they raced for the ruined gate.

The foreknowledge of her own passing did not trouble her.

In a way it was comforting. Hers was a borrowed life, one that should have ended two centuries ago but for the intervention of Felix Jaeger. It was destiny, she supposed, fully conscious of the irony in that, and at least in living it she had guided Be'lakor towards his own great work.

The death of this world at the hands of the Everchosen, Be'lakor's child-in-darkness.

And its rebirth.

A future unseen but *felt* lay before them all. What it held, what form it would take, she could not say, but it was there and the sim-ple fact of not knowing thrilled her.

Summoning her own power to her fingertips she moved into a burning street – shadows rushed to envelop her – and stepped out onto a tower that had lost its roof to an aerial blast.

Fires blazed all around her, ravaged buildings poking through like islands in a sunset sea. Screams rose around her like smoke.

A persistent drone passed overhead and she looked up at the sleek belly of the dwarf airship. Gun-barrels fixed within rotating metal bubbles swivelled and boomed. From the corner of her eye she watched as one of the gunners noticed the mutant sorceress over-looking the battlefield and pivoted his battery towards her. With a sigh she clapped her hands sharply, the impact foreshadowing the small explosion that blew the gun turret and a spurt of shrapnel from the side of the airship.

Sometimes she wondered why she still bothered to fight, but it was not yet her time. One minute away or a hundred years, what was the difference? She had seen this moment coming all her life. If she was going to give up now, then she would have done so decades ago. She had even felt the change that came next, but even without forewarning it would have been impossible to miss.

For a moment the magic that swirled down from the polar warp gate in the far Northern Wastes was overwhelmed by another source. It came from deep below ground, spearing through a fissure in the rock of reality as though the world had been cracked and molten light beamed from its core. It was the polar gate that Grimnir had long ago vowed to close, and a doorway onto his road lay here.

And it had just been opened.

Be'lakor threw back his head and roared in triumph, vanishing mid-cry with an implosive *clap* that sucked in the surrounding flames to the abruptly voided space.

Morzanna felt herself relax. She had played her part, but the future lay in the hands of others now. She looked to the inner walls of the fortress, noting with an almost maternal pride that the tribesmen continued to pour forward despite the departure of their infernal lord. Several swung grapnels like lariats above their heads and launched them over the parapet, jumping from the backs of their galloping horses and slapping into the walls before grinning and starting to climb. The handful of missile troops left on the walls loosed their last panicked shots before jumping down. As far as she could see, only one man and a huge, strangely-outfitted dwarf Slayer remained to defend the wall.

She had often heard it said that dying was like falling asleep.

The dwarf raised his long firearm. A flash of red light shone in her eyes and blinded her for one crucial second as an explosive shot raced ahead of its accompanying bullet.

Morzanna smiled.

It was time to dream her own dreams.

She had always wondered how it would feel to sleep.

'Retreat! Everybody back to the temple!'

Gustav waved men back as he retreated up the wide steps to the temple of Grimnir, yelling until the thin air and the smoke turned his voice into a rasp. The smoke was so thick he could no longer make out *Unstoppable*. The sharp points of light that cut through the murk might have been the vessel's guide lights or could just as easily have been stars. Only the relentless rolls of thunder assured him that the airship was still there at all. While the mighty craft remained aloft and firing he had hope, but he would gladly have traded a handful of its cannons for half as many good men on the ground.

Horsemen in iron and leather scales galloped in and out of view, cheek flaps and leather skirts slapping their sides, shod hooves clattering on stone. Gustav flinched from the whine of arrows. A man in soiled burgundy and gold and a breastplate slowly turning to rust caught an arrow through the leather padding between armour and shoulder and went down with a scream. Another took an arrow in the back of the leg, dropping to his knees and making a wild shot with his blunderbuss only to be beheaded by an adze-wielding rider charging in from the side.

Everywhere he looked his men were dropping, men he had led since Badenhof, people he had come to consider as something more than mere friends.

Smoke clinging to his enormous armoured frame, the Slayer-Abbot barrelled towards a group of marauder horsemen. The riders flowed away, teasingly out of reach, calling out to the enraged dwarf as they riddled him with arrows. White and brown feathers bristled like a hedgehog's quills from every part of his body when he took one last despairing lunge and crashed over.

'Laddie, catch.'

Gustav snatched up his hand instinctively as a blocky dwarf-made pistol flew through the air towards him. From the weight of it, it was already loaded so Gustav swung it round immediately and fired, winging the pauldron of a Chaos knight who had been thundering across his line of sight towards the last pocket of Slayer-Monks battling with the marble statues at their backs.

Malakai Makaisson was a few steps below him and backing up, shrugging off the shoulder strap of his longrifle and muscling up his big handcannon. With calm proficiency the engineer ignored the incoming marauders, slotting a crank handle into the right hand of the stock and feeding a belt of what looked like ammunition into a hopper on the left. He began to turn the crank and, slowly at first but with his hugely muscled right arm quickly building speed and power, the cylindrical gun-barrel chugged and span, spitting out a torrent of shells. Laughing maniacally, the engineer swept his gun from left to right, mowing down the first rank of the cavalry charge before they made the bottom step. Horses screamed as they fell. Men jerked as the relentless stream of missiles pumped bloody craters into their bodies, many somehow remaining in the saddle only to be crushed by their falling mounts. The cannon flashed with every shot, spent casings raining from the hopper and tumbling down the steps. Makaisson's single goggle lens shone like the eye of a daemon. And then he raked his fire back the other way, cutting through the second rank with even greater glee than he had gleaned from the first.

Gustav held up the pistol and shouted over the onslaught: 'You have any more shot for this?'

'There's five mair already in the chamber.'

Gustav took another step back, aimed at a de-horsed marauder and took out half of the man's face and the back of his head with a well-placed shot.

A six-shot pistol. Remarkable. A pity the Empire would never get to see them in service.

'Ma ain invention,' Makaisson yelled up.

Gustav aimed again and fired again. And again. And again. Until the pistol returned his pulls on the trigger with empty clicks and he stood at the top of the steps with his back to the colonnaded frontage of the temple itself. He threw the gun away and hefted his sabre two-handed. Malakai's weapon stalled. The engineer shook it with a curse, then took a bomb from his backpack, pulled the pin in a fountain of sparks and let it bounce down the steps as he ran to rejoin Gustav at the top.

The explosion was small but fierce, sending bodies flying left and right. The damage to the stairway itself was minimal however and before the smoke had cleared, mounted warriors were already clattering up. Makaisson threw Gustav a wink, cleared the jam from his handcannon with brute force, unused ammunition drizzling through his fingers, and then re-attached the munitions belt to the hopper.

'Ye're nae the oath-swearin' kind are ye, young Gustav?'

Perhaps it was the imminence of death that tickled him. Or perhaps it was the preposterous pointlessness of it that made him chuckle.

Him a rememberer to a Slayer – in what mad world?

'How do you say "go to hell" in Dwarfish?'

'Ach, laddie,' Makaisson grinned, bringing his weapon to bear once more and setting his tattooed hand to the crank. 'We dinnae huv all day.'

Cavernous hallways echoed to the shriek of daemons. The stone walls of bottomless stairwells rang with the impact of rune-axe and claw, bodies tumbling endlessly down or piling high before those that fought to follow. Slender marble bridges arced over rivers of abyssal darkness, fiends and horrors raining from them as Gotrek and his axes ploughed remorselessly across. Felix stuck close, stabbing out at anything that encroached on the Slayer's back. His arms were numb and his chest burned, and he could barely see for the sweat pouring from his brow. When he did get the chance to mop his arm across his eyes all he could see was a wave of dark, distorted creatures scrambling down walls or surging up corridors from adjoining chambers. Gibbering cries screeched from every stone.

Gotrek savaged a hole and punched though.

With an axe of Grimnir in each hand, the Slayer had become an unstoppable force, an avatar of bloody-minded vengeance as the Ancestor had predicted he would be. Felix was fighting as hard as he could just to keep up. Part of him wanted to remind the Slayer that they hadn't all had the good fortune to be imbued with godly power, but he was too occupied by his own concerns to spare even that much effort.

There wouldn't be much left of him if he fell behind now.

At the end of another long hallway there was something different – a door – and Gotrek cut them a path towards it. It was high enough for a giant to pass through untroubled and sufficiently wide to accommodate a rank of Reiksguard Knights. Its carved, red wood panelling depicted images of struggle, encompassing oceans and nations and the void above, and was banded with brass. Finials in the form of vanquished daemons appeared to gnash their teeth and rage, surrounded by runic inscriptions like warding circles. Felix darted around the Slayer to try the handle. It gave an iron rattle, latched and bolted from the other side.

He shook the handle, then kicked it and cried out in frustration. 'Of all the useless...'

'Let me have a try, manling.'

Felix ducked around again, raising his sword to the slavering hordes as Gotrek at the same time spun the opposite way, like clockwork dancers on a dwarfish music box, to face the door. Felix parried a rust-edged knife, a three-bladed pincer, an axe crusted with blisters, his sword moving faster than he could control. He gave ground, keeping his back square to Gotrek's as the Slayer advanced, axes whirring.

The pair of them roared with one voice as the air around them dissolved into brass shards and splinters. Max had given his life for this. Snorri and Ulrika and Kolya and Kat had died for this. But despite the best efforts of daemons and demi-gods, they had made it.

Their last adventure.

They were going to save the world.

And they would do it together.

NINETEEN

The Doom of Gotrek Gurnisson

A silver radiance bathed the inner sanctum of Grimnir's temple with a spectral shimmer. The air resonated with a limpid hum that hinted at forces only barely held in check and that thrummed against Felix's inner ear. Looking around was disorientating, like trying to locate a silver schilling at the bottom of a wishing well while a flautist played a single out-of-tune note beside him.

The chamber was of a similar size to the courtyard above it and with the same circular design. There were no weight-bearing columns here, nothing to divide the temple into more discrete spaces, nor to provide any hiding place from that light. The high ceiling was vaulted with ribs of iron and stone that crossed each other in a pattern that resembled a field of stars, a single ruby glittering in the centre of each one. There was a mezzanine level at the opposite end of the chamber, supported by nothing more obvious than dwarfish ingenuity and the two marble staircases that swept around the curve of the temple's walls towards it. A chandelier hung over each staircase. Each was an iron latticework of geometric forms, squares coming together to form stars, which assembled in turn into pyramids that lay atop one another in the confines of the final, square shape of the chandelier. Precious glowstones, rather than candles, shone from them, but the ambient light around them washed out their colours and brightness.

Felix looked up to the mezzanine itself. There was the origin of the light and the fluting hum. An enormous silver portal rippled and swirled. It was identical to that shown to him by Grimnir during his trials, but rather than standing free in the air the distortions that it put out were mitigated by the huge stone dolmen that had been constructed to contain it. The marble uprights were carved into the stylised semblances of dwarf gods. They were not of Grimnir, Felix realised, but of the other two members of the dwarfs' holy triumvirate: Grungni the smith and Valaya the hearth-maker.

Of course, Grimnir had likely built this shrine himself. And the Vengeful Ancestor was not so boastful as to ornament it with his own likeness.

The argent surface was semi-translucent, a film rather than a barrier, and the visions that passed within it were in a state of constant flux. The only object of permanence was Grimnir himself. Locked in his eternal battle, the Ancestor was a true colossus. The being that Felix watched through rippling silver was greater even than the avatar that had vanquished Gotrek so off-handedly in the halls above, his scale more readily comparable to large buildings or small hills than mortal flesh. How much of that impression was due to Grimnir's own godly proportions and how much was affected by the portal's distortions, Felix could not say. However, in the brief period Felix had to observe he saw the Ancestor grapple with a two-headed daemon whose own rust-red torso was muscled like a mountain, levering the bawling monster to its knees and cracking its spine with his knee before moving on, all in utter silence but for that charged hum.

Felix wanted to see more. There was something hypnotic about the endless flow. But there was no time and he forced himself to look away.

He turned back the way they had come, raising his sword with a frustrated hiss as semi-feral daemonic footsoldiers poured in through the ravaged door. They swarmed around the walls, forming a horseshoe-like body of gibbered taunts and twitching claws, but avoiding the central floor space as a night goblin would the sun.

Felix backed away from them, risking a glance over his shoulder and noticing only then that his companion was no longer with him. Gotrek was a few paces ahead, just about at the centre point of the circular chamber between the two hanging chandeliers and glaring up at the portal.

No. Not at the portal. Something in front of it.

Hidden within the portal's radiant light, enthroned upon a seat of brazen skulls, sat Be'lakor. With the light shining fiercely behind him, the Dark Master was a void from which the eight-pointed star of Chaos blazed, as if the portal shone through him for the sole benefit of illuminating that ill-starred sigil of ruin. Upon his horned head was a crown, and at the foot of his throne four huge and equally terrible figures abased themselves before him.

One was ruddy-fleshed and bestial, clad in archaic armour of rune-scored bronze and clenching an axe that seemed to keen in hunger over its bent knee. Where the first was a brutal knot of blood-caked armour and savagery, the second was supple and slender, a subtle suggestiveness to the bend of her leg. Felix felt an unsettling alchemy of desire and self-disgust gurgle within him. He wasn't even sure what made him label the creature 'her' but nor did it seem to matter; *her* hideous, inhuman beauty transcended such prosaic delimitations of lust. The third was as different from the preceding two as one monster could be from another. Too bloated to kneel, it squatted, a miasma of brownish gases rising from its pestilential hulk. Rusted chains hung from its horns like jewellery. Maggots crawled through its flesh. Buboes swelled and popped, disgorging buzzing flies that swarmed around its head, settling occasionally to lay eggs under sagging folds of dead flesh. Nauseated, Felix turned to regard the final figure. Its avian physique was strangely jointed, bobbing lightly as if it stood upon a raft. It was wrapped up in robes that shimmered like an oasis under the Arabyan sun. A long, bird-like beak protruded from its hood. Above, hidden within the shadows of the hood, deep blue eyes glowed with enlightenment. It held a staff in one scaly, four-clawed hand. It was dazzling, and even before the brilliance of the portal it shone with every colour of the rainbow plus a few extra that Felix had not previously been aware existed.

Greater daemons, Felix thought, an unsteadiness of nerve creeping into his sword's grip. *Four of them!* One for each of the Great Powers. *This is my destiny,* Felix reminded himself. He swallowed hard.

He had always hated prophecy.

Be'lakor clasped the arms of his skull throne and rose, to the thrilled murmur of his infernal supplicants.

'Your greatest wish is granted, Gotrek Gurnisson. Your name will ring down the aeons, but as he who opened the doorway to divinity for the fifth Great Power. You are witness to the commencement of a new era, when four powers unchanged since the birthing cries of creation must bow and admit the Master of Darkness to their pantheon.'

Be'lakor laughed coldly, stepping from the throne and spreading his arms as if eulogising to the daemon hordes that were still piling into the rear of the chamber. 'I am the Dark Master. Prodigal. Pariah. Everchosen. Only I can unite the forgotten servants of the Four and at long last put an end to Grimnir's eternal war.'

The Bloodthirster snarled, turning its animalistic visage towards Gotrek and Felix. Fire dribbled from its maw. Hatred burned in its eyes.

Be'lakor gestured back to the stone dolmen. 'Here is where the banished fall, this purgatory, here to rage in mindlessness and hunger for millennia or else to relent and perish on Grimnir's axe. Only I can free them. Only I can lead their legions to ash and hell-fire upon your world.'

The exquisite daemon-woman of Slaanesh climbed languorously to her feet and stretched, running her gaze over Felix and then Gotrek. A knowing half-smile played on her lips. 'I prophesied that one greater than I was to die killing you, Slayer, do you remember? He has killed you. And now he must die. You opened the door for the Dark Master, my jewel, and now your death will be the death of Grimnir himself.'

'Come on down here, daemon,' Gotrek shouted, brandishing both his axes. 'One at a time or all together, this here is as close to Grimnir as you'll come today. Don't make me walk up those stairs or on my oath it'll go harder on you.'

The Bloodthirster bristled and made to rise, only for Be'lakor's firm hand on its shoulder to hold it at bay.

'The leash suits you,' Gotrek leered, drawing a vengeful snarl from the daemon of Khorne.

'I will feast on your brain yet, mortal. Do not for one second of your short life believe that I will not.'

'Leave these two rats to the dogs,' said Be'lakor, releasing the Bloodthirster and raising a beneficent claw to the rabid daemon pack that gibbered and howled, inching forward in response. Felix tightened his grip on his sword. 'You have greater concerns. Rally your legions. You all know what I require of you.'

The androgyne, the plague hulk and the shimmering oracle

bowed their heads and rose – each to their abilities – before turning towards Grimnir's dolmen.

They were going after Grimnir!

'When I give the word, manling, you run.' Gotrek had turned his body so one axe was held ready for the daemonic foot-soldiers behind them while the other remained on Be'lakor and the remaining greater daemon. With his eyebrows he gestured to the alcove beneath the mezzanine. It was about man-height, separated from the portal by a layer of stone and from the daemon tide by Gotrek and his axes.

It was probably the safest place in the temple, although all things were admittedly relative.

Setting his jaw, Felix slid up against his companion's back and raised his sword. 'Not this time. We'll fight them together.'

'It's your funeral,' Gotrek grunted, and then, with a grumbling melancholy: 'This isn't getting into my death poem, is it?'

'Probably not, no.'

'Pity.'

One after the next, the greater daemons passed through the silvery waters of the portal and Be'lakor turned to the unmoving Bloodthirster. The Khornate daemon was still glaring down at Gotrek and Felix, pinions flexing as though mentally powering it through the air towards its hated foes. Be'lakor's regal features twisted with impatience, but before he could utter a word of admonition the Bloodthirster exploded forward, giving vent to a soul-tearing howl as it pounded towards the balcony's edge, flung out its wings, and leapt.

Felix felt his courage shrivel as its wings blacked out the portal's light.

The daemon's cloven feet punched into the flagstones. Felix felt the impacts shake him. He watched as the berserker shook off its wings, whipped up its axe, and bellowed. Blood and flame spittled its knife-edged teeth. The runes of its armour shone. The fire-crack of its whip startled Felix out of his horror that he might cower before it more completely, but he didn't get the opportunity.

As if given a signal, the daemon mob bayed and surged forward.

Without a word spoken between them, Gotrek gave a roar and charged towards the Bloodthirster while Felix spun around to address the lesser daemons galloping for his back.

There was an apocalyptic clang as meteoric iron clashed against infernal brass, and then every last one of Felix's senses was overwhelmed by a tidal wall of scabs, claws, eye-sacks and twisted blades.

He parried the first blow, a meat cleaver smeared with bilious juices, and exerted the least possible effort to divert it across his body. He had to conserve his strength if he was going to last more than a few seconds. Unable to fight the momentum of the tide, he gave ground. A brown-skinned daemon with three asymmetrically positioned horns and a swinging ball-and-chain lunged for him. Felix sidestepped. The spiked mace-head swept across his turning body as a well-timed elbow from Felix caused the daemon's soft jaw to erupt. White maggots slopped over Felix's arm and he backed hurriedly away. A squat, simian horror armed with nothing but its maul-like fists barrelled straight past Felix towards Gotrek. Felix stuck out a leg and brought the daemon crashing down. A vicious satisfaction gave him the strength to hold his ground a minute longer; short, economical cuts making the tiniest of nicks in the unending body of the horde.

Ignore Felix Jaeger, will you?

Parry, feint, riposte; his sword whipped out as though drawn to the blades and weaponised appendages of his attackers. His arms were numb up to the shoulders. His breath came in rasps that his chest seemed to resist accepting, as if doing so was a burden it could do without. Every so often the opportunity presented itself to slide Karaghul through some monster's belly, but more often than not he let it pass – better to live a moment longer than risk it. No two daemons were even superficially alike, he knew, and it was impossible to say which would have entrails that would tighten around his sword like a boa, or which would have abdominals of iron that would ring the blade from Felix's hands.

Something tore open the mail beneath his left armpit and gouged into flesh. Felix didn't see what it was. He barely even felt it. If he survived, then he would look forward to feeling it then. Under the circumstances, that passed for optimism. If he were to some-how find the strength and the luck to fight on all day there would still be thousands of enemies left to kill, and for every daemon he blocked or cut down, dozens more swarmed past him.

He was just one man: waist deep in the sea, holding out his arms, trying to defend the beach from the rising tide.

The ground beneath him went from being flat to being tiered. He backed up a step and then another, realising only after taking the third step that despite his efforts he had been driven back onto the left-hand staircase. He sought out Gotrek, whose back he was at least notionally defending, and found him almost exactly where he had left him in the middle of the chamber.

The Slayer was a runic ghost within a swirl of starmetal, the iron core within a firestorm of raging brass and crimson flesh. Fiery ropes of saliva spooled out from the melee, scalding the lesser daemons that came too close. Others were pulped under the Blood-thirster's feet or else carelessly eviscerated by stray lashes of its axe and whip. Its weapons beat against Gotrek's axes like hammers striking an anvil. Conflicting magicks produced sparks of scarlet and gold, and occasionally the almighty coming together of blades evinced a shockwave that sent daemons flying and cracked the surrounding stone. The presence of both of Grimnir's axes and the activation of the Rune of Unbinding had made a more even contest than had been the case when these two had last crossed paths within the bowels of Karag Dum, but to Felix's snap impression the raw ferocity and overwhelming power of the Bloodthirster still held the advantage.

A molten-faced monstrosity came for Felix with a pair of spike-arms working like pistons and he was forced to look away from his companion and attend to his own peril.

He didn't know what he was doing now, but he couldn't call it fighting. He was dodging, backing off, only occasionally parrying. It was a dance, a drunken, fumbling, exhausted parody of a dance, one that had been described to him in a hurry but that he had never had the chance to practise before the most important performance of his life. He retreated another step.

The whine from the portal grew incrementally more focused and shrill. Its radiance shimmered across the corner of his eye, and he turned his face towards it slightly to prevent the glare from straining his eyes. In so doing he unwittingly caught sight of what was happening on the other side of the portal.

The image was garbled and difficult to make sense of, forcing a vast, perhaps infinite field into two dimensions upon a rippling, semi-translucent pool of silver. Rolling distortions confused things further. There were random bursts of light. Magical attacks, Felix realised, almost constant volleys cast from the daemon hordes towards Grimnir. A concentrated burst blistered the surface of the portal as if a source of heat had just been turned upon it. Distance did not exist within the image insofar as Felix could discern, but he saw what looked like the three greater daemons advancing on Grimnir's back, unleashing a concerted salvo of magical fire. The

Ancestor staggered. It all occurred without sound, but Felix saw pain ripple across Grimnir's face.

Felix didn't want to believe that Grimnir might really be in danger, but it looked like Be'lakor might actually achieve what he had boasted – rally the warring daemons to one leader and bring the mighty Ancestor down.

What would that mean for the world if he succeeded?

A sense of despair rose up to fill Felix. He was mortal, human, what could he do to fight something capable of bringing down a god?

A despairing *mittelhau* slash opened the throat of a black horror, bringing it down mid-leap and spraying corrosive blood over the near wall. A disgusting centipedal thing scrambled over its body. Felix kicked down at it with a sobbing cry, backing up, lashing out, making it to the edge of the staircase about seven or eight feet off the ground, and looked across to the cratered ring of bodies and gore through which Gotrek and the Bloodthirster still fought.

'Grimnir, Gotrek! We have to do something.'

The Slayer bared his teeth, possibly an indication that he'd heard, but he was hard-pressed to do anything about it with the frenzied Bloodthirster raining down blows.

Felix quickly looked around for something he could do to help. Anything that was more than simply buying time for Sigmar alone knew what. He looked up. The iron chandelier swayed overhead. He bit his lip, glancing from the chandelier to where Gotrek fought in the middle of the floor. He made a quick mental calculation and cursed himself. Gustav had been right about him.

He really was a pitiably heroic old fool.

Clearing himself a space with a wild sweep of his sword, he dropped to his haunches and then leapt with his left hand outstretched for the base of the chandelier.

He caught an iron bar and swung on it, straining until his face turned red and his body shook, hauling up his armoured weight on the strength of his unfavoured arm alone. A jowly daemon-thing made a grab for his hanging leg. Felix buried his foot in its face, pushing off against it for the lift he needed to swing his sword arm over the iron latticework and pull himself up into the chandelier.

Quivering with exertion, Felix got up. He was in a cage of iron illuminated by tiny glowing stones. It was just spacious enough for him to stand and, provided he wasn't careless about it, there were enough bars of sufficient width at the base for him to move within it. The chandelier rattled on its sturdy dwarf-made chain. Looking down through the bars, Felix saw dozens of his foul pursuers aping his actions, leaping up and grabbing on, swaying for a moment before being dragged down by others seeking to use their hanging bodies to climb. Still more surged right on up the stairs as if Felix had always been an utterly incidental concern against the portal. He saw Be'lakor, standing before the dolmen beside his throne of brazen skulls.

The daemon prince raised a claw towards Felix, a sneer on his lips.

Felix swore, charging head down through the lattice of stars and triangles until he reached the end overhanging the chamber floor.

He leapt clear, just a breath ahead of the whine of superheated air that *whooshed* behind him and ripped a fireball through the chandelier.

A hot rush of displaced air flung him clear, mangled bits of iron firing across him like a hail of crossbow bolts. His cloak tatters fluttered. Below him, the Bloodthirster tore into Gotrek, armoured hide riddled with twisted and still-glowing iron quarrels. He fought down the urge to panic, enough to control his arms and legs and to bring up his sword, upended, blade down.

And then he began to fall.

Felix gripped Karaghul's hilt in both hands, turning all his strength and the full weight of his fall to plunge the sword into the Bloodthirster's shoulder.

The brass clasps between breastplate and backplate split open, the enchanted blade sinking through meat and tissue to the jewel-eyed dragonhead hilt. Flame gouted from the wound, as if the likeness within the sword breathed fire, and the Bloodthirster unleashed a seismic bellow of pain. An arch of the back and a buffet of its bloody black wings threw Felix from its shoulders.

He sailed backwards through the air, arms swimming against the current, still grasping for a handhold as his back thumped into the wall.

His mail shirt stiffened painfully against his back and shoulders and the back of his head cracked against the stone. He bit through his tongue, tasted blood, then dropped back down onto the stairs on his knees, almost pitching down them except for the fact that his hands were still flailing and managed to seize a hold of the marble balustrade.

Dizzily, he stood up and patted himself down. He was bruised, but alive, and aside from the damp smear of blood under his left armpit he seemed more-or-less in one piece. The Bloodthirster had flung him onto the bottom of the right-hand stair. The daemons had avoided this side of the chamber thus far, drawn up the left hand side after Felix and like grist to the bloody mill that was Gotrek and the greater daemon down in the centre.

Gotrek backed away from the thrashing Bloodthirster. The Slayer wiped blood from what looked like a broken nose across his bicep, threw Felix an almost accusatory glare and then threw himself into the torrent pouring up that left-hand stair with a berserker howl.

Noting every daemon warrior that was gutted, hacked in two, or kicked over the edge with a deepening snarl, Be'lakor drew his long black blade. Energy crackled along its length.

The Slayer was submerged in Chaos, but Felix was convinced he saw the dwarf smile.

Felix's hand moved instinctively to his belt for his own sword.

It wasn't there.

Swallowing the lump in his throat, he looked up.

The Bloodthirster was ablaze with fury. It was a red star, licked by a corona of bloody fire. It clenched its fists, infernal muscles bulging where its brass plate left arms and neck exposed, tendons hardening like steel cables as it drew back its head and roared. It was a cry that would make itself heard across an abyss and cause its darkest denizens to wail. Felix staggered from it. And he saw his sword. It shone white hot in the daemon's neck, embers spurting around it, some amalgam of daemonic blood and binding magicks.

Sigmar, what now?

Felix's hands scrambled through his clothing for a weapon. He had a small knife inside his left boot. He took it. And a liberated Hochlander's pistol for which he had no shot. He took that too, gripping the barrel in his left hand to wield the walnut stock like a club. He retreated until his back was to the wall and gulped.

With a final bark of fury, the Bloodthirster stomped towards him, broad shoulders swaying with the intent to rend and sever and bleed.

Felix swore, spun away from it and ran up the stairs.

The Bloodthirster's roar pounded after him, its footfalls shaking the staircase as it too broke into a run in pursuit. The monster had wings, but it wanted to run him down. Either that or it was simply too maddened by killing rage to do anything more considered than give chase and kill.

'*Gotrek!*' he yelled, taking the steps two at a time.

A warning? A cry for help?

Felix wasn't sure, but at that moment it was all he could think of to say.

He practically threw himself onto the mezzanine, breathing hard of air that stung the back of the throat with the taste of ozone. The drone of the portal was intense and the radiance it put out almost blinding, doubly so when blisters of intensity shone across its surface. Gotrek and Be'lakor were painted chrome and battling over a carpet of skulls that had previously been the daemon prince's throne. Dark lightning arced between Gotrek's axes and Be'lakor's outstretched claws, reducing every lesser daemon that drew close enough to ash. The Slayer grunted and pushed as if engaged in a straightforward contest of strength. Electricity flashed across Be'lakor's silvered form. Warpstone ice crystallised across the walls and stitched over the Ancestor faces of the dolmen.

From some deep reserve, Felix found the strength to stagger forward. A skull crunched underfoot. There was no time for horror.

Enormous muscles straining, Gotrek drove through the lightning field to hack at the daemon prince. Be'lakor's blade met his, shards of darkness breaking off, misting around the two fighters as their battle swirled through it. Be'lakor chuckled, fading into the darkness just as Gotrek's axe swept through the emptiness he had that moment abandoned. Gotrek growled murderously, axes tearing up the mist even as it flowed away from him, reforming before the portal into the shape of Be'lakor, hand outstretched and an incantation of power on his lips. A withering volley of black arrows burst from the daemon prince's claws and battered away at the protective barrier afforded by the Rune of Unbinding. It glowed golden-red, projecting a shield of the same hue around Gotrek. It looked thinner than that which Max had previously conjured for himself. It flickered alarmingly under the barrage and, much like a mail shirt deflecting and absorbing a blow but leaving a horrible bruise beneath, left Gotrek struggling to get up off his knees.

Felix couldn't believe his senses.

After everything they had been through, everything they had lost and every edge they had paid for in blood, Gotrek was losing.

He gritted his teeth and brought up his knife. Not while his rememberer still breathed.

Be'lakor noticed him standing there; battered, aged, hair curling from the electric heat and paltry weapons in hand. The daemon prince lowered his sword a fraction. His obsidian-black hand, part-way through the form of another spell, left it to smooth a cruel laugh from his lips.

'Felix Jaeger. If it is not my downfa–'

The sneer disappeared from his face.

There was a crash from behind Felix, as of a brass foot-guard punching into marble and grinding deep. There was a sense of heat, of pressure, and terrible, terrible rage, and in what felt like devastatingly slow motion Felix turned his head to look around.

The frenzied Bloodthirster roared, storming up the steps, blinded to everything but what lay within arm's reach of its wrath. Karaghul's hilt blazed from its shoulder like the lance of a charging knight under the setting sun. It swept up its brass axe and threw itself forward.

Acting on instinct, Felix dropped to the ground. The daemon passed over him by inches, his skin reddening under its infernal body heat. It didn't stop. It was too far gone for that.

It was charging straight for Gotrek and Be'lakor.

The daemon prince snarled, black eyes boring hatred into the charging Bloodthirster as his hands traced a rapid sigil through the air between them. It became treacly and dark and Be'lakor began to fade into it.

Gotrek's crest rose through the murky soup. The nearness of the portal gave him a metallic lustre, an Ancestor idol worked from a jagged piece of tin. His axes glittered.

A measure of Be'lakor's amusement returned as he continued to disperse.

'What is it they say in those melodramas your companion is so inexplicably fond of – it's behind you?'

'You owe me the life of a rememberer, daemon, and a dwarf never forgets.' The Slayer raised his own long-serving axe high, betraying not the slightest hint of concern at the flame-wreathed nightmare bearing down on him from behind, vengeance glittering diamond-hard in both of his eyes. 'An eye for a bloody eye.'

He hacked down, burying his axe-blade in Be'lakor's thigh. The daemon prince howled, a note of panic buried there in the outpouring of pain. The god-slaying Rune of Unbinding throbbed, like a swallowing throat, gorging hungrily on the shadow magic with which Be'lakor had wreathed himself. Until it was gone. Gotrek wrenched his axe free in a gout of something ethereal and grey.

Be'lakor extended a hand to the Bloodthirster; not to ravage the daemon with magic, for Gotrek's axe had left him with none, but to appeal to the brute's reason.

But Felix had left it with none.

Gotrek sneered, nodding to something in the portal that only he could see. 'It's behind you.'

Felix pushed himself up off his chest to watch in open-mouthed horror as the Bloodthirster trampled over Gotrek and ploughed through. The swipe of its axe severed Be'lakor's outstretched arm at the elbow and bit into his hip, its brazen horns impaling the daemon prince's chest and sending them both – and Gotrek with them – tumbling into the portal.

'Gotrek!' Felix screamed, all three of them disappearing in a flash of light that sent ripples racing each other across the surface.

The lesser daemons throughout the chamber and – inconceivably – still arriving in impossible numbers through the outer door gave voice to a keening lament.

Felix scrambled to his feet, clutching his pistol and his knife close to him, but none of the creatures seemed inclined to attack. There was no telling how long that would last. He studied the portal, breathing hard. He needed only a moment to think. He kissed the ring on his finger and muttered a prayer to Sigmar.

It was simply habit. He doubted the God-King could hear him here.

Then he took a running leap and dived after his friend.

A plain of black glass stretched out for a million miles. In another life, Felix had been a merchant's son; he knew how to see the curve of the earth in the gradual appearance of a homecoming merchantman's sail over the horizon. But not here. Here the plain went on until Felix's eyes could follow it no further. The sky was tormented, riven by flashes of sheet lightning, thunder that mocked the benighted ground like the laughter of gods and daemons. The air tasted bitter on the tongue, like sucking on a coin, and it was dry. Felix doubted there was a river or a lake within... he shook his head and gave up. Whatever measure of distance he could recall or contrive would be inadequate. His long journey had brought him to the one place he had thought even Gotrek would never try to take him.

He was in the Realm of Chaos.

The hot core of the universe.

The home of the gods.

He turned around, partly to reacquaint himself with a mortal sense of scale - six and a half feet, give or take an inch, to the portal - but largely to reassure himself that he could still leave if he chose to. He could see the temple through it, flat and distorted just as this place had been from the other side. He could see the feral daemon-things crowding on the far side. For now they seemed content to stay there, which suited Felix fine though it did rather take a hammer to his cherished thoughts of returning back to his own world.

With a sigh, he drew his long hair away from his eyes and crunched back around. There was no sign of Be'lakor, nor any of the greater daemons that had temporarily united under him with the aim of slaying Grimnir and leading a daemon army out through Kazad Drengazi.

Unless one counted the crimson, severed head that Gotrek was in the process of messily wrenching from his axe.

The Bloodthirster's eyes were glassy. Its red tongue lolled out from its open mouth. Felix was accustomed to daemons dissipating back into the aethyr upon their destruction and he had to remind himself that he was currently *in* the aethyr. It was not a pleasant thought. From what he had been able to gather of Be'lakor's self-indulgent monologue, a daemon killed here could stay dead for a long, long time.

The head came off with a slurp and fell face down in the glass.

Felix found that very reassuring. He just wished he could see Be'lakor's body somewhere out there too.

He beaked his eyes with his hand to shield them from the lightning flashes and searched the distance. The horizon – it comforted him to call it that – seethed like an angry sea. The daemon hordes that Be'lakor had sought to marshal had not gone away with his departure, but it looked as though the combined efforts of Gotrek and Grimnir had driven them back.

Possibly for the first time in ten thousand years.

Was that a cause to hope?

Felix brought his ring to his lips and prayed for it. By every god still standing, he hoped so.

'Welcome to my home!' Grimnir shouted, his dwarf blood still hot from an eternity of battle, cheeks flushed and eyes bright. He was closer to normal-sized now, a larger than average dwarf rather than the titan he had seemed through the portal. He wielded an axe in one massive hand. There was nothing overtly magical about this weapon. It was just an axe, but then he required nothing grander. His presence alone was empowering and merely standing in it helped Felix to stand a little straighter and look on the world with more steel in his heart.

'Gotrek,' said Felix, wanting to go to his companion's side and draw him back, but loath to venture too far from the portal lest it somehow disappear or succumb to the warped dimensions of this place. 'Let's take the weapon, or the artefact, or whatever there is for us and get out of here. It might not be too late to use it to help Gustav and Malakai.'

Grimnir lowered his face. He smiled benignly as he shook his head. 'You still don't understand. *I* am the power, lad. Me. Long ago, I came here to fight the gods and end the threat of Chaos forever. I failed, though not completely. I stand yet.' He turned to Gotrek with a shrug that on a figure less mountainous might have been construed as self-deprecating. 'But now the End Times are here and there's naught I can do to stop it. It's my time to rejoin the world once again, to fight the final fight as I always intended to – to relinquish my burden to my heir.'

Felix stared at the two Slayers aghast, thunder's laughter ringing in his ears.

'You mean give Gotrek a portion of your power? That's what you mean, isn't it?'

Grimnir jerked a thumb back around his head to the daemons

gathered in the distance. 'They'll be back, and someone has to be here to fight them when they do. You're my heir, Gotrek, if you'll take it. This is where fate's been taking you since you first took shelter in that cave and picked up my axe. You're a Slayer after my own example. I promise you battle, for eternity and without respite, and I promise you doom.' The Ancestor bared his teeth in a smile. 'The mightiest doom ever achieved by a Slayer. *My* doom.'

Gotrek looked thoughtful. He glanced to the portal, then ground his jaw and turned towards the daemons that filled the vastness of the horizon. Then he nodded.

Just once.

'No,' Felix yelled, striding forwards now and to hell with the portal assuming they were not already lost there with it. 'We need Gotrek. The world needs him. I–' His voice caught. His fist bunched over his mouth, then he yanked it away and beat his chest with it. '*I* need him. He swore to come with me to Middenheim. He swore!'

Felix backed up again, eyes blurring with the tears he'd forgotten he had. He wiped his eyes and sniffed.

'The world is dying.'

'Aye,' said Grimnir. 'Maybe it will die, and maybe I'll die trying to save it. But there are worlds beyond this one, lad. Worlds that will have need of their gods.'

Gotrek's passing will be the doom of this world, the seeress in Felix's dream had told him, *but it may be enough to save the next.*

Tears were streaming unchecked down Felix's cheeks as Gotrek turned to him, blurring his vision and scattering the glare from the lightning flashes so that it appeared the Slayer was surrounded by a silvery corona of light. The Slayer looked him up and down as though committing him to memory, as if the timescales he envisioned expanding before him would tax even the legendary memory of a dwarf.

'No,' Felix sobbed. 'No. He's not offering some glorious afterlife filled with maidens and wine, Gotrek. There's not a foul thing we've faced together that I'd wish this fate on.' He extended a hand to Gotrek, but for some reason his feet continued to back him away towards the portal. 'I've lost too much to lose you now too. It's too much. Come back with me. I'll fight beside you to the end, I'll-'

'Felix,' said Gotrek, cutting him off gently.

Felix gaped, stunned silent, as Gotrek produced a saw-toothed smile that said all that needed saying. It was carefree, reminiscent of one that had once belonged to a dwarf yet to bear the burden of a never-ending quest. Light was streaming off him and Felix roughly rubbed his eyes dry, expecting the effect to clear with the tears but to his surprise it remained. Too late, Felix recognised the cool touch of the portal on his back. He had backed into it, and the world was turning silver. He resisted the urgent pull of the current, the demand of his native plane, to throw his luminous companion – his *friend* – one last imploring look.

Haloed in silver, Gotrek raised his axe in farewell, in salute.

'Remember me.'

CODA

It was dark; the dark of the deep earth, of grief, of the lonely space inside the walls of Felix's mind. The portal was gone, buried under the same cave-in that had accounted for the daemons and snuffed out the ceiling glowstones under a mountain of rock. Only Felix, it seemed, had been spared, sheltered under the sturdy stone arch of Grimnir's dolmen. The sole, faint source of light emanated from the ornate runeblade partially buried under a heap of marble. It was Karaghul. It still glowed from its altercation with the Bloodthirster, albeit dimly, and its gradual decline was Felix's only external confirmation of the passage of time.

How many minutes – or was it hours? – he had spent watching it fade he could not guess.

From somewhere within the collapsed structure, Felix could hear the trickle of water. Whatever pseudo-dimension this place had once inhabited, it was now firmly a part of the mortal realm with the departure of Grimnir's power. There was another sound too, a scratching, like something tiny digging far, far away. He listened.

And were those voices he could hear? It almost sounded as though they called his name. He shook his head.

No. He was alone now.

Out there, the End Times continued, but they would do so without him, and without the Slayer. In short, it no longer felt like his concern.

Aching all over, aching inside, he bent slowly forward to play out the ties that held his mail shirt tight. With his other hand, he reached inside the loosened shirt to withdraw the oilcloth-bound parcel that rested against his heart. He set it upon his lap, carefully unwrapping the protective covering to reveal his leather-bound journal, a quill pen, and a small vial of iron gall ink. He let them be undisturbed a moment more, took a deep breath.

The air tasted stale, used. He had lived half of his life amongst dwarfs, and he had spent enough time underground to know what that meant.

He didn't have a lot of time left.

Unwinding the string tie that sealed the precious pages of his journal, Felix opened the small book. Its spine creaked, aged beyond its years by disuse. At the same time he unstoppered the ink vial, sharpened a tip into the quill with his thumbnail and dipped it gently in the ink. Then, in the dying light of his sword, he began to write.

Gotrek Gurnisson had found his doom at last.

And Felix Jaeger had an oath to keep.

'If this journal is found, if the day was won,
then remember this – here a Slayer lies.'

ABOUT THE AUTHOR

David Guymer is the author of the Gotrek & Felix novels *Slayer, Kinslayer* and *City of the Damned,* along with the novella *Thorgrim* and a plethora of short stories set in the worlds of Warhammer and Warhammer 40,000. He is a freelance writer and occasional scientist based in the East Riding, and was a finalist in the 2014 David Gemmell Legend Awards for his novel *Headtaker.*

WARHAMMER®

ROB SANDERS

ARCHAON

LORD OF CHAOS

An Extract from

Archaon: Lord of Chaos

by Rob Sanders

Leading the way with the faintly glowing blade, Archaon moved through the rib-lined chambers and rachidian passageways of the palace. He was focused. He was ready. Should any daemon servant proceed from the darkness or rush him from the strange architecture, the dark templar would cleave them in two. There was nothing, however. No horrors haunted the palace. No things waited for him in the shadow. The Forsaken Fortress seemed empty. Yet Archaon felt like he was being watched. The darkness that afflicted the lengths of bone-lined corridors was a mirror through which he could not see but could be seen.

You are far from home...

The voice was everywhere. The boom was bottomless, like the abyss, and the words seethed like hellish flame. It was a voice he had known his whole life yet had never heard... until now.

The Chaos warrior moved across a large chamber, looking about him. He slowly turned and swished *Terminus* all around. He peered into the dark recesses of alcoves. He crooked his neck to look back the way he had come, the path now lost to shadow. As he moved through the nightmarish interior of the palace, the murk receded to reveal a large figure in the centre of the chamber. Like the Forsaken Fortress, it was horned, cloven-clawed and broad of wing. To Archaon, it appeared to be a replica of the fortress in miniature.

At first, he took it for the daemon overlord of the palace itself, but as his shuffled steps and defensive turns took him closer, he saw the infernal figure for what it was. A throne. Crafted from the same rough stone as the palace in which it sat. The daemon prince's crouching legs formed the seat, its star-scarred chest the back and its clasped talons the arms. The horned horror that was the daemon's grotesque head formed a kind of crafted crown, while the leathery, outstretched wings, hewn from volcanic rock, gave the throne a hellish grandness. For all its imposing abomination, the throne was empty, like the palace.

'I am where I need to be, daemon,' Archaon answered back finally. His words returned to him with a strange quality, echoing through the torturous skeletal structure of the daemon palace.

That is more true than you can ever know. Though not many who have sought out the Forsaken Fortress have found it.

'I am Archaon,' the Chaos warrior spat, angling his helm about the dark entrances to the chamber. 'I am the chosen of the Dark Gods and the end to the entire world. Nothing is beyond me.'

I am beyond you, chosen one.

'And yet here I stand, *Be'lakor*,' Archaon spat. 'I have your name, daemon. I have all your names. Shadowlord. Dark Master. Cursed of the Ruinous Gods. You, who have watched me from oblivion, like the craven being you are. I stare back, abyssal thing. I see you now, daemon prince, though there be little or nothing to see. And here I stand, before your cursed throne within your cursed castle.'

Archaon waved *Terminus* at the darkness in invitation. The blade smouldered with expectation. 'Time for us both to take a closer look, don't you think? If I'm lucky, as with your palace, I might get to see inside.'

As Archaon turned, his weapon ready, his good eye and the dark-sight of his ruined socket everywhere, he set his afflicted gaze once more on the mighty throne. In it, crafted in his own image, sat the insanity that was the daemon Be'lakor within a rocky palace that was the same.

'Daemon,' Archaon told it. 'You have an undue fascination with yourself.'

The beast laughed. It was horrible to hear. Like the deep torment of rock and earth, as the land quakes and continents heave.

And with you...

As the creature spoke, the blue inferno burning within him escaped his ugly maw.

'I'm here to put an end to that, creature,' the dark templar told it, moving slowly and steadily in on the thing in the throne. A great infernal blade of jagged black steel stood upright before the throne, held in place by the loosely clasped talon of the stone arm. The daemon prince's own claw rested on the pommel spike of the weapon.

Oh, you are, are you?

'But first you will give me the satisfaction of all that is unknown to me, but known to you,' the Chaos warrior threatened.

You want secrets...

'I want truths,' he told it. 'And I'll have them, even if I have to cut them out of you, dread thing.'

The living truth that is Archaon, chosen of the Chaos gods.

'Aye.'

Archaon moved in. The daemon prince reared from his throne of stone, dragging his colossal blade with him. The beast's wings spread and he thrust his ferocious daemon head forward, shaking the crown of horns as he spoke.

Well you can't have it, mortal, Be'lakor roared at him, his words searing with hellfire. *You impudent worm – bold of word but feeble of flesh.*

'I thought you might say that,' Archaon returned. As Be'lakor dragged the tip of his infernal blade across the floor of the throne room and turned it upright in his claws, the Chaos warrior did the opposite. Turning *Terminus* about in his gauntlets, he aimed the point of the crusader blade at the floor. 'See, you can't give what you don't have, daemon.'

Archaon stabbed his Sigmarite sword straight down into the floor of the throne room. Instead of turning the blade tip aside like the smooth rock it appeared to be, the material admitted its length with a shower of sparks. The blade steamed with the honour of its past deeds in the name of the God-King. The stone about it began to bubble and churn. Be'lakor let out a roar that descended into a hideous shriek. The palace trembled about Archaon and the daemon. It shuddered. It quaked. The daemon prince clutched his chest and crashed to his knees. The Ruinous Star scarred into his flesh steamed also. The infernal blade tumbled from his grip, falling straight through the floor with a splatter of stone, as though it had been dropped into a lake.

Archaon turned his greatsword in the broiling stone of the wound. Be'lakor screeched. His wings flapped and his spine arched. His knees sank into the floor and his claws trailed stringy stone where he had splashed the morphing material in his infernal agonies.

'Now we're talking,' Archaon told the daemon. 'This is a language that both of us can understand.'

Be'lakor's claws tore at his daemon form. He was becoming one with his surroundings. In the throes of white-hot pain and the purity that still afflicted the crusader sword's steel, he was changing. The palace was also losing its consistency. Liquid rock glooped and streamed from the ceiling while the ribs and bones contorted within the structure. Be'lakor and palace were as one. Except neither were Be'lakor.

'Your name, daemon,' Archaon demanded as his sword burned in the monster's flesh. Its wings and features dribbled away. The creature sank into the floor. Into itself. It splashed like a flailing swimmer before thrashing beneath the surface of the stone. Its face rippled through the horrific visage of a thousand other diabolical things. Archaon pulled *Terminus* from the daemonflesh. For a moment everything was silent. The shrieking agony that shook the palace was gone. The Forsaken Fortress had melted to a ruptured, contorted mess.

Archaon lost his footing as the floor seemed to sink through the palace. The Chaos warrior turned the greatsword about in his grip, aiming its tip back at the floor at his feet. Like a corpse in a river, the daemon floated to the surface of the stone. It was a lesser thing now. A thing of arms and hidden form, lost within the twisting folds of a hooded shroud. As the colour of the stone bleached from it, the daemon began to move.

Archaon lifted *Terminus* higher, indicating his intention to bury the Sigmarite sword in the creature's extended form once more, but the walls liquefied about him. The palace cascaded around him towards the ice floe. The fingers of one puny arm begged him to desist. The razor gales of the Southern Wastes and blizzards of splintered ice once again intruded on the scene. Archaon was standing in a sea of stone. The sea retracted to a lake. Then the lake to a puddle about the daemon until finally the thing held only its own form. Archaon stepped forward, holding his shield before the maelstrom and *Terminus* high above his head.

'Enough of your tricks, dissembler,' the dark templar told it. 'Your name.'

'Long forgotten,' the creature managed. 'Along with the face that it belonged to.'

'Well, Changeling,' Archaon roared through the howling wind. 'It matters not that you are known. Only what you know.'

'You sought me out?'

'Yes, daemon,' Archaon said. 'It is said by the bestial shamans and diabolical creatures of this land that you are a deceiver and that you meddle in the great affairs of this dark world. That you hold a looking glass to both the damned and the damning and that you become what is seen.'

'I have my questionable gifts, Archaon,' the Changeling hissed, 'as the chosen of the Ruinous Powers must have his own.'

'Then you have held your glass to the infernal prince I seek,' Archaon said, circling the prostrate monstrosity with his sword as snowfall gathered about the daemon.

'I have studied him.'

'Why, darknid thing? Speak and live to hold your mirror again.'

'It pleases my master...' the Changeling told him. '...the great Lord Tzeentch, to have the Dark Master's ambitions frustrated.'

'And so you impersonate Be'lakor, his form, his fortress.'

'To god-pleasing perfection.'

'You are a twisted thing, Changeling,' Archaon told the daemon, 'on a crooked path to nowhere.'

'It is my fate,' it told him. 'It is the fate of all the Great Changer's servants.'

'So I was told by the monstrosities that led me to you,' Archaon said. 'Your damned journey, your twisted path, might not be any use to you, lost one. But it might be to me. Archaon, chosen of all the Dark Gods. Choose, Changeling. Assist me or accept that your journey ends here, with my sword as your grave marker, at some Byzantine crossroads on your lost path.'

Archaon grabbed the daemon by the lengths of its twisted shroud and dragged it over to a black snowbank that offered a little shelter from the storm. In the depths of the snowbank's shadow, the blizzard died to a whisper. Archaon stared at the daemon. About them the southern continent was a blasted winter wasteland of warped confusion. The shredding splinters of ice drifted to the ground and stopped. The snow began to creak and freeze about them as the temperature plummeted. Archaon's plate scorched his skin with the abyssal cold. He tensed as the daemon creature before him got to its feet in the snow. Subtle but horrific changes were taking place inside the depths of the thing's hooded shroud. Something more resilient to the benumbing surroundings. 'Don't test me, warped servant of Tzeentch.'

'As I said,' it told him, ever at change beneath the frosted folds, 'it pleases my master to frustrate the daemon prince you seek. How may I assist you, great Archaon?' The Chaos warrior nodded. Satisfied.

'You have studied Be'lakor?'

'As I have studied all whose flesh I assume,' the Changeling said. 'As I have studied you, Archaon, whose boundless ambition surpasses even your ageless father-in-shadow.'

'What did you say?'

'I say too much, perhaps,' the Changeling tittered. Archaon shook his helm slowly. The Chaos warrior had crossed the surface of the known world and had travelled to hell and back. His experiences – the dark truths, the betrayals and the slaughter – had long washed anything approaching sentimentality from his cursed bones. There were truths he must know, however, even about himself, if he were to proceed in his apocalyptic quest.

'You say what your Ruinous master wants you to say,' Archaon told the Tzeentchian monstrosity. 'You are a miserable messenger. No more. So, let us play your dark lord's game. You mentioned my father. To which I am supposed to reply, "I never knew my father". Or my mother, for that matter. I'm an orphan. Abandoned on the steps of an Imperial temple. A temple of the thrice-cursed God-King.'

'Your mother was a nothing,' the Changeling told Archaon. 'Baseborn. Simple. Unremarkable. Unclouded of heart in a way our foetid kind abhor. The kind of heart our masters revel in corrupting.'

Archaon burned into the Changeling with an unswerving gaze.

'But they never got the chance.'

'No,' the Changeling said. 'Her blood is on you, Archaon. She died in birth. In the labours of delivering the apocalypse to the world.'

Archaon's gauntlet creaked about the hilt of *Terminus*. The Tzeentchian servant was enjoying this.

'And my father?'

'You have had several, Archaon,' the creature told him. 'The wretch whose wife you took and then left to raise your youngling brothers.'

'I have brothers?'

'Half-brothers,' the Changeling cackled. 'But they are long dead, Archaon. You have outlived them, chosen one.'

'My father?'

'Is Be'lakor, of course.'